The Opposite of You

Opposites Attract Book One

Rachel Higginson

The Opposite of You
Opposites Attract Series, Book One

Rachel Higginson

Copy Editing by Amy Donnelly of Alchemy and Words
Cover Design by Caedus Design Co.

Other Romances by Rachel Higginson

The Five Stages of Falling in Love (Adult Second Chance Romance)

Every Wrong Reason (Adult Second Chance Romance)

Bet on Us (NA Contemporary Romance)
Bet on Me (NA Contemporary Romance)

To A, B and K,
You're not victims. You're survivors.
And the strongest women I know.
You deserve all the happiness.

Chapter One

"*B*eautiful."

I turned my head and smiled at my best friend since fourth grade. "She is, isn't she?"

Molly pushed her dark curtain of bangs back from her eyes, revealing her heart-shaped face and determined expression. "She better be after everything I've done for her."

My heart stuttered in my chest, my pulse sped up and hammered excitedly beneath my skin. This was my baby. *My life*. And after today I was one step closer to opening. "*You've* done for her?"

Molly turned and her bright blue eyes widened, twinkling with humor. She waved her still wet paintbrush in the air. "*To* her. I meant *to* her." Ignoring my glare, she brought her paintbrush back to her messy palette and swiped the tip in the gloopy paint. "You'd be nothing without me, babe. Who cares what kind of magic you can do inside the Shaggin' Wagon? Nobody would be able to find you without my perfect signage."

I couldn't help but laugh. Molly Maverick was a ridiculous person, and the only reason I still had my sanity after the past year.

"Can we not refer to my truck as the Shaggin' Wagon? It makes me sound like a hooker."

Molly's sideways glance revealed her thoughts. "You could use some hookin'."

I turned back to the fresh paint glinting in the sunlight, my whole body shivery with anticipation. "The smell."

She snorted indelicately and paused her paintbrush midair. "What?"

"They'd find me by the delicious smell. Like little cartoon characters. They would follow their noses right here." I pointed at the ground beneath my feet.

She tossed her head back, her long black hair dancing across her back, and laughed. "If you're planning on also hooking, you might not want to advertise the delicious smells."

I poked her arm. "You're a pervert, Molly Maverick."

"But you love me, Vera Delane."

We shared a conspiratorial grin acknowledging both truths until the bright red lettering Molly had just finished painting on the side of my truck captured my attention once again. I couldn't turn away from it. Or at least not for long. There was finality in naming something. And hope. Something burrowed in the action, pulled from the decision and conviction that said, "This is mine. I claim you."

The fresh paint glistened against the silver siding. Most of the aluminum sparkled in the afternoon sun, except for the shaded part where my brand new black and white striped awning stretched along the row of windows, the frilly edges danced in the stifled summer breeze. The sliding line of windows were all clean corners and modern efficiency, but the rest of my newly acquired "wagon" winked with a kitschy vintage vibe that I liked to think mirrored my style.

She really was beautiful. Only made more perfect by the bright splash of fresh red paint. My insanely talented friend was an artist by nature and a graphic designer by trade, but her true passion was painting. And she was absolutely incredible at it.

Which was why I felt no shame exploiting our friendship. Not that Molly had taken much convincing. She was the first person I'd shared my crazy food truck idea with, and she was also the first person to offer her help when I'd returned home.

Now her retro-inspired design on the side of my truck would attract customers from all over the plaza. My most optimistic fantasy pictured them stumbling drunkenly in droves from the bars and clubs that dotted the trendy part of downtown.

Hungry droves.

Probably wishful thinking, but I didn't have much to hope for these days. My endeavor with *Foodie* the food truck was my last ditch effort to salvage the remnants of my career that had gone terribly wrong in the last few years. In fact, my truck—*my very own food truck!*—was pretty much all of my dwindled goals and remaining aspirations and savings all tied up into one final push.

If Foodie didn't make it, I failed too.

Which meant what?

I stared at the name I'd carefully picked after months of planning and dreaming and hoping and tried to picture a realistic future if this desperate venture fizzled—or worse, if it went up in flames just like everything else I'd built my life on.

I couldn't see anything beyond this truck. I couldn't imagine anything but *Foodie* working out for me. And it wasn't for lack of trying.

I thought about this all the time. Concerns, anxiety and the fear of failure kept me awake at night constantly. Most nights I couldn't stop staring up at my dark ceiling, trying to reimagine my life without food or cooking or creating.

And I honestly couldn't.

This was who I was.

Life could take everything else from me—my stable future, my expectations, my dream of becoming a noteworthy, decorated chef before I hit thirty, my last dollar... all of it.

But I would not give up on my goal of becoming the chef of my own kitchen.

I would cook out of trash cans in an alley if I had to.

Just kidding.

That was a metaphor.

Nobody would eat food made in trashcans.

"Vera?" Molly asked in that small, careful voice I was coming to realize meant she was trying not to startle me.

I blinked until the world around me came back into focus. I already knew what she was going to ask before the question formed in her mouth, so I cut her off at the pass. "I'm good."

"You spaced out," she stated the obvious, looking concerned.

I let out a sigh and told her the truth. "I'm freaking out. This is scary."

One corner of her mouth lifted in a smug smile. "This truck is going to be amazing. Your food is going to be amazing," she promised. "This city is going to be crazy for you. I predict lines down the block and hour long waits and rave reviews."

I allowed a wobbly smile that didn't feel real or honest. "Everything I've always wanted." I turned away before she noticed the tears that threatened to spill from my eyes. Sarcasm wasn't enough to mask the truth in my words. Those were the things I honestly wanted.

Or had wanted.

Once upon a time.

Before everything went to shit.

Now I wanted them again, but on a smaller scale. Instead of a gleaming, five-star kitchen, I was settling for a shiny thirty-foot galley on wheels. Instead of a fully staffed, well-oiled machine, I was giving up my original ambitions and taking on this endeavor solo.

I hadn't buried myself in massive student loan debt to cook out of a rescued Airstream that I'd gone into even more debt for. But four months ago, I'd moved back home with sharpened skills, an intense year of experience and Plan B.

Foodie was Plan B.

I'd put myself through culinary school to become a world renowned chef. I'd fought and battled my way through a male dominated profession to work in the best restaurants around the world. I'd slaved and sacrificed to build a resume and reputation that would open doors to any kitchen I wanted. And I'd hoped and prayed that I would be able to learn from the best chefs, to be accepted in their circles and maybe even, hopefully, someday be considered one of them. I'd promised myself awards, Michelin stars and industry-wide respect.

Only that hadn't happened. My dreams had been delayed because I made a poor decision and got distracted.

I still felt distracted.

No matter how hard I'd worked over the last year to heal, I still felt the nagging pressure on the back of my neck, the hitch in my breathing and sickly feeling deep in the pit of my stomach.

I still felt the presence I couldn't ignore hovering just over my shoulder. A dark specter I couldn't quite see… couldn't quite forget.

This truck, as beautiful and inspiring as she was, didn't represent the person I thought I would become. She was the culmination of everything that I'd let happen to me. She was dreams abandoned and futures lost.

And she was all I had left.

Bells jingled in the distance, drawing my attention toward the shop I shared the parking lot with—Cycle Life— when the owner stepped outside. I smiled at him since he was one of my favorite people on the planet. A small business guru, a total hipster in denial and my older brother, Vann was everything I looked up to and admired. He held up his hand against the blinding sun and started walking toward Molly and me with a nod.

Molly returned a halfhearted jerk of her chin and then went to stand on the ladder so she could finish the last touches on Foodie. She was all confidence and comfortable-in-her-own-skin until she had to show someone else her work, then she became as insecure and unsure as the rest of us mere mortals.

12

"Hey, Vann," I greeted before he'd made it to the shade of the awning.

He gazed seriously, assessing Molly's handiwork. Usually, Molly didn't have anything to worry about. Her art was always perfect, her talent moving and breathtaking to anyone lucky enough to see it. But my brother wouldn't hold any punches, especially not for Molly. Molly and Vann were as close to being siblings as Vann and I were. "You got the name on it?"

Nervous energy tingled through me. "What do you think?"

Vann was super critical of every single situation he ever encountered. He had no filter. And he had no sense of empathy. He always said what he meant. And he meant what he said.

That made him an intolerable asshole the majority of the time.

Which meant his opinion was super important to me.

"Looks good, Vera. You're a legit business now."

"Hear that, Molly? I'm like legit."

She turned toward us, balancing on the ladder rungs and smiled. "You're impressed. Aren't you, Vann? Go ahead and tell me how amazing I am."

He waved her off but nodded in agreement. "I like it. I'd eat here."

"I hope so," I groaned. "I need at least one paying customer."

Vann let out a low chuckle. "Oh, I didn't say I'd *pay* to eat here. I just mean because it's so close to the shop and mooching by parking in half of my lot. Plus, it's run by family. For those reasons, I would stop by once in a while for a meal on the house."

I gave him a look. "I can't afford meals on the house. I can't even afford meals that people are paying for yet."

His face crumpled, disappointed. "Not even lunch?"

Giving his shoulder a shove, I shook my head. "All I have today is paint. But I'm happy to whip you up a bowl of red."

"Barn Red to be exact," Molly added helpfully.

"You're such a smart-ass these days," Vann said to my back. "You used to be so nice. Hey, Molly, remember when Vera used to be nice?"

Molly paused in her work again and looked down at me with pretend pity. I ignored the real emotion lurking in her sarcasm.

I could handle sarcasm.

I did not want to face the real stuff.

"It's because she thinks she's better than us," Molly agreed. "She's all world-traveled and cultured now. We can't compare to Europe, Vann, no matter how awesome we are."

"I love you guys," I told them honestly. "Europe, despite how good the food was and how fantastic the fashion was and even how easy the public transportation was, cannot compare to you." I paused with one foot on the step leading to the guts of my new business. "Have I told you about the architecture, though? They have buildings that are older than our entire country."

"You've mentioned it," Vann grumbled. "Once or twice."

"Or three thousand times," Molly added.

Smiling to myself I disappeared up the stairs of the truck and paused to check out the inside of my new venture.

I'd gone to one of the best culinary schools in America. I'd spent the last year of my life bumming around Europe tasting the best food and putting together the best flavor profiles. I had experience, education and a whole bunch of shattered dreams.

Europe had been safe and I'd been anonymous. Nobody had known anything about me or where I'd gone to school or who I'd dated before. I hadn't had to worry about being blacklisted because of malicious rumors or turned down for a job because of the enemies I'd made.

But now that I was back home, I could feel my past stalking me like a hungry alligator getting ready to spring. Working somewhere prestigious was no longer an option. Pursuing my dreams was no longer possible. So I had to come up with a contingency plan—another way to do what I loved and piece together my broken life.

Why not open a food truck?

Inside Foodie, everything gleamed in stainless steel. From the ceiling to the floor, the cabinets and refrigerators, the stove, fryer, and dishwasher—every single piece of my new kitchen shined. Looking at the countertops, I could see my blurred reflection in the flawlessly smooth surface. The lines of my freckled cheeks and narrow nose were unfocused and soft, hiding my makeup free face and tired, gray eyes. My messy hair mostly hidden underneath a black bandana, chestnut curls spilling down my back like Medusa's snakes. Only wilder. And much frizzier. My formerly white t-shirt splattered with red paint and sweat from working hard. I was not my most attractive.

I looked more like me than I had in years.

Now to feel like me, too.

Tearing my eyes from an image that still made me uncomfortable, I marched over to the coolers that lined one corner of the small, narrow space and checked the thermostat. Despite my unconventional design, they were keeping the temperature evenly. Thank God.

I hadn't brought food to store on the truck yet. To be honest, I still hadn't finalized my opening night menu. I was months out of practice and terrified to make final decisions, petrified I would get it wrong or make the wrong thing or mess up. All my best recipes ping-ponged through my head along with the possibilities and potential failures. How to pick one out of all of them? How to know which one people were most likely to take a chance on? I was too overwhelmed to decide.

And on top of that, I needed to take the kitchen for a test run, to see what was possible in this confined space. I also had to decide what I would have to make beforehand at the commissary kitchen—the industrial kitchen I rented that was health code safe and rich with storage space.

My goal had been gourmet cuisine with street food flare. I'd even imagined my first food blogger or magazine write up to include exactly that phrasing. Now I was contemplating serving frozen french fries and hot dogs—I knew I couldn't screw those up. Plus, they were tried and true crowd favorites.

If my efforts to revolutionize this section of downtown with fancy truck food failed, I always had the classics to fall back on.

But I wouldn't.

Fisting my hands into determined balls of confident strength, I steeled my resolve for the umpteenth time. I had already failed as badly as possible. I had already crashed and burned.

Foodie wasn't going to be a leap toward greatness, but it would be a step out of hell. It would be a lunge in the direction of salvation and the redemption for my first love—food.

Good food.

The best food.

I opened my eyes, not realizing I had closed them, and my gaze immediately fell on a white-washed square structure across the street. Most of the buildings lining the cobblestone plaza were tall, red brick and accented with iron. Lilou stood like a lone beacon of farmhouse fresh in a sea of early nineteenth century architecture.

The acclaimed restaurant was delicate and gentle while the other buildings in the plaza shouted loud, strong and imposing. Soft when everything surrounding it was hard and unyielding. Cultured when strobe lights poured from basement windows and heavy bass bounced around the plaza once darkness fell.

Lilou was the culmination of all my past dreams and forgotten ambitions. The kitchen was the best in the city. The reservation list was scheduled a month out. The wait staff was rumored to have to go through restaurant boot camp before they were even considered for employment. The owner, Ezra Baptiste, was a shrewd restaurateur famous for three successful restaurants all allegedly named after past girlfriends.

15

And the current chef? A legend in the industry. At thirty-two, he'd already earned a Michelin Star and the respect of every major restaurant critic, food blogger and worthy food and wine magazine across the country. He'd made executive chef of his first kitchen by twenty-five. By twenty-eight he'd been given the James Beard award for Outstanding Chef. By thirty-one he'd grabbed Lilou an Outstanding Restaurant award. Rumored to be a total ass and dictator in the kitchen, Killian Quinn's dishes were inspired and fresh, perfect to the point of obsession, but most of all, his refined recipes and plate presentation were copycatted all over the country.

Or so I'd read in the latest issue of *Food and Wine*, and the hundreds of articles I'd perused online during my research once my brother offered his parking lot for *Foodie*—directly across the street from Lilou.

I'd watched Quinn's rise to stardom closely during my culinary school days, fascinated by his luck and success. But over the last couple of years my interest in his career had faded along with the other important things in my life. Only when Vann mentioned my potential "competition" across the plaza did I remember Lilou and where it was located, forcing me to also remember the powerhouse chef that I would possibly share customers with.

I found myself gazing across the parking lot, admiring the simple design of Lilou; the subtle, simple banner that declared its famous name and the uncomplicated design aesthetic so different from my flashy, trendy truck across the street.

"He's not my competition," I mumbled to myself, swearing it like an oath.

And he wasn't. Our clientele wouldn't be the same. Or if they were, we'd be serving them at different times. He would get them for dinner service and I would lure them in later, after they'd been drinking and dancing all night.

I didn't want his customer's extravagant tips; I wanted their business when they left the nightclubs and made bad, late night decisions. Decisions that more than likely included searching for a late night, greasy fourth meal.

Killian Quinn offered them a once in a lifetime dining experience. I offered comfort food that would cure hangovers.

Lilou might be the precise image of everything I'd given up, of the dreams I'd pissed away and the life I could have had... but a restaurant like that wasn't my competition.

So why did I feel so intimidated standing in its shadow?

16

Chapter Two

I wasn't supposed to open until this weekend. Molly and I had been furiously working to get the *Foodie* signage and kitchen ready since I'd returned home with only a tiny bit of savings left to my name, the promise of an early inheritance and this crazy, absolutely insane idea.

Thank God, Molly had missed me during my European escape. She put up with my obsessive planning and preparations just to spend time with me. I couldn't have gotten this far without her, but she couldn't hold my hand forever. Especially when go time was here.

Molly could paint the ceiling of the Sistine Chapel blind, one hand tied behind her back on banana leaves but she couldn't make toast without setting the fire alarms off.

And maybe I was exaggerating her talent a teensy bit, but only because seventeen years of friendship and undying loyalty swayed me.

Vann's head popped through the open door, his face scrunched up with concern. "Were you serious about no food?"

I tore my eyes off Lilou and gave him an apologetic shrug. "Thursday," I promised him. "I'll be firing all engines for an entire day's worth of food testing. You can be my guinea pig."

"Fine," he huffed. "But I expect breakfast, lunch and dinner."

"You're a workaholic," I accused him. "That store is going to ruin your life."

He gasped and shook his head back and forth in wide-eyed disbelief. "That store is my life." He looked around pointedly at the shiny inside of my desperate business venture. "Besides, you're one to talk."

"Hey, I'm not a workaholic yet! Give me at least three more days before you start flinging accusations."

His mouth twitched with a smile he wouldn't let loose. "Fine, you can be my apprentice for the afternoon. I'll show you how all the best workaholics take lunch breaks."

"Really?"

He jerked his chin toward the parking lot, "You're a chef. You can't exactly starve yourself."

"I run a food truck." I grabbed the edge of the stainless steel counter and squeezed. "I'm *going* to run a food truck," I amended. "I'm basically a fry cook. Hardly worthy of the chef title. And I can starve. I can very easily starve."

His usually intense gray eyes softened, followed by a patient sigh that was so out of character for him, my insides went squishy with sisterly affection. "They're going to love you, Vere. And your truck. And your awesome food. This is a brilliant idea."

"And if they don't? If I fail?"

"You won't," he promised. "Besides, I'll send all my customers to you. Guaranteed business."

I snorted, a smile finally breaking free on my face after acknowledging Lilou across the way. "Your crunchy granola loving crowd is hardly my ideal clientele, Vann. Besides, opposite business hours, remember? That's why this whole thing works."

His mouth tilted into a rare smile. "Hey, even crunchy, granola-loving, tree huggers drink too much on occasion. We even stay out late once in a while. Sometimes past midnight."

My eyes bulged in mock surprise. "No, Vann! Past midnight? I can't even imagine. That's just... so crazy. You're really living life on the edge."

His smile disappeared, and his voice flattened, back to the super serious big brother I knew and loved. "I'm rethinking my offer to buy you lunch."

"You're buying?" I grabbed my purse from the wire shelf overhead and followed him out the door. Pausing to lock the door behind me, I added, "You should have led with that."

"Wait!" Molly stopped me with my key still in the deadbolt. "I need to store my paints."

She'd already packed away the bright reds and taken care of her paint pallet, but her brushes still glistened with crimson. I eyed them skeptically.

She let out a longsuffering sigh. "I promise not to stain your pristine sanctuary. Seriously, Vera!" She gestured at the sign she just painted for me—for free—then waved around her expensive brushes in exasperation.

"No dripping," I sternly warned her.

She rolled her eyes but nodded compliantly. "I promise to leave it as shiny and new as I found it."

I unlocked the door again, and pulled it open for her. She pushed past me without waiting for me to drop the outer step so her climb into the truck was awkward and wide. She didn't seem to notice.

"Yeesh," Vann mumbled. "And I thought I was anal."

I turned to give him the evil eye. "I guess she could have washed her brushes off in your store."

He cringed, seeing my point.

My brother was as meticulous and OCD as they came. We were products of our environment. And by that I meant, raised by a single father that hardly remembered to run the dishwasher let alone clean things like bathrooms or clothes or really anything. Vann and I had emerged from our childhood home desperate for order and good hygiene. We were the opposite of everything Dad had been.

But not out of spite.

We loved our dad fiercely. He'd sacrificed everything for us and then managed to raise us to be decent, successful grownups. Or at least that was how he'd raised Vann. I was still finding my sea legs on the functioning adult ship. But I hoped to make him proud soon.

Really soon, since I didn't have much time.

The sound of an engine interrupted our quiet afternoon, growling through the plaza. Most of downtown was a busy mix of one-way streets and constant traffic, but the center strip, with its border of brick industrial buildings turned into trendy lofts and high-end businesses, was the busiest part.

Three separate plazas, one right next to the other, boasted restaurants, bars, clubs, lofts and businesses successful enough to pay the exorbitant rent. This section of town was all millennials clubbing until ungodly hours and high rollers throwing their money around for extravagant dinners and designer clothes.

I was neither cool enough to have real estate here nor rich enough for the rent. But Vann's custom bicycle shop fit in perfectly and after begging, pleading and selling my soul to the city council, I'd been given temporary and reluctant approval to operate on the same property.

At this time of day, the plaza was busy but not as boisterous as it would be later this evening. The sound of a motorcycle zipping through the plaza rumbled above all the other noise. Vann and I watched with equal interest as the sleek black crotch rocket zipped through the alley beside Lilou and slid to a stop, like the driver was from some kind of British spy movie.

It was obnoxious how cool he looked.

Goosebumps skittered over my arms, despite the warm summer sun. Keen awareness rocketed through me, and my stomach flipped with nervous anticipation.

"That's him," Vann confirmed my suspicions. He turned, his eyes glinting with mischief. "Your competition."

Swallowing past the fist-sized lump in my throat, I grated out, "He's not my competition."

I felt Vann's smirk even though I refused to look at him. I couldn't take my eyes off the black helmet and lean body that had dismounted from the motorcycle with a level of grace I'd never, ever achieved.

I gulped and tried not to hyperventilate.

He stared in our direction. If my neighbors in our plaza were curious about the silver RV taking up residence in front of the bike shop, splashing *Foodie* across the front in bright red paint was a pretty good indication of what was going on.

He pulled his helmet off and let it dangle in one hand. I flinched, taking an instinctive step back. I couldn't make out the finer details of his features, but *I hate you* was pretty much written all over his squared shoulders and angry aura.

Killian Quinn knew what moved in across the street from him and it was safe to say he was not a fan.

I'd been advertising on social media and in local papers since I'd gotten approval and all the necessary permits required to open. I had a fair amount of positive interest, but Vann had stayed tight-lipped with his neighbors. He told me it was because he preferred the element of surprise. I was confident that meant he was terrified to tell them that he'd opened his lot to a late-night food truck, afraid of what they'd think of him.

"Then why do you look like you're about to throw up?" Vann teased.

My voice was a choked whisper. "That's really him?"

"Killian Quinn in the flesh." Vann had never cared about food. Growing up we'd been mostly responsible for our own meals. If we wanted to eat, we had to scrounge for ourselves. Our dad worked two jobs, first shift and third shift, and never had the energy for family dinners or grocery shopping. Vann survived on the bare minimum.

It was why he was so happy with granola bars and protein shakes. They were several steps above his childhood diet of ramen noodles and Kraft mac and cheese.

I'd taken the opposite approach. Denied basic meals and balanced food groups, food became fascinating to me. I dreamed of the day I could eat something that tasted good. I became obsessed with food that didn't taste cheap or convenient.

Good food became a goal that sprouted wings and grew talons during my junior high Home Ec class. My goal grew to be a living, breathing monster when I got to high school and found a teacher that had once been a chef at a European bistro before she'd met the love of her life and moved here to start their family.

She'd settled in her husband's hometown and turned to inspiring the next generation of chefs when she should have opened her own kitchen and made a name for herself. She'd always laughed when I told her that, insisting that love, marriage and raising a family was the greatest thing she could ever do.

Moral of the story? Kids ruined everything.

Just ask my dad.

All that to say, Vann wasn't intimidated by Killian Quinn in the least. He didn't read *Food and Wine* obsessively or troll online food blogs every single day. He didn't have to compare himself to the greatness across the plaza or wish that his life had gone in a similar direction as Quinn's, instead of the fiery train wreck mine had become.

From across the busy street, I watched Killian Quinn staring back. I didn't have to be close to know it was him. I'd cyberstalked him enough times that I could recognize his dark, wild shock of hair and the signature beard that stood out in an industry filled with cleanly shaven men.

He continued staring at us while we stared back. Vann didn't move to say hi to him, and I felt frozen in place, waiting to shatter from the presence of someone so prolific and talented.

I couldn't be certain, but I could have sworn his eyes narrowed at the freshly painted Foodie declaring my business to the world. I could have sworn his gaze moved over my paint-splattered white t-shirt and black and white apron tied around my waist. I could have sworn I felt his gaze on me, assessing, calculating, taking in my black bandana, assessing my face, arms, body before looking at the food truck behind me again.

I could have sworn Killian Quinn absorbed every one of my weaknesses and insecurities, including the fragile faith I put in the truck behind me. He had weighed my worth and my talent, or lack thereof, then disregarded me as anything but a fleeting annoyance.

His body jerked as if awoken from a trance and he turned his attention to his bike, pushing it to park on the side of Lilou and storing his helmet in a side compartment. His motorcycle jacket stretched over broad shoulders as he stretched his arms wide and then across his chest as if working out kinks.

I stayed transfixed, watching this hero of mine as he fiddled around for another minute, then pulled keys from his pocket and let himself in the side door of Lilou. The door slammed shut behind him, and there was no more Killian Quinn.

Letting out a slow breath I hadn't realized I'd been holding back, I shivered despite the heat of the day.

"You're really that intimidated by him?" Vann asked, surprise and some amusement lacing his tone.

"He's a big deal," I told him.

Vann shook his head and turned to offer Molly a hand as she jumped down from the RV. "If you say so."

"If I say what?" Molly asked.

"Not you. Me. We just got our first glimpse of *him*," I explained, turning to Molly with *ABORT MISSION* written all over my face.

Molly was momentarily perplexed. "Him? Oh, him! And I missed it! Why didn't you call me out here?"

Vann made a choked sound, clearly disapproving our interest. "I really don't get what the big deal is. So he's a good cook. So are you, Vere. You've got nothing to be afraid of."

Molly nodded enthusiastically, patting me on the shoulder. "Vann's right. You're the best. Killian Quinn's got nothing on you, babe."

"If that's what you think then why are you so interested in him?" Vann asked Molly curiously.

"Uh, are you serious?" She laughed. "Because he's smokin' hot! Didn't you just see him? He could make burnt oatmeal, and I would pretend to be amazed."

"More likely you'll be the one to make him burned oatmeal," I laughed.

"If he's as good as you say he is, my cooking might be a deal breaker, huh?"

"You're cooking is a deal breaker for every guy," Vann muttered.

Molly punched him in the kidneys, causing him to jerk forward and grunt. Vann reached up and grabbed a fistful of Molly's hair, yanking it backward. The two of them were like a Three Stooges routine.

"Stand up for me, Vera!" Molly demanded.

"I can't," I told her honestly. "Vann's right. Your cooking is so bad it's almost a deal breaker for *me*."

"I hate you both," she pouted. "And just for that, I get to pick the restaurant."

I tried to protest. Molly's taste ranged from Junior Whoppers with cheese to filet mignon- cooked well done. *Ick.* "But—"

"Am I buying your lunch too?" Vann squinted at her.

She squinted back. "Are you offering?"

He shrugged and decided, "I'll put it on the business card and call it a client lunch."

Molly and I grinned at each other. "Make it someplace nice, Molls." She started to point across the plaza but I cut her off before she got ahead of herself. "Except Lilou. They're not open for lunch. And we don't have a genie, so there's no way we're getting in before the next solar eclipse anyway."

Her face fell, disappointed, but it was a universal truth. Until something better popped up or a zombie apocalypse occurred, there was no way we were eating at Lilou without doing our time on the reservation list.

"Vincenzo's it is!" Molly decided.

"I'm going to have to fight a carb coma for the rest of the day," my ultra-healthy brother complained.

Molly pinched his waist, looking for pudge that wasn't there. "And it's going to feel so good."

I laughed, despite my fresh onslaught of nerves and pending failure. We walked across the plaza past Lilou, on our way to the next block of buildings and cobblestone square. I couldn't help but stare at the darkened windows as we passed, taking in the rustic white washed brick and vibrant green ivy snaking around the windows. I couldn't see him, but I knew he was in there and my pulse quickened with insecurities.

Until this moment, opening Foodie had felt like the craziest thing I'd ever done.

But I realized that wasn't true. Now I was forced to acknowledge that Killian Quinn resided less than a football field away from me and I realized that this was the craziest thing I'd ever done. And the stupidest.

It wasn't the truck that was foolish. It was opening a pseudo fast food restaurant across the plaza from one of America's rising chefs.

I let out a breath and forced myself to get over it. It was sink or swim time, and besides that, I'd already hit rock bottom.

A nervous breath escaped me as I thought, *how bad can it really be?* Maybe I'd even learn a thing or two from my illustrious competition...

Famous last words.

Chapter Three

"*D*ad?" It was late when I got home. Well, late for my dad. He usually went to bed by eight, and it was already past nine.

When he didn't answer, I set my purse down on the cluttered, Formica table and weaved my way through the small house.

My childhood home—a cozy three bedroom, two bath with tight corners—had furniture packed in every available space. My dad bought this house for my mom when they were first married. They'd planned to upgrade when they had kids. But shortly after I was born, my mom got sick, and their plans halted.

After my mom passed away, my dad never considered leaving. Plus, there wasn't any reason to with only the three of us.

Where my dad and brother were content to be cramped and close in the old, museum of a house, I had wanted to flee somewhere since I could remember. I'd moved out as soon as possible, headed for school and the big goals I'd set for myself.

Coming back here after everything that had happened felt strange, misplaced. I was too big for this house. Too old. I had shed this skin a long time ago, but somehow had to figure out a way to wear it again.

I had nowhere else to go.

Plus, Dad needed me.

I found him asleep in his favorite chair, a faded blue recliner that creaked every time the footrest popped up. The TV remote rested loosely in his hand and one of his house shoes dangled precariously from the tip of his toe.

Quietly, I slipped the remote from his grip and grabbed the nearest throw blanket, gently tossing it over his legs. He barely fit in the recliner meant for normal-size humans. My dad was tall, bulky and built from a lifetime as a mechanic. He routinely had to duck under doorframes and squeeze into tight spaces like cars, hallways and the Grand Canyon.

But that was my dad, oversized and larger than life even if he was more likely to shy away from conversation and people. He was absent a lot when Vann and I were younger. He had to work all the time just to make ends meet, and after my mom died, it was hard for him to come home anyway.

There were too many reminders of mom. Every room was touched with her decorating style and framed pictures of before she got sick. In a corner of the backyard sat the remnants of her abandoned garden. The ground had never recovered, tangled with weeds thanks to our neglect, but reminiscent of her all the same. And us— Vann and me— spitting images of the woman he had loved so deeply and lost so early.

So he stayed away, isolating himself from the aching memories and painful present. We had everything we needed, but never enough of what we wanted. And so my lonely childhood had turned into an adolescence filled with desperation to escape. But now my exodus had turned into a last-resort homecoming to take care of the man that had done everything he could to take care of me.

These were things I accepted a long time ago. And whatever bitterness or resentment I felt during those earlier years had faded in the light of his real love for us.

I had come to accept his distant role in our lives, even count on it. It was easier to have a father that loved me but didn't want anything to do with me when I was doing things I shouldn't—when I was living a life he would never approve of anyway. His love was real. I told myself that was all that mattered.

And now, looking down at him while he slept in his favorite chair, I actually believed it.

He stirred, probably sensing me staring at him. Heavy eyelids fluttered open, and he rubbed his face with one of his big, rough hands.

When I was a child, I was morbidly fascinated with his huge hands. As a mechanic, his hands were constantly black, streaked with dirt and oil and whatever else he worked on. He would stumble through the kitchen door at the end of his shift smelling like the equipment he worked on and covered in grease. Those big, dirty hands of his would lift to give us all a weary hello, and then he'd turn to the sink and start scrubbing.

They were clean now. He had to retire two years back when he first got sick. It wasn't cancer yet, but he was too sick to keep up his manual-labor lifestyle. Thankfully, his pension could cover all his medical expenses.

"Vera May," he mumbled sleepily.

"Hi, Daddy." My voice stayed a whisper even though he was awake now.

"Just getting home?"

I gave him the tired smile I imagined he gave me all those years. Our roles were reversed now. I was the one wandering in after a long day's work, exhausted and filthy. My clothes were covered in dried paint and my skin in salty sweat from working in the heat all afternoon.

"Yeah," I affirmed through a yawn. Sliding down on the couch nearby, I plopped my bare feet on the coffee table and tipped my head back. My eyes closed without permission.

His warm chuckle floated through the quiet room. "You're working yourself too hard. You haven't even opened yet."

I lifted one droopy eyelid and shot him a stern frown. "Says the man that worked two jobs his entire life."

He chuffed a laugh. "Not because I wanted to. That was for survival."

I tilted my head back against the couch and closed my eyes tightly again. "Yeah, well this is for survival too."

I heard the creak of the recliner as my dad sat up as quickly as he was capable of. "Why do you say that now? Have you heard from him? Has he been bothering you again?"

I shook my head, keeping my eyes closed. "No, it's not him. I haven't seen or heard… He hasn't bothered me." Banished memories flooded my mind unbidden. My heart kicked into a gallop, pounding against my chest, beating to break free from the nightmare of my past. I opened my eyes, hoping to escape the thoughts that seemed to imprison me even after a year of freedom. Meeting my dad's worried gray gaze, I said, "This is for me. This is all for me."

His forehead scrunched, pulling his wrinkled skin into deep lines. "I'm proud of you, Vere. You know that, don't you?"

I looked at my dad, a shadow of the strength and stability he used to be. He was so sick now. He quite literally worked himself to death. But, he was still the same man I grew up trusting. He was still the same man that provided for Vann and me when all he wanted to do was crumble and give up. He was still the man that had given me his approval when I ran away

27

to Europe, even though he was the one that had to stay to fight my battles and banish my demons.

My dad was a survivor. A lot of my life had been spent running from this house… running from the things that I thought I didn't want. But I wanted his strength now. I wanted to be a survivor, too—exactly like my dad.

I cleared my throat, so he didn't hear the emotion clogging it. "I know, Daddy."

He leaned forward, earnest for me to understand. "And not just about the food truck, yeah? I'm proud of you for all of it. For getting out. For knowing when to get out."

I swallow back more tears and the lies I felt coating my tongue. My dad only knew part of the story. He only knew the sugar-coated version I could bear to give him. But what he knew was bad enough.

"I'm proud of you, too," I told him. Because it was true. And because I desperately wanted to change the subject.

He waved his hand in the air and leaned back in the recliner. "Bah," he mumbled. "There's nothing to be proud of me for."

I stood up and walked over to give him a kiss on his shiny bald head. "That's where you're wrong."

He grabbed my hand and looked up at me, surprising me with the tears clinging to his lashes. Hank Delane was not an emotional man. "Glad you're home, baby girl."

I sighed, and this time when I spoke, it was the whole truth. "Me too." Squeezing his hand, I looked around the dimly lit living room. Book shelves were pushed into the corners and a muted TV flashed brightly along one wall.

The furniture had all been here since my mom. But the floors and paint were new. Despite cancer, my dad was still thinking about Vann and me. He'd been slowly remodeling the house so that we'd be able to sell it easily after he was gone.

It was a sweet and thoughtful gesture, but also super morbid. Vann and I had been begging him to quit, to let us take care of everything *if* he goes. But he wouldn't listen.

The man was too stubborn for his own good.

But mostly I didn't think he knew how to do anything but take care of us. At least in his own way.

"Do you want me to help you to your room?" I asked him.

He yawned and shook his head. "Nah, I'm more comfortable here. Plus, the TV's already on."

I handed him the remote again and told him goodnight. His snores filled the air before I could even check the front door to make sure it was locked.

Making my way through the rest of the house, I flicked off lights and picked up my things that were scattered throughout every room.

When I moved out on my own I became an obsessive neat freak. First by choice, and later by necessity. But since I moved back in with my dad, old habits had popped up out of nowhere. I couldn't seem to remember to pick up my socks off the living room floor or put my dishes in the sink. It wasn't that big of a deal, but I couldn't help but feel the panicked dread every time I noticed one of my belongings out of place or dirty dishes on the counter.

It was silly. And if anything I should be grateful there were no real consequences to leaving my things strewn about the house.

I *should* feel better.

But I couldn't. Not yet.

Moving back home with my dad at twenty-six was never something I planned for, but I was grateful to be here now. He needed me, and I was not afraid to admit that I needed him—for as long as I could keep him.

I showered, then changed into yoga pants and a tank top and spent a few minutes in the bathroom brushing my teeth and adding product to control my excessively thick hair. By the time I shut myself in my old room, exhaustion had settled in my weary bones.

I blinked blearily at the clock and forced myself to do another hour's worth of work. I desperately needed to finalize the menu for Friday night. And once that was done, I needed to figure out my grocery list and where I could pick up all the ingredients around town. I still needed to wash all of my equipment and lug it over to the truck. Plus, I needed to write up the menu on my chalkboard and figure out how to hang it next to the window.

Panic swirled through my belly. *What am I doing?*

I can't do this.

What makes me think I can do this?

I glanced at my knives still in their case on my desk. The clean black cloth was nicely folded, velvety in perfect softness and hiding the tools of my trade. They were a graduation gift from Vann and my dad. And the most expensive thing I owned. I had always been suspicious that my dad took out a loan to pay for them. But I'd always been too grateful for them to ask.

My knives stared back at me tonight, asking silent questions and looking sorely neglected. I hadn't cooked since I'd been back home. I hadn't tested recipes or flavors or even made myself a grilled cheese sandwich.

And I hated the reason why.

I was afraid.

No, it was worse than that. I was crippled by fear. I was drowning in the terror of failure and the realization that I might have bet my entire life on a false sense of self-worth.

Old insecurities slipped into my thoughts like thunderclouds on a sunny day. They covered the sun and blocked out the blue sky. They darkened every positive thing and left me feeling cold and lost, without a sense of direction.

My breathing staggered and my hands turned to ice. I felt the pressure to succeed—the pressure not to screw this up like I'd destroyed every other thing in my life—like serial killer hands around my throat.

I shook my head and threw my notebook off my lap. I'd been sitting on my bed with my legs tucked under me hoping to find inspiration, but that hadn't worked. And I couldn't make myself face my knives yet. I couldn't even use my desk because I was afraid to move them.

How pathetic was that?

Pulling my laptop onto my lap, I let out a slow, steady breath. Fear and self-doubt still tugged at my confidence, trying to unravel everything I'd worked to regain over the last year. I wouldn't let them win.

I wouldn't.

It was sheer determination that my breaths evened out and my vision cleared. My hands still shook as my laptop came to life.

I intended to research some food for my menu, but my Facebook homepage popped up because I never closed out of it the last time I used my computer. I was instantly pulled into the newsfeed, even though it wasn't very interesting.

When I left for Europe, I closed my personal page. Actually, I did more than that. I shut off my phone and deleted my email. I went as off the grid as possible. Well, not actually off the grid, since I did get a new cell and email account. But only so I could keep in touch with dad, Vann and Molly. I'd skipped Facebook to stay hidden.

As soon as I decided to open Foodie, I knew I couldn't run a small business without a social media presence. It was the only reason I opened new profiles on social sites under a different name. Vera May instead of Vera Delane.

Unfortunately, there weren't that many people left in my life to friend other than Vann and Molly. And quite frankly, I was tired of all of Vann's healthy lifestyle, extreme sports posts. *Blah, blah, blah, Vann. We get it. You like to torture your body and eat cardboard. Hooray for you.*

Finding nothing interesting on my personal Facebook page, I clicked to Foodie's business page. I'd been spending a minimal amount of money on advertising, thanks to Vann's small business expertise. He'd been showing me how to make the most on a small advertising budget.

Because of that, Foodie had several hundred likes. *Woo hoo!* Okay, it wasn't much, but I had to start somewhere. I'd been super lucky to find a graphic designer who gave me the hottest promo pics for free—*thank you, Molly!*

Plus, food trucks were trending around the country and Durham didn't have many yet.

I smiled at a few posts from people excited about Friday's opening. Their enthusiasm was contagious, and I couldn't help the excitement that began to bubble inside me. I nibbled on my bottom lip, unable to hold the superstition at bay, afraid of having too much confidence at this point. But hope still bloomed, washing away the lingering nerves and fear of failure.

The message box indicated someone had contacted me and it grabbed my attention. I eagerly opened it to find my first business related private message. It was sent this afternoon, and I instantly felt bad for not checking sooner. I would have to do better at keeping up with this page now that Foodie was finally becoming a reality.

I skimmed the message first, too nervous to dive into the content. My spirits jumped off a cliff and landed in a fiery explosion when I forced myself to go back to the beginning and read it word for word.

Checking out the name of the sender, I clicked on it and quickly skimmed through what I could see of his private profile page. Fear of being discovered burned at the back of my neck, but I promised myself that my business page kept my identity hidden. It was there to promote my food truck and nothing more. There was no personal information or picture of me. It was just the truck, Molly's gorgeous promo material and my mission statement. The sender could glean as much information about me as I could about him. Which was virtually nothing.

Although clearly, he didn't like me anyway.

James Q: I don't understand the point of your food truck. There are already restaurants in that area of downtown. What are you hoping to accomplish? The other restaurants are going to crush you. Save yourself the pain.

My chest felt hollowed out by embarrassment. It was like he'd read my mind and thrown all of my insecurities and fears back at me, asking the same questions I was too afraid to say out loud.

Vann's parking lot was the only real estate I'd looked at because he let me park there for free. Plus, I could park beside his building with access to power and water, promising to pay my portion of the utility bills of course. And I was in accordance with the city laws that pertained to the distance I needed to be away from brick and mortar restaurants. Lilou was the closest restaurant, and I parked exactly the required distance away.

The spot had been perfect. Unfortunately, it was also surrounded by other established restaurants. I consoled myself with the knowledge that none of them served what I would offer. My truck and menu were all about late night comfort food. The other six restaurants in the plaza catered to the high-end dining experience. My food would come in a box with unlimited napkins. Theirs required a dress code.

Insecurity was quickly replaced with outrage. Did this guy not know anything about the food industry?

I tapped out a response to James Q. And could we be honest for a second? That didn't even sound like a real name.

Foodie the Food Truck: Thanks for the unwanted advice, James Q. But you missed the point, idiot. Go back to trolling the internet and living in your mom's basement.

I quickly backspaced before my itchy fingers accidentally pressed send against my better judgment. The customer, or *potential* customer, in this case, was always right.

Foodie the Food Truck: Thanks for your concern, James.

We were obviously on a first name basis by now. He'd lost his right to the Q and any formality by being a complete jackass.

I continued my message response.

Foodie the Food Truck: But, I am not interested in competing with the other restaurants. In fact, I wouldn't even consider myself a restaurant. I'm offering a completely different service that I'm hoping will be very popular in that particular section of town. Thank you for reaching out to me. I hope you give Foodie a try sometime soon!

I pressed send, impressed with my professionalism.

The cursor started blinking immediately, telling me he had started his reply.

Well, James. That was fast. Maybe he really was hanging out in his mom's dingy basement.

A sense of dread filled me. If this guy was a troll, I might have just set him off. Both Vann and Molly warned me not to engage with people just looking for attention.

Just ignore the bad reviews, Vann advised. *Interacting with them makes you the douche.*

I scanned my message again, assuring myself that I didn't add any douche-ness to it. I hoped I was good. James Q already seemed to have made up his opinion of me from his first message, so this could be bad.

James Q: The other restaurants might beg to differ.

I huffed at the screen, not liking James Q's reply at all. So what if they thought I was competition? I didn't move to the plaza to make friends. At least, not with the other restaurants.

I was across the street from Lilou for God's sake. Nobody would ever put my food next to Killian Quinn's and call it equal. Any sane person would feel sorry for me.

I felt sorry for me.

I tried appealing to James's softer side. That's right, I was going to win him over with my upbeat attitude and indomitable spirit. *Kumbaya, James Q. Namaste and all that.*

Foodie the Food Truck: The goal of Foodie is to make good, late night food that people can enjoy after a fun night out!

I worried over my exclamation point. Was it too much? Was James going to assume I was a hyperactive chipmunk?

James Q: So, you're catering to hammered club rats by serving greasy street tacos?

Oh, my God, James Q was a real asshole! Forget that his estimation was almost exactly what I was trying to do. It was rude coming from a total stranger on the internet.

And what's wrong with greasy street tacos?

Nothing.

Not a damn thing.

Hoping to wrap this up, I replied as politely as possible.

Foodie the Food Truck: Thanks again for getting in touch with me. I hope you change your mind about Foodie and give us a try!

Are you kidding me? Did I just use another exclamation point? What was wrong with me? This guy didn't deserve exclamation points!

Oops. I meant, this guy didn't deserve exclamation points. Please note the angry period at the end of that sentence.

James Q's reply was short and to the point, but at least the conversation officially ended when he typed out a terse, **Not likely.**

I stared at those two words for a long time, waiting for them to trample my hopes and dreams, and force me to give up. Those words eventually would. I knew they would.

I was weak these days. Maybe I had always been weak. I had never thought of myself as a pathetic person growing up... but the decisions I'd made in and after culinary school… the way I'd been taught to feel about myself and my inability to find my confidence again was disheartening.

I spent a year traveling around Europe trying to "find myself" again, and I came home dejected, whimpering and ten pounds heavier. If Dad hadn't needed me, I'd probably still be hopping from job to job trying to find the girl I'd been before. Before I became the girl that traded in her bright future for an illusion because it had promised instant gratification.

A dirty look from a hamster could send me into a tailspin of self-hate and tears these days. My self-confidence was fragile.

Until James Q. His words lit a fire that had been dormant for way too long. I glanced at my knives wrapped up like a Christmas present on my desk, feeling something stir inside me, feeling my old ambitions come to life with the ferocity that sent me to culinary school in the first place.

I could cook. I could *really* cook. I had proved it by being at the top of my class in culinary school and as I worked my way through Europe last year, hopping from one great kitchen to the next. I proved it with every dish I made. I proved it with the hours I poured into perfecting my craft. I proved it by not giving up. By not letting other forces make me give up.

And Foodie wasn't just going to serve greasy tacos and french fries. I was going to revolutionize the whole damn late night dining scene in this city.

Watch out world, or at least Durham, I'm coming for you.

Chapter Four

I spent the entire next day cooking in my truck's tiny kitchen. I got up with the sun and made myself presentable, knowing I would have to interact with other humans. Humans that weren't related to me or obligated to love me because they were my best friend.

I started the day by transferring equipment out of my dad's house to the truck. Even though Vann had great security and surveillance gear guarding the bike shop inside and out, I had been nervous about moving my expensive pans and knives to the truck, but I needed to test recipes and the workspace. I realized somewhere in the middle of the night that I wouldn't be able to execute all the dishes from my repertoire in the limited space of the truck's kitchen. That significantly narrowed my recipe playlist.

After I left the equipment in the truck, I headed to the supermarket and spent the next couple of hours rifling through mediocre meats, and overpriced and under-ripened vegetables.

Belatedly, I realized I should have done more research on where to buy fresh ingredients. But I'd been crazy busy since I got back to town. First with Dad's treatment, and then learning what it would take to get him healthy. Followed by opening the business and everything that entailed putting a food truck together. The cooking part was almost an afterthought.

Still, I should have found a good farmer's market by this point.

Even though Durham was my hometown, I hadn't been back since shortly after graduation over two years ago. I'd attended culinary school in Charlotte. For the last year, I'd polished my skills by jumping from job to job in cities all over Europe. Working in Durham was going to be a completely new experience.

Finding my place here would be difficult, but not impossible. Every decent sized city had hidden treasure troves that grew the freshest produce and butchered the best meats. It would take time to hunt them down.

But currently, I didn't have the time or patience to search for greatness. Today and this weekend, I would work with what I could find at the supermarket. And pray it would be good enough.

By the time I got back to the truck with my grocery finds, it was after lunch, and the summer sun burned hotter than Hades. I had to crank the AC in my old Taurus on the way to the truck to feel anything but sweltering.

I parked my car behind Cycle Life, so I didn't take up any more of Vann's parking lot and got to work unloading the groceries. My stomach dipped at how much everything cost, not just because my funds were severely limited, but because I wasn't going to make any immediate profit on what I cooked today. This was a test run. I needed to nail down my opening dishes and decide on a cuisine aesthetic for Foodie.

Hopefully, Vann was hungry. At least I would be paying him back for lunch from yesterday.

His shop was surprisingly busy for a late Thursday afternoon. If I were honest, I didn't understand how he stayed in business. How many people needed bike parts on a regular basis? But Vann made it work.

He'd skipped college and went straight to owning his business. Well, not straight there. He'd worked at a bicycle shop all through high school. The store was ancient and a pillar of my childhood neighborhood. Vann had gotten the job to make extra money, but fallen in love with the sport once he started. He continued to work at the shop for a few years after high school.

When Vann started talking about opening his own business, doing the same thing except in a trendier, more hipster-cluttered part of town, dad offered him the same deal as me. Vann took dad's startup cash, filled in the blanks with a business loan and voila, Cycle Life was born.

Things had been rocky for Vann at first, so he ended up taking a few night classes in business management. The classes had helped, plus he'd managed to grab some real estate in a downtown hot spot. He'd been slowly growing his name and reach ever since.

I knew he stressed about money all the time, but he was still successful. He just had the kind of personality that couldn't relax. His apartment was trendy and close to his shop, and he'd bought an almost new car last year with cash. So maybe he wasn't rolling in cash, but he worked hard. And he was bound and determined to make his business work.

Basically, he was my role model in everything, but especially for owning a small business. I hoped for just a small slice of the success he'd managed to grab.

I smiled at Foodie, balancing my grocery bags precariously in one hand and unlocking the door with the other. I nudged the drop-step down with the toe of my flip flop and propped it open to let the breeze in.

She—because obviously, my gorgeous truck was a girl—looked so pretty in the sunlight, all clean lines and smooth surface. I wanted to take a thousand pictures of her and post them online, but I refused to be one of those annoying new parents.

That thought stretched my grin even wider. "Hey, baby," I cooed to her as I swung my bags ahead of me and squeezed my way through the narrow door.

I set my ingredients down on an empty counter and quickly unloaded everything that needed to be refrigerated or had the potential to wilt in the blazing heat. Grabbing the keys, I decided to keep her locked up until I could return with the second round of bags.

As I locked the door, the same grumbling engine from yesterday zoomed through the plaza. I turned to watch the sleek motorcycle weave in and out of traffic, disregarding traffic laws and angry drivers alike. A subtle feeling of disappointment gurgled in my belly.

I wasn't necessarily a rule follower, but it was kind of annoying how Killian Quinn just ignored lanes and traffic lights and pedestrians that were in his way. His face was a mystery behind his sleek black helmet. But his lean body broadcasted relaxed disregard for everyone around him. He simply didn't care.

Or at least that was what I assumed as I watched him like a stalker pressed against the side of Foodie.

The engine cut off abruptly when he reached Lilou. I strained my neck so I could watch him hop off and store his helmet like he had yesterday. His head whipped my direction as if he could sense my gaze on him. I didn't think he could see me, but he stared with that laser-like focus at my truck for a long time.

What kind of chef was he? I wondered. Everything I knew about him was from a distance, food blogs and magazine write-ups. Nothing personal. Nothing that hadn't been edited and filtered. I wanted to know what he was like as a human. His personality and work ethic. Was he outgoing? Or an introvert? How short was his fuse? How perfect was his perfectionism?

Most of the chefs I knew were arrogant and overly self-assured. You kind of had to be in our industry. If you didn't believe in your food, nobody was going to pat you on the head and convince you that you were good. You either came out of the gate swinging, or you faded into the background.

It was a monstrously competitive industry and not only did you have to convince your peers that you were worth your salt, but you had to convince your diners as well. And the critics. And the food blogs. And the staff that had to stand behind you.

And everyone got to hand out stars. Serious industry professionals gave awards and accolades. There were critics in newspapers, blogs, magazines and every other place online. And your customers had a crack at you with Yelp and Zomato—even Google had business star ratings now, and restaurants were included. Every single person had the authority to judge you. Some were obviously more qualified than others, but all of them were given the power. And most people exercised that power. Fairly or unfairly, it didn't matter. The only thing that mattered was what made it to the internet. That was the world we lived in these days.

It wasn't that I was expecting a chef of Killian Quinn's caliber to be humble. But I found it completely repulsive when professional confidence tipped over into grossly exaggerated arrogance. And, okay, I hadn't met the acclaimed Mr. Quinn yet. But everything about him screamed icky conceit and aggressive superiority complex.

I realized he was still looking in my direction and that he could see me—half leaning around my truck bumper to stare back at him. We were yards apart, but I hated that I'd been caught watching him.

At least today he could tell I was a girl. My wild hair hung down to the middle of my back, angry with unruly curls and humidity-induced frizz. I'd sported another white t-shirt, but I'd tucked it into red, high-waisted shorts and zebra-print flip flops, knowing I would get hot in my food truck with the fryer running. And my figure could be described as nothing but generously curvy after a year in Europe.

I had never been skinny. I loved food too much. I loved good food. I couldn't even stomach the idea of Vann's diet of green plants and quinoa. So, my thighs had always touched, and my hips had never not flared and my boobs had never been anything itty bitty or manageable.

A year ago, I hated the way I looked. A year ago, I would avoid mirrors and reflections and anything that reminded me that I couldn't change me.

Insecurity, my old friend, had convinced me that I was fat instead of curvy. My demons were embarrassed of my weight, jeans size and diet instead of comfortable in my own skin. And the voices I'd let into my life only fanned the flames of self-hate and shame.

I'd shed some of the debilitating emotions once I reached Europe, but that lack of confidence hadn't yet disappeared. Although it was quieter now.

Maybe it was because I was as independent as I'd ever been, or maybe it was because I'd spent a year trekking through France and Italy and Spain with their never-ending glasses of wine and constant supply of carbs. One thing I realized—this was how I was built. I was thicker than most, built more like my dad than my mom. And no matter how much exercise I forced my body to submit to, my ass hung onto carbs like it would shrivel up and die without them.

And I wasn't about to give up carbs.

I mean... that was obviously an insane expectation.

So, curvy it was. And since I only had myself to please and planned to keep it that way for a very long time, I decided to be happy just the way I was.

Still, Killian's glare from across the street made me self-conscious. I turned away, stepping away from the truck. I hurried back to my car and out of his sight. I should ignore him anyway. Watching Killian Quinn and comparing myself to him was only going to get me into trouble anyway.

I hated how nervous he made me. I knew what I was getting into before when I asked Vann to let me park here. I wasn't his competition. We ran opposite kinds of kitchens. There was no reason at all to let him intimidate me.

None.

Not one.

Okay, there were probably a hundred reasons to be intimidated by him. But it wasn't like I was going to meet him. Ever. He was a food god.

Or at least a legend.

At least in my circle.

Not even in my circle! In restaurant circles. Fine dining restaurant circles that I was not included in because I ran a food truck. A food truck that hadn't even opened yet. And he ran a world-class five-star restaurant. They were two totally different things. Plus, I had zero interest in other chefs. Dating them or befriending them or hell, even meeting them.

Like I said—opposites.

I needed to start ignoring him and the monster of a shadow Lilou cast, and worry about my own thing.

I nodded to myself, mentally patting my resolve on the head, and grabbed the last of my heavy crates from my shopping excursion. I stacked them on top of each other, so I only had to make one last trip. I was practically crushed under the weight of everything I carried, and my left hand kept slipping because I'd held onto my keys to make unlocking the door as easy as possible.

By the time I staggered back to the truck, beads of sweat had speckled my forehead and trickled down my spine. I cursed creatively as I shuffled to a stop in front of the door, but before I could open it, I noticed the legend himself leaning against the silver siding.

My mouth dried up and I nearly dropped everything. "Son of a bitch!" I hissed against plastic.

I didn't know whether to run back to my car or keep walking and pretend like I didn't own this truck and these weren't my crates overflowing with ingredients. He probably wouldn't notice if I made a fast U-turn. Or threw myself in front of the oncoming traffic.

What could he possibly want?

Be brave, Vera, I chanted to myself. *Be confident. You're not spineless. You're not insecure. You're not a pushover.*

I waited by the door, not knowing what to do or say. I should have been normal and said hi or something, but I was starstruck and obnoxiously jittery instead. I realized it was stupid to be nervous because it wasn't like he knew I knew him. I could totally play it cool right now. Pretend like he was just a normal nobody, and I wasn't melting in a pile of awe and jealousy.

Except I'd lost the ability to use my mouth or motor functions. My arms had started shaking from the weight I was carrying, and I was sweating and hyperventilating because Killian Quinn was two feet away from me and hadn't said a freaking word and I didn't know what he wanted and—

I set the crates on the ground before I dropped them. Or puked inside them. Well, mostly I set them on the ground. I managed to get my foot trapped beneath one. "Ow!" I yipped reflexively. I slipped my foot out, but my flip-flop slipped off and stayed stuck under the box. I tried to casually hook my toe around the back and slide it out from under, but the boxes were too heavy, and it wouldn't budge.

Panicking and refusing to look at Killian until I had both shoes firmly in place, I balanced on one foot, swooped down and snatched the damn thing free. I plastered on my best smile, while I hopped around trying to grapple with the same feisty shoe.

"Hi," I finally said.

Killian's gaze flickered to my stack of crates before he dragged it back to me.

I nearly blurted, "Thanks for the help," but managed to bite my tongue. I didn't need his help.

Mostly.

I was an independent woman, running a new small business, about to take names and kick some ass.

Mostly.

He didn't greet me in return. Instead, his mouth pinched into an unhappy frown, and he huffed an impatient breath. "This is your truck?"

I licked dry lips and patted my forehead with the back of my hand, discreetly trying to wipe away droplets of sweat. My styled hair was sticking to my slick neck, and I cursed myself for not putting it up like I usually did. I resisted the urge to glance down at my white t-shirt and inspect it for sweat spots or coffee stains or alien blood.

Obviously, not a likely scenario. But working in a kitchen in white attracted all kinds of unidentifiable stains.

God, I was such a hot mess.

Literally and figuratively.

Killian Quinn, on the other hand, was perfect and smooth and so cool it hurt to look at him. He also wore a white t-shirt, but his clung to toned muscles and a hard chest. His black pants that were industry standard ended at stylish black shoes and looked way out of place for a greasy kitchen.

Maybe his kitchen wasn't greasy?

Because that could be possible for someone like him. Someone that seemed to defy all other laws and rules and universal continuums out of sheer will and smoldering looks.

Tattoos snaked up his forearms and over hard biceps, disappearing beneath the sleeves of his t-shirt. I wanted to inspect them, gawk at them until I could describe each one in detail. But I was too self-conscious to stare.

His hair was a little tousled after removing his helmet. His eyes were green and sharp and so intense I could only hold his gaze for a few seconds before mine dropped away. Straight to his beard.

I licked my lips again and tried to swallow but my mouth was suddenly very dry, and my throat had a fist-sized lump in it.

That beard. It was shocking. Longer than I expected even though it was neatly trimmed.

I got the strongest urge to touch it. I wanted to know what it felt like against my fingertips, feel it scratch my palm and test the texture. I sucked in a quick breath and met his ferocious gaze again, just to stop myself from fixating on that ridiculous beard.

He cleared his throat as if he could sense my inappropriate thoughts and I schooled my expression just in case it gave anything away—like me holding back fangirl screaming and desperate pleas to have his baby. "Yep. My truck. I'm Vera," I answered, pasting a smile on after the fact, hoping that I sounded friendly and not spastic.

Killian stared at me. Or maybe *glared at me* was a more appropriate description. "Vera," he repeated, my name spitting out of his mouth like a curse word. "Vera what?"

I tried to swallow again. I barely managed. "Delane."

Killian's eyes narrowed, and this time when he said my name it was more of a growl than a curse. "Vera Delane. I've never heard of you."

Fire zinged through me, setting the remaining shreds of my backbone ablaze. "That doesn't surprise me. We've never met before."

His eyebrows rose in surprise but not in kindness. "Do you know who I am?"

I barely restrained an eye roll. I was not over my awe. I mean, this was Killian Quinn. But it irritated me that he was turning out to be every cliché I'd expected him to be. Cocky, self-absorbed and rude. Seconds ago, I was practically drooling over this man, and now I could barely force a polite response. "Killian Quinn?"

He jerked his chin down in a nod and sliced his gaze to Lilou, then back to mine. "Yeah, and that's Lilou. You've heard of Lilou?"

I swallowed my rising frustration. "I've heard of Lilou," I confirmed. "I've even seen it before. We're practically neighbors."

His mouth pressed into a frown and his lips got lost in his full beard. "Well, then, *neighbor*, let me give you some friendly advice. Your eyesore is out of its league. A food truck doesn't belong in this neighborhood. Or anywhere near Lilou. Who told you this was a good idea?"

Something happened to me. I couldn't explain it. I'd taken a lot of shit over the past couple of years, and I'd always reacted in the worst possible way—meaning I laid down and took it. I didn't stand up for myself. Recently, I'd concluded that I just wasn't capable of standing up for myself. Some people were fighters. Some were doormats.

I was a doormat.

Until now.

42

Until this moment.

Until Killian Quinn opened his big mouth and made me see red.

My hip popped out, and I slammed my hand on it, cocking my elbow with every bit of attitude I didn't know I had. "First of all, nobody told me this was a good idea. I came up with it all by myself. And do you know why?" I didn't wait for his response. It wasn't a question I wanted to hear the answer to. "Because I'm perfectly capable of coming up with my very own ideas all by myself. I'm sorry that your fragile ego feels threatened by a chef you've never even heard of before, but the reality is that I open tomorrow, so you better get used to the idea of some competition. If you can't hack it, then maybe you should find a different profession." He slid his bottom jaw back and forth, forcing a frustrated muscle to pop. His green eyes became lasers intent on smoking me on the spot. I just told one of the hottest chefs in the country to quit and do something else. *Oh, my God.* But before I could rein in my temper or leash my tongue, I finished my angry monologue with a barely contained threat. "And this food truck isn't an eyesore, it's my life. So, I don't welcome your insults or your prejudice. You stick to your side of the street, and I'll stick to mine, and we'll manage to go on with our lives without any problems."

It took a moment for him to recover. He couldn't seem to figure me out, and I was so proud of finally, *finally* sticking up for myself that I nearly ruined everything by smiling.

But even that died when his angry glare began to move over me. His eyes were hot and dangerous, and as he swept them from my head to my toes, I felt him take me in, weighing and measuring and deciding my worth in one scathing glance.

My skin prickled and my insides turned to mush. Whatever fight I had, died under his crushing intensity and couldn't do anything but quiver as he prepared his retort.

His mouth finally broke from his hard frown, kicking up into a cruel, mocking smile. "Do you really think you stand a chance? You can't out cook me. You can't compete with Lilou. What are you trying to do?"

"I'm not trying to compete with Lilou," I answered honestly, proud of myself for not losing my edge after all. "And I'm *really* not competing with you. But I do have a lot to do today, and I'm sure you have… things to prepare or whatever." I glanced over at Lilou, hoping he got the hint. My chest clenched at the sight of Lilou in all its glory, and my heart kicked against my breastbone, just like every other time I'd looked at it.

"Yeah, I've got a restaurant to run," he bit out. He took a step back without turning around, without removing his glower.

The way he said "restaurant" was the final insult. If he wanted to get to me, he finally landed the right punch.

Because I'd never be a restaurant. Because nobody would ever confuse my food truck with his five-star kitchen. Because he was a chef and I was a glorified line cook.

"Thanks for welcoming me to the neighborhood, *Killian Quinn*." My smile was overly sweet and subtly vicious. My nose stung and I knew I was just seconds away from crying. I needed him to leave before that happened—before he saw how much his words wounded me.

His steps paused, and I was forced to look at him again. He shook his head, a bitter expression of disbelief twisting his handsome features. "I don't know what to think about you, *Vera Delane*."

"Then don't," I bit back.

"What?"

"Don't think about me. Pretend like I don't exist, and I'll do the same to you."

He stared at me for a few moments longer, probably trying to decide if I was serious. Which I was. I didn't even feel like crying anymore. That was how serious I was. Whatever pedestal I'd placed him on had disintegrated beneath the weight of his ego. He was no longer the revered chef I hoped to be some day. He was just your common asshole that thought too highly of himself.

Making a sound in the back of his throat, he didn't say another word. He finally turned his back to me and marched across the street, back to Lilou, back to the fame and glory he was used to. His shoulders didn't sag in defeat, and his long legs never lost the swagger of a man completely confident with himself and his talent. Just because I got the last word didn't mean I won anything.

In fact, snapping at Killian was far less satisfying than I thought it would be. A gritty, sickly feeling settled in my stomach as guilt pressed down on me. Killian deserved all of that. I knew he did. He was mean and a bully and completely out of line.

But that didn't mean I had to stoop to his level.

I pressed my palms to my temples, hoping to clear the sticky residue of our first and hopefully last interaction. I was serious when I told him to ignore me. I hadn't expected him to ever do anything but ignore me.

With extra care, I opened the door to Foodie gently, as if she was as wounded by that exchange as I was. "It doesn't matter," I whispered to her. "He doesn't matter."

And I meant that.

44

Lilou would always be one of the best restaurants in Durham, maybe even in the nation. And Killian would always be a phenomenal chef. But those weren't the things I wanted anymore.

Those weren't my dreams or my goals.

They were only memories.

And Killian Quinn finally pounded the last nail in the coffin of my former life. I'd moved on. I'd worked really, really hard to move on.

Now I was going to do the two things I was great at—hide, and make damn good food.

Chapter Five

Friday night opened with more fanfare than I expected- especially since I didn't finalize my menu until well after midnight the night before. I'd cooked all day. My tiny counter space was covered in potential dishes, some epic failures, and some surprising winners. And yet I still couldn't pull the trigger and decide on my final weekend menu.

Insecurity and legitimate fear clouded my judgment and twisted my insight. I'd done my research. I knew my expertise. The opening night menu should have been obvious. Or at least manageable. And yet I couldn't make myself commit to side dishes, let alone the main fare.

I had been a sweaty, exhausted mess when I decided to give up and forget this entire thing. A cool breeze had finally breached the small kitchen space. I was about to throw in the towel, not only for the night but on this stupid dream completely, when Killian Quinn had zipped by on his motorcycle, leather jacket tight around his lean torso, black helmet obscuring his pretentious face.

Lilou had shut down over an hour earlier, and I had been telling myself I wasn't waiting to catch a glimpse of the rat bastard, even though I couldn't stop throwing hateful glances his way all day. His staff had filtered out a half hour before, but Killian was the last one that left the building.

He didn't stop by the truck again. And I expected hell would freeze over before he ever spoke to me after our earlier altercation. Which was more than fine with me.

But something about the way he flew through the plaza without once turning his helmeted head my direction lit a fire in me once again. He was a jerk. An arrogant jerk! So caught up in his sycophantic world that he couldn't see a good chef if she punched him in the face...

Before I knew it, I had a decent menu picked and mentally prepared.

My whole philosophy was modern Americana comfort food with a twist. I'd played with burgers and mini meatloaves, chicken fried steak and ribs all day, but inspiration hit like a lightning strike, and I knew exactly what I wanted.

Grilled cheese and tomato soup. Only my grilled cheese would come with fresh mozzarella, pancetta and strawberry-jalapeno jam on brioche. And my tomato soup would be served as a cooled drizzle over the sandwich. Hand cut fries for the side with the same tomato soup served for dipping instead of ketchup. Messy, but not overly so. Familiar, but interesting enough to feel different.

Pulled pork sandwiches. Only instead of traditional American BBQ, the sandwiches would be Korean BBQ with an Asian slaw and sticky buns. With fried green beans and a teriyaki glaze for the side dish.

Done.

I'd smiled down at my list, knowing both dishes could be made quickly and easily enough. I'd start my pork early in the morning so it would be done ahead of time and the rest was easy enough to handle by myself.

The menu would have to stay small for now, but I could change it when things didn't work or weren't selling. Or hell, whenever I felt like it.

I'd gotten used to cooking quickly over the past year as I moved from kitchen to kitchen wherever I could find work. I had never been in charge before, but Friday night was as good a time as any to take the lead.

Fast forward twenty-ish hours or so and my pride-fueled optimism had evolved into full-fledged panic.

The line in front of my window stretched six people deep while three other couples waited for their food.

I scrambled around my tiny kitchen like a mad woman, carefully balancing taking orders and filling orders. If I ignored the window for too long, the people waiting would leave. If I ignored the orders waiting, those people would leave too and drop scathing reviews all over the internet.

Or shout their complaints straight to my face.

I wiped my hand across my damp forehead and ignored the hard pounding of my heart. Adrenaline coursed through me. I couldn't decide if I wanted to dance in triumph or puke in early defeat.

"Hey, anybody home?" A voice called through the window sounding cartoonish in its dramatic impatience. "I've been waiting forever out here!"

I finished slapping together a grilled cheese and set it on the stove before I hurried over to the window. Vann grinned at me through the open window.

"Look at you." His smile stretched across his face, and his eyebrows danced on his forehead. "I'm impressed, sis. Opening night and you're killing it."

"Oh, thank God," I panted, ignoring his compliment. "I need your help."

His eyebrows stopped waggling and drew down in concern. "Do you need me to get something from the store? I'm not sure what's still open, but I can-"

I cut him off, desperate to get him inside. "I need you to take orders. Inside. Now." I turned back to the stove to flip the grilled cheese. Glancing back at Vann, I tacked on a quick and panicked, "Please."

He shook his head, fear reflecting in his eyes. "I can't go in there. You've seen me in a kitchen! I'm a disaster."

"I don't need you to cook anything!" I reached overhead for a disposable cardboard basket and a butcher paper square to line it. "I just need you to take orders and money."

My brother's voice trailed after me. "Are you serious?"

I threw a desperate smile over my shoulder. "I'll owe you one!"

"You already owe me!"

Gently placing the toasted grilled cheese on one side of the basket and dumping a handful of fries on the other, I gracefully added the tomato soup drizzle as well as a plastic ramekin of the sauce for the fries. With a small sprinkle of parsley for garnish, I stepped to the other window and handed it to the man waiting.

"Here you go." I smiled again, hoping he didn't notice the lines of sweat coating my face or the way my hands shook as I passed him his late night meal. "Thanks for stopping by."

Thankfully his bleary eyes were fixed on his food. "This looks amazing."

I had a line of people and more plates to make, but I couldn't help soaking in his compliment. "Thank you."

With his mouth already full of a bite of sandwich he shook his finger at the truck and crooned, "This was such a good idea. This area needs more late night food."

My grin stretched across my face. "That's exactly what I thought."

"Okay, what do I do?"

49

I glanced to my left to see Vann tying on one of the extra aprons I had hanging near the door. He didn't need to wear one since he wouldn't be handling food, but I didn't waste time telling him that.

"Thanks again," I hollered to the customer and then spun around to make the next meal. To Vann, I said, "Just take orders. Write them down here." I pointed to a pad of paper. "Put them up here." I pointed to the order line over my head. "And don't get them out of order."

He leaned out the window. "Just a second." To me, he asked, "And payment?"

"Use the pouch for cash and my PayPal thingy for cards." I slid my phone to him with the card reader attached to it. "Everything's five dollars tonight," I explained while my hands flew with superhuman speed to make two pulled pork meals.

The cunning businessman in my brother perked up, and he couldn't help but ask, "I thought you wanted to make money?"

I smiled at the sandwich in my gloved hand. "Opening weekend special. I'm hooking them on good, cheap food. I need them to come back. Even when the prices double."

"Huh," Vann grunted. He didn't say anything more so I couldn't tell if he thought that was a good idea or a bad one. Regardless he started taking orders and payment, and I stopped freaking out.

I exhaled a slow breath and finally let myself settle into making good food. For the past three hours, it was nothing short of a relentless scramble. I hadn't been able to breathe, let alone enjoy the thing I loved most in this world.

Now I could finally find my stride. I was used to full menus to cook from, so limiting myself to two dishes became an easy routine I glided through effortlessly.

I was happier with my dishes too. Even though I knew they tasted fine, they weren't always the prettiest things to look at in my haste to shove them at the customers. With Vann's help, I could take the time to make each order look as good as it tasted.

Which made me immensely happy.

I finished up the orders practically twirling around in the kitchen, and when we finally got a second for a break twenty minutes later, I threw my arms around Vann and squealed against his t-shirt.

He hugged me back, squeezing me affectionately. "Has it been like this all night?"

I blinked back happy tears and pulled away with a huge grin plastered on my face. "It was slow at first, but once it got dark, things really started to pick up."

"You're going to have to hire someone," he murmured practically. "I can't moonlight as your cashier every night."

I narrowed my eyes, playfully negotiating with him. "How about just the weekends?"

"I'm already giving you the space for free, Vera! Good God."

I laughed at how affronted he was. "I'm just kidding. I know you can't, but I appreciate your help tonight. I don't know what I would have done if you hadn't shown up."

"No kidding," he grunted.

I glanced out at the plaza. It was getting close to midnight, and only the late night venues were still open at this point. The shops and businesses closed hours ago, and the restaurants were dark now, with only their staff remaining.

Seeing no one wandering our direction, I turned back to Vann. "Are you hungry? I can at least pay you in food."

"That *is* why I came over here."

I smiled at him and his sarcasm. I couldn't help it. Not even Vann's surliness could put me in a bad mood tonight. I was high on endorphins, unexpected success and the feeling I got every time I stepped into a kitchen. "Pulled pork or grilled cheese?"

"You pick for me," Vann said, letting go of a small, amused smile. "Grilled cheese, though? You really know your clientele."

"If you mean drunk people, I told you. It's all about catering to their need for greasy comfort food to soak up all that alcohol."

He snickered at my honest answer. Granted, there would never be enough drunk people to keep me in business forever, but it was a start.

I finished making him a plate of one of everything and set it down on the counter next to him while he prepared to take another order. Glancing out the window, I saw there was a group of people staring at the menu, all dressed in white or black t-shirts and black pants. Some of them were wearing bandanas to hold their hair back. All of them look tired. And hungry.

They were clearly the kitchen staff from one of the nearby restaurants, but I didn't recognize any of them nor did I know the area well enough to guess which one.

My gaze flickered to Lilou, but I highly doubted anyone from that kitchen would deign to grace me with their superior presence.

Stepping away from the window so Vann could take their orders I moved to the back of the truck and slipped my plastic gloves off for a second. My hair was in desperate need of a redo, and I wanted a second to take a deep breath.

In the back of the truck, I stepped up to the small mirror over the sink, and I fixed my hair in a knot on the top of my head. Using a few paper towels to pat my face, I felt refreshed and ready for more. I could hear Vann still talking at the window, so I let myself assess my face with a critical eye.

I'd definitely been working hard tonight. My cheeks were red, blotchy from excitement and effort. And yet the blush stain did nothing to cover up my freckles, in fact, it only enhanced them. My chocolate brown hair was darker near the roots where I'd been sweating. I grabbed a fresh bandana and folded it quickly so I could tie it like a headband and cover the evidence of my hard work.

Universal fact—nobody wanted to look at a sweaty chef.

Second fact—all kitchens were hotter than hell.

The only makeup I fussed with tonight was waterproof mascara, and that was holding strong, even if the rest of my face looked like I'd been running a marathon in the Sahara desert without sunscreen.

For one painful moment, I saw myself through *his* eyes and my stomach dropped to my feet. His voice whispered up my spine and wrapped around my new sense of confidence. I was too heavy these days. I had at least fifteen pounds to lose. My hair looked crazy on top of my head in a fat messy bun that was truly messy. I should have worn eyeliner to hide how tired I was, how haunted my eyes still looked. My chef's coat was unflattering. My ears were too small. My lips too big.

On and on, the criticisms swirled around in my head, poisoning my good mood and flaring the insecurities that plagued me constantly.

"Vera?" Vann called from the other side of the truck.

My brother's questioning voice broke the evil spell, and I shook myself out of that negative head space. Those were his thoughts. Not mine. Those were his words.

Never mine.

I was stronger than that.

I was confident.

Secure.

Not the doormat any longer.

I loved my hair, despite it being a pain in the ass. I was happy with the weight I'd gained, with the progress I'd made.

"Coming," I hollered back at Vann. Turning the cold water on, I splashed water on my face and then spent a significant amount of time washing my hands.

I turned back to the kitchen and experienced a renewed sense of peace, a sense of being home, the thrill of anticipation and bite of nerves.

I let those mixed feelings wash over me, mingling into a healing balm that I would never get enough of.

Cooking was the thing that saved me before, and this kitchen was going to be what saved me now.

Ignoring the orders Vann was still taking, I grabbed at the first ticket, glanced at it and got to work. I had filled three orders before I started handing them out the window.

The people waiting stood in friendly comradery, laughing at inside jokes and commiserating over their brutal night.

"He's a beast," a tiny woman with a lip ring growled. Her dark blue hair was cut in a hip pixie style, with shaved lines etched into the sides. I was instantly intimidated. She was way too cool for me.

A tall, lanky guy with full sleeve tattoos that reached all the way to his ears countered with, "He's the best."

"And he knows it," the woman argued. "He's a nightmare to work for."

"Nobody's making you stay," another guy laughed. He was thick, built like a linebacker. His hair was hidden behind a black bandana, and huge gauges stretch his earlobes big enough to make me wince. "I hear Applebees is hiring."

The woman glared at him, and I dangled their food out the window before they noticed I was eavesdropping. "Grilled cheese?"

The huge guy stepped up with a tight smile. "That's me."

I reached back for the two pulled pork orders. "These must be yours." The tall guy and the short girl stepped up next.

"You know I'm not going anywhere," the girl continued their conversation. "I just like to bitch."

Both of the guys mumbled, "We know," at the same time.

I got back to work, filling the next three orders. When I turned back to the window to hand them off, the tall guy was standing close by, waiting for me. His food was only half gone, and he held it close to his face, inspecting it thoroughly.

I called out the orders, handed them off and then turned to him. "Is there something wrong?"

His gaze bounced up to mine and I saw surprise written all over his features. "It's good."

My mouth dropped open at the tone in his voice. He was really surprised. Genuinely shocked.

"I mean, it's really good," he repeated.

"Thanks?" What was this guy's problem? It sounded like a compliment, but it wasn't. It wasn't even close.

He must have seen the sneer on my face because he laughed a little and stepped closer to me. "I didn't mean to offend you, I just wasn't sure what to think."

I started to say something about how the food I made wasn't anything especially difficult, but, "You were expecting garbage?" came out instead.

"I was expecting grease and cooking one oh one." I wanted to stay pissed at him, but his expression was so open and honest that I couldn't hate him after all. "You know what you're doing."

Not wanting to get his expectations up, I said, "For a food truck maybe."

He smiled at me. "He's going to hate you even more now."

"Who?" I asked, even while dread curdled my insides and my gaze jumped to Lilou involuntarily.

He smiled wider and held up his basket. "Thanks for the meal." Turning his back on me, he joined the rest of his friends or peers or whatever. They all talked animatedly and laughed loudly, but no one else came back to compliment my food.

A few minutes later, they left, and I went back to filling orders for the people filtering out of clubs and bars, people I was much more comfortable serving. I heard Killian's motorcycle roar through the plaza, but I was too busy making progress on my new life to care.

By the end of the night, I couldn't stop smiling. I was utterly exhausted but in the very best way.

I did it. I moved on. I started over. And I got to do something I loved more than anything else.

There was no better feeling in the entire world. And nobody was going to take that away from me.

Or distract me.

Or ruin it for me.

Chapter Six

Saturday night, I recruited Molly to take orders instead of Vann because I thought it was cruel to force him to volunteer two nights in a row. Part of me wondered if I would even need Molly, though. Maybe Friday had been a fluke?

The night even started slowly, but I blamed the weather. For early June, the heat was nearly unbearable. And locked away in the closed space of the food truck with the stove and fryer working hard to overheat us to death, Molly and I could barely breathe.

Since it wasn't much cooler outside, I hoped people were staying close to the air-conditioning for now.

"I quit," Molly groaned. "These conditions are unacceptable. I'm calling my union representative."

I snorted a laugh, too weak from the heat to work up real humor. "You can't quit! You're fired."

"You can't fire me. I'll see you in court!"

I gave her my meanest glare. "You can burn in hell."

She grinned at me, then immediately started fanning her face with both hands. "I think I'm already there. How do you work like this, Vere? I'm dying."

"You know what they say? If you can't stand the heat, get out of the kitchen." I winked at her to be obnoxious.

She patted the back of her fingers over her flushed cheeks and breathed out slowly—as if that would help cool her down. "Seriously, this heat is an abomination. How are you going to cook in it night after night?"

"It won't always be this hot. There are other seasons." She mumbled *brat* under her breath. "But it's just something you adjust to. I've cooked in some crazy conditions over the last year. Hot, cold, tiny, ancient, makeshift. You name it. At this point, I'm pretty sure I could make you a five-course meal on a broken Bunsen burner."

Molly propped her head in her hand and tilted her face toward the small fan above her. "I have full faith in you, my friend."

I adjusted the clip-on fan so that it pointed directly at her head. Hey, what were friends for if not to save each other from heat stroke?

She sighed in relief. Wisps of black hair danced around her forehead from where they'd escaped her high ponytail, mixing in with her heavy bangs. For all her complaining, she didn't look uncomfortable. But that was so quintessentially Molly. Always unruffled. Forever cool, calm and collected.

Where my pale skin turned splotchy and red when I was hot or frustrated or angry or embarrassed or feeling any emotion of any kind, Molly was all even-keeled and perfectly tanned skin. Her hair remained unfrizzed, sleek and straight like she'd intended. I already felt the natural disaster mine had become in the few hours we'd been here. Even hidden beneath a bandana, it exploded out the back like live wires.

But usually, I could count on Molly to be together where I was perpetually falling apart. She was the kind of person I wanted to grow up to be someday. Smart and talented and without baggage. Responsible, driven, wholly comfortable with who she was. Except when it came to her art, but other than that she was basically my adulting hero.

"So, has *he who shall not be named* been over to check out the competition?" Her eyes popped open, glittering with interest.

I made a sound in the back of my throat. "He knows I'm not competition."

"Apparently not," she singsonged evilly. "From what you told me the other day, it sounds like he's shaking in his little chef booties afraid you'll put him out of business."

A self-deprecating laugh burst out of me. "Which is so ridiculous. He's just not used to other people playing in his sandbox. Killian Quinn might as well walk around with a giant **Does Not Play Well With Others** sticker plastered to his forehead. He's an asshole. They're all assholes."

"Chefs?" she clarified.

"Men," I muttered.

She hummed a sound of agreement but worry furrowed across her forehead, and I looked away before she turned this conversation into a heart to heart.

"Anyway," I continued offhandedly. "He's already forgotten about me. And I plan to do the same. If I start worrying about him and Lilou, I'll forget why I'm here and what I'm trying to do."

"And what is that, Vere?"

I hated the concern in her voice. She was being lovely and a good friend, but the only thing I heard was my resounding failure. Her worry reminded me of where I was, where I'd put myself and why this converted Airstream was now the closest thing I had to redemption.

"Comfort food." I chose to be obtuse even though I knew what she was asking. "I'm trying to make fancy comfort food."

I felt Molly's eyes on the back of my head, but I refused to turn around, opting to do more prepping even though we hadn't had a customer in twenty minutes.

"Not every guy is him," she whispered.

I immediately knew she was not talking about Killian Quinn. I turned around, unable to back down from this fight, but stubbornly steering it in a different direction. "The big ones are. Every top chef I've met is just like him. Arrogant. Pretentious. Snobby. They're all intolerable."

"Him who?" Molly asked gently. "Killian Quinn? Or Derrek?"

Bitter fear coated my tongue and slid down my throat, making me feel queasy and unstable. I hated his name, hated the memories that imprisoned me and the threat I felt behind them. Still, I answered, "Both."

Her tone became scolding, and her face pinched with equal parts concern and reproach. "Don't lump them together. No one is like Derrek."

"That's true." Hot tears pricked the backs of my eyes and my nose stung as I forced them back, down into the deep pit of my repressed emotions and fears that were too scary to face. "He's definitely one of a kind." I glanced back at Molly, not even trying to hide the raw feeling scraping through me. "Or at least according to *Gastronomica*."

She rolled her eyes. "Hacks! They're all hacks. Which is why your transition to a food truck is so genius. You'll show them."

And by them she meant *him*.

God, I hoped she was right.

"He's cute, though."

I whipped around, knife still clutched in my hand. "What?"

"Killian Quinn," she said quickly, carefully.

My knuckles were stretched, bleached white with the tightness of my grip. Realizing my reaction was more than over the top, I tried to shrug casually. I was jittery from our conversation, exposed and itchy in my own skin. I said the first insult that popped into my head. "That beard is gross."

She turned to look at Lilou across the plaza. "That beard is *not* gross. You're a bad liar."

"I'll introduce you two," I teased. "I think he really respects my opinion."

Her laugh eased me back into normal head space, and I sucked in a deep, steadying breath.

"Not for me, silly. He's not my type."

"You have a type?"

She ignored me. "You don't think he's hot?"

I stared down at the potatoes I'd started to dice into itty bitty pieces that couldn't be used for anything. I decided to tell her that he's too obnoxious to be hot, but that was just another lie. And when I moved back home, I promised Molly I would always be honest with her. No more secrets between us.

No more dangerous half-truths.

No more lies. Period.

"Sure, he's hot," I reluctantly confessed. "In a purely obvious way. He's like the kind of glossy hot that looks good in magazines. Except when you meet him in real life, and he starts talking, he loses all of that necessary airbrushing."

"So, you're saying you wouldn't date him?"

"Date him?" I laughed. "Hardly. And not just because I've sworn off men for the rest of all eternity. He's too… He's too familiar. I don't want a guy like Killian Quinn. I want the exact opposite of him."

Molly didn't respond, and I realized she'd turned her attention to a customer. We had little time to talk after that. It was late enough that restaurants were starting to close and the bar crowd had begun hopping to different destinations around the plaza.

The night picked up and was even busier than Friday. I busted my ass to make orders as perfectly as humanly possible. There were a few complaints, but usually about the kind of food I served, not the quality.

I couldn't make someone enjoy strawberry-jalapeno jam. But it was enough that they tried it. Right?

Or at least that was how I consoled myself.

Vann stopped by again, and I realized he planned on eating all his meals here. For free. Which I supposed was his right. My dad had planned to swing by too, but halfway through the night, he sent a text saying he was too tired. I promised to bring him home something good.

Around ten, a familiar face popped into the window. The tall, lanky guy from last night—the one that complimented my dish in a backward way. I heard him order two grilled cheese meals and a pulled pork.

Not thinking anything of it, I got to work on his order, taking extra care to get everything right. He obviously worked at a restaurant around here, and I had a sneaking suspicion it was Lilou. I told myself I wasn't trying to impress him. But if he hailed from that good of a kitchen, he would obviously have high expectations. And he would naturally be critical of all food he paid for.

I would try to meet his standards at a professional level.

"Do you want me to bag these up for you?" I asked him at the pick-up window.

He stepped forward so that we were face to face. "It's okay. I'm going to eat this one." He reached for the grilled cheese. "I can handle the other two without a sack."

Unease unfurled in my gut, warning me to snatch his order back. I'd even refund him out of sheer, unfiltered paranoia. "You're from Lilou?"

He nodded around a big bite of sandwich.

"And they don't feed you there?"

He chuckled with a mouth full of food and shook his head. "Sure. But I'm on break. And I wanted something different."

"Don't tell your boss what you had," I warned him, wagging a finger back and forth between us. "Pretty sure this is grounds for termination."

He gave me a funny look. "What do you mean?"

I ducked my head as if I was sharing a secret with him. "I'm the enemy. And you're currently fraternizing with me."

His gaze narrowed and that thoughtful look didn't leave his face. "What makes you think that?"

I glanced over at the two people waiting for me to make their food. I needed to wrap this up, but I couldn't help saying, "Because he stopped over here the other day to tell me that. I'm an eyesore. And an abomination to the food industry as a whole."

"He said that?"

I shrugged. "More or less."

His lips quirked up in a smirk. "I'm not surprised. I once heard him call Marco Tempest, the head chef at Bleu, a microwave-loving fraud."

I couldn't help but laugh. "Why?"

"I'm not sure," the kid laughed too. "Something about carrots." He shifted his food to his left hand and stretched out his right to shake mine. "I'm Wyatt Shaw by the way."

"Vera." But apparently, he'd already been briefed.

"Vera Delane." He grinned at me. When I lifted one eyebrow in confusion, he shrugged and took another bite of the grilled cheese. "What? I did my research."

"Checking out the competition?"

"Something like that."

"Let me guess—this was a homework assignment from your boss? He wants you all to familiarize yourself with the rival food truck. Steal my secret recipes and smuggle them back to your kitchen?"

He tossed his now empty basket in the nearby trashcan and reached for the other two plates he'd set down on the ledge near the napkin dispenser. "You have no idea how close you are to the truth." He lifted the baskets in a kind of wave and started walking backward, scurrying away to his kitchen of the damned. "Thanks for these," he called out. "Don't hate me."

"Don't hate you?" I was truly confused. "Why would I hate you?" But he had already turned around and started jogging back to Lilou. I stared after him for a second longer before I got back to work as well.

I couldn't shake the weird feeling that crept up my spine after Wyatt disappeared. What I should have asked him was who the food was for.

The truck stayed busy enough that I was forced back into my routine. I realized I truly might have to hire permanent help to take money soon. It wasn't fair to only rely on my brother and best friend to fill in when they were doing it pro bono.

But that was the problem. This was only day two. I hardly had enough profit to cover my operating expenses. I wasn't exactly in the best place to start taking on employees.

Wyatt returned an hour later. There was a lull, and Molly and I had our faces an inch away from fans, trying to cool off.

"You're not secretly serving my food to your customers, are you?" I joked. "Because you better be upcharging the shit out of it if you are."

He laughed nervously, but it didn't reach his apologetic eyes. "I'm so sorry," he mumbled, and I panicked thinking for a second that he really was serving my food to his diners. No, wait. He only took two plates. Unless he was Jesus, miraculous food multiplication was impossible.

That anxious feeling crept back over me and I felt sick again. I didn't know him, but he was nice enough earlier. What did he possibly have to feel sorry about? "Sorry for what?"

He held out a folded piece of paper. "I didn't think he'd have notes for you. I swear."

"Notes? Who had notes?"

Molly was tight at my side. She'd tensed, ready for a fight. But all I could do was look between Wyatt's downturned face and the white piece of paper he held out to me.

"He wanted to try your food, but I swear, I wouldn't have done it if I'd known he was going to send me back here."

My mouth dried out and my thoughts started bouncing against the impossibility of what I didn't want to believe just happened. It was like I was a bumper car trapped in the corner. I knew what I had to do. I knew what was happening. But I couldn't get the car turned around in the right direction.

This wasn't happening.

"Who?" I asked, still calm, still disbelieving. "Killian?"

Wyatt shook the paper at me. "He's my boss."

I snatched the note out of his stupid fingers. "Yeah, well you're not a mindless minion," I snapped.

Wyatt took a step back and shrugged helplessly. "He's my boss," he repeated.

With that, he scurried back across the street and Molly and I were left to stare at the folded piece of paper. Apparently "boss" included spying on the nearby food truck and acting as a carrier pigeon.

"What just happened?" she asked.

I glared at Lilou, mentally wishing it would burst into flames. "I think I just got my first review."

Molly glanced back and forth between the same restaurant and the paper in my hands putting the pieces together. "No," she disagreed. "No way."

I unfolded the paper, and sure enough, handwriting scratched across it, the quick, slanted lines of Killian's expert opinion.

"He didn't," Molly continued to deny. "I mean, the nerve of someone to do that. So what, he sent that guy over to take him back food? So he could critique it? I can't even imagine what kind of ego you'd have to have... I mean, think about it! What if I sent every other marketer my opinion of their work? It's so ballsy!"

Molly continued her tirade while I finally scrounged the courage to read the words meant to put me in my place.

Grilled Cheese- too sweet. The pancetta, jam and brioche are way too much. It could be a dessert if not for all the goddamn salt. The tomato drizzle could have been good, but it's ruined by the cluster fuck of everything else.

Good grief. I wanted to scream at him. What an asshole! Hadn't I said it before? He was an asshole! And apparently, he was only getting started...

Pulled Pork- I can tell the pork is a day old. Amateur. The green beans are soggy. And the teriyaki sauce is pedestrian.

And if that wasn't bad enough, he moved on to attack my garnishes.

Stop with the parsley. For God's sake. What's the point??

Try harder.

Molly's gasp of outrage was loud in my ear when she finished reading over my shoulder. "This can't be real."

I saw red. Anger boiled my blood and pulsed in my temples. "Try harder? *Try harder?* Is he kidding me? He doesn't even know me!" I realized that was a ridiculous thing to say. My diners didn't know me; they judged me purely on the food I made them. And that was all I expected from them.

But Quinn was different. This felt personal.

He didn't review my food, he attacked me personally.

"He called my teriyaki sauce pedestrian," I hissed, surprised when I didn't breathe fire. "He called my grilled cheese a cluster fuck!"

"He's an asshole," Molly conceded. "A complete and utter asshole. I see what you mean now about the whole glossy hotness thing. It's over. That beard is gross."

I would have smiled if I wasn't so utterly pissed off right now.

Laughter floated over to us, and we looked up to see people wandering our direction.

"Customers," Molly whispered as if I'd forgotten my entire purpose for being here. "Are you going to respond? What are you going to do?"

My eyes were hot inside my head, furious with tears I desperately held back and hatred for a man I once admired beating like a drum inside my throat. "I'm going to cook the shit out of my pedestrian sauces and overly sweet sandwiches." I whipped around to the stove, game-planning as I moved. "And tomorrow I'm going to make us reservations at the top restaurant in the city. He's not the only one with an opinion."

Molly shot me a menacing smile and then turned to the people waiting to order. "How can I help you?" she asked, sweet and friendly once again.

Thank God she was there to deal with customers while I angry cooked my way through the rest of the night. Like so many other things in my life, I didn't know what I would have done without her. Besides, her help gave me plenty of space to plot my revenge.

Two can play at this game, Killian Quinn.

Chapter Seven

*B*y Tuesday afternoon I was still exhausted from the weekend. I realized sometime Sunday afternoon when I finally rolled out of bed that my entire schedule was going to have to change.

I was used to late nights from working in various kitchens for the last several years, but by the time I cleaned and closed Foodie, it was four am before I got home.

And I was exhausted. I knew how to bust my ass in a kitchen, but I didn't expect the stress of running my own, however small, would be so taxing. Saturday night I ran out of pork. But had way too many sticky buns and green beans left over. But without the pork, I couldn't serve them.

Good thing Dad appreciated leftovers!

When he was hungry enough to eat them.

I had until Thursday to analyze sales, expenses and goals. I learned so much over the weekend, but I had a sinking feeling that I had a ton to figure out. This was not as simple and clear-cut as I'd hoped it would be.

I also decided to change up my menu. Not because of Killian Quinn.

Or mostly not because of him.

But because I was my own boss and I could do whatever I wanted. Killian's criticism might have been complete bullshit—or mostly bullshit—but he was right about one thing. I could try harder. I could be better.

I'd let myself get away with easy meals because I'd been afraid to push myself only to crash and burn. I had been afraid to push my customers, worried they wouldn't come back if the food wasn't familiar and easy to like. I'd been too cowardly to be the chef I wanted to be, and so I'd let myself play it safe and get away with mediocre.

An ugly feeling settled in my chest. I didn't want to acknowledge the shame I felt burrowing through me, like worms in gritty dirt. Or the embarrassment.

It wasn't even embarrassment. It was utter humiliation.

Killian Quinn had tried my food, under false pretenses, and found it lacking.

Found me lacking.

Found my whole business lacking.

Good grief, I hadn't felt this shitty since... well, okay, it hadn't been that long. But I *hated* feeling this way. I hated that less-than feeling that hollowed out my chest cavity and churned in my gut. My body felt empty, boneless and bloodless, nothing but an empty shell that couldn't do anything right. The words rang over and over and over in my head while my thoughts tumbled together, never forming useful ideas or coherent sentences.

Before it had always been Derrek's opinion that hurt the most. And always because it was aimed at personal things about me. I wasn't good enough. Pretty enough. Smart enough. I wasn't ever going to be anything. Amount to anything. Accomplish anything. My soul wasn't worthy. My very humanity unqualified.

At least I could call that for what it was—an attempt to manipulate and control me. And I'd let it. I'd let those ugly, filthy words twist my spirit until I was wrung so tight I started to unravel.

Killian's insults weren't nearly as bad. He'd offended me on a professional level. He'd taken my hopes and fears and thrown them in my face. And he'd called me out.

But he hadn't dedicated years to breaking me. He hadn't trapped me in his world where he could poison me, where he could direct my slow death. He hadn't abused me.

He'd just pissed me off.

I had two days to finish a new menu and prove him wrong. And I would.

I'd prove them both wrong.

"Well, if it isn't Sleeping Beauty." My dad's gravelly voice greeted me in the kitchen. He stood over the sink with a store-bought danish halfway to his mouth.

I wrinkled my nose at the processed food, but didn't say anything because they were his absolute favorite. This picture of my dad, one hand braced against the scuffed sink basin, the other holding some variation of manufactured pastry, crumbs dusting his chin, was one I would always remember. *This* was my dad.

"Sorry," I mumbled through a yawn. "I'm not used to working so late."

He winked at me. "I remember those days. Man, do they mess with your internal clock. It always felt weird to drink beer at seven in the morning. But then again, you can't end the work day without a beer." He finished off the second half of his pastry in one giant bite. "It used to be quite the conundrum." His words were muffled by his full mouth, and his eyes were so thoughtful, so rich and deep with years of life and experience and wisdom.

"I don't think it would be hard for me to decide."

My dad chuckled. "Yeah, it was never too hard for me to choose either. Besides if you pick the light stuff, it can be considered breakfast too."

"Is that how it works?" I smiled at him and moved to the refrigerator. My hand closed around the orange juice carton, and it was all I could do to keep from popping the top off and guzzling it straight from the carton. Partly because of thirst, but also because of old habits that hadn't died. I never expected to have to move back here at twenty-six, and there was just something about drinking straight from the carton that brought out the fourteen-year-old kid in me.

"What are your plans for the day?" Dad asked after he'd washed and dried his hands.

"I don't even know where to start," I told him. "I want to talk to a few distributors, and there's this farmer's market I found online that I'd like to wander around."

"You're not open tonight, though, are you?"

I shook my head and enjoyed a long gulp of orange juice from a tumbler. "Nope. Thursdays through Saturday. For now."

"You wanna get dinner with me tonight?" he asked. "We could go down to the Riverwalk and grab tacos at that place you like."

Worry pitted in my stomach, quickly growing roots and spreading out under my skin. "Are you sure you're up for it?"

He waved me off. "I'm fine. Besides, haven't you heard of the curative powers of tacos? For as smart as you are, I wonder sometimes."

There was a twinkle in his eye, and I couldn't help but laugh. "You know, I hadn't heard of that before, but who am I to argue with medical science?"

"My thoughts exactly. Invite your brother. He'll get jealous if we leave him out again."

"Again?"

My dad gestured at the kitchen. "You know, because you're living here with me. He feels like he's missing out on something."

My mouth unhinged. "He doesn't live here because he has an actual apartment. Because he can support himself at his actual job. What is there to be jealous of?"

Dad let out a long-suffering sigh. "Well, you know your brother. He's more sensitive than you."

I laughed again and felt encouraged at his surprising burst of energy. "That's true," I agreed. "Fine, I'll invite my poor, delicate brother to tacos. I better go then. I've got a lot to do in a short amount of time."

"Don't rush for me, baby girl. I can eat a late dinner."

I let him see my eye roll. "Dad, a late dinner to you is like four-thirty. That gives me all of three hours to run my errands and stop by the truck for a bit."

He waved me off again. "Go on then, get out of here."

I kissed his cheek and grabbed my purse off the counter. "Love you!"

"Love you," he called back. "And don't forget your brother!"

I promised to invite him and headed out. The city felt sticky with summer heat. The tar on the street had started to melt, and the air smelled like metal and sweat. I blinked at the aggressive daylight, groaning in resignation. Coffee was at the top of my list today.

Before Europe, I had a decent size savings account. It wasn't anything to retire on, but it got me to Amsterdam and helped fund my journey to self-discovery. When I go there, I had convinced myself that I would work my way through the best restaurants in the best cities and keep my savings padded so there would be nothing to worry about.

The reality was a crash course in foreign work visas and my ignorance of the languages—all the languages. So instead, I ate my way through the most mediocre kitchens in cities that had reputable hostels and worked wherever anyone was willing to pay me cash under the table. Still, I saw and experienced a ton.

Sleeping in skeezy dorms and working in even worse kitchens wasn't what I set out to accomplish, but I wouldn't trade that year for anything.

When I got home, Dad put up some capital for me to start Foodie. He'd cashed his 401k since he claimed he no longer needed a retirement and told me it was my early inheritance. I used what remained of my bank account and a decent size business loan to fill in the gaps. I'd made money over the weekend, but I had student loans and bills and expenses to pay.

Basically, I couldn't afford to buy coffee.

And yet, I needed one.

Blame it on poor impulse control.

I grabbed my favorite latte from my favorite local coffee shop and headed into the heart of downtown.

The heat only blazed hotter here. The humidity sat in the air like a wet pillow, trying to suck all the air from my lungs. I wasn't planning on cooking today, so my breezy, floral maxi dress was supposed to combat the high temps. And yet it stuck to my back and stomach as I tried to pretend I wasn't melting.

I met with a butcher I thought could help me out with better meats than the grocery store. He was an older guy, built like a truck, and thick, caterpillar-like black eyebrows. I'd read about him in an online forum. A lot of the nearby restaurants used him, so he knew popular cuts of meat and always offered his most interesting proteins to his favorite customers.

Which I planned to be soon enough.

He was polite, even though I had a feeling he was upcharging me. Still, he would be cheaper than the supermarket. And he agreed to do business with me even though I was a tiny account compared to the other venues he worked with.

Next, I stopped at two bakeries, hoping to find one that was willing to partner with me. I wanted to offer something in the way of sweets, but I wasn't a baker. I mean, I could bake, but it wasn't my specialty. Plus, I didn't have the time for it.

My hope was to find a local shop that wanted to team up with me. I would sell their product and advertise their bakery, and in return, they would make enough of a sweet offering for me to stay stocked. And ideally, they would also advertise my food truck in return.

I left a note at one of the bakeries for the owner to call me and was flat out rejected at the other one. Not even a possibility there.

I wanted to shake off the rejection. I knew I was asking a lot. Besides they didn't know me. I didn't have a reputation. Or experience. Or any redeeming resume-related qualities. But I wasn't expecting a decision or anyone to lock in today. I just wanted to start a conversation.

My spirits dipped even further after tracking down the farmer's market. It was on the edge of downtown where a lot of art galleries and hipster secondhand stores could be found. I had gone there hoping for fresh, organic veggies, but found organic flowers instead.

It was a cool place filled with original art and jewelry. I picked up a pale pink nail polish that was supposed to be better for me than my store-bought ones. But there were no vegetables in sight.

By the time I left, I was cranky and disappointed. It wasn't until I was halfway to the plaza that I realized I should have asked one of the vendors if they knew where I could go for better produce.

I bounced my forehead on my faded steering wheel and ignored the frustration biting underneath my skin.

This was my hometown, but I had been gone awhile. Culinary Art Institute of Charlotte was in Charlotte, only a few hours' drive from here. But after school, I'd stayed there with my boyfriend playing house and designing a life I didn't want.

It had been almost impossible to find an excuse to get home to visit Dad and Vann even though it was so close. It wasn't until the tail end of my European sabbatical that my dad had emailed about his failing health. I'd finally come home to Durham and came clean to Molly. Dad and Vann got only the dark highlights, but those were enough. This city was the only place for me after I landed back in America.

I didn't know the city of Durham at all. I knew the familiar childhood haunts around my house and enough about the city to drive to most areas without getting lost. But I didn't know the ins and outs of the city that you learn when you're an adult. And I didn't know all the little secrets that someone in my profession would need to survive.

I parked behind the bike shop and grabbed my notebook. I needed to take inventory before I decided on this week's menu. Plus, I was hoping my beloved truck and staring down the devil across the street would spur some much needed inspiration.

Poking my head in the bike shop's door, I smiled at Vann. "Hey. Are you alone today?"

He looked up from the cash register where he sat on a tall stool reading a fitness magazine. "Scott is late, and Maizy couldn't wait for him to get here, so I'm filling in."

"That's good for you," I told him. "You can see how the rest of us peons live."

He frowned at me. "I have three employees. I'm not exactly living large."

I leveled him with a look, "One man's barely-surviving small business is another man's kingdom, Vann."

"Says the small business owner to the other small business owner."

I wrinkled my nose at him. "Yeah, but I don't even have one employee. I just have people that I manipulate into helping me for free food."

"I think you need more people." He made that sound in the back of his throat that I found irritating. "Molly and I aren't going to always be available."

I slumped against the doorframe. He was right. "I need more friends."

He barked out a laugh. "You need a boyfriend. Slave labor is part of the deal."

He was joking. I knew he was joking. Still, a sick feeling rolled through my stomach, and my heart immediately started punching my chest. "I'd rather figure it out myself. Thanks for the advice, though."

His face fell at my terse tone, and I saw his regret immediately. "I didn't mean anything by that—"

"Don't worry about it," I cut him off. "I know."

He made a thoughtful face and shook his head. "Vere, not every guy is a bad seed. You can't write us all off."

I cleared my throat and tried to make a joke. "Well, I'm writing you off obviously. You're my brother. Gross."

"That's not what I meant. You know that's not what I meant."

"I'm going to get to work. I'll see you later."

"Vera."

"Oh, Dad wants to take us for tacos later. You in?"

His forehead wrinkled, but he let it go. "When?"

"Um, later? I have some work to do. And he says he's not in a hurry. Just whenever you're ready."

"I'm done about six. I can pick you and Dad up?"

I let out a slow breath, thankful we had moved on from relationship talk. "That works."

"K, see you then."

"Bye, Vann. Keep up the good work."

"Go away."

Despite our tense moment, I smiled as I walked to the truck. Vann didn't abandon dad like I did when I moved away, but he still wouldn't have made time for tacos before the diagnosis. Until six months ago, my dad had health complications with his bladder that were worrisome. But that was it. We worried. We hoped for the best. And then we huddled together when the prognosis became cancer instead of polyps and preventative care. Now that Dad was fighting stage four bladder cancer, we both felt the pressure of how little time we had left with him.

I missed the cool air from Vann's shop as soon as I stepped back outside. God, this heat. *I can't wait for fall.*

It was even worse inside Foodie. I quickly turned on the fans and opened the windows. The tiny air conditioning unit kicked on, grumbling

70

under the strain of trying to work in these conditions and letting go of a smelly blast of cool air. I once again praised Vann for the convenience of my parking spot. I didn't have to drive the truck around town or store it at a commissary and deal with paying rent. Vann's shop couldn't have been more perfect for my needs.

Giving up on cooling down, I tossed my hair into a low ponytail with a hair tie from around my wrist. Then pulled out a pen from my purse and got to work. I was halfway to a brilliant idea when a sound at the front door had me spinning around and letting out a startled squeak.

Killian Quinn glared at me from just outside. "You quit?"

A hundred horrible things rolled around in my mouth. I settled on a confused, "What?"

His green eyes glinted at me, and his fingers clenched the doorframe, knuckles turning white from the pressure. "You had one bad weekend, and you quit?"

A dangerous emotion started to bubble up in my throat. "I didn't have a bad weekend. I had a great weekend." My angry thoughts all tried to push out of my mouth at the same time, and I had to take a breath to make a coherent sentence. "And I didn't quit. I'm just getting started."

"You haven't been here since Saturday."

I swallowed despite my dry throat. He looked even better than I remembered him, which sucked since he was an awful human. His black t-shirt clung to his raised biceps, and his beard had been recently trimmed into cleaner lines. Basically, he was obnoxiously hot, and I hated him.

His accusation penetrated my heat-addled brain, and I narrowed my eyes belatedly. "I haven't been here since Saturday because I'm only open Thursday through Saturday."

"Why?"

"What?"

"Why are you only open three nights a week?" His patience was obviously wearing thin, but I didn't understand why he'd bothered to walk all the way over here just to pester me.

So, I asked him. "I'm so confused. Why are you here?"

For the first time since I turned around, he glanced away. For a second, I thought I saw an emotion other than loathing in his intense expression. I

71

even thought maybe his cheeks turned a little red, but it was hard to tell because of his beard. And it was so damn hot that it could have been because of that.

"I thought maybe my suggestions..." he started. Clearing his throat, he tried again.

Suddenly, I was so angry I was sure I could breathe fire if I needed to. "You thought your nasty little note drove me to quit my business?" I made a sound in the back of my throat that reminded me of Vann. "I'm not that insecure."

Liar, liar, pants on fire. But I sounded convincing, and that was all that mattered.

His glare snapped back to mine, pinning me under the concentration of his irritation. "Nasty little note? You make it sound like I was jealous."

I couldn't stop the ridiculous words before they flew out of my mouth. "Maybe because you are."

His eyes widened with incredulity, and I realized how stupid I sounded, how completely idiotic my accusations were. "You think I'm jealous of you?" he demanded. "That's what this is about? I'm jealous of a food truck?"

"God, you're a pompous asshole. Do you hear yourself?"

He laughed, but it was bitter and humorless. "You open up a food truck across from the greatest restaurant in this city and call me pompous? Unbelievable!" He moved his head in a slow shake that sent embarrassment spiraling through me. "That's the last time I try to help a—" He held his hand up and took a step back. But then quickly stepped forward again, crowding the doorway. "You know what? I felt sorry for you. You show up here in this expensive... thing. You're obviously spending money on marketing and logos, and then I tasted that... God, that food. It's not that you don't have potential. It's just that it's completely wasted on easy, fast food that I could find anywhere."

"Out." His eyes widened again, only this time it was from surprise. "Get out. I don't have to listen to you insult me. Not everybody can be the great Killian Quinn. Not everyone has food critics wrapped around their fingers and a team of chefs at their disposal. I'm doing the best I can. This food truck is my life, and I'm not going to let you or anyone else push me around just because they feel threatened by a little competition."

He glared at me, his gaze sweeping over my length, taking my measure, determining my worth. "You're not my competition."

My tone was knife sharp, unwavering when I told him, "And you're not mine."

I swallowed against a jagged bolt of dread when his bright eyes narrowed with challenge. "We'll see." He leaned toward me, and I accidentally inhaled him, spice and mint and something that was neither of those things, something that made my mouth go dry and my belly heat. "Good luck, Vera. You're going to need it."

I was too shocked that he remembered my name to get a good last word in. He didn't wait around for one anyway. He left me staring at him, clinging to my courage and anger. I couldn't let them go. I needed them, needed to wear them like armor.

I hated that I watched him cross the street and disappear inside Lilou. I hated that I stared at the door for another ten minutes waiting for him to come back and apologize.

I hated that he was this complete opposite of me, that he had everything that I'd ever wanted and would never get. I hated that I couldn't want those things anymore.

I couldn't let myself.

Because if I remembered what I used to want, the things I was forced to give up and let go of… I would crumble.

I would shatter.

Most of all, I hated that after how awful Killian Quinn was, his opinion meant everything to me.

Chapter Eight

"Don't serve him!"

Molly glanced back at me like I'd grown a second head. "Vera?"

Wyatt stood at the window with an amused grin pulling up his too wide mouth. I'd noticed him step out the side door of Lilou and hoped he was just going for a smoke. Somehow, I knew better.

I glared at him, irritated with the way he didn't seem to care that he'd pissed me off. Was I a joke to everyone around here? "I have no idea why you're here, Wyatt."

He raised his hands defensively. "Don't be mad at me. This is one of those don't shoot the messenger situations."

I leaned over the messy counter, littered with shredded lettuce and feta cheese from tonight's spicy gyro slider and growled at him through the window. "Too late. You've been blacklisted."

One of his dark eyebrows lifted, the silver ring at the end glinting in my bright lights. "You can afford to blacklist people?"

"Oh, my God, you're just like him."

"Wrong," he argued immediately. "He's Killian Quinn. I'm just a poor, insignificant sous chef. We could not be more different."

The humbled awe in his tone when he murmured Killian Quinn's name so reverently made me roll my eyes. "I don't want to hear it, Wyatt. You're going to have to eat out of your own kitchen."

A line had formed behind him. It wasn't big, just a couple and another set of club goers behind them, but I didn't want them to walk away because Wyatt wanted to draw me a pie chart of all the ways Killian Quinn was superior to the rest of us posers.

Wyatt's gaze followed mine and he glanced over his shoulder at the people standing behind him. When he turned around the arrogance was gone, replaced with puppy dog eyes and an overly exaggerated pout. "But the lamb smells so good, V! I have a thing for gyros. It's practically sexual."

"And I have a thing for not being told I'm doing everything wrong."

He clasped his hands together in front of him. "Please, Vera. I'm starving. You wouldn't deny a starving man a good meal, would you?"

Molly covered her mouth with her hand, hiding her smile. But her hiccup of laughter gave her away regardless.

Unlike my forgiving BFF, I held my poker face. "Go away, Wyatt."

I half expected him to drop to his knees and beg, but his next offer surprised me. "I'll trade you."

"What?"

A satisfied gleam lit his eyes, and he leaned into the window as if the people behind him cared what he had to say. He was just tall enough that he could peer inside the truck, his large fingers curling around the metal window frame. "I'll bring you dessert."

Curiosity sparked inside me, but I needed more of a verbal contract. "From where?"

He jerked his chin toward Lilou. "From where do you think?"

"What is it?"

"Lemon and lavender cake bars or dark chocolate mousse with a salted popcorn crunch."

I puffed my cheeks out, thinking about his offer. "I want both."

"I don't know if I can—"

"All or nothing, Wyatt. You did this to yourself."

Wyatt glanced helplessly at Molly. "She's so mean to me. Is she this mean to you?"

Molly laughed and shook her head. "I've never sold her secrets to the antichrist."

Wyatt glared at her but turned back to me, resigned. "Fine. Both. But if I get caught I need you to testify in court that you held me at gunpoint."

My lips twitched, but I suppressed my smile. "You're stalling, and I have customers."

His head dropped back, and he let out a frustrated growl. "Fine. Two desserts." He looked at me once again. "Can I order now? Please?"

"You have to eat it inside the truck."

"What?"

I pointed to the space behind Molly. "I don't trust you, Wyatt. If you're ordering it, you're eating in here."

"Woman!" He pulled out his wallet despite his frustration. "Fine, but hurry. My break's almost over."

I stepped back from the window and moved to open the door for Wyatt. He marched inside, eating up all the small space with his lanky frame.

Sensing his hurry, I rushed to make his gyro sliders. I had made meatballs instead of the traditional shaved lamb and let them simmer in Mediterranean gravy all day. They were amazing. And perfectly spiced.

It had only taken me the entire week to get the recipe right.

And it had absolutely nothing to do with Killian Quinn's criticism.

Nothing at all.

Wyatt leaned over my shoulder, crowding me. "Don't be stingy with the feta."

I threw him a glare over my shoulder and almost ran into his nose. "Back off, buddy. You'll get what I give you."

He took a step back, his mouth splitting into a charming grin. Unease curled in my stomach, and I turned back to his order.

It wasn't him. Wyatt was nothing but adorably friendly. Despite his tattoos and piercings, he was way too chill to be a threat. But my past had broken me. Had twisted my trust and turned my personal bubble into an impenetrable steel cage.

Molly added orders to the ticket line, so I didn't have time to pay Wyatt any attention after I handed him his meal.

"Holy shit, Vera," he mumbled through a mouth full of food. "This is insane."

I smiled down at the pita pocket I'd made from scratch. "I know." And I did. But it was still nice to hear it from someone else—someone that knew what he was talking about.

"I want another," he demanded.

"I thought you had to go?" Smiling at the people at the pickup window, I handed their sealed to go containers over and spared Wyatt a glance. He stood hovering above the small staircase as if deciding what to do.

"When I bring your desserts back I need another one."

"You're going to have to eat it here again," I told him. His eyes bugged comically. "I'm not kidding. I'm not dealing with him again."

His crooked smile made me release one of my own. "Do you know how many kidneys I would give for him to try my food and tell me what he thought? Both of them. I would give both of them."

I rolled my eyes. "You're ridiculous."

"And you're crazy. He was being nice."

"He was being an asshole, and you know it. Now get back to work before the asshole fires you."

He glanced nervously at the street before tossing his hand up in a quick wave. "You're right. He will fire me."

The door slammed shut behind him, but I was already working on the next order. And the next. A whole fifteen minutes passed before Molly found a second to give me her opinion.

"He's cute."

I scanned the plaza, playing dumb. "Who?"

She slapped my arm with the back of her hand. "You know who. Tall, dark and tattooed."

"You're going to have to be more specific," I told her.

Making a sound in the back of her throat she pointed at Lilou. "Wyatt the Gyro Lover. He's hot, and you know it."

I chewed on my bottom lip to keep from smiling. "He's not ugly. I'll give you that."

"And those piercings."

I nodded. "They make him even less ugly."

"So?"

Cutting my attention back to my meatballs and the next order, I avoided eye contact with her. "So what?"

"So… you should hit that."

"Oh, my God, Molly. You have a weird obsession with my sex life, you know that?"

A laugh bubbled out of her, but she didn't deny it. "I just want you to move on, Vere. And the fastest way to get over someone is to get under someone else."

This time I couldn't help it. I stopped what I was doing and gaped at her. "Molly Maverick, I thought you were a lady."

Her head tipped back as she continued to laugh. "Don't look so scandalized. You know it's true."

"I know nothing," I argued. "And even if it were true, which it's not, I wouldn't be into Wyatt. He's not my type."

"Your type is…what? Not hot guys?"

I rolled my eyes and turned to my station, wiping it down and cleaning it up while I had a break in customers. "My type is anyone not in my industry. I'm not dating another chef."

"I didn't tell you to date him. I told you to—"

Cutting her off quickly, I said, "I know what you told me. But I'm telling you, even a one night stand is completely off the table. Especially with someone that works across the street from the business I own. No more drama, Molls. And no more difficult relationships. I won't survive it."

She turned back to the window. I knew I'd shut her up by reminding her of my past. Instantly, I felt guilty. I'd promised myself months ago that I wasn't going to let my awful history ruin my present. I wanted to move on. I wanted a life. I wanted to get over my bad mistakes and not be afraid to try new things.

But dating wasn't an option. Especially not a chef.

Not that they were all like my ex. But generally, we were egotistical, narcissistic people. It was just the way of things.

I could admit to being that way. I could also admit that two people with those personality traits did not a healthy relationship make.

Molly's soft admonition filled our suddenly quiet space. "You will survive it, Vera. You're stronger than you think. Stronger than anyone I know."

I didn't answer her. She was wrong. I wasn't strong. I was weak. Too weak. So weak, I'd let myself be abused, mistreated and trampled on for two years of my life. When I should have been taking important steps advancing my career I'd shrunk behind the shadow of a great chef and shitty human.

It wasn't until I had absolutely no other choice that I left. It wasn't until my dreams had been stripped from me and my confidence battered and burned that I'd finally, desperately escaped.

And even then, I hadn't confronted him. I'd removed his name from my savings account and ran away to Europe.

Those weren't the markers of someone strong, someone courageous.

I was a coward, and we both knew it.

But at least I'd gotten away.

Two hours later, Molly and I had shrugged off the weirdness that descended whenever we tried to talk about my last relationship. There were very few things that had ever come between us, but Derrek Hanover was always one of them. I knew she didn't blame me for what I'd been through, but she also didn't understand how I'd let any of it happen.

I didn't understand either, to be honest.

And that was why I chose to think about it as little as possible.

"Oh, shit," Molly hissed, instantly pulling my attention to the order window.

I stared out the window unbelieving. He couldn't be serious. Hadn't I made myself clear enough?

Killian Quinn approached Foodie without one single hesitant step. He walked up to the window like he had a right to be there. Like he couldn't be bothered with my hatred of him.

"I thought you banned him," Molly whispered quickly.

Shaking my head slowly I admitted, "I thought I did too." I bumped her with my hip. "Move over. I'll deal with him."

Leaning forward and resting my elbows on the windowsill, I told him firmly, "We're closed."

His narrowed gaze darted to my latest customers still finishing their meals. They stood in a wide circle, eating over their cardboard containers, laughing and talking animatedly. At least they seemed to be enjoying the food.

He quirked an eyebrow at me. "Then I should throw these away?" Like a poker player revealing his winning hand, Killian set two golden takeout containers on the small ledge in front of me.

"What are those?"

"I was told goods had been exchanged." His long, gorgeous fingers dipped into the seam of one of the containers, pulling back the lid to reveal rich, creamy mousse. "Desserts for meatballs."

I popped up to my full height, deciding to never trust another sous chef again in my life. "My deal was with Wyatt."

"Deal?" Killian let out a sound that almost sounded like a laugh. "You blackmailed him and then held him hostage in your tiny truck."

My fingers curled around the windowsill, the sharp edges biting into my palms. "And you're here to avenge him?"

His lips twitched, but his facial expression—bored annoyance—didn't change. "I'm here to remind you that you've committed two felonies already. Are you sure you want to commit a third?"

"Felonies? Hardly." I wanted to slam my window shut and turn off my lights, so he finally got the message but I couldn't help myself. I had to know. "What's the third?"

This time his mouth did turn up in a cocky smirk. "Stealing." He tapped the top of the gold box with one finger and I momentarily found myself mesmerized.

Blinking, I tore my gaze from his stupidly perfect hands and focused on his beard. It seemed like the path of least resistance. "You think I'm trying to steal your dessert recipes?" My gaze dragged upward, over his full lips and crooked nose to those deep green eyes.

He shrugged. "It wouldn't be the first time it's happened."

"I'm not," I told him honestly, quickly, adamantly. "That's not what the deal was about. The deal that Wyatt walked into willingly. With his full consent."

Killian tipped forward, pressing all his weight onto his hands. "Make it with me."

There was something in his tone, in the way he softened his voice and looked at me so intently. A wicked curl of heat coiled through my belly. I ignored it. "What?"

"Make the deal with me. Desserts for meatballs."

I glanced at the boxes, hating that my traitor of a stomach wanted to agree. I had something of Killian Quinn's right in front of me. Something of Lilou's. I was just an inch from touching two desserts I knew would be beyond amazing. All I had to do was sell my soul to get them. "You're delusional."

"Why? Because I want a…" He stepped back and read the chalkboard menu. "A gyro slider and Greek fries?"

God, he was so tempting. Not just the offer… but *him*. Everything about him. The playful look in his eyes, the lift of his mouth, the fullness of his beard. It simply wasn't fair that he looked the way he did *and* acted the way he did.

"No, because you won't be able to keep your mouth shut. Contrary to what you think, I don't hate myself. I'm perfectly happy never to hear your opinion again."

He crowded the window. I could smell him again. He smelled how I imagined his kitchen smelled—a blend of unique spices, grease from the fires and that purely masculine scent that had to be his soap underneath it all. "What are Greek fries anyway?"

I glared at him. I was proud of my food tonight. Despite his assholery, I had put a lot of effort into making sure my flavors were on point. The plating was as pretty as to-go plating could be. And my Greek fries were both creative and delicious.

I had nothing to fear from him.

I ignored his question. "Where's Wyatt?"

A muscle near his eye ticked. "Working. Like he's supposed to be."

"Did you fire him?"

"I just told you he was working."

"Are you going to fire him?"

"Why? Because he abandoned his post so he could flirt with the food truck girl for a half hour? I should fire him. We're booked the entire night." I opened my mouth, but I didn't know where to start. So many of the things he'd said were… annoying. He didn't give me a chance, though. "Would you fire him?"

"Excuse me?"

"Not him. Not Wyatt. But if you had a sous chef, someone you counted on to get you through each service, someone you trusted above all other people in your kitchen, and they left you for thirty minutes in the middle of an important night, would you fire him?"

Killian was trying to trap me. He knew my answer—it was obvious. Yes. Wyatt had made a big mistake. "I don't know," I said instead, choosing my words carefully. "I've never had a sous chef. Or run a kitchen. I don't know what I would do."

"I do," Killian was quick with his response. "You'd fire him."

My cheeks heated with emotion, I just couldn't tell which emotion. Killian brought out so many- anger, frustration, embarrassment, insecurity, irritation, lust. Stupid, stupid lust. "You don't know that."

He ran a hand through his beard, messing it up and then tugging it back to its shape. "You're a hard-ass, Vera Delane. Of course you'd fire him."

My guilty heart thumped hard for Wyatt, despite my earlier claims that I didn't want anything to do with him. "Is that what you're going to do?"

"Didn't you hear me? I trust him. It's too hard to find a sous as good as him. He's safe for today. As long as he can give up taking his breaks locked away with you."

I slammed my eyes shut in frustration, hating his implication. "He wasn't locked away with me. I just didn't want him sneaking his food back to you so you could rip it apart."

He stared at me so hard that I felt it all over my skin. I opened my eyes and shivered beneath the heat of his glare. "Then let me rip it apart now."

"You're out of your mind."

He tapped the boxes again. "It's a fair trade. I'll even keep my opinion to myself."

"Did Lilou run out of food? Can't you get your sous chef to make you a snack? God, you're aggravating."

"Come on, Delane," he persuaded with a lilting voice. "The lemon lavender shortbreads are insane. You know you want them."

Curiosity didn't just kill the cat. It killed the stupid chef that was willing to sell her soul just to get a tiny taste of one of the greatest chefs in the city.

He held up a hand as if he could read the denial swirling in my head. "And before you go claiming that these are already bought and paid for, let's just consider that Wyatt really would have gotten fired for smuggling these out of the restaurant. The only way you're going to get to try these is if you make a deal with me."

A deal with the devil.

"I could always make a reservation. I'm sure it's not that hard." That was a lie. I'd already made a reservation after he'd written me that scathing note, but the earliest they could get me in was still six weeks away.

"Delane, by the time you can manage to sneak inside my restaurant, we'll have changed the entire menu."

I shifted my shoulders, hating the way I felt every time he used my last name. And not because it made me feel bad. Because it made me feel the opposite. "I don't even like lemon."

He leaned closer, erasing the space between us. "You're such a liar," he murmured on a dark chuckle. "Just make me the goddamn slider."

He was right. I was a liar. And where the hell had Molly gone? Why wasn't she coming to my rescue? I was about to make a very stupid mistake, and she had promised that she'd intervene the next time I tried to ruin my entire life.

"Fine," I relented. Letting out a slow, measured breath so he didn't see how nervous I was, I said, "One meatball."

"And fries." He smiled victoriously. "Greek fries."

Stepping over to the counter I started putting together his box. "What is your fascination with Greek fries?"

He poked his head through the window so he could watch me. "I'm intrigued."

"You're obnoxious." I jerked my head to the other side of the truck. "You can wait down there."

"You're not going to make me come in and eat it in front of you?"

Snapping my head up, I glared at him. "Sorry, friends and employees only. It's off limits to you." I held back an evil laugh and asked, "Unless you're looking for a job? I need someone part time to help with prep and orders. Interested?"

His eyes narrowed at the insult to everything he'd worked for and accomplished. "I'll wait down here."

"Good idea." The thrill of victory bubbled in my chest, but I also hated that his smile disappeared. It was a silly thing to miss since I couldn't stand this man. But he was always so serious. I barely knew the guy, and I could tell that his smiles were rare and hard-earned.

Focusing on perfecting his order, I threw myself into the very thing I loved, the thing that had saved me—cooking. I heated his pita on the grill top then added the house tzatziki sauce, and pickled red onions, carrots and cucumbers. Next, I plated the fries fresh from the fryer and topped them with generous portions of all that I put on the slider. I scooped out a simmering meatball and set it very carefully in the middle of the pita, careful not to rip the flatbread, finalizing everything with a sprinkle of feta cheese everywhere.

My hands shook as I carried the box to the pickup window. I tried to convince myself that I already had his worst, that he couldn't say anything else to me that would be meaner than his note or make me feel less than. Still, my traitor of a heart soared with anticipation and hopeful optimism.

He might have been right about my grilled cheese and pulled pork, but I'd stepped up my game. He had to acknowledge that.

That's when I realized I wanted this. I wanted him to try my food again. It was foolish and masochistic. But Wyatt was right, Killian Quinn's opinion mattered.

When I leaned out the window, he had his phone in his hand. The bright light lit up his mouth and that beard, highlighting the contrast of his dark, trimmed facial hair to the red fullness of his lips.

"Order's ready." My voice came out breathier than I intended, weak and afraid. I cleared my throat and waited for him to acknowledge me.

He tucked the phone into his pocket and traded cartons with me. Without saying anything else, he grabbed a fork and napkin from the cutlery container I had next to the window and dug in.

I stepped back into the truck, unable to stop myself from obsessing over his reaction. I convinced myself I would move just as soon as he took his first bite. I couldn't stand there all night watching him chew. That would be weird.

Right?

Yes. Obviously. Yes, that was weird.

He dug in, wrapping his mouth around the pita and I stared at him, determined to read his expression instead of listening to his words. Only it gave nothing away. He was as mysterious as always, and neither looked at me with approval or verbalized his thoughts.

Spinning away from him, I decided I'd tortured myself enough. The desserts went into the cooler because I could not even begin to enjoy those with him outside, eating and judging my food.

Judging me.

"What are you doing?" I whisper yelled at Molly, making an expression that showed her just how furious I was that she'd abandoned me.

"I, uh, had to text my friend," she answered.

I raised an eyebrow. "Your friend?"

She nodded once, barely restraining her smile. "I meant my mom."

"You're a terrible person," I told her.

Her grin broke free, and she looked so ridiculously happy I wanted to punch her. She bounced on her toes and pointed toward the window mouthing, "He's so hot!"

"Stop!" I mouthed back. I took a step towards her, keeping my voice low. "He's the worst!"

"Delane!"

I whirled around at my barked name. It only took three steps until I reached the window. He stood there with my meatball completely dissected.

My stomach dropped to my toes. He hated it. I instantly knew he hated it. "You promised to keep your opinion to yourself."

He mashed his lips together, glaring at the meatball and clearly frustrated that he'd done that. His eyes flicked up to mine. "Do you hate salt?"

"Excuse me?"

"Salt? Do you hate it?"

Fire and anger and pride seared beneath my skin, setting my bones ablaze and my blood to boil. "No, I don't hate salt."

He jabbed his hand at my food. "Then why do you abuse it like you do? It's a supporting actor, not the star of the show. It should enhance flavor, not slap you in the face with it."

My gasp cut through the plaza, high and shrill. "Stop! Stop it right there! I don't want to hear your opinion or your thoughts or your criticism. No more, Killian! I mean it."

His attention moved so quickly from the meatball to my face that I stumbled back a step. There was so much intensity to him. So much aggression and focus and emotion. He wasn't someone you could forget. He left an impression in seconds. Or an imprint. He was a force like the wind, or a tornado. He blew over you with destructive intent, annihilating everything you thought you knew about the world with his brutal opinions and cocky confidence.

When he just stared at me, I began to shrivel. My hands and knees started trembling, and I felt the immediate urge to bolt, to just run away.

Finally, he stepped forward, scooping up a bite of pita and meatball with this fork. He held it toward my face. "Try it."

My voice was nothing more than a breathless gasp. "What?"

He jerked the fork toward me again. "Try it. Try the meatball."

"I did—"

"Humor me."

Unwilling to give this difficult man everything he wanted, I crossed my arms over my chest and said, "Don't you have a kitchen to run?"

"Yes, I do. So take the bite."

"No."

He stepped closer, losing some of his hard edge. "Humor me." After a beat of silence, he added, "Please?"

It was his please that did it. My body reacted to the softly spoken plea before my brain could intervene. I closed my mouth around the fork, *his* fork, and took the bite. A shiver rolled down my spine when I realized how strange the gesture was, how intimate.

I didn't make a habit of eating off other people's forks.

"See?" His question brought me back to reality, and I remembered to taste the food that was in my mouth.

I had spent hours over this recipe. Hours and hours. I'd put every last bit of my talent into creating the perfect lamb meatball. I had made sure it was well spiced, a good, solid texture with just the right notes of earthiness and comfort. The gravy was my own recipe, and it was thick and creamy but not too rich. I'd pickled the vegetables myself and made sure each dice was exactly even and consistent. They were tangy and just barely still crisp—just the way I wanted them. And the pita was a trick I'd learned from a Greek grandmother in Italy. I'd worked with her son at a small bistro, and I'd convinced him to let her teach me how. The pitas were perfection.

And yet now that he brought up the salt…

"Goddamn you," I hissed at him after I swallowed.

He poked at the fries. "The fries are clever and would have been the highlight if not for everything else. The flatbread is fine. But the vegetables are bland, and the meatball is too salty. Your tzatziki is stringy."

"I hate you."

He shook his head, ignoring me. "You hate that I'm right."

If I didn't before, I did now. "Go away, Quinn."

By now a line had formed again, and Molly had filled the ticket line with orders. I needed to get back to work and serve people that didn't care that I'd slightly over-salted the meat. They wouldn't even be able to tell.

Yes, fine, Killian was right. But only a professional would be able to tell.

At least that's what I told myself. The sweet tasting lie would give me the courage to finish out the night at least.

Killian opened his mouth like he wanted to argue with me some more, but Wyatt appeared in the side door of Lilou. "We need you, Chef!"

88

I seized the opportunity to get rid of him. "Your kitchen needs you, *Chef*. So get out of mine."

He grinned at me, as if enjoying my hatred. "Enjoy the desserts, Vera. It was worth the trade."

He tossed his half-eaten meal in the trash can and sauntered back to his restaurant. If I didn't know any better, I would have even said there was a spring in his step.

"God, what an asshole," I growled once he was out of earshot.

When Molly didn't immediately agree, I turned to look at her. She shrugged innocently. "I think he's used to getting his way."

"It's obnoxious."

She fanned herself with her notepad. "And so damn hot."

I should have disagreed with her. But that would have been a filthy lie.

Chapter Nine

I hoped Killian had gotten the message that I didn't want anything more to do with him. It was weird hating a chef of Killian's caliber, but the guy was intolerable. I couldn't stand him.

He had to realize that by now.

I didn't like to think of myself as an opportunist, but in culinary school I'd made it a point to get to know as many notable chefs as possible. Whether they were teachers or guest speakers, I wanted to glean as much technique and talent as I could from them.

It wasn't anything more than a desire to get the most out of my expensive education. But in the end, it had backfired.

I'd gotten to know one guest chef too closely. And then I'd fallen in love with him.

Instead of getting a foot in the door of an ultra-competitive industry, I'd traded my goals and aspirations for a toxic relationship that inevitably ruined any chance I had at making a name for myself.

But even if it weren't for my firsthand experience with self-absorbed, verbally abusive chefs, I still would want nothing to do with Killian Quinn. He was rude, intrusive and insensitive. I didn't ask him for his opinion.

And I certainly didn't want it.

What I wanted was for him to leave me alone.

Apparently, that was too much to ask.

I'd seen him arrive at Lilou an hour earlier. It was Saturday afternoon, and I was deep in prep work for this evening's dinner service. The second I saw him pull up, I had ducked out of view, where I watched him like a weird stalker from the shadows.

He'd dismounted his motorcycle with the same careless ease he always did and tugged the helmet from his head. Only this time instead of going straight inside his restaurant, he stared at the food truck for a solid two minutes.

My heart pounded inside my chest, afraid he would walk over here. I scrunched back against the cooler, praying he couldn't see me as I hid like a coward. But his gaze stayed so intent that I started to wonder if he had super-vision.

Finally, he propped his helmet on his bike and disappeared inside Lilou. I took a deep, stabilizing breath and contemplated trying to convince Vann to move the bike shop. Like across town. Or to a different city. Maybe, possibly, the moon.

I already knew my brother would never do it. *Selfish bastard.*

The sauce in front of me simmered in the pan, bubbles bursting every once in a while. Dipping a clean spoon in it, I lifted it to my lips and tasted. Not salty enough.

Damn it.

I needed to get the meatballs in the sauce, but now I was afraid of ruining the flavor. The self-doubt wasn't natural for me, and I hated it even more because it was inspired by the idiot across the street. It wrapped around me like cracked, too-tight skin I desperately needed to shed.

A sharp knock on the door interrupted my internal freak out, and I spun around ready to face Vann or Molly and ask them to restore some of my confidence with flowery, over the top compliments.

I wasn't ashamed to beg for verbal affirmations. Sometimes a girl just needed to hear how freaking awesome she was.

Before you judge, I gave out verbal affirmations in return. Because I was a good friend and a good sister. And because Molly and Vann truly were freaking awesome.

Unfortunately, it was neither of them.

"Do I need to get a restraining order for you to take the hint?"

Killian stared at me, his mouth just barely twitching. "We're neighbors. Our kitchens aren't even one hundred feet apart."

I snorted. "And wouldn't it be a pity if you lost your job because you can't leave mine alone?"

His cocky expression turned into a scowl. "I knew you were green, Delane. But I didn't think you were a baby."

"I'm not taking your bait, Quinn. You might as well leave."

92

"The thing about baiting is that sometimes it takes a little persistence. You'll give in. I'm not worried."

I slammed a hand on my hip, remembering that I hadn't changed into professional clothes yet. The weather still sizzled around the temperature of the sun, so I'd worn loud, yellow, flowery high-waisted shorts because they were every girl's best friend, and a navy blue lacy crop top.

"I've got work to do, Killian. What do you want?"

He stepped inside the truck but didn't come further than the entryway. "I wanted to..." He took another step toward me, his gaze catching on the simmering pan. "Are you reworking your gravy?"

I swallowed against the offended lump in my throat. "No."

He sniffed the air and moved closer to me. "Are you sure?"

"This isn't gravy," I lied to him. "I'm trying to figure out your shortbread recipe."

His low chuckle slid over the back of my neck and whispered down my spine. "You could have just asked."

I whipped around to face him, jumpy from feelings I shouldn't be having. "And you would have given it to me?"

He shrugged. "Sure."

I wasn't planning on making my own desserts, but I wanted to test him. "Okay, give it to me."

"What do I get out of it?"

"Who says you get anything out of it?"

He held my gaze, his mouth quirking at one corner. Good grief, he was unfairly hot. Molly was right about that.

Standing this close to him in daylight I could finally check out his tattoos. And I did, uncaring if he caught me staring. We were well beyond polite shyness.

An anatomical heart had been strikingly etched on the inside of one forearm with a giant, bloody butcher knife piercing its center. Celtic designs wound around the rest of the space disappearing underneath the sleeve of his black t-shirt. On the other forearm, a large compass stretched from the inside of his elbow to his wrist, filling up almost the entire space. Instead of arrows pointing toward the direction markers, kitchen utensils had been cleverly used. A spatula pointed west, and a whisk pointed north, like a clock telling time.

He crossed his arms over his chest, breaking the momentary spell his tattoos had put on me. "That's how we play this game, Delane. You give me something. I give you something."

I blinked at him. "We're not playing a game."

93

"Are you sure?" His tongue swept over his bottom lip, and I bit the inside of my cheek to keep from mimicking him.

"Yes," I told him firmly.

"Try it," he suggested. "Ask me for something. I'll tell you what it costs."

"So how do I stop you from giving me any more unwanted advice?"

His mouth broke into a full grin. He watched me for a few, long seconds as he debated something internally. "It doesn't matter. The shortbread recipe isn't mine. I can't give it to you."

I would have been surprised had it been his. He wasn't known for his desserts after all. "I didn't want it anyway."

"But you do want my help with the sauce."

"I don't."

He reached past me, brushing my waist with his hand, uncaring that I was standing between him and the stove. "If you'll just..." Unable to reach a clean spoon, he gripped my hip with two hands and physically moved me to the side.

"What the—"

Outraged I watched him try the sauce and then tap his nose with the tip of the spoon. He stood there in thought before grabbing a meatball out of the cooler and biting into it. He got a different spoon and tasted the gravy again before finishing the meatball.

He slammed around my kitchen, rifling through shelves and opening metal cabinets. Finally, he moved to the cooler and pulled out fresh mint.

I bought it for the tzatziki sauce. I'd contemplated putting it into the meatballs, but I hadn't. I didn't want that particular flavor to be overwhelming.

Killian moved back to the counter and pulled down a clean cutting board. Then he helped himself to my knives.

My hands clenched into fists. "What are you doing?"

He glanced at me over his shoulder. "Oh, do you mind if I just..." He gestured at the cutting board with the knife already in his hand.

"I—wha-"

He turned back to the mint and started chopping it into minuscule pieces. "This is a nice knife." He read the brand and went back to work. "At least you know how to take care of your tools."

"What a dick thing to say."

His shoulders shook with a silent laugh. "I just gave you a compliment."

"You gave me a backhanded compliment. And you know it."

He moved the mint to the white sauce and added dill. Then he went back to the cooler and pulled out a lemon. "Take the compliment, chef, and stop assuming that everything I say is an insult."

He called me chef.

He called me chef!

My ego perked up at the unexpected accolade and I tried to remember all the horrible things he'd done to me in the short time I knew him.

"You're making it too much like the tzatziki," I complained.

He shook his head, his lips quirking up in a private smile. "Have a little faith." He then grabbed the red pepper flakes and tossed in a generous amount.

He stood over the pan and stirred while I watched him. Neither of us said anything for a long time. I couldn't guess the thoughts in his head, but I was trying to come to terms with how comfortable he looked in *my* kitchen.

He should have been too big for the small interior. But he hunched his broad shoulders when he worked, curling his long torso over his food protectively… thoughtfully. His muscles rolled with every small movement, every stir of his whisk or lift of a new spoon to taste his progress.

His ego should have made him seem pretentious and out of place in my humble space. But he moved around with a natural ease that was at once alluring and intimidating. He guessed where things were, but most of the time he was right. He mastered my knives like he'd used them all his life. And he worked the sauce like it was his original recipe.

He was too good for my kitchen and yet he didn't act like it. No matter what we'd said to each other leading up to now, he was being nice.

Even friendly.

And it was weirding me out.

Panic twisted in my gut, warning me that this was dangerous. *He* was dangerous. "What do you want, Killian?"

He turned around with a spoon in one hand, the other making a cup underneath. "For you to try this."

He all but shoved the spoon in my mouth. I closed my lips around it because there was no other choice.

It was too hot, but I still had to stifle a groan. He'd taken my good sauce and made it a masterpiece. He'd transformed my modest recipe from necessary to essential, from dead to alive, from anonymous to five-star-worthy. I stepped back, keeping hold of the spoon. His eyes followed me, waiting, expecting. "It's too similar to the tzatziki," I told him.

"That's the point," he explained. "Only use the gravy. Save the tzatziki for the fries. You'll separate the flavor profiles and make it more interesting."

I clenched my teeth so hard, my jaw ticked. He was a pushy, intrusive asshole. And completely right. *Damn him*. I shoved my way between him and the stove, grabbing for the red pepper flakes, just to make a point that this was still my kitchen.

"You went a little light."

He peered over my shoulder, his chest pressing momentarily against my back. His deep voice rumbled in my ear. "Careful, chef."

I shivered. I couldn't help it. He made the relentless summer day feel frigid compared to his body heat. His breath danced along my earlobe and despite the savory sauce filling the kitchen with Mediterranean scents and tangible defeat, all I could smell was him.

The whisk in my hand trembled once, twice. I leaned back into him, unable to resist exploring what it would feel like to be pressed against his hard chest, how he would make me feel against his body.

I had to know.

He leaned closer, and my shoulders settled against him, his hand landing on my hip with the lightest touch. A ripple of uncertainty vibrated through me. I should pull away. I shouldn't have gotten this close to begin with.

I started to step to the side, and Killian's fingers dug into my hip, holding me in place, taking the decision away from me. His touch was light only seconds before, but now it was strong, familiar, possessive. He was used to getting his way, and I'd suddenly stopped coming up with reasons why I shouldn't let him have it.

"Sorry, I'm late, Vera!" My dad's voice boomed inside the truck and Killian and I jumped apart like we'd been caught cooking completely naked.

Dad ambled inside, catching Killian and I avoiding each other's eyes and shuffling to opposite sides of the small space. "Oh, sorry," Dad murmured. "I didn't realize you had company."

"I don't!" I rushed to explain, knowing my eyes were wild with guilt. The reality of how easy it had been to let myself touch Killian crashed down on me carrying the burden of my abandoned dreams and failed relationship. "I mean, he's not company. Or a friend. Or really, anything." Dad and Killian shared similar expressions of confusion. Translation: I was acting like a lunatic. "What I mean is he was helping me, but now he's leaving. Killian runs the kitchen across the street. He was just, uh, giving me his opinion on my sauce for tonight."

Killian thrust out his hand for my dad to shake. "Killian Quinn. Like Vera said, I run Lilou just over there."

My dad followed Killian's pointer finger before taking his hand. "Hank Delane. Vera's said nice things about that restaurant. She's the only expert I know, but she always knows what she's talking about. You must be proud."

"Very, sir." He half turned around, staring at the sauce I stirred absently. "I'll see you later, Vera. Good luck tonight."

Not wanting to seem rude in front of my dad, I mumbled, "You too."

Killian left quickly, taking all his weird energy with him. I let out a shaky breath and glared at the gravy.

"He seemed nice," Dad said. "You made him out to be such a superstar. I wasn't sure what to expect."

I snorted and felt a tingle of relief as I remembered how I really felt. "He's not usually so welcoming. You brought out the decent human in him. Most of the time he's obnoxiously combative."

My dad snickered, taking a seat at the tall stool I'd bought for Vann and Molly when they helped me out. Neither of them could be here tonight, so my dad offered to take money instead- even though I was positive he didn't fully understand what that entailed. I felt beyond guilty asking him to stay up hours past his bedtime, but he insisted. I loved him more for it, plus I needed him to look at my cooler and work his mechanical magic. "I don't think I'm the reason he was over here *helping you with your sauce*."

My face flushed tomato red. "Oh, my gosh, Dad!"

"Well, baby girl, honestly."

I stared harder at Killian's creation—I couldn't even call it mine anymore. "Are you sure you're up for this tonight? I hate risking your health."

He waved me off with his meaty hand. "Vera May, there is no place I'd rather be than right here with you. If I have to go, at least let me spend my last days with the people I love most doing the things they love most."

Hot tears pricked my eyes, but I refused to let them fall, not yet. "Dad, you're not going anywhere, so stop talking like that. Besides, I'm going to teach you how to use a fancy phone and then you'll realize how much you have to live for."

He grunted and said something that sounded suspiciously like, "Jesus, take me now." I finally lifted my face to smile at him. "You can do it, Pops. I believe in you."

"Alright," he finally grumbled. "Show me how to work the hoozywhatsit."

I filled out the sauce to accommodate all the meatballs, following Killian's additions, hating him every second of it. Then I showed Dad how to use the PayPal card swiper on my phone. He practiced with his credit card while I finished the prep work.

By the time we had our first customer, he'd deposited two hundred dollars of his own money into my account, claiming that he couldn't resist the opportunity to invest in such an exciting business venture.

"I'm paying you back," I told him sternly.

He didn't bother to take me seriously. "What for? I can't take it with me."

I hated that he kept referring to his death as if it were going to happen tomorrow. I wanted him to fight his cancer. Fight it and win.

That said, with dad helping take orders, it was the roughest night I had so far—even worse than the first night when I had to do it all myself. He loved talking to the customers, but got most of the orders wrong or mixed up. He kept accidentally deleting apps from my phone when it sat too long, and he had to pull up the pay app on his own. And he ate more meatballs than I sold.

Or at least it seemed like it.

But we had so much fun. My dad was funny, and he kept my customers and me entertained. I didn't remember that about him from my childhood. Or I guess I did, but it was in a distant way.

I had been so excited to flee this town and his house, that I hadn't let myself appreciate him or his sense of humor. I should have spent the last few years getting to know that about him, getting to know him.

Instead, I'd let myself get locked away. Derrek had never wanted to visit, never wanted to let me come back here. At first, I blamed his job. He was an executive chef after all. He had to work late and be up early. He didn't get weekends or holidays off. He couldn't leave his kitchen.

Later, when his abusive nature made itself known, I realized he preferred the control. He didn't care about my family and didn't want me to care about them either. He wanted me for himself. Where he could keep an eye on me. Where he could dictate my every move and thought.

Dad had always been polite to Derrek, but just barely. I knew I hid what was really going on the few times Dad and Vann had come to visit us, but they both saw that I was unhappy.

And for those reasons I'd kept Dad at a distance. I felt like I was only just now getting to know him since I'd moved back. But now my time with him had an expiration date. Dad was dying, and I couldn't make up for all the time lost.

I closed the truck two hours early. I was nearly out of meatballs and Dad looked tired. Besides that, *I* was exhausted from trying to babysit him at the window and get through all those orders.

Dad helped me clean up and carry what I needed to my car. I walked by Lilou wondering what Killian would think when he came outside and I was gone. Usually, he left before me.

Shaking my head, I realized how ridiculous that was. He wouldn't care. Or notice. Whatever we were, we weren't friends. We weren't even enemies.

Enemies implied that we were on equal footing of some sort, but he had made it clear time and time again that he was the superior chef. What had he called me in that note?

Pedestrian.

Dad followed me home and went straight to bed. He barely made it through his bedroom door before I heard the deep rumble of his snores.

I couldn't fall asleep easily after a shift. I was always too amped up.

Plus, I usually smelled like the inside of a deep fat fryer. I took a shower and washed work off me, all the different smells from the night and the shadow of failure I couldn't shake.

I blamed Killian Quinn for that.

Or at least tonight I did.

After I'd put product in my hair and brushed my teeth, I sat on my bed and pulled my laptop out. I tried not to get too obsessive with my business page or the reviews that popped up every other day, but I couldn't help it. Feedback was addicting. And thankfully, so far the response had been so positive that it was hard not to bask in the glow.

Besides, after putting up with Killian for two days in a row, I deserved a little glow.

There was a message waiting for me, and my heart sank when I saw that it was from James Q, the same heckler that had originally reached out to me.

James Q: How's business? He'd asked. Like he knew me.

I thought about ignoring him completely. But this guy had assumed I would fail from the start. He needed a verbal lashing.

Or at least an *I told you so.*

Foodie the Food Truck: Fantastic. It's been better than I could have ever expected. And it had been. It wasn't a lie.

His response came quickly. **James Q: I'm impressed, Foodie. I honestly didn't think you had it in you.**

I wasn't sure how to respond. **Foodie the Food Truck: Uh, thank you? James Q: It was a compliment.**

My brow furrowed. How had I gotten sucked into another conversation with this guy?

Foodie the Food Truck: I assumed.

James Q: I've been told I don't give very good compliments, so I just wanted you to be sure.

This conversation echoed too closely to Killian, and I immediately clicked on his name to cyberstalk him more closely. There was no profile picture, although from his feed and small friends list it was clear this guy was involved in the food industry somehow. I scrolled through past posts and pictures of the dishes he made both at home and in an industrial kitchen. But his posts were few and far between, and there were never any face shots.

He could have been any chef.

He could have been Derrek.

He could have been Killian.

I shook my head, hating how absorbed in Killian I was. I obviously needed sleep. Anything to stop thinking about him.

Foodie the Food Truck: Well, thanks again, James. I hope you get to check out Foodie sometime soon.

He sent me back a thumbs up, releasing me from the conversation. I clicked off the message box and shut my computer down.

Putting aside the message, and Killian and Lilou, I lay back on my bed and rubbed my hand over my heart.

It burned in my chest, punching against my breastbone, wanting something I couldn't define. I hated this feeling. I hated that it followed me around like a specter, taunting and poking and never leaving me alone.

I'd felt it in high school the second I realized I wanted to be a chef. Every time I researched schools or made plans for my future, it was there, spurring me on to chase my dreams. I'd had a momentary break from it during culinary school, but it returned in full force once I was tied to Derrek and realized my dream of becoming a famous chef faded in the long shadow of his illustrious career.

In the beginning, I had hoped Derrek would help me in my career. I hadn't wanted to use his connections for unfair advantages, but he'd been an opinion I trusted, a gentle critic that would both inspire me to do better and point out my flaws. Until we moved in together. Then he'd quickly made it clear that I could cook in a kitchen, but not one that I ran. He didn't want to compete with me. He didn't want me to suffer a schedule like his. He didn't think that we would survive both of our career goals.

So, I'd blended into the background while he continued to accomplish everything he wanted to.

My heart started hurting again the day I was offered a sous chef position in an up and coming bistro. I'd come home elated and so proud. Derrek had been excited for me too, but then started asking questions carefully crafted to make me doubt myself. By the end of the conversation, I'd believed I wasn't ready to be a sous chef. He'd helped me realize that if I took that important of a position, then I wouldn't be able to see him or take care of our apartment. It was a great kitchen, but not one on the top of my list. If I settled now, I would always be settling.

I turned down the offer and worked part time at a bigger, more commercial kitchen. The food wasn't interesting, and the head chef was obstinate and self-absorbed. I would never have moved up there. I would never inspire new and creative dishes. I would make the same generic crap over and over again under the thumb of a man that didn't even know my name.

But I did get to see Derrek whenever he was home or needed me. I did get to play house with our apartment.

And that was just the beginning of how things went so wrong.

I continued to rub my chest, wondering when the ache would go away. Derrek was gone. I ran my own kitchen. I owned a business.

I'd been forced to change my dreams since my young culinary days, but I'd recalibrated and made new dreams. Set new goals.

And I was reaching them.

So why did it feel like settling?

Chapter Ten

*T*he next four weekends became a circus routine of trying to make the best damn food on the freaking planet and Killian sending one of his spies to infiltrate my very carefully vetted line of customers every time I changed up the menu.

It was infuriating.

He was infuriating.

I would have denied access to every single one of his moles except I couldn't screen as thoroughly as I would have liked. Not while I was busy cooking. And not while he dressed them in disguise—or at least made them take off their chef jackets.

Not to mention, when it came down to it I was afraid to refuse service to anyone just in case they didn't work for Killian. Refusing to serve customers based solely on my irritation with the man across the street would obviously be very bad for business.

So, to combat Killian's ruthless criticism, I kept the menu at one option instead of two. And I honed every one of my techniques to master level. I became a freaking black belt at cooking.

The notes still didn't stop.

The weekend I made meatloaf burgers on onion buns he sent this back: *Mushy and over seasoned. I'm taking away your salt privileges. And if you don't stop using parsley as a garnish, I'm suing. I will sue you for defamation.*

The next night, Friday night, I chopped up four cups of parsley out of spite and sent it over to Lilou in a to-go container. I made Wyatt give it to Killian. Actually, I tried to get Wyatt to throw it in his face and yell, "Make it rain, motherfucker!" But Wyatt was a giant, skinny chicken. Basically, Wyatt just handed it to him and explained my evil plan. And then apparently, they had a nice chuckle over it. I hated them both.

Lesson learned, never send a man to get a woman's revenge.

That Saturday night, I'd removed the parsley from the dish—mainly because I used it all in my flop of a prank—tightened up the spices and added a thorough fry to the meatloaf burger on the grill top to make it less "mushy." Killian stopped by after Lilou closed to suggest I use Panko in the burgers instead of regular breadcrumbs, add turmeric to the seasoning mix, and top them with fried onion rings instead of sautéed onions.

His suggestions were obnoxious.

And genius.

The weekend I served a mashup of poutine and pot roast with slow-cooked chuck roast over French fries with fried cheese curds, gravy and a side of roasted balsamic carrots, he sent this lovely note: *What is this, Canada? Make it taste better, Delane.*

I'd actually sent a note back that time that said, *What does that even mean?*

He didn't waste any time. Not five minutes later he wrote:

1. Chuck roast—cheap. It's so cheap. Why are you so cheap, chef?

2. Fries—soggy.

3. Cheese curds—stringy.

4. Carrots—how are those working out for you? That's what I thought.

5. ...

Well, to be honest, I already knew what number five was going to say, and I didn't want to read it. Or care about it. Or bother with it.

5. Gravy—I'm sending someone over to confiscate your salt. Don't fight this. It's the best thing for both of us.

That Friday morning, I stopped by Tractor Supply and picked up a twenty-five-pound salt block for $6.99. I made Wyatt take it over to him later that night. It had been as satisfying as I imagined it would be.

He stopped by around midnight and tricked Vann into letting him order. I'd made his food and had it halfway out the window before I realized it was him. Before I could pull it back, he'd grabbed it and taken off across the street.

I shouted after him, "You better run, Quinn!"

He'd turned around to flash me a smug grin and almost got hit by an oncoming Volvo.

The weekend I tried a play on Reubens by stuffing biscuits with pastrami, Swiss cheese, house-made sauerkraut and Thousand Island aioli to dip it in, Killian made a traffic ticket out of an order pad and fined me one million dollars for "Forcing soggy biscuits on unsuspecting customers."

One million dollars.

I copied his ticket on an order paper of my own and fined him one billion dollars for being such an asshole. (Molly's idea!)

He stopped by that Saturday night to add ketchup to my aioli, and I quote, "Because nobody ever expects ketchup." Then he showed me how to bake the biscuits halfway so they didn't get mushy and squeeze the excess juice from the sauerkraut—something I had known how to do once upon a time. But let's be honest, I didn't work with sauerkraut a whole bunch. I was bound to forget something every once in a while.

This weekend I'd picked chili dogs to feature, and I was keeping those pretty straightforward only because my chili kicked ass. My butcher had gotten me a sweet deal on spicy kosher hot dogs, and they had a fair amount of heat to them. I'd pickled my pickles two months ago and then quartered them for the hot dogs. They were the perfect blend of spicy and sweet, crunchy and soft.

When Killian sent back his criticism, I was beyond being surprised by his notes or him as a human. I'd accepted this as my new reality. Yes, I owned a business, set my own hours and made whatever I wanted! Yes, I also had to deal with Killian Quinn every day—my punishment for living the dream.

I could never catch who took him my food. To be honest, I didn't try that hard. Whoever they were always paid, so at least there was that. I had my suspicions, but there were close to two hundred customers nightly, and I only recognized a couple of people from Lilou, specifically. Regardless of who took Killian my food, Wyatt was always the one that brought the note back.

I glared at him as he walked up to the truck, shoulders slumped in acceptance. I couldn't help needling him. "The messenger I'm dying to shoot."

He pouted. "I miss eating here."

"Yeah, well, you've been banned." I reached out of the order window and tapped the siding next to the chalkboard menu. I'd made Molly hand draw wanted posters of Wyatt and Killian. Although they were a little worse for wear since they'd been taped outside for three weeks. I probably should have laminated them.

Wyatt frowned at his faded, windblown picture. "If it makes you feel any better, tonight he chewed my ass on three separate occasions. Once he even threatened to call animal control."

I suppressed a laugh. "On you?"

He nodded, resigned. "On me."

"Oh, poor Wyatt. We don't think you're an animal. You should quit Lilou and come hang out with us. We're way more fun!"

Molly leaned over, "We also have a two ass-chewing maximum. So the most you ever get your ass chewed is twice per night."

His head tipped back, and he closed his eyes. "That shouldn't sound amazing, but it does." Meeting my eyes once again, he looked like he was considering it. "What do you pay?"

I opened my mouth to speak, but Molly cut me off. "I can answer that since I'm her highest paid employee." She leaned back on the stool, resting the book she'd been reading between customers on her lap with her finger in place to hold the page. "Nothing. She pays us nothing."

Wyatt grinned at her. "Slave labor? I like the way you roll, Vera."

"Like it enough to become a minion? The position also comes with hugs!"

"I'd love to defect and join the resistance," he told us seriously. "But I need dental."

Molly perked up. "You have insurance?"

He leaned in conspiratorially, "And mental health days."

Molly stared dreamily across the street as if she were the one considering defection. I cocked my head back and glared at my delusional best friend. "Molly, you *have* health insurance. And mental health days. At your real job. Remember the fancy marketing firm you work at every day?"

She picked up her book again. "Oh, right. Sorry. Sometimes I get so sucked into the drama here, I can't remember what's real and what's foreplay between two insane chefs."

Wyatt barked a laugh, his entire body rocking with the force of it. She smirked, proud of herself. And I contemplated creating a Tinder profile for her. Because revenge.

"*Anyway.* Why are you here, Wyatt?"

He held up a folded over piece of printer paper. "Same old."

I snatched it from him and waved it at Molly. "This isn't foreplay. This is motive. Which is a pity since pale people shouldn't be forced to wear orange."

106

Molly rolled her eyes, but she set her book down again. "This is like... if I had a favorite daytime soap. Wyatt, we're going to need popcorn and Twizzlers."

Ignoring them both, I opened the note. *Congratulations on the least original food truck idea ever. If you're hard up for inspiration, you can always ask me for help.* Just when I thought he'd leave the salt out of it, he added a quickly scrawled, *Be real, is salt holding you at gunpoint right now?*

I lifted my head, "Huh."

Wyatt cringed. "What does it say?"

Molly gaped at him. "You mean you don't read them?"

He stared back at him. "He trusts me. At least with this."

"You're a better person than me," she told him. "I'm too nosy."

Wyatt turned back to me, apparently just as meddlesome as Molly after all. "Care to share?"

"I feel weird saying this, but I think he liked it tonight." I read the note again, waiting for the missing soul-crushing put down, but I couldn't find it. I mean, it wasn't like the nicest thing I'd ever read, but it lacked Killian's flare for sending me to therapy. He'd even offered to help me.

Wyatt snorted. "He likes everything you make."

I tore my eyes from the note and gave Wyatt a look that questioned his sanity. "Obviously, he loves everything I make. Which is why he's always insulting me. I'm sure it's just how his tiny, cold heart shows affection."

"Vera, seriously. Last month he fired a dishwasher because they turned the kitchen radio station to country during clean-up. He doesn't tolerate bullshit."

"He didn't really fire someone for liking country music."

Wyatt's lips twitched. "Okay true. He was constantly late and had three no-shows. He might have had it coming. But the country station thing was the last straw."

I considered my revenge for a long time before settling with something as equally anticlimactic as Killian's had been. Turning the paper over, I scrawled back a response. It would have been better if I could have written it in magazine cutouts, but there was no time, man!

Salt wants me to say that I'm not being held against my will.

I mean, I love being held against my will.

I mean, I love salt.

I think it's Stockholm Syndrome.

Send help.

I passed the note back to Wyatt and capped my pen before sticking it somewhere in the dangerous abyss of my hair.

He looked at the note, then at me. "That's it?"

"That's it."

"No diabolical present? No maniacal threat? No trip to the feed store?"

"Go away, Wyatt."

He touched the corner of the folded note to his temple and meandered back across the street to his side of the fence.

We watched Wyatt disappear through the side door of Lilou in silence. As soon as the door slammed shut behind him, Molly asked, "Really, what did the note say?"

I turned around to stir my chili. "He called me unoriginal and made a lame joke about salt."

"Huh."

"My thoughts exactly."

"So do you think he'll stop by later?" she asked quietly since a few customers had stepped up to the menu board.

"Yeah."

Her feet hit the ground emphatically. "You do?"

"He's stopped by before," I reminded her.

"You sound super sure tonight. Did you invite him over?"

"Don't be ridiculous."

She couldn't let it go. "Then how do you know?"

I shrugged. Because he offered help and I jokingly asked him for it. But I didn't tell her that. For some reason, it felt like an inside joke between Killian and me and I was reluctant to share it with anyone else. "Gut feeling."

She let it go, but couldn't help herself. "He's so into you, Vera."

I started laughing because honestly that was hilarious. "He's so into *food*. And I think he's really bored with his life."

"Why do you think that?"

"Because he lives at Lilou. Seriously, he works every single day. His life consists of that square building and the troll bridge he sleeps under. I kind of feel bad for him."

Molly fell quiet again, probably trying to figure out the logistics of Killian's life. She could join the club. In the time that I'd opened my food truck, he'd only been absent for dinner service a handful of times.

He started his morning early at Lilou with deliveries, of which he was always present for. Probably to ensure the food being delivered was up to his standards. Then sometimes he disappeared during the middle of the

108

day, and sometimes he worked straight through lunch. But even if he took a break, he was almost always back in time to prep for the night.

Not that I was stalking him or anything.

Besides, that was the price you paid for running a kitchen like Lilou. That was the life we lived. We were all workaholics. Even chefs who didn't work every single night, like me, couldn't ever let it go. It didn't end. We never let it end.

Just like I predicted, he showed up an hour later after my late-night rush. He walked right up to the window and said hi to Molly. I pretended not to notice him. I had chili to stir. And other stuff.

Apparently, he couldn't stand not having all the attention. "I didn't realize you were getting your best ideas from concession stands."

Do not engage. Do not engage. Do not engage.

I spun around, totally engaging. "The chili dogs have been a huge hit, so..."

I had no willpower. I would have made a terrible ninja.

"So, you're catering to the masses now? How revolutionary."

Leaning forward, unable to restrain the snarky biotch he brought out in me, I said, "Hey, the masses pay the bills. I'll leave the food revolution to you. If only you could combat climate change by taking away everyone's table salt."

His lips twitched, and I could have sworn he wanted to smile. But he didn't. "It wasn't overly salted tonight. I'm impressed, Delane."

"It's never overly salty," I returned. "You have an overly sensitive palate."

He stared at me, those green eyes glittering with something he wanted to say, but for some reason, he held back. Which wasn't fair. I wanted to know what it was. And I wanted to know why he held back. And I wanted to know a hundred other things I shouldn't want to know.

Another minute passed before I realized we were just standing there, staring at each other, locked in some kind of weird hate spell. People started walking up and standing in line behind him, and we were simultaneously released from the enchantment.

"Did you come over here for another one of my underwhelming chili dogs? Or was there something else?"

His voice dropped low, sending a tingle of something through my belly. A single butterfly leaped inside me, flapping unwelcomed wings and sending uninvited shivers down my stiff spine. He ran a hand through his hair, pushing it back from his face. "I just stopped by to see if you needed help. That's all."

My breath caught. He was so sweet at that moment. Gentle. Reserved. Open.

Fear curled inside me, fueled by his gesture of kindness and the way his hair fell in tousled waves. I wanted to run my fingers through it like he had. And that terrified me.

I didn't have time for him. Or this unwanted attraction. I'd sworn off men. All men. Including, no wait, *especially*, arrogant, pigheaded, pushy chefs like Killian Quinn.

"I'm good." I cleared my throat and gestured at Foodie. "We're good."

He took a step back, withdrawing physically and emotionally. Not that he was emotionally involved or anything. But it was like he closed back up behind shuttered eyes, closed up and retreated from our innocuous conversation. "Of course you are."

"See you later, chef."

He bobbed his head, seeming to decide something. "Lay off the salt, Delane."

I watched him walk away, wondering how I could get us back to the place where I hated him. Nothing had changed tonight. Nothing significant or life-altering or obvious. And yet something had changed. Because I wanted to hate him, but I didn't.

I wanted him to stay away.

But I so didn't.

And I didn't know what to do with any of it.

"He's so into you!" Molly gloated after he'd gone.

I wrapped my arms around my waist, annoyed by the lump in my throat. "He's not. For real. Sorry to burst your bubble, but I'm right about this, Molls."

I proved it two hours later when Killian closed Lilou and left with a pretty blonde on the back of his motorcycle. They'd walked out of the kitchen together, but she was dressed in tight jeans and sky-high stilettos, obviously not one of his employees. He'd given her his helmet, and she'd wrapped her arms around his waist. They'd driven off, his engine roaring through the plaza, and not once had he looked in my direction.

See? I was right.

Chapter Eleven

"*W*here is he?"

"Shh!" I ducked down, flattening myself against the table.

Molly giggled and continued to look back and forth around the restaurant. "Is he going to bring out our food?"

I snorted. "Killian Quinn associating with commoners? Highly unlikely."

"Welcome to Lilou, ladies."

I snapped upright and flashed a tight smile at the waiter hovering over the table. He wore a serene expression despite our suspicious behavior. I caught Molly's eye from across our small table and used every ounce of self-control to keep from laughing.

"My name is Shane, and I'll be serving you this evening. Have you been to Lilou before?"

"No," I mumbled.

Molly sounded significantly more put together. "It's our first time. We've heard such great things about the chef."

Shane beamed, nodding his head toward the kitchen. "Chef Quinn is truly the best. You won't be disappointed."

"We'll see about that," I murmured under my breath.

Shane gave me a curious look, but it was brief and replaced with the bland, professional look all the servers sported. "Chef Quinn is introducing a new menu this evening." His hand swept gracefully toward a rectangle of creamy cardstock. The cursive letters arched across the smooth surface, freshly printed. "Please take your time perusing, and I'm happy to answer any questions you might have."

"I do have a question," I blurted before he walked away. He waited patiently while I found the courage to snoop. "Does Chef Quinn change the menu regularly?"

Shane had no reason to distrust me. Killian was well known enough that industry insiders ate here all the time. I could be another food blogger for all he knew. "Seasonally," Shane finally admitted.

It was the end of July. Hardly a new season. "Is this the fall or summer menu?"

He didn't know exactly how to take me. "I'm so sorry. Were you hoping to try something from the last menu? If you'd like I can see if he'll accommodate you, although I can't promise anything."

Oh, God, the last thing I wanted to do was draw attention to myself. "No! No, thank you. It's just that it's the middle of summer. How new is the menu?"

One of his eyebrows raised, suspicious. "You're right. Up until two weeks ago, we served a different menu, but Chef Quinn felt that a change was necessary. We trust he knows best."

I was like a dog with a bone. "Any particular reason?"

Shane released a short, nervous laugh. "Inspiration."

"Excuse me?"

"Inspiration," Shane emphasized. "We were told he was inspired to change it. I'm afraid I don't know what that means, only that it's one of his best menus to date. I'm positive you'll be pleased with it."

Forcing a relaxed smile, I agreed with him. "I'm positive I will be too." Even if I would never tell Killian that.

"The wine list." Shane tapped his finger on a golden, shimmery folder in the middle of the table. "Our sommelier has selected the very best bottles to accompany your meal. Or if you'd prefer, our bartender is a master craftsman with cocktails." He took a step back and bowed his head. "I'll give you a few minutes to look over the menus. I'll be back soon."

Molly leaned forward smiling, "Waterboarding might be more effective."

I followed Shane, watching as he walked around the restaurant. "But how to get him to meet me in the bathroom?"

She laughed. "You're ridiculous. Why don't you just ask him all these questions yourself?"

I met her gaze. "And let all of my detective talents go to waste? It's like you don't even know me."

112

She pushed the wine list toward me. "At least pick out something good to drink. If I have to endure this amazing dinner while you try to steal all of Killian Quinn's secrets at least let me get drunk."

I didn't argue with her because she had a point. "What do you feel like? Cocktails or wine?"

"What's cheaper?" she whispered.

Quickly scanning the menu, I whispered back, "Water."

"Cocktails it is."

Molly did well for herself, meaning she could pay all her bills and afford her cute downtown apartment and newish car payment. But she didn't have unlimited amounts of cash sitting around. Or enough to justify tonight's meal.

Neither did I for that matter.

Just one more reason I loved her—she splurged with me just for the hell of it. Some girls went shopping together. When Molly and I wanted to blow all our savings, we went to five-star restaurants and gallery openings. When we wanted new clothes, we hit our favorite thrift stores and raided each other's closet.

Shane reappeared to take our drink orders, two variations of the bartender's signature Moscow Mules, one with pomegranate and the other with elderflower, and I ordered the pork belly and wagyu beef heart kabobs for an appetizer.

He disappeared again, and with another look around, I relaxed into my seat, secure in the feeling that Killian had no idea that I was here. And there was no reason for him to know I was ever here.

Lilou was as charming as I imagined it would be. The white brick looked just as quaint on this side as it did the outside, especially with the dimmed overhead lights and candles set on the tables. The tablescapes were elegant, classy, without being over the top. The linens were pristine. The cutlery was perfectly modern. The atmosphere engaged and whimsical.

I loved it.

It was the kind of restaurant I had dreamed of working in. I imagined what it would look like in the daytime with the lights fully up. The servers would hustle from table to table, setting up for supper service. The phone would ring constantly as last minute diners tried and failed to get reservations. The clatter from the kitchen would fill the restaurant like a theme song, the never-ending background music as Killian prepared for the evening and his army of chefs obeyed his every command.

My heartbeat picked up speed, dancing in my chest, responding to the electricity humming in the air. Killian was probably too arrogant to realize what a gift a kitchen like this was. Entitled and spoiled, he was used to this level of success. But from where I sat on a pile of ashes that used to be dreams, I knew he held a rare and precious thing. For as many restaurants as there were in this city, he had the privilege of running one of the nicest. For as many chefs as there were in this industry, he had the honor of being one of the best.

And still, I couldn't find it in me to be jealous of him. Maybe at first I had been. But that had been a generic jealousy, born from the bitter taste of my mistakes. Now that I knew him a little better, I realized he deserved this kitchen. He'd earned it.

Even if I hated admitting that.

"What are you thinking?" Molly asked quietly when I'd been silent for several minutes.

I shook my head, curling my shoulders forward and playing with my linen napkin. "Nothing, really. I was just taking it all in."

"It's pretty, isn't it?" Molly agreed. "Almost too pretty. From everything you've said about Killian, it doesn't seem to be his kind of place."

Shane arrived with our drinks and first course. "I guess we'll find out."

He went over the dishes, explaining the crispy pork belly over grits with basil crème and oyster mushrooms. My mouth started watering as I took in the food, inhaling the savory scents. He pointed to the beef kabobs, explaining the Mediterranean take on them and the tzatziki inspired sauce.

My gaze narrowed on the skewers with laser focus. He wouldn't.

He didn't.

Before Shane could walk away, I'd already dragged my finger through the white sauce and tasted it. "That bastard!" I hissed.

"What?" Molly asked, leaning forward with alarm at the same time Shane panicked. "Is something wrong?"

I sucked my finger clean because damn it if he hadn't made it even better than the one he'd helped me with. "No, nothing. Sorry." My cheeks turned red with embarrassment. "It's just *so* good."

Shane smiled, appeased by my compliment. "It really is. I could drink that sauce by itself."

Molly tilted her head curiously, but waited to try anything until Shane had walked away again.

"That's my sauce," I told her. "The one he stopped by to improve."

Her voice dropped, and she immediately plated one of the kabobs to try it. "He stole it?"

I wished. "No, not really," I admitted. "Mine was good. His is from a different planet of good. But it's definitely similar to mine."

114

"Could we call it 'inspired' by yours?"

I ignored her sly grin and shook my head. "Only in the general sense of he realized how awesome he could make it and how not awesome I had made it. Besides, I keep changing up my menu, so it's not a huge deal. Those meatballs were so last month."

"You're not mad? Really?"

Honestly, I was flattered, but I didn't want to admit it. "I'm always mad at him. The man is obnoxious." Although I hadn't expected him to ever steal something from me. Killian Quinn was a complete original. I got the vibe that he loathed doing the popular thing. He wanted to be the first, set the tone, create the trend. Not follow in someone else's footsteps.

We were going over the rest of the menu, trying to narrow our main courses to a couple of options we could share, when Wyatt stepped out of the kitchen. He walked over to Shane, who pointed in our direction.

"Oh, no! Molly, we've been made!"

She ducked down, holding the menu to the side of her face. "I told you we should have worn disguises!"

"Well, well, well," Wyatt crooned, stepping up to our table. "If it isn't our nosy neighbors."

I peeled the menu from the front of my face and braved looking at him. "I would have had you bring me something, but I felt sorry for you and didn't want to get you fired."

The high planes of his sharp cheekbones turned pink. "Thanks for that."

Offering him a genuine smile, I made a show of glancing around. "I mean, I don't personally understand why anyone would want to work here, but I guess if you need to pay your bills or whatever."

He laughed and held out the tray I hadn't noticed yet. "Yeah, I just need the basics really. Like electricity, water, cat food."

Molly and I shared a look. *Cat food?*

"I think you need better priorities, but hey, I'm not one to judge." I leaned toward the tray, pulled in by the interesting bites of food he'd brought with him. "What do you have there?"

He grinned at me. "A little amuse bouche, compliments of the chef."

"How generous," I mumbled.

"He wanted to thank you for stopping in. He always loves another chef's opinion."

I resisted the urge to roll my eyes. "We were hungry," I explained. "We didn't have anything else going on tonight." Lie. "We're not here to spy." Another lie. "Besides, if anyone has been spying lately..." I pointed to the remnants of the tzatziki sauce that hadn't yet been licked off the plate. "I think I'm the one with the right to complain."

Wyatt chuckled, not taking me seriously. "You know the entire kitchen blames you for the new menu."

"What? Why?" Panic jumped around inside me. My insides became a mosh pit of confused emotion. The very notion seemed too absurd even to consider, and yet the sauce sat there glaring at me, proving that it wasn't entirely impossible.

"The last time Killian changed the menu in the middle of a season, was after a Jarod Campbell review. Killian had all but lit the menu on fire and started from scratch. It was terrifying."

Jarod Campbell was one of the toughest critics in the country. He never gave glowing reviews. He preferred scathing criticisms with a few positive notes sprinkled throughout. But I was surprised even Killian had suffered Jarod's harsh opinion.

My eyebrows jumped to my hairline. "So you're saying he hates me as much as Jarod Campbell?"

Wyatt gave me a goofy look. "That is not what I'm saying at all."

I didn't know what he was saying. Nor did I want to know. "You better get back in there before he realizes how much he doesn't need you."

Wyatt chuckled again and turned to Molly, setting down the fancy little bites of food on a fresh plate. "Enjoy." To me, he said, "He'll be out when he can catch a break."

"He doesn't need to bother! I swear we didn't come here to visit."

Wyatt backed up a step. "But you did come all this way. It's only polite."

Before I could embarrass myself further, Wyatt was swept away in the current of bustling servers and trays of food. He disappeared into the kitchen with his now empty tray, and we were left with our amuse bouches that suddenly felt like less of a friendly gesture and more of a deal with the devil.

"Well, this was nice of him," commented Molly—poor, sweet, naïve Molly.

"Killian Quinn isn't capable of being nice. He's just rubbing his superior skill in my face."

She picked one up; it had a small toast on the bottom with a thin piece of prosciutto and maybe mascarpone on it? There was a brown drizzle that I suspected was balsamic based. "Oh, my God," she groaned after consuming it in one bite—like it was intended. "He's such an asshole. I hate him."

"Liar."

She grinned at me. "I'm sorry, but a man that makes that cannot possibly be entirely evil."

"That's the whole point, Molly! He's tricking you with his good looks and delicious food. Meanwhile, your soul is damned to hell."

"Stop being difficult, Vere, and try the damn food before I eat yours."

I gasped, immediately picking up a flakey piece of white fish with a perfectly peppered crust on a lavosh-like cracker. I couldn't stand the man, but there was no way I was giving away my food. "Fine," I huffed. "It's more ammunition for the Yelp review anyway."

Molly just shook her head at me, her mouth too full for her to verbally respond.

Shane didn't return to take our order. A bus boy cleared our plates, but nobody checked on us until Shane reappeared with a tray full of plates, the bartender at his side replacing our drinks with new ones.

"We didn't order this," I pointed out.

Shane smiled politely, his eyes darting around the table afraid to meet mine. "The chef wanted you to enjoy a variety of dishes." He stepped back so the server with him could start setting the plates down. "And drinks," he added.

"That's unnecessary—"

Shane held up a hand. "He insisted. He also said that you should stop arguing with him."

"I didn't—" But at Shane's look of complete helplessness I backed off. It wasn't Shane's fault that Killian was so heavy-handed. "Alright, fine."

Shane watched me for another minute, probably trying to figure out why we were getting such special treatment.

Honestly, I wanted to know too.

Finally, after every plate had been squeezed onto our tiny table, he asked, "Would you like me to thank the chef for you?"

"No." I tore my eyes from the feast in front of me and smiled apologetically at Shane. "Thank you, but no. I don't want you to thank him for me."

"You'd like to do it yourself?" he guessed.

"I'd like to punch him in the throat, but I'll have to settle for icy silence."

Molly snickered, already plating for both of us, while Shane floundered for a response. "I, uh, well, if you need anything else, please don't hesitate."

"We won't," Molly answered for me. "Thank you so much."

"The nerve of that man," I grumbled while I consulted my menu and matched the dishes with the plates in front of me.

"Should we send it back?" Molly had already started eating from the plate in front of her, not even bothering to disguise her blissed-out reactions.

"Are you kidding? I'm irritated, not crazy!"

She waggled her eyebrows at me, and we dove in. I tried to explain the dishes to her so she knew what she was eating, but she didn't care about the individual components of each plate. She just wanted to eat in peace.

So, I let her. Meanwhile, I dissected every single thing in front of me, studying it, examining it... enjoying it. Killian wasn't just a good chef, he was a phenomenal one. I couldn't help but picture those strong fingers of his, carefully crafting each dish, putting it together with all that dynamic focus, refusing to let even one peppercorn fall out of place.

The meal wasn't simply sustenance. It wasn't even as simple as a memorable experience. This was a work of art, the masterpiece in front of me reaching all five senses and even further than that, down into my soul where I would remember this meal for the rest of my life.

Everything was perfectly cooked, perfectly crispy, perfectly moist, perfectly whatever it needed to be to make the flavors explode in my mouth and burrow deep down in my bones. Braised rabbit legs, creamy truffle risotto, slow-cooked bone-in duck breast with fig sauce, succulent filet with duck fat fries, golden trout with leeks and pineapple and heirloom tomatoes.

This wasn't just a meal, it was a religious experience. I would never be the same after this, unequivocally altered by the sheer genius of each bite.

I tried to ignore the warmth blooming inside my chest. Killian wasn't trying to rub his food in my face; he had given me a gift. Only I didn't understand why.

When we were halfway through our meal, the table looked more like a massacre than an elegant evening out. A tingle of awareness prickled the back of my neck. I suppressed the urge to run. I wouldn't be able to hide my admiration or trick him into believing I was anything but completely enamored. With his food.

Only his food.

He pushed through the kitchen door, striding through the dining room with domineering steps. His gaze went straight to our table. Straight to me. His mouth was all but hidden behind his full beard, but there was a satisfied smile sitting in his eyes. He didn't have to see my reaction to know how I felt.

He already knew it. Before he'd even stepped foot outside of his kitchen.

And I just sat there staring at him, shivery and impressed and awestruck.

He owned this restaurant. Maybe not literally, he had a boss after all. But he commanded it. He was the captain, and this was his ship.

This was his empire, and he was the king.

Patrons swiveled to watch him move through the narrow aisles. Everyone recognized him, if not because they already knew who he was than because of his presence—because you couldn't mistake him for anyone besides the man in charge.

He walked directly over to us and by the time he reached our table, my mouth was dry, and all the delicious food I'd inhaled had been turned to dust in my stomach.

I was nervous. And slightly turned on. It was so out of place and ridiculous that I wanted to face plant in my risotto. Instead, I pasted on a charming smile and said, "You stole my tzatziki sauce."

His green eyes flashed with surprise. He gestured at the half empty plates on the table. "So what are you going to steal from me?"

I had already decided on about a half dozen things, but to him I said, "I don't need to steal anything from you. I'm good." His gaze narrowed and I knew he didn't believe me, but he didn't call me on it. "Have you met Molly?" I asked him.

"Not formally." He turned to her. "Hi."

She took his hand, eying him warily. "Hi."

"Molly this is Killian. He's the chef I keep telling you to call the cops on. The one that keeps stealing all of my dishes."

He turned back to me, fire in his gaze. "Inspired."

"What?"

"My sauce is inspired by your cute little meatballs. It's plenty different, and you know it."

His admission of truth was such a surprise that I momentarily lost the ability to speak. When I finally found my voice again, I said the first stupid thing that came to mind. "Where's your charcuterie board?"

Killian's eyebrows shot to his hairline. "Excuse me?"

"They're all the rage," I pointed out. "Doesn't Lilou want to be on trend?"

His lip curled back in disgust. "Lilou likes to go against the grain, not with the masses. Risks get you noticed, Delane. Or were you planning on cooking chili dogs for every meal?"

Before I could argue with him, another man called his name from a short distance away. "Killian."

119

We all turned and watched the most gorgeous man I had ever seen approach the table. Black, wavy hair, perfectly tanned, flawless skin, tall, lean, muscular—he was perfect. Completely perfect. And the absolute opposite of Killian.

Clean cut where Killian was basically a lumbersexual. Business sleek where Killian was tattooed and wild. Sophisticated and reserved where Killian was… upfront and unapologetic.

I preferred Killian in every way.

Still, I couldn't stop staring at the newcomer. He was the kind of beautiful that demanded attention.

"Ezra," Killian greeted. "I thought you were spending the night at Bianca?"

Not to be confused with spending the night *with* Bianca.

Ezra Baptiste- that's who this was. Lilou's owner. Killian's boss. Restaurateur, businessman, model.

Okay, I made the model thing up.

"I had to get out of there before I did something impetuous," Ezra explained. "That little shit is begging to be fired."

Killian murmured his agreement, glancing at me, gauging my reaction. "Do you want a plate?" he asked Ezra, and if I didn't know any better, I would have thought it was his attempt to get rid of his boss.

"Yeah, later." Ezra turned to the table, his smile transforming his entire face from handsome, to devastatingly so. I heard Molly's audible intake of breath and felt the urge to pat my forehead with the clean side of my napkin. "What's brought you out of the kitchen? I hope there's not a problem?"

Because only a problem would pull Killian from his kingdom?

"No," Killian denied immediately. "Well, not in the traditional sense."

What was that supposed to mean? Before I could ask, Killian introduced me to one of the most important people in the restaurant industry. "This is our new neighbor, Ezra. Vera Delane meet Ezra Baptiste."

I stuck my trembling hand in Ezra's and gripped firmly, attempting professionalism. "Nice to meet you."

"Likewise," he smiled. "Which property is yours?"

Embarrassment swept over me from head to toe. "The truck," I replied weakly. "Foodie."

Ezra's expression lit with recognition. "Ah, now I see. You're the chef *my* chef can't stop talking about."

For the second time tonight I wondered if coming here was a big mistake. "Oh, no. I'm definitely not that chef. I just run a food truck."

Ezra's smile widened. "I've heard."

I forced myself to hold his gaze when all I wanted to do was stare at my shoes. "This is my friend Molly," I told him, finally diverting his gaze elsewhere. "She's an artist."

Ezra's eyes lit up when he took her in. "Really? An artist of what variety?"

If I would have been standing next to her, she would have pinched me. "Graphic designer by trade," she explained taking his hand when he offered it to her.

He seemed disappointed in her answer. I was too. But I couldn't force her to acknowledge her talent.

Leaning toward her, Ezra asked her opinion on something design oriented. She answered, and he immediately pulled out his phone. Just like that, they were talking shop.

Ezra walked around Killian so he could show Molly his screen and she started pointing at it, explaining nervously.

Knowing Killian would have to get back to the kitchen soon, I stood up and turned to face him again. He still towered over me, even though I'd worn my slutty heels tonight. The red stilettos gave me four inches of height but I still only reached the middle of his beard. "Thank you for dinner. You didn't have to—"

He shrugged, cutting me off. "I figured you should have the most information at your disposal."

"I didn't come here to spy on you."

His gaze narrowed. "Then why did you come?"

"I needed to see what the fuss was about."

"And?"

"Don't tell me you're one of those guys that needs his ego coddled?"

He leaned in, brushing his shoulder against mine. "Every guy is that guy. Don't single me out."

I tried not to smile. Really. I gave it my best effort. "Honestly?"

He pulled back, holding my gaze and nodding. "Why do you think women always hold the power?"

If I didn't know better, I would have thought he looked nervous. His eyes moved over me tentatively, and his hands were tucked into his pockets.

"Honestly, I think everything needs a little more salt."

Shock hit his entire body at once, rocking him back on his heels. He'd expected me to fawn over him, to fall to my knees and praise him for being a god in the kitchen.

But I was done kissing ass to great chefs who didn't need to be told they were great.

Before Killian could respond, Molly's sharp voice captured my attention. "I suppose it's up to you," she snapped at Ezra. "It's your website. Your logo. You should do what you want to do."

"Even if it looks like shit?" Ezra snarled.

"I didn't say that."

The two of them glowered at each other, and it was so shocking that I couldn't even figure out a way to rescue the conversation. Molly didn't snap at people. Molly didn't glower at them. Molly was sweet and shy and always professional.

Always.

Ezra stepped back, disentangling himself from conflict. "I'll let you get back to your meal. Thank you for your advice." To Killian, he said, "I'll be at my usual table."

Killian nodded. "I'll find you later. We can talk about Bianca."

Bianca was one of Ezra's other restaurants, closer to the suburbs. And it sounded like they were having chef problems. I immediately wondered who they would hire.

Killian hovered a second longer before nodding toward his kitchen. "I should get back. I just wanted to make sure everything tasted fine."

"Thanks for checking on us," Molly gushed before I could answer. "I didn't know food could taste this good."

I kicked her shin under the table.

Killian tugged on his beard, somehow acknowledging me without looking at me. "I don't believe you." Finally, he turned back to me and said, "I'll have Shane clean this up and bring you dessert. You can stay as long as you'd like, the meal is on me tonight."

"You don't have to—"

"Just tell me what you're making this weekend," he countered as if that would be fair play.

I stood for almost thirty seconds not knowing what to say or how to react. He couldn't possibly be that interested in my cooking. Or my menus. When logic failed, sarcasm swooped in to save the day. "I'd rather pay my bill," I told him.

His hand swiped over his mouth, hiding his brief smile. "I guess I'll have to stop by and find out for myself then."

"No, that's not what I—"

He'd already turned away from me. "Molly, it was a pleasure to meet you. Forgive my friend, he's a bigger asshole than I am." Molly tried to apologize for her behavior too, but Killian cut us both off and said, "Goodnight, ladies."

Then he was gone. Like a dragon back to his lair.

I turned to Molly. "What just happened?"

Her eyes cut across the restaurant to where Ezra had disappeared. "I'm not totally sure I know."

"Men are weird."

She gave me a sympathetic smile. "I think you might be on to something with your vow of celibacy."

"So, are you saying you're taking the vow with me?"

Her head tipped back with the force of her laughter. "No, God, no. I was just admitting that you're smarter than me."

I leaned back when Shane showed up to swap our third course plates for a buffet of desserts. "Would you ladies like to see the coffee menu?"

I winked at Molly. "Absolutely."

Chapter Twelve

*T*hree days later, I got a call from Vann while I was in the middle of prepping tonight's crispy pork belly pot pie, which was not at all inspired by Killian or Lilou or the dinner Molly and I shared Tuesday night that I hadn't stopped thinking about once. I wiped my hands on my apron and tucked my phone between my shoulder and chin.

"Is everything okay?" I asked instead of a regular hello.

"I just wanted to go over everything again before I pick him up."

My brother sounded scared and unsure. I could count on one hand how many times Vann had been afraid of something growing up. But my dad's illness was one of them.

Steadying my voice and doing my best to sound casual, I explained the chemo treatment area. "You'll be in a private room, so you won't have to deal with anyone else except the nurse. There's a TV. He'll probably sleep through most of it."

"And when will he get sick?

"Not until Sunday." Dad was getting sicker with each treatment. He'd started out handling them like a champ, but recently the two days following his treatment were bad.

Thankfully, I had Sunday off so I could sit with him and wait on him when he needed me. Dad's treatments were usually on Tuesday, so I always took him. But this week, they asked him to come in on Friday. He had ten weeks of treatment left. Vann offered to take him today, so I could work.

125

Vann was quiet for so long that I had to look at my phone to make sure the line was still connected. "Is he going to be okay, Vera?"

I leaned over the counter, curling my fingers around the edge and squeezing tightly until I was positive I wouldn't crumple on the ground. When I'd first come home, we'd only had to face the diagnosis. Dad didn't want surgery, but he'd agreed to chemo.

Fine. That was his choice. But he'd still looked healthy. From the outside, it was impossible to tell that something monstrous was destroying him from the inside out.

Now, he looked sick. Now, he looked like a cancer patient. Now, I wanted to beg and plead and demand he live.

"I don't know, Vann," I whispered into the phone.

He cleared his throat and changed the subject. "Let's have supper together Sunday night. I know dad won't feel up for much, but I'll bring over chicken noodle from Rusty's and that bread he likes."

I pressed the back of my hand to my forehead, doing my best to hold it together. "That's a good idea. We can play Scrabble and watch *60 Minutes*."

"This is dumb," he groaned. "I hate this."

Sniffling, I agreed. "Me too. But he'll be happy you're taking him today. He's worried you're jealous that I moved home."

Vann didn't respond to that, making me wonder if it was true after all. "I love you, Vera."

I didn't know what to say for a minute. Vann and I weren't overly demonstrative. Dad's sickness had put things into perspective for us both. "I love you too, Vann." Then I thought of something. "He likes HGTV. He'll tell you to put on whatever you want, but he wants the house hunting and remodeling shows. Even if he's asleep."

Vann's chuckle was relieved but fragile. "Midget house hunters it is."

"I don't think that's what it's called."

"Here he comes. I'll call you after."

"Give him my love." We hung up, and I stared at the phone for a minute, wondering if I shouldn't just abandon service tonight and meet them at the clinic.

I was just about to pack up shop when the door swung open, scaring the absolute crap out of me. I clutched my butcher knife and spun around.

Killian prowled into the small truck, shrinking everything under the strength of his anger. He held up his phone, shaking it back and forth at me. "Fussy? Pretentious?"

I bit my lip to keep from smiling. He'd found my Yelp review.

"What's going on?" I asked innocently.

126

He glared at me and my knees nearly buckled under the force of it. Clearing his throat, he turned back to his phone and began reading. "I went to Lilou despite everything I knew it would be. And unfortunately, it lived up to every one of my expectations. I knew the atmosphere would be stuffy. And it was. I knew the food would be fussy. And it was. I knew the chef, Killian Quinn, who is raved about in some circles, but otherwise known to be a total douche, would be snobby. And he was. The garnishes were all a little much for my standards. And I can't remember one dish that wasn't overly salty. Not to mention I was looking forward to a charcuterie board and disappointed to find that they did not offer one. Obviously, nobody would call Lilou cutting edge, but I would have felt comforted knowing they at least tried to keep up with current trends. All in all, while the food was executed well enough, I was underwhelmed. To be fair, the desserts were incredible. But I heard they outsource those. In the end, I expected more from a chef with Quinn's reputation." Killian looked up at me again, his green eyes hot and furious. "That's my latest Yelp review," he explained. "Posted by someone with the screen name *Nanananabooboo.*"

I cleared my throat and checked the exits. He was blocking the doorway, but maybe I could throw myself out one of the windows?

Deciding on guiltless ignorance, I threw myself into the role. "Yikes. That sucks."

"Vera."

"I mean, why even write something so vicious?" I gulped nervously but just kept digging my grave. "Although, *Nanananabooboo* does bring up some valid points. Would it be the worst thing to—"

"Vera," Killian growled. "Are you kidding me?"

"Yes?" Licking dry lips, I tried again. "No. I mean no. I'm not kidding you."

His voice dropped low, menacing. He did not find the review hilarious at all. "What is this, Delane? Is this your idea of a joke?"

It was my idea of a joke. Or payback. After all his helpful notes and midnight tutoring sessions, this was exactly my idea of vengeance. Only now, with him standing across the food truck looking so big and scary, I wasn't so sure that it was my brightest idea ever.

To be fair, Molly had even tried to talk me out of it. But we'd gone back to her apartment after our life-altering meal at Lilou, opened a bottle of wine and I'd lost the ability to make rational decisions.

My gaze jumped from Killian to the door, to Killian back to the counter behind me, to Killian then up to the ceiling. If this was my "act casual" look, I should probably give up my dreams of being an international spy. "Come on, you can't think that's me."

His expression hardened, his mouth pulling down in a frown. "I don't think. I *know* it's you." He took a step forward. I retreated instinctively.

"You can't *know* that it's me."

He took another step towards me. "I can."

I changed tactics. "It's just Yelp. Who reads Yelp anyway?"

"It's the first thing that shows up on a Google search!"

He'd stopped moving right in front of me. I could feel his body heat and smell his skin. My heartbeat skipped in my chest, desperately trying to run away.

"You were Googling yourself, weren't you? That's how you found it." I narrowed my eyes, trying frantically to turn this into a joke we could both laugh about. "I bet you have alerts set up. I bet it pinged you when it went live."

His eyes darkened, and his mouth pressed into a straight line, disappearing behind his beard. Belatedly, I found the nerve to run, but he was faster than me. Or maybe he'd been expecting me to run and so he was prepared.

I darted away from him, ready to throw myself out the front door, but he grabbed my wrist and yanked me back to his body. I landed in a surprised heap against his chest, my cheek smooshed over his chiseled pectoral muscle.

I rested there for a second. Maybe two seconds.

There was a good possibility it was at least thirty seconds.

Hot awareness zinged through me with my body pressed so tightly to his. He was breathing heavily, worked up by the review, and I couldn't help but imagine what it would be like to be plastered over his well-defined body in other circumstances.

Like if we were both naked, for example.

Replacing my cheek with my hand, I quickly pushed away from him, desperate for space. He kept hold of my wrist and caged me in against the cool counter.

My butt hit the edge, and my back bowed to put some space between my now looming neighbor and me. Killian's hands rested on either side of my waist, making an impenetrable prison while his body leaned over mine, holding my full attention.

I tried not to smell him again, but he was everywhere. And so very close. His thighs rested against mine. His stomach against mine. Our chests were just inches apart. If I leaned forward just a smidge, I could head butt him. Or bite him.

Or kiss him.

I swallowed through the dysfunctional lump in my throat. "What are you doing?" I whispered.

"Forcing a confession."

"Wh-what?"

"Confess, Vera. Confess that the review was yours and that you didn't mean it."

I rolled my eyes, faking bravado. "Never."

His head dropped, the heat warming, shifting, evolving from one kind of frustration to another. His gaze dropped to my mouth. "Vera," he warned.

I shivered at the way his deep voice curled around my name. He was so close. So intimidating. So something I wouldn't let myself admit.

"Tell me it's yours," he demanded.

Shaking my head, I realized I should have been afraid of him right now. The trauma of my past should have triggered all kinds of fear and panic and desperation. I should be kicking and screaming or at the very least curled up into a helpless ball of uselessness.

Instead of freaking out, I felt something different, something fluttery and hot and hungry. At the same time, I realized I was taunting Killian on purpose, seeing just how far I could push him, I admitted that I wasn't afraid of him. That I even might have, sort of, trusted him.

At least I trusted him not to hurt me.

If I would have imagined this scenario yesterday, I would have denied it. I would have stood by the fact that every executive chef, maybe every man on the planet (except my dad and Vann), were the same. They all had excessive egos and the need to be coddled, worshiped and obeyed. And when they didn't get their way, they took it out on whomever could be hurt the most.

Yesterday, I thought all men were assholes, and the lead asshole of them all was Killian Quinn.

Today, he'd made me acknowledge the truth. Killian could be an asshole, but he wasn't only an asshole. And he was a man, but he wasn't a bad man.

Most of all, he wasn't anything like one man in particular.

And that was huge for me. Not only did I not distrust Killian, but I trusted him. I trusted him not to hurt me physically, verbally or emotionally. Maybe he'd said some exasperating things in the past, but they hadn't been meant to manipulate or control me. He hadn't been spiteful or mean for the sake of being mean.

Most of all, they hadn't destroyed whole pieces of me at a time. If anything, I'd become a better chef because of him.

That didn't mean he was completely forgiven for past actions or that my Yelp review wasn't completely justified. But it did mean that maybe I wasn't completely broken after all.

"Make me," I dared him.

His eyes dropped to my lips again, and I resisted, but barely, the urge to lick them. "Admit that it's yours and I won't have to torture you."

I raised my eyebrows in surprise. "I'm terrified. Really."

Half his mouth lifted in a cocky smile. "Good." Then he extracted his revenge. By tickling me.

The bastard.

One hand clamped down on my right hip. I was so surprised at first, that I squeaked. But then he pressed his thumb into a sensitive spot, and I started to wiggle. His other hand grabbed my other side, and I looked like a lunatic trying to shake him off me.

I gasped for air as his hands moved over my torso from hip bones to ribs, poking, squeezing and prodding until tears leaked from the corners of my eyes. He didn't let up. He tickled me until I didn't think I could breathe—until I was positive that I was going to die from being tickled too much.

"Okay!" I panted. "You win! You win!"

"Admit that you wrote the review," he demanded.

And since he hadn't stopped tickling me yet, I nodded furiously. "Fine, I did it. I'm *Nanananabooboo*!"

He backed off a little, but not enough. "Now, tell me you're sorry."

"I'm sorry," I laughed, now that it was easier to breathe. "Oh, my God, I'm so sorry."

He stopped tickling me, but his hand remained on my waist, and I realized my fingers had grasped his t-shirt in a desperate attempt to shove him off me. It hadn't worked. Apparently, I'd decided to cling to him instead.

We were intimately close. Our bodies draped over each other from our tussle, hot everywhere we touched, buzzing with new energy and new interest.

He had what he wanted, but he didn't pull away. "Now I'm going to need you to remove the review completely."

His intense, serious expression stole my amusement and revenge fun. I wanted to wiggle under his stare, but we were too close. Wiggling would only lead to more trouble. "What if I really feel that way?"

His eyes flashed with uncertainty. "Do you? Feel that way I mean?"

I nibbled my bottom lip, but couldn't convince myself to lie. "No," I whispered. "Not even a little bit."

His head dipped toward mine again, closer, within biting distance.

Within kissing distance.

"Then will you remove your mean review? Please?"

It was the please that did it. His please would always do it. The word sounded too fragile for his filthy mouth, too sweet to come from someone so hard. I didn't stand a chance.

I patted the counter blindly until I found my phone. Making a show of unlocking it and pulling up the Yelp app, I went about removing my review from the site.

I hadn't planned to keep it up anyway. But I had been curious to see how long it would take him to find it.

Three days.

Apparently, I wasn't the only one obsessed with reviews.

I showed him the confirmation screen. "There. All gone."

He dropped his head in relief, his forehead brushing my cheek. "Thank you."

"I hope your ego recovers," I joked to untangle us from this spot—figuratively and literally. He was still leaning over me, making all my neglected girly parts wake up and pay attention.

He chuckled, his chest vibrating against mine with the sound. "My ego is never safe around you, Delane." Lifting his head, he caught my gaze and held it. His hands brushed over the counter and over my hips. For a second I was afraid he was going to start tickling me again, but then his fingertips dipped beneath my white t-shirt and his hands wrapped around my waist instead. "Thank you for removing the review."

"You already said that," I whispered, nervous and excited and confused all at once.

"I mean it, though." The corners of his mouth lifted in a sincere smile. "I just wanted you to know."

All I could do was blink. I knew he was going to kiss me. I just knew it.

And I was right. He closed the distance between us, his lush mouth finding the corner of mine and placing a sweet, lingering kiss.

I squirmed when his beard scratched my skin, brushing over it with an interesting mix of soft and rough. I decided very quickly that I liked the feel of his beard on my skin.

I liked it a whole lot.

He kissed me one more time along the jaw, then he pulled back, separating us entirely. I shivered again, but this time it was because I missed the heat of his body, the cover of his skin against mine.

131

"Break a leg, chef," he murmured, sounding as hot and bothered as I felt.

"You too," I croaked.

He gave me one more searing look before he hopped down from my truck and ambled back across the street to Lilou.

I stared at his back in complete wonder as he walked away. I didn't think my fake review would bring out that kind of reaction from him. I wasn't even sure what to do with that reaction!

Well, I wasn't sure until my phone pinged with a notification. What I should have done was shake off Killian's skin and scent and get to work on dinner service. Instead, I stupidly checked my phone thinking it might be him.

I swiped my phone open and instantly regretted it. The notification wasn't from Killian.

It was from Derrek.

He'd messaged my personal account on Facebook. The one I'd been reluctant to create just because I was terrified of something like this happening.

The message, from the familiar profile picture of Derrek Hanover, simply said, "Where did you go?"

That was it. That was all he said, but it was enough to have me contemplating running off to Europe again. All I wanted to do was run away. All I wanted to do was deactivate my account and set my computer on fire. My smartphone too, while I was at it. I wanted to curl into a ball on the floor and cry for the rest of the night. Maybe the rest of the week.

But most of all I wanted to go back to before the message, to when I was lusting after Killian Quinn and considering that maybe life wasn't full of lemons and sour moments. That maybe there was something good out there too.

Only my heart knew better. My hope was wiser than that. Because if I'd learned anything in twenty-six years, it was that if something bad could happen, it would happen.

And Derrek Hanover was the bad thing that just kept happening to me.

So maybe his message was a good reminder. It made me wake up where Killian was concerned anyway. It made me realize that I didn't want a relationship or to ever be put in a position where I had to trust another man ever again.

I had moved on from Derrek. I had opened a business and learned to manage my life. The only reason for Derrek to be anywhere in my life these days was as a cautionary tale of failed love. And nothing else.

But that's all Killian would be too. A bullet dodged. An awkward circumstance avoided. I friend that would always stay a friend.

Chapter Thirteen

*T*he next weekend I stood at the pickup window, listening to a customer list off everything he hated about my buttermilk fried chicken and jalapeno waffles. It was Friday night, and so far, things had not gone smoothly at all.

They hadn't gone well Thursday night either. I contemplated giving up this dish altogether and abandoning profit for the weekend. But I was too stubborn to admit defeat. Plus, I couldn't afford to give up.

I could agree with the guy that my fried chicken was nothing like his grandmother's. I'd used a tempura fry on chicken tenderloins. Because they were easier to eat than a hunky breast or thigh. And to be honest, because they were super cheap this week.

My waffles were also nonconventional. I'd grabbed my dad's ancient waffle iron that hadn't been used since my mom was alive and made the batter with diced jalapenos and sriracha. I'd been going for a savory/spicy/sweet kind of mashup.

I'd been optimistic in my test run. My waffle had been fluffy. Maybe a little too spicy, but it looked pretty. My chicken had been crispy. And the maple syrup tied everything together.

Unfortunately, made in mass quantities, I wasn't nearly as proud. I'd made the executive decision to ban all future chicken and waffle ideas until the end of time. Forever and ever, amen.

I just had to get through the weekend first. And then the cleanup process. The interior of my truck was coated in maple syrup, thanks to

Molly's offering to fill up the to-go ramekins. And waffle batter had dried in big, bulbous clumps all over the counter, the floor and me.

And this wasn't the first customer to complain. My entire night had been one upset customer after another.

Okay, maybe that was an exaggeration. But there had been enough complaints to send me into a tailspin of existential crisis. What was I even doing with my life???

I still had at least two hours left. *Jesus, take the wheel.*

"Sir," I tried gently at first. Gently didn't work. "Sir!" He paused in his tirade. "Would you like your money back?"

He snorted. "Obviously."

I picked the remnants of my dignity off the ground and accepted the ten dollar bill from Molly. "I apologize again for the waffles being so hot." I offered him a genuinely sincere smile when I handed his money back to him. "The menu is different every weekend, though. I hope you give us another shot soon."

He snarled a terse, "Not a chance in hell." Luckily for me, it was easy to pretend he'd said, "I'd like that as well," instead.

What separated humans from animals? The incredible ability to plant our feet in denial. Beautiful, blissful denial.

"Is it a full moon?" Molly asked, stretching her neck out the window. "People are cranky tonight."

I looked back at my fryer and batter-covered station. It hadn't just been the complaining customers that made the night difficult. I had been overly ambitious trying to fry chicken fresh *and* make hot waffles for every order. I'd been bouncing around the narrow space all night like a pinball. "Lesson learned, Durham. No more chicken and waffles for you."

"How about one more?"

I spun around, surprised to see Killian at the window. His gaze moved over me, quick, assessing, amused.

I brushed my hand down my front, realizing how disheveled I must have looked. My white chef's jacket was covered in grease and syrup and sriracha. I had been fighting my bandana for hours, pulling clumps of batter out of wayward hair that wouldn't stay tucked away.

He had worked tonight too. But in a white t-shirt that hugged his tattooed arms and low slung black pants, he looked tired, but not like he'd spent hours in the kitchen slaving away.

More like he'd had a grueling day shooting Armani underwear ads.

"No." I hadn't meant to sound so serious, but he was pissing me off already, and he'd just got here. I didn't have the energy to listen to him pick apart my dish. I already knew it wasn't a keeper.

He laughed, but it was unsure and nervous. "Excuse me?"

I shook my head and tried one more time to muster up manners. "No, you can't have one."

Killian stepped closer to the order window, peering inside. "Hey, Molly," he said as an afterthought.

"Hi." She stood up, taking a step back from the window. Killian made her nervous.

He made me nervous too. But he also pissed me off. Usually, the anger canceled out the nerves.

His attentive gaze found mine again. "Rough night?"

I resisted the urge to kick the stove. "Chicken and waffles," I sighed. "I should have known better."

I could have sworn his lips twitched, but it was hard to tell since they were hidden behind that beard. "Let me try."

"No."

"Can I come back there?"

"Why? So you can fix everything? Make it better and remind me how much I suck?" The words tasted like vinegar, whiney and self-pitying.

"Geez, you're in a mood tonight. It can't be that bad."

I turned away from him, pulling a towel down to start wiping up the counter. "It's fine," I said to the hard balls of batter that had crusted on the stainless steel.

His voice dropped to a low murmur as he addressed Molly. "How bad was it?"

"Mean customers," Molly explained. "That last guy was a real jerk."

Embarrassment sharp and stinging sliced through me. It wasn't that I cared about Molly or Killian's opinion of me. But it bothered me that I cared at all, that a few harsh words had upset me so completely.

The door opened, and Killian stepped inside uninvited. His footsteps echoed around the space while neither Molly nor I moved.

I wanted to remind him that he wasn't invited. That I didn't want him in here, but I couldn't find the courage to even look at him. If I would have been closer to the pick-up window, I would have jumped out of it by now and ran away.

Never to be heard from again.

"I hate bad reviews. I mean, I *really* hate them. I don't think there's a single other thing I hate, actually." He stepped up next to me, his words honest, but his tone gentle. "Except maybe eggplant. I also hate eggplant."

I stilled, remembering his reaction to my Yelp review. It wasn't hard to imagine just how much he hated negative feedback. Even the joking kind.

137

He'd walked over so he could stand right at my side, not touching, but close enough that his presence invaded every single one of my senses, burrowing so deep I felt him in my blood, my bones… my breath.

"It's one thing when they come from a critic," Killian went on. "But it's physically painful when it comes from a regular, or someone who doesn't know you at all. Then you know it wasn't a small technicality or minuscule mistake. Then you know you just suck."

I smiled, it was small and barely there, but I felt a chink in my pissed-off armor. "I thought you came in here to make me feel better."

His tone turned teasing. "You're so young, Delane. So very young. And so very naïve."

"Stop with all the compliments. Seriously, my ego is like—" I made an explosion sound, mimicking the motion with both hands.

He turned, propping his hip against the counter. "How old are you? Fifteen? Sixteen?"

"Gross, stop."

His lips twitched again. "What I'm trying to say is that I'm older than you. Wiser. I've been doing this for a lot longer than you, and I can honestly say they all sting. Every last one of them. There's no way to get around the pain. There's no way to ignore the feeling of incompetence. You just have to ride it out and show up anyway."

I knew he was right. I'd been here before. It wasn't like this was my first bad night. Or even close.

But this was the first shitty night that was mine completely. I wasn't working for someone else. A different chef didn't have their name on the final project or banner. This was mine. Completely. And I'd screwed up.

"Name them," he demanded.

I raised my gaze to find his. I'd been perfectly happy staring at his beard, but now I needed his eyes, the strength that was always present there… the courage. "Name what?"

"Name your fears. Your insecurities. Name the truth you heard in the complaint, the thing that's got you so wrapped up you're ready to quit."

Logic started to dawn in my otherwise dark night of pity. I realized he was right. My fears had become a roadblock inside my chest, a tangle of lies and fears and uncertainties. I opened my mouth to say them out loud, but I couldn't get them out of my mouth. They stayed lodged in my throat, an inconvenient lump growing into a jagged boulder.

"My chicken was tasteless."

His eyes widened, revealing his surprise. He hadn't thought I could do it. "You forgot salt. Didn't you?"

I hated him just a tiny bit more for teasing me. Hated him and liked him. "I didn't forget it," I growled. "I just... ugh, I just didn't use enough. And my waffles were too doughy. I overcooked half of them tonight trying to manage everything."

He grinned at me. "What else?"

"I don't think I can do this. It's too much. Too hard. I don't know what I'm doing. I've never even been in charge of my own kitchen. I don't know why I thought I could run my own goddamn business." I slapped my hand over my mouth, surprised that I'd said so much.

Surprised that I felt so much.

Killian had lost his smile, his amusement. Those green eyes glittered brightly above the darkness of his beard, seeing more of me than I ever wanted to show him. "Now do you realize how absurd those thoughts are? You had a bad night. So what? You learned something. You pushed yourself to your limit and found out what you're capable of. What works. What doesn't work. And now you can go on with your life. You won't make this dish. You won't ever use that antiquated piece of shit waffle iron again." He did a double take, his eyes widening at the sight of it covered in dried batter, rusted near the rubber feet. "Good lord, what is that thing?" He nudged the chipped handle with the tip of his finger as if he was afraid it would give him some kind of disease. "And you'll remember the fucking flavor. Yeah?"

I nodded even while I said, "I hate you almost as much as I hate salt."

His lips twitched with an almost smile. "You don't hate salt." He stepped closer. "And you really don't hate me."

"I do too," I insisted. But it was an unconvincing whisper. And a dirty lie.

He ignored me. "You don't have to worry about doing this, Delane. You *are* doing it. We'll rework the menu and tomorrow will be a better day."

"Does that always work?"

"What?"

"Naming it like that, calling yourself on your own crap. Is that all it takes to move on?"

The hint of something played over his features. Regret maybe? Disappointment? It was hard to say, but whatever it was made me feel cold all over again inside. I knew the answer before he vocalized it.

"No, it doesn't. But when this therapeutic bullshit fails, we do what we do best."

"And that is?"

"We cook, Delane. Come on, we're chefs. So, we cook. Not for them, not for the people judging us. We cook for us. We make whatever reminds us of how fucking amazing we are."

I laughed, and it was the first time all night I finally felt like myself again. Hell, maybe it was the first time in years I felt like myself again. Not the shadowed, broken version I'd been since Derrek, but the real me. The one that had been rescued by cooking and empowered by the kitchen. "I thought you were going to say drinking," I told him. "That when all else fails, we drink."

He chuckled, reaching for a bowl of spices. "Well, we do that too."

"Hey, Vere?" Molly called from behind me.

Oh, my God, I'd completely forgotten she was here. I whipped around to her, hoping she didn't comment on how red my cheeks flamed or how absorbed in Killian I'd been for the last ten minutes. "Hi, sorry. Gosh, Molly, sorry."

She gave me a pointed look, silently calling me out on everything I hadn't wanted her to see. Her eyebrows danced over her eyes, and she made a silent gesture toward Killian—kissing and then something more vulgar. "Do you care if I take off? I have an early morning tomorrow, and I'd like to get home."

She was a liar. She had brunch with me tomorrow morning because we'd made plans less than an hour ago.

I narrowed my eyes at her. "Are you sure?"

Smiling innocently, she nodded. "Super sure."

"You don't want to wait around just another hour or so?"

She started walking toward the door, collecting her things as she went. "Nope, I'm good. I'll uh, see you tomorrow, Vera. Bye, Killian."

"Bye, Molly," Killian called over his shoulder, fully absorbed in his new and improved spice blend.

I didn't say anything to her. I was pretty sure I was never going to speak to her again.

Or at least not until tomorrow morning when I met her at brunch.

The door shut behind her and Killian and I were left alone. Suddenly feeling awkward, I moved away from him and focused very intently on anything else. Like my cleaning rag and the greased-over fryer.

"Where did you train?" he asked when I found more surfaces to scrub.

"CAI, Charlotte," I told him.

He whistled between his teeth. "That's a good program. You finished?"

I nodded. "Yeah, with a Bachelors. Geez, that was almost five years ago."

His face scrunched up while he worked through my answer. "So, I met your dad, and your brother owns the bike shop, right?" I nodded, not liking where this was going. "And your mom?"

I rubbed my hand over my heart, feeling that same hollow ache I always got when the subject of my mom was brought up. "She, uh, died when I was little. My dad raised us."

His silence was a tangible thing that filled up every single space in the truck. It sucked up the remaining oxygen and reached across the galley to touch me, wrap around me... hold me. "I'm sorry," he said so very tenderly my heart skipped.

I tilted my head, avoiding eye contact with him. "Thank you." We were silent for a minute while he let me step out of the sharp but also distant grief that came with losing a mother I could barely remember. I only had a handful of faded memories of her. Watching her put on perfume. Laughing while she pushed me on a swing. A family vacation at the beach. There weren't many of them, but I treasured each one.

People never knew what to say when I told them my mom died when I was young. They usually tried to fill in the emptiness with useless clichés or words of encouragement. I appreciated Killian's silence. There honestly wasn't anything to say. Nothing made it better or okay. Nothing said could change what happened. It just was. This was part of my story, the reality I lived with. Killian seemed to get that better than anyone else.

I wanted to ask about his family, but he changed the subject before I got a chance. "Durham is home for you?"

"Born and raised."

"And the truck is a new venture, right?"

"Right."

"Where have you been since CAI? Not in a kitchen around here. I would have heard about you."

I shook my head. As flattering as that statement was, I also knew it wasn't true. I'd worked for plenty of chefs happy to give me busy work without any real responsibility. "I stayed in Charlotte for a while. Last year, I worked my way across Europe."

Interest sparked in his bright eyes, darkening them, deepening them. "Worked, as in cooked?"

"Yeah, you know I just hopped from kitchen to kitchen. Nothing fancy or famous. Just your average bistro or café. I wanted some perspective. Some flavor for my resume."

"You couldn't get that in Charlotte?"

"Not like that." Charlotte had a great food scene. There were plenty of notable kitchens to work out of. Theoretically, I could have built a great

141

resume there. Except that hadn't been in the cards for me. I skipped over the sordid details of my past and told him the truth. "Charlotte was a great place to start. But come on, Europe? Last June I was in Barcelona. Then Paris. Then Rome. Then Tuscany. Vienna. Berlin. All the little towns in between. So, no, I couldn't get that in Charlotte."

"That explains your flavors."

"You hate my flavors."

He held my gaze, unflinching, showing me something I hadn't seen before. "You don't get it. Or maybe you don't see it. Your flavors are going to be legend, Vera. They're going to make *you* a legend."

"If I can remember to get the salt right."

His lips twitched again. "Ideally, yeah. If you can be careful with the salt."

"So what about you then? How did you find your footing?"

He shook his head, crossing his arms over his chest. We were as far apart as we could be in the small space. He leaned against one counter, and I leaned against the other.

He was such a man. Not in the sexist sense, but like the anatomical sense. His long, lean body was all muscled frame and virile strength. His tattoos only added to his hard edges, feeding that masculine presence and making me feel very, very female.

Delicately feminine compared to his intoxicating male-ness.

I yanked the bandana off and retied my hair in a messy bun on the top of my head. Killian watched me, fascinated.

He waited until my hair was situated before he spoke. "Chicago," he explained, although I already knew that from my prior years of light cyberstalking. "I cut my teeth at Americana under Toby Manier." He crossed his feet at the ankles, leaning back against the counter, a nostalgic smile playing at the corners of his mouth. "God, those years were hell."

"I've heard horror stories about his kitchens," I empathized.

He looked up at me from beneath those long lashes, and I felt my heart jump in my chest, surprised by the boyish expression and warmth waiting there. "Whatever you've heard, they can't compare to the truth. He was psychotic. And paranoid like you would not believe. Before he died, I would get regular cease and desist letters from him. Ezra had to keep a lawyer on retainer just to fight my legal battles with him."

"You're kidding!"

"I wish." He laughed again, the sound all melty chocolate and cozy firesides. "But I learned how to clean a kitchen working for him. And I learned how to bust my ass for every single thing. In his kitchen, there was no small task. Every single thing meant something bigger, greater. He was a slave driver for sure, but I don't regret those days."

I felt some of my awe for him return. Not many people could live through Toby Manier and thank him for his strident obsessiveness. But it was clear, despite legal issues and slave labor, Killian still respected the man. "What made you leave Americana?"

He rubbed at his beard again, shaping it with two hands until it made a point. "It was clear very early on in my career that I needed to run my own kitchen. I've always struggled to follow the rules and listen to authority. Once I got my feet under me, I decided what I wanted to do, and there was little to stop me after that. I moved to New York and tried working in a few other kitchens. Etienne Immanuel, Sasha Goering and Christopher Perry to name a few. It was the same song and dance in every kitchen, though. I learned, I studied, I grew and then I needed to move on."

"Do they all hate you for it?"

He laughed and looked at his shoes. "They should. But other than Toby, I somehow convinced them all to stay friends."

"What brought you to Durham?"

"Ezra," he said easily. "We're from here. When he told me his plan for Lilou, I couldn't resist."

"We're? You and Ezra?"

"Born and raised. We grew up together."

"So what, one day you were on the playground at recess and just decided that he would open restaurants and you would become a world-renowned chef?"

The look in his eyes turned wicked. "That's exactly how it happened."

"Nu-uh!"

"Okay, no it didn't really happen that way. Ezra and I hated each other as kids. He can sometimes be a bit of an asshole."

I couldn't help myself. "Unlike you, who's *always* an asshole?"

"Ha! The girl has bite."

I blushed, avoiding his gaze. Because the truth was I didn't have bite. Not even sometimes. I was always a pushover except when it came to Killian.

For whatever reason, my rubbery spine decided to stand up straight whenever he was around.

"Anyway, Ezra and I couldn't be more different. I always knew I was going into food. He fell into it by accident."

"How does one come to own three restaurants by accident?"

"Four," Killian corrected. "He's a silent partner in his first restaurant thanks to his first wife." A sly smile lifted one half of his mouth. "And by marrying the owner. That's how you accidentally get involved with your first restaurant. When she leaves you for another man, that's when you open three other restaurants as revenge."

I gaped at Killian, unsure how to respond. "So you're part of the plot?"

"When he opened Lilou, I was the only chef he trusted not to break up another one of his marriages."

"She left him for a chef?"

"Their chef. The chef at Quince."

"He owns Quince!" My voice just kept getting louder, but in my defense, Killian's story kept escalating.

He chuckled at my theatrics. "Silently. And out of spite. He won't let her buy him out just to torture her. Lilou, Bianca and Sarita are the projects he's truly passionate about."

"And now it makes sense why he names the restaurants after his ex-girlfriends. Wow."

"Anyway." Killian stood to his full height, making a show of looking around the kitchen. "How are we going to rescue tomorrow's menu?"

"I thought we'd already decided I was going to quit?"

"Enough of that," he demanded with steel. "You're not quitting. You're too fucking good to even joke about it." He glared at me until I held up my hands in surrender. His eyes softened, but just barely when he said, "I'll give you the advice the late, great, Toby Manier gave me all those years ago. Are you ready for it?"

I felt the urge to smile, but repressed it. "Yes. I'm ready. Give it to me."

"Stop being a loser and make something better."

"Are you serious?"

"I swear. He said that to me at least three times a night." He lifted one of his shoulders casually. "It worked."

I nodded, feeling the motivation in my joints, spreading to my bones... bleeding into my veins. *Stop being a loser*. I could do that. *Make something better*. I could at least try.

I moved to stand beside him at the prep counter. "Why are you being so nice to me?"

He looked at me out of the corner of his eye. "I'm not being nice. I'm afraid if you start making shit food, you'll drive all my business away."

I restrained the urge to elbow him in the ribs. He was flirting with me, and all I wanted to do was flirt back. The need swelled up inside me, bursting through my fingers and toes, spiraling straight to my core. This was dangerous. He was dangerous.

He threatened everything. My business. My sanity. My vow of celibacy. The carefully constructed walls I'd built around my heart. My fragile courage I'd only just regained. He'd bulldozed into my life and shaken up everything I'd thought was true about men and chefs and people. And I didn't know what to do with him.

Plus, I didn't think he understood the baggage I carried. I wasn't emotionally available anymore. I wasn't an attractive offer. I was used. Broken. Scared.

He had a weird obsession with my food truck, but that was it. He liked the attention I gave him.

Things for me weren't so simple. I couldn't flirt carelessly or without consequence. Despite everything I'd been through, everything I'd pulled myself out of, I wasn't the kind of girl that didn't get attached.

I got very attached. And then when everything inevitably went wrong? I stayed attached.

So, Killian Quinn needed to stop or move on or do anything but flirt with me.

I wasn't going to fall for this guy—this man that was everything I didn't want. I'd sworn to let my heart heal, to give myself a break from toxic relationships and bad decisions.

But beyond that, even when I put myself back on the market or whatever, Killian still wouldn't be my type. I'd already dated the egomaniac. I'd already had a relationship with the famous executive chef. I'd already given up my dreams so someone else could pursue theirs.

And I'd lost everything in the process.

I didn't want a guy like Killian Quinn.

I wanted the exact opposite.

Chapter Fourteen

"Are you comfortable, Mr. Delane?"

Dad eyed the young nurse with one eye open and one sleepily shut. "Fine for now. Thanks, Leanne."

She smiled at him, patted his shoulder and left the private chemotherapy room.

"You could have been a nurse," he said to me once we were alone again and his eyes were both firmly closed.

I stared at him, taking in the smooth recliner Leanne had set him up in. He was attached to an IV pumping him full of drugs, both toxic and necessary to his survival. He'd lost weight over the last couple of months, but not his hair. He'd lost that a long time ago. And somehow he was holding onto his eyebrows and lashes.

He looked fragile in his chair, sicker than he should be. I wanted to drag him back to the car and drive away from here as fast as I could. He didn't belong here. This place was for dying people. Sick people. And even though I knew my dad was both of those things, I refused to come to terms with them.

"Why?" I responded to his last comment. "Because I'm so nurturing?" I tapped my fingers on the back of his arm to prove my point. Dad hadn't wanted me to come today. He didn't want me to remember him like this, "strapped to a chair with tubes sticking out of me every which way." But I'd insisted. I was a coward in a lot of ways, but this wasn't one of them.

Not when it came to my dad.

He peeled one eye open again. "Well, yes. You've always been so quick to help others. Heal those that needed to be healed. Save those that needed saving." He smiled softly, finally giving into the conversation and opening both eyes. "Remember when Vann got mono? I would have accidentally killed the boy had it not been for you."

I smiled too. He wasn't lying. Vann had been sick for over a week before my dad had taken him to the doctor. And it was only after I'd logged his symptoms and convinced them both that Vann wasn't getting better. Then I'd missed three days of school to take care of my older brother so Dad could work.

I'd been fourteen at the time. Even then I knew that Dad hadn't been neglecting Vann. He couldn't stand the sickness, watching someone else suffer. Vann was just like him.

That left me. I wasn't nurturing because I wanted to be. I learned to be nurturing because I had to be.

"Well, I'm amazing, what can I say?"

His mouth quirked up in a tired smile. "That you are, baby girl."

I rubbed my hands over my thighs, then tucked my feet into my gray maxi skirt. The chemo center was freezing compared to the brutal heat outside. I'd dressed to spend the morning with Dad and the afternoon in my truck, prepping for tonight, but my scoop neck black tee wasn't cutting it. "So, other than being nurturing, why else should I have been?"

He settled back in his chair, adjusting until he was comfortable. For a minute, I didn't think he was going to answer me. And when he did, it was not the answer I expected. "It's a stable job, Vera. You wouldn't have to stress like you do."

Crossing my arms over my chest, I leaned back in my chair, mimicking his position, but not on purpose. I tried to smile, but it was wobbly and weak. "I'm pretty sure nurses get stressed out too. Especially dealing with difficult patients like you." I took a deep breath, sensing he needed reassurance over sass. Gentling my tone, but adding steel, I promised, "I love what I do, Dad. I love cooking."

He made a sound in the back of his throat that made me feel like he didn't believe me. "I worry about you. I worry about what will happen to you when I'm gone."

"So don't go anywhere," I dared him stubbornly.

He shook his head and looked at me once again. "I'm doing my best here."

Breath whooshed out of me, emptying my chest with a defeated sigh. "I know." I cleared my throat and tried to take away some of the heaviness of the conversation. "The food truck is doing fine, old man. I'm figuring it out."

His mouth pressed into a hard frown. Apparently, that wasn't enough to erase his fears. "The food truck was never what you wanted, kiddo. What happened to working in a restaurant? You spent all your money in Europe and came back with funny ideas."

My gladiator sandals were suddenly the most interesting thing in the room. I'd come back from Europe to be with him. If Dad hadn't gotten sick, I didn't know that I would have ever returned. I would have cooked my life away with cash under the table in ancient, greasy kitchens where nobody recognized my ex-boyfriend's name.

"I came back from Europe to settle down."

"You were settled down," he reminded me. "Isn't that what you were doing with that stuck-up boyfriend?"

I shivered at the memory of Derrek, a sickly feeling rolling over my spine and curdling in my stomach. "Derrek was a mistake."

"And what was Europe?"

My salvation. But I didn't say that out loud.

Dad had never given me a hard time about Europe before. He'd barely said anything about Derrek, even though I knew he didn't like him. So, what was this all about?

I held onto my patience, but barely. "Europe was an effort to expand my craft."

"So you could open a food truck? I love you, Vera, but I'm not going to be around forever. I just..." His expression changed, twisting with grief and regret and something that hurt to look at. When my heart squeezed, and it became hard to swallow, I realized it was fear. My dad was afraid for me. "I just want to know that you're going to be okay."

"I'm fine." And I tried to sound fine. I thought I might have even pulled it off.

But dad's pained expression only darkened and the pang in my chest only sharpened. "No, you're not, baby girl. I don't know what you're keeping to yourself, but those demons must be pretty evil for you to have run all the way across an ocean to get away from them. I'm sorry I made you come back."

"You didn't make me," I whispered, but neither of us was convinced. "I wouldn't give up this time with you for anything."

That didn't appease him. Before we could continue our conversation, though, Leanne stopped by to check on him. When she asked how he was doing, he asked for a blanket. "And one for my daughter too. She's bound and determined to see this through with me, but she shouldn't have to turn into a popsicle."

Leanne smiled at me, kindness shining through for my commitment to my dad. "I'll be right back."

When she'd walked away again, I surprised myself by admitting, "I'm happier than I've been in a long time." Dad focused on me, searching my face for the truth. "And when Derrek and I ended... or even before we ended, I wasn't sure that I would ever be happy again. Europe helped. I won't ever regret going. I can't regret it, not when it did so much to help me move on. But I'm glad that I'm back. I'm glad I get to spend so much time with you and Vann. I'm glad that Molly and I are in the same city again. And I love my food truck. Honestly, Dad. I'm not as much of a tragedy as you think I am."

My confession helped him relax. His shoulders lost their rigid lines, and his barrel of a chest breathed easier. "I love you, Vera. More than anything in this world. I'm fighting this damn disease the best I can, but if I can't win, I just need you to know that you deserve all the great things in this life. You don't ever need to settle, baby girl. Not ever."

Hot tears pricked at my eyes, quickly spilling over my lashes to my cheeks. I tried discretely to brush them away, but they just kept falling. "I love you too, Daddy," I sniffled. "You've already given me great things. You should never worry about that. I have them. And because of you, I have my truck too. If you're worried about me being prepared to be on my own, I am. You made sure of that."

And as I said the words, I realized they were true. I had been stupid with Derrek, but not because my dad hadn't taught me better. He had. He'd made sure I knew how to be a successful adult.

I just hadn't listened.

Dad finally dozed off, filling the quiet space with light snuffling. Leanne stopped back over when dad had reached REM and I was getting bored with my phone. Derrek's message still lit up my message box, but I refused to open it... refused to acknowledge its existence. There were more messages now. I'd lost count how many time a new notification popped up on my phone. Apparently, he'd decided that I was the Vera he was looking for. But I wouldn't read them.

I couldn't read them.

"Is he still doing okay?" she asked, checking him out.

I inclined my head toward him. "He's basically Rip Van Winkle."

She smiled fondly at him. "I'm always impressed with how quickly he can fall asleep. It always takes me forever to wind down."

"He's always been like this. My brother is the same way. They just pass out."

"Men," she murmured with a tilt of her head. "They don't worry about things like we do." I laughed politely, but she wasn't exactly right. My dad worried better than anyone I knew. And maybe sometimes he was justified in it. She turned to me. "Can I get you a paper or magazine?"

"Sure. I'd love a paper. Thank you."

She returned with the Herald-Sun a few minutes later. Most industry gossip was found online, with food bloggers and online magazines. But newspapers could always be counted on to print reviews. I flipped straight to the Living section, anxious to see if there was anything new in the Durham area and maybe, possibly, see if something had been written about Foodie. It was a long shot, and nobody had contacted me about it or anything, but a girl could hope.

Instead of local news, a familiar face stared at me from the flat pages. It was a write up for a newish restaurant in Charlotte making a splash in the southeast.

I tried to swallow around the gritty lump in my throat, but I couldn't seem to manage.

Derrek leaned against an industrial cooktop, surrounded by smooth steel and shiny accessories. His crisp white chef's coat had no wrinkles, his name and restaurant name perfectly embroidered over the right breast. His eyes looked kind in the picture, creasing in the corners and glittering with pride. And his face. His face that was so good looking it almost hurt.

Unlike Killian, who screamed danger and mayhem and broken rules, Derrek was all-American- blonde, blue-eyed with clean-cut, chiseled features. After I'd moved in with him and things had turned for the worse, I used to wonder if his success had more to do with his appearance than his skill in the kitchen. He was a good chef, but he wasn't phenomenal.

But it wasn't just his looks and mediocre talent that propelled his career skyward. Even I could admit that the man had charisma. He was charming, alluring, he made everyone feel comfortable and cared about. Nobody could resist him.

Especially not me.

Not until I'd learned my lesson the hard way.

Now he'd managed national acclaim. I wasn't surprised. Disappointed in the American people as a whole, but not surprised.

My stomach churned, and chills crawled over my body, making me paranoid. My fear was silly and unfounded. It was just a picture. He couldn't see me. He didn't know I'd found this article or bothered to read it.

151

He didn't know anything about me anymore.

I sucked in a deep breath and clenched my hands into tight fists to keep them from shaking. I didn't like to think about him anymore, or the time I spent with him. But once in a while, when I was afraid of the future or disappointed with how little I had done with my life so far, I allowed myself to imagine what my life would have been like if I'd have stayed with him.

Would he have proposed by now?

Would he have made me quit my job by now?

Would he have hospitalized me by now?

Would he have killed me by now?

A sour feeling of dread snaked through my stomach, threatening to make me toss up my breakfast, followed by a flash of heat and sweat. God, I was a mess when it came to Derrek. One part relief that I wasn't still with him. One part embarrassment that I'd become a victim, that I'd let myself get sucked into an abusive relationship to begin with. One part hate—pure, raw, violent hate. And one part fear. Fear that he would find me again. Fear that he would suck me back in, remind me that I was nothing without him, that I would never be anything without him. Fear that he wouldn't give me the choice. That he would demand my obedience.

And I would give it to him.

Again.

I felt like an addict in the worst way. And it was the sick addiction that scared me the most. Because I knew what I wanted and he wasn't it. I knew how to be happy again, and he wasn't the way. I knew how to stay healthy and go after my dreams and be my own, independent woman. And yet the threat of what he could do to me, how he could destroy every single thing, was very real.

And knowing that still didn't take away the fear. Because I didn't trust that there wasn't some way he could convince me to go back to him.

He had stripped me of self-worth and confidence and everything I needed to be me. He'd turned me into a submissive, weak, shell of a woman. He'd broken me.

What if he did it again?

What if he didn't *turn* me weak? What if I'd *always been* weak?

And he had simply been stronger?

When Leanne came back at the end of my dad's treatment, I still clutched the Living section in my sweaty hands. She woke Dad and unhooked him. His sleepy gaze swept over the paper. I didn't know if he recognized Derrek or not, but he didn't comment on him.

He wrapped his heavy arm around my shoulder, and we walked to the car. It wasn't until we were buckled and headed back home that he reached over from the passenger's seat and settled his warm hand on my still-chilled shoulder. "I'm proud of you, Vera. No matter what I said earlier, you should know that I'm proud of the woman you've become and all that you've accomplished. I only worry because it's my job."

I gave him a watery smile, unable to speak past the lump in my throat.

"And you don't need him," he went on, surprising the hell out of me. "I know you've kept what happened a secret because you think you're protecting me, but I see it, Vera. I see that he hurt you badly. Hell, I had to deal with him after you left, calling the house twenty times a day. I know that he damaged you somehow and I hate him for it. I'd like to kill him for it. But I know I don't need to. You're stronger than that boy. And you deserve better. You deserve the best. I've never known anyone more deserving than you, baby girl."

"Thanks, Dad," I hiccupped on a mushy sob.

He squeezed my shoulder, his large hand engulfing me, making me feel small, protected. "You'll get your picture in the paper soon enough. You just watch. He'll be reading about you soon enough."

I nodded, accepting his comfort without explaining that recognition was the last thing I wanted. Well, at least now, after I read Derrek's feature.

He'd inadvertently put things into perspective for me. I wasn't trying to make national or even statewide news. I needed to stay under the radar, do my thing quietly, inconspicuously and without drawing attention to myself.

Derrek could make the paper all he wanted; I just hoped he wasn't dating anyone new.

Not for my sake.

But for hers.

****

That afternoon, after I had dropped Dad off and made sure Vann would be by later to check on him, I headed to the truck. I had about ten thousand things to do for the weekend, especially after the chicken and waffle flop. I needed to up my game. I couldn't have any more train wrecks like that.

I'd learned so much in the few months that I'd been opened, but business could be better. My business management skills could be better. My food could be better. Basically, every single thing could be better.

153

I hadn't heard back from any of the bakeries I'd stopped by, and I still hadn't found a produce vendor I was happy with. So far I'd managed with the closest organic grocery store, but it was gouging my budget. I needed a place with fresh fruits and vegetables without breaking the bank.

All in all, though, I'd learned a ton since I'd opened. Nothing had been smooth or easy or natural, but I was getting the hang of it. Mostly.

I opened the windows and propped the door open. The truck hummed with electricity while the fans whirred to life. I stepped in front of one and tried to cool down.

Vann's bike shop buzzed with activity around me. Cyclists from all over the city had shown up for a weekly group ride. There was a little Mexican restaurant outside the city where they went to celebrate Taco Tuesday. I'd told Vann I would serve tacos to them, so they didn't have to go all the way to Mama Bonita, but Vann said that defeated the purpose. Clearly, cyclists were crazy.

Enough of them stopped by to see if I sold power drinks or energy bars though that I seriously contemplated stocking them for the future. I offered them cans of soda, but they looked at me like I had lost my damn mind.

When someone knocked on the door, I assumed it was another one of them. "I don't have anything made by Gatorade. I'm not even open."

"No, I, uh, I wasn't looking for anything. I just saw you were here."

I spun around. Killian stood in the doorframe. His arms were braced on either side, but he had yet to step inside.

"I thought you were one of them." I pointed to the human-size bumble bees behind him— because of all the yellow and black spandex. "They want me to whip them up some go bars and energy squeezies."

He wrinkled his nose, as unimpressed as I had been. "That's disgusting."

"My brother is one of them, and I can safely say they don't know the difference between cardboard and what they keep in their refrigerators. If it's not tasteless and full of protein, they don't want it."

He nodded, but didn't say anything else on the subject. Instead, he seemed to watch me for a minute, thinking something over. When he finally spoke again, he said the very last thing I ever expected him to say. "I've never asked, and it's kind of silly to do so now, but I gotta know, Delane. Do you have a boyfriend?"

My heart stuttered, tripping over uneven beats and panic. Derrek's article flashed in my head, and I worried that Killian knew. How did he find out I'd dated Derrek? Had he seen the article? Did Killian know Derrek?

Did he know what Derrek was really like? Or did Killian respect him like the rest of the industry?

I inhaled slowly and answered as evenly as I could. "I don't have a boyfriend." I looked down at the knife in my hand and swallowed thickly. I sounded nervous, unsteady. And apparently, Killian thought so too because he just stood there staring at me. His eyebrows squished together over his nose and I could feel the concern bubbling up inside him. I rushed to rescue the conversation and cover my jittery behavior. "Unless you count the truck. Then things are new, but we took out a loan together so I guess I'm stuck with him." I tried for sarcastic, but my voice sounded brittle and unconvinced. I hiccupped an awkward laugh and then just started spitting out words in an anti-effort to salvage my dignity. "And thank God for that, because I honestly don't want a boyfriend. The only thing I'm capable of committing to right now is food." Oh, God. The words just wouldn't stop. "I mean, clearly I'm a walking disaster. A guy would have to be insane to date me. Or be one of those guys that likes crazy girls. And what does that say about them? Besides how hypocritical is our culture that a girl that's high drama gets labeled as crazy, but a guy that enjoys high drama is what? Nothing? Applauded for putting up with her? It's such a double standard."

Killian stared at me for a minute, not saying anything and not doing anything. I turned back to the counter and put the knife away. Talking about boyfriends made me stabby. I didn't want to be responsible for what happened to Killian if he pried any further.

Not that he pried.

He just asked a question, and I verbally vomited all over him.

After a long, uncomfortable silence, he said, "Uh, I came over to ask if you wanted to go out with some of us from the restaurant tonight? It's Wyatt's birthday."

Surprised by his offer, I turned around and leaned against the counter. If I was honest, I was surprised that he was still here. He hadn't fled. He'd witnessed some of my crazy and hadn't abandoned me. He stood there as calm and patient as always.

Something warm and bubbly burst through me. I crossed my arms, trying to ward off the sensation, but I couldn't manage to banish it. I tried to convince myself that it was just nice to be included with the staff at Lilou, but even my stubborn heart saw through the lie. It had nothing to do with Wyatt or his birthday and everything to do with the cocky, self-absorbed chef standing in my doorway. "Where are you going?"

Killian inclined his head toward the other side of the plaza. "Probably Verve or Greenlight. It could be cool."

"Yeah, it could be."

Half his mouth lifted in a coaxing smile, partly hidden behind his beard. "You don't sound convinced."

"No, it's not that. I mean, Wyatt's cool. And I should probably get him a gift for all he's put up with from me anyway. I just don't know anybody except you and the birthday boy."

He shrugged, playing cool, but his shoulders were rigid, and he'd crossed his arms over his chest. "Yeah, but you do know me. We could hang out. Away from food and our places of employment."

I licked my suddenly dry lips and avoided his gaze. God, I wanted to say yes. My first instinct was to say yes. To jump at the chance to see what he was like away from a kitchen. To get to know him without the pressure of performing. But Derrek was too fresh in my mind, a dark shadow that lingered in every corner of my new happiness.

Killian sensed my hesitation and threw me a life preserver. "You don't have to decide now. Just see how you feel later."

"How will I find you?" Not that I was thinking about going. Because I wasn't.

"Here, hand me your phone. I'll give you my number."

I blinked at him, unable to believe he was seriously hitting on me. He had such a poker face. "Okay, smooth operator," I mumbled.

His lips twitched into a reluctant smile. "What?"

"Don't act so casual. I see what you're doing."

It became harder for him to hold back his smile. "I'm just saying; then you can text me later."

"Mmm-hmmm."

The smile won, breaking through and transforming his face from ruggedly handsome to *I can't breathe when I look directly at you.* "I probably need it anyway, you know, for like work stuff."

I raised an eyebrow. "Work stuff?"

"That way I can just text you tips and salt warnings."

"You wouldn't."

He reached up to tug at the side of his beard, forcing it into shape. Then he curled those long fingers at me, gesturing for me to give up my phone.

Apparently, I'd also lost my mind. I grabbed my cell from the shelf over my head and walked it to him. "If I get a text about salt, I might punch you."

He took the phone from me after I'd tapped in the password, our fingers brushing in the exchange. It wasn't anything. We barely touched, but a burst of sensation sizzled up my arm, sending butterflies in a craze

156

inside my belly and flushing my cheeks with heat. What was wrong with me?

I'd sworn off men.

All men.

Including him.

Especially him.

But honestly, did I even stand a chance when it came to him? His bright green eyes were warm beneath thick lashes. His dark hair was wavy and full, pushed to one side in a disheveled sort of delicious mess. He was just a step shorter than me, since he still hovered near the doorway and it was the first time I looked at his face where his beard wasn't the prominent feature. From this angle, I noticed his tanned, perfect skin and the wrinkles his forehead made when he raised his eyebrows.

I swallowed and took a steadying breath. *Get it together.*

He punched in his number and then called his phone from mine. "It's done," he said simply, handing it back to me. "Just text me when you decide about tonight. I'll tell you where to meet us."

"Do you go out with your staff a lot?" I knew I was being nosy, but whenever they came to the truck, they seemed to be terrified of him. Wyatt especially had a delirious case of hero-worship grounded in substantial work-related terror. I wondered if Killian was a different person with them outside of work.

Although it was hard to imagine Killian as anything but domineering.

He lifted one shoulder. "Yeah, I don't know. Sometimes."

"That's nice of you. I bet they like that."

His dry look disagreed with me. "Sure. Everyone loves hanging out with their boss."

"Hey, my employees love hanging out with me. Maybe it's just you."

He shook his head, calling my bullshit. "Your employees are your friends."

"Exactly. Yours could be too."

"No, they're your actual friends. They want to hang out with you because you're who they hang out with."

"You're just jealous." Oh, my God, why was I flirting with him? I needed a sedative. Like one of those tribal spit-shooter darts. I should have planted Molly in the bushes so she could blow one at me in case of emergency.

This was obviously an emergency.

His smile was earnest and made his eyes crinkle. "Maybe. Are you sticking around to work today?"

I shook my head, determined to pull back and disentangle myself from this weird place we'd accidentally stumbled into. "No, I have some errands to do. And I have to figure the menu out for the weekend."

"Writer's block?"

I wrinkled my nose, trying to pinpoint it. "I need more inspiring produce. I've been going to Wagner's, but it's just not good enough."

"Have you tried the Morning Market? On Franklin Ave.?"

My ears perked up. This was the tip I needed. "No. Is it good?"

He gave me a look. "Do you doubt my judgment?"

"This could be sabotage."

"This is a favor," he countered. "And you're going to owe me your first born son when you realize I just changed your life." I made a "ha!" sound, but he ignored me. "It's only open in the mornings from seven to tenthirty. The earlier you get there, the better. There's coffee, though. And a kolache stand. It's legit. You'll love it."

"Killian, thank you. I've been searching for a great place to go, but I've never heard of this one."

"Yeah, it's kind of an insider secret."

I could have hugged him, but I held back. I was confused enough and wrapping myself around his body like a spider monkey didn't seem like the best decision.

"Thanks again." I waved my phone back and forth. "I'll text you what I decide about tonight."

"Sounds good. Bye, Vera."

"Bye, Killian."

He stepped down from the truck and turned toward Lilou. I told myself I wasn't watching him walk away, but then he turned back around and caught me staring at him. He didn't call me on it, though.

"Meatballs," he called out.

Fine. I'd been staring at his ass. *Whatever.* Regardless, I was incapable of coherent thought. "What?"

"You should make meatballs again. Your lamb ones were the best meatballs I've ever had."

The professional side of me exploded in a surprise orgasm. Just kidding. But I was almost too shocked to reply. *I mean, what?!?!* He didn't wait around for me to reply anyway. He crossed the street without another word.

"Is that why you stole the recipe from me?" I shouted after him, but he was already to the side door of Lilou. He didn't even bother to turn around and defend himself. He just disappeared inside with that impish grin mostly hidden behind his thick beard.

It wasn't until my cheeks started hurting that I realized I had been grinning too. For like a solid half hour. Especially after I double checked my phone and saw that Killian's name appeared under the title **James Q**.

Which explained a lot about my nosy internet friend.

It also made me extremely, irrationally happy for some unexplainable reason.

I pulled the Living Section out of my purse and stared at Derrek's smug face. My dad's words echoed through the narrow galley of my truck. *You'll have your picture in the paper someday.*

But not if I got distracted.

Perspective, Vera.

I went home an hour later. And six hours later when Killian texted to see if I'd decided to go out or not, I told him I had a headache.

He didn't text back.

I was safe from losing myself again.

I was back in neutral territory with Killian.

I was a coward.

Chapter Fifteen

*T*he next morning, I felt like shit. It might have been because I stress ate my way through a half pan of double fudge brownies. The box kind. I'd sold out for two-dollars-worth of anxiety-induced desperation.

But just so we're clear, no matter how many good meals I'd had, or how high my standards for food were, boxed brownie mix was the best kind of guilty pleasure.

Or, my exhaustion and icky feeling of disappointment could have stemmed from the lack of sleep. I hadn't been able to fall asleep until close to three.

I blamed my weekend hours. Thursday through Sunday I stayed up until ungodly hours and by the time I got home, showered and decompressed it was always after four before I finally closed my eyes.

The important thing to note was that this had nothing to do with the lame ass text I'd sent to Killian the night before.

Despite my sleepless night, I still dragged myself from bed early enough to get to the Morning Market by the opening. I'd had to Google it for the exact address and found pictures of what to expect. Killian had definite rights to my first born. This market was everything I was looking for.

The market sat nestled in the corner of an industrial area, neighbored by a tool and die designer on one side and a lighting palace on the other. It spread out in an abandoned parking lot, covered by mix-matched tents and just as diverse vendors.

In one section, fragrant flowers in every color burst from buckets with hand drawn price tags hanging off them. In another, eggs and farm-fresh milk in coolers spread out between artisan cheeses and all manner of jerkies.

But the majority of the market? Fresh produce. Fresh produce everywhere. Fruits, vegetables. More fruits. More vegetables.

It was glorious.

And Killian hadn't lied about the kolache stand. I stopped there first, picking up an egg and spicy bacon pastry and a cup of hazelnut coffee with the perfect amount of creamer.

My weird mood faded in light of the possibilities in front of me. And the coffee.

The coffee definitely helped.

I'd just stepped up to a pepper stand with bins of every single pepper I could think of. Colored bells, spicy habaneros, shishitos and jalapenos, and my favorite—hatch. Plus so many more. The vendor even had hybrids he'd been breeding himself.

My eyes got a little misty, but I blamed it on the pollen in the air.

"Let me guess…" I nearly dropped my coffee when Killian stepped up next to me. "Anchos. You're all about the anchos."

Embarrassment for my awkward text from the night before burst to life inside me, flushing my cheeks a nice, dark, strawberry red. But at the same time, the achy feeling in my chest faded. I stopped feeling mildly queasy. I stopped hating myself for not going out the night before. I stopped missing Killian and hating myself for being such a coward. Most of all, I stopped analyzing every single thing I did, said or thought.

He was here! And I was determined not to be a giant weirdo.

"Really? We've been friends for three weeks now, and you pick anchos? Do you not know me at all?"

We turned to face each other. His expression remained cautious, thoughtful. I didn't know if it was part of our game or if he had taken my blow-off text to heart. "Three weeks? We've been friends longer than that."

I hid my smile behind a drink of coffee. "No, I've been friends with James Q for longer than that. You've only just recently decided to be nice."

He gave me the side eye. "James Q was kind of an asshole. *I've* been nice to you for at least three months." His hand moved up to tug at the side of his beard. His other hand held a cup of coffee just like mine. Except without creamer. Because apparently, he hated himself.

162

I wrinkled my nose in thought. "Then you should know better than ancho. And you should have told me you had a secret internet identity."

"It's only secret from the general public. I thought it would be better not to give angry diners a platform to hunt me down." I could actually understand that since I also went by a variation of my name.

"So, it's Killian James Quinn?"

He nodded. "And you're Vera Foodie the Food Truck Delane?"

"May," I confessed. "Vera May Delane."

We acknowledged each other's full names with a shared look of satisfaction. Turning back to the table, he tilted his head, examining the table of peppers once again. "Hatch?"

"Ding, ding, ding." A warm feeling fizzed through me, like my insides were suddenly carbonated. "They are my favorite. But I'm actually interested in the shishitos."

His gaze found mine again, so green, like freshly mowed grass or Christmas-worthy evergreens. "What are you thinking?"

"Skirt steak tacos with roasted shishitos, crumbled cotija cheese and braised lettuce."

His eyebrows shot up at the same time his eyes flashed with something like surprise. "You should squeeze fresh lemon over the top instead of lime."

It was my turn to be surprised. That was a great idea. Different enough to be interesting. Acidic enough to bring the dish together. "Good idea, Quinn. You should be a chef or something."

He chuckled at my lame joke. "Are you telling me there won't be any meatballs for me?"

I shrugged and tossed a casual, "Sorry, you're in charge of your own balls this weekend," before I turned to the vendor and talked pepper quantities and prices.

Killian laughed outright but let me haggle in peace. As soon as I finished and paid, agreeing to pick up my purchase at the end of my shopping, he jumped in with his own questions.

Where I'd been mostly interested in being able to afford the peppers I wanted, Killian had a long list of questions to ask. He didn't care about price—and he wouldn't have to since he wasn't paying for these peppers out of his pocket. He was more interested in soil quality and sunlight exposure. He wanted to know spice variants and hybrid procedures. He spent the next twenty minutes tasting them raw, deliberating over each bite.

I watched him with unfiltered awe. He let me without calling me on it. Instead, he generously offered to give me bites as well, asking my opinion, discussing the crispness or heat or sweetness of each one. He asked question after question about the future of each breed. What would the hatch taste like in the fall? The serrano?

Then he turned to me and hinted at dish ideas he was mulling over for the autumn menu. He wanted to know my thoughts on pepper-protein combinations. What did I think would go best with flank steak? With frog legs? With tofu?

I blinked at him. "Tofu?"

"Ezra's idea," he explained. "He wants a more vegetarian/vegan-friendly menu. He says we're ignoring a huge consumer base."

"Is that true?"

He lifted one shoulder. "People do not come to Lilou for their diversity-friendly menu. They want the best meal of their life. Not tofu."

His frustrated resignation laced each word, broadcasting his feelings on the topic. "Ezra won't listen to you?" I guessed.

"Ezra is a businessman. A damn good one. But he doesn't know the first thing about food." He picked up a jalapeno by the stem and examined one side of it, the cracked, brownish lines that snaked over it like veins. You could tell just by looking at those dried out vines that it would be a spicy one. "That won't stop him from getting involved, though."

"Does he always give you input on your menus?"

Killian reached out to shake the vendor's hand, then inclined his head, indicating I should follow him. We threw our empty coffee cups away and wandered through the clustered aisles of the market, stepping over the larger puddles on the wet asphalt.

It took a minute before he answered my question. "Always. I don't think I can even call them my menus. They're his. They follow his vision for his restaurant. I work for him."

We stepped up to a stand with different variants of greens and root vegetables. "It almost sounds like you don't like working at one of the best restaurants in the city, Killian Quinn. Good thing I know better."

"Do you? Know better I mean."

"Ezra might needlessly put his hands on everything you do, but he can't cook for you. You're the one that makes the food. You're the one that's responsible for the restaurant's reputation. That has nothing to do with Ezra."

He shoved his hands in the pockets of his jeans. "But it does. It's not really my food. It's not really my restaurant. As far as reputations go, I'm just good at cooking other people's ideas."

164

Frustration boiled in my chest. "You could put a thousand other chefs in your position, and they wouldn't accomplish what you're doing over there. You've forgotten I've eaten there. I had 'Ezra's' food. And it changed my life on like a spiritual level."

His mouth quirked up in a reluctant smile. "Spiritual level, huh?"

"I had an existential experience with the braised lamb. I think I actually left my body and went to some other plane of existence."

"You're such a liar."

His humility was so out of place with everything about him that I wanted to call *him* the liar. Everything I knew about this man screamed confidence to the point of arrogance. But he was so damn good at what he did that I couldn't even fault him for it.

But now he wanted to play shy?

What a weirdo.

An adorable, sexy, gorgeous weirdo.

I kind of hated him for being so irresistible.

Turning back to a bushel of iridescent rhubarb, I pushed those thoughts out of my head and dropped some knowledge on him. "The point is most chefs would kill to be in your position. I bet you don't even have to worry about a budget. Yeah, maybe Ezra gets final approval, but you pretty much have complete freedom and notoriety to create whatever you want."

"You get to create whatever you want," he pointed out.

I made a sound in the back of my throat. "It's not even close to the same thing, and you know it. I'm cooking out of a tin can. You run one of the best kitchens in the state, possibly the entire country. We couldn't be more opposite." Realizing something shocking, I turned around to face him, dropping my hand on my hip. He was already looking at me, all masculine strength and hard body. The sun exposed his twining tattoos and tanned skin. He was perfect—not just at what he did, but how he looked too. "You know that, by the way. I have no idea why I'm padding your ego. It's not in any danger of being squashed."

His head dipped toward mine, and a sly smile lifted his mouth. "This isn't about ego, although I don't mind your compliments. Feel free to keep them coming."

"You're impossible."

His grin widened.

I turned back to the produce.

When he spoke again, he sounded more serious. "I thought your food truck was your dream come true? Didn't you say something about it being everything to you?"

165

I nibbled on my bottom lip for a minute while I compared prices of carrots and turnips without really seeing anything. I vaguely remembered stepping over here to look at lettuce, but my thoughts were a jumbled mess at this point, and Killian prying into my life didn't help.

Finally, I braved some truth. "I said it was everything I have left. Not all of us get handed our dream kitchens because our childhood friend hands it to us."

"Friendship had nothing to do with it. The only reason Ezra hired me was because I deserved that kitchen. Neither of us wants to be reminded of our childhood. Neither of us can stand looking at the other," he shot back immediately.

It was defensive enough that I couldn't help but be curious.

"And he didn't hand it to me," Killian added. "I worked my ass off to earn a kitchen like Lilou. And I continue to work my ass off to keep it."

"I thought you said—"

He cut me off by reminding me that he'd said they grew up together. That apparently didn't imply friendship. "Honestly, I'm not sure if you could even call us friends yet. He's someone I owe a lot to, someone I would probably die for. But I don't know if that makes us friends or not."

Men. "It makes you friends," I told him, hoping it would help him in some way. "If you're willing to die for him, then you're friends."

"Ezra's complicated," Killian explained without explaining anything.

"*You're* complicated," I countered.

"That's adorable coming from you, Delane."

I glared at him with narrowed eyes. "I'm not complicated. I'm easy. As long as you don't get in my way."

He shook his head, not sparing me a glance. He was too focused on the turnips in his hands. "Then stop changing the subject on me and tell me why you're running a food truck when you clearly want a kitchen."

The will to speak dried up in my throat. I wasn't ready to say those words to anyone yet. Let alone Killian Quinn. He wouldn't understand throwing away my career like I did. He wouldn't understand turning my back on my dream for someone else. And he really wouldn't understand being trampled for years because I lacked the backbone to escape.

"It's complicated," I admitted, the word tasting like dirt in my mouth. Maybe I wasn't as simple and straightforward as I had hoped.

His warm hand wrapped around my wrist. His fingers circled my smaller bones completely, touching his palm and making me feel so small, so fragile next to him. He made me feel sheltered, protected. He made me feel valued in a way that took me off guard every single time he treated me so kindly.

166

And yet I couldn't shake the worry, the old fear that stayed with me no matter what.

I was the exact opposite of him. He was sure and stable, where I was fickle and shaky. He was confident when I was only insecure. Strong where I was only ever weak.

I kept my gaze trained on where his hand touched me, using him to steady the wild beating of my heart. When I first left Derrek, leaving the country had felt like my only option. I had been skittish around all people, jumpy and paranoid. My hands shook regularly, and my expectations for human decency were lower than low. But during my year in Europe, I'd worked on some coping mechanisms to help me heal.

I hated them. And I hated being weak. But I refused to give this part of me to Derrek. He'd taken so much. He didn't get to take my sense of peace either, my ability to be normal and interact with other people. But it was easy with Killian, easier than I expected. He made me feel normal again. Safe.

Killian stepped closer, demanding my attention. His body heat swept over me like a tidal wave, covering me completely, all at once. I swallowed so loudly he had to have heard it. "You're all mystery, Vera. Half-truths and bold statements, but you hide everything about you." His grip around my wrist tightened, demanding my attention. I looked into his eyes, but it turned out to be a mistake. He was too intense. Too overwhelming. He was everything hot and exciting, interesting and new. I wanted to get to know him. And I wanted to be known by him. "Tell me something real," he demanded.

I should have walked away. I should have turned around and ignored him for the rest of the day. For the rest of forever. But instead, I told him the truth. The stupid, ugly truth. "The food truck wasn't ever something I wanted. I pictured myself like you. I wanted the big kitchen. The acclaimed restaurant. I wanted a staff and name recognition and all of it. I wanted everything. Instead, I got a five-foot galley and twelve hundred Facebook likes. I don't have any clue what I'm doing. And I moved back home with my dad. I'm twenty-six years old, and I live at home." The words left my mouth in a rush of confession and connection. I felt him absorb them, take them in and get to know me. I felt this tug between us grow tauter.

I wanted to take them all back, erase the closeness between us. I wanted to remember that I was done with men. That falling for Killian would only hurt me.

Hurt my career.

But I couldn't. The damage was done. I saw it in his expression, the way his eyes warmed and softened and saw me—really, truly saw me. "If you want a restaurant, Vera, you could have one. You have more talent in your pinky than most chefs have their entire career. Why did you give up?"

"Can I help you guys find anything?"

The vendor's voice broke the spell over both of us. We took an instinctive step back, neither of us realizing how close we stood.

I tugged my arm from Killian's grasp and took another three steps away, thankful I didn't have to answer his question.

"Lettuce," I sounded breathless, shaken up.

And I was.

The vendor went over his different variations and their quality. I half listened. No, that was a lie. I tried to *look* like I was half listening while my brain tumbled in my head like it had been put on a dryer setting.

I finally picked out iceberg. It wasn't the most inventive of greens, but it would braise well. I paid him and promised to come pick it up before he closed for the day.

Killian took over, grilling the guy like he had the first vendor. He asked no less than a thousand questions. I just watched him, mentally taking notes on everything he said.

He didn't end up buying anything. The vendor was just as surprised as I was. Killian thanked him but didn't make any promises to come back.

"Did I buy bad lettuce?" I asked when we'd turned away from the stand.

"There's not a whole lot to lettuce. You'll be fine."

I stared at him. "What was wrong with everything else?"

He shrugged that casual one shoulder shrug. I wanted to whack-a-mole it. "Nothing is wrong with it. It's just not… Here, I'll show you."

My poor battered heart lurched. His words felt heavier than our simple morning at a farmer's market. I should have left.

Run away.

Instead, I did something simple and utterly irreversible, something that would be the beginning of the end for me. I didn't walk away.

I let him show me.

Chapter Sixteen

Killian reached down and grabbed my hand, pulling me after him. I stared at our interlocked fingers for a minute while he weaved through cluttered aisles and clumps of shoppers inspecting produce as thoroughly as Killian had.

His hand wrapped around mine, hot with his body heat, strong with all those sinewy muscles. I shouldn't have let him get his way so easily. I should have put up some kind of fight or stood up for myself or something, but I couldn't do anything besides let him lead me.

My past had damaged me. This was something I was well aware of. But for whatever reason, Killian Quinn felt like healing.

My last year in Europe had been a buffet of available men; men that hadn't been looking for something serious or committed. Men I could have used to help me move on after Derrek.

And I'd been unable to open myself up to any of them. I couldn't risk being vulnerable with someone again. I couldn't gamble with my heart and lose, falling right back into an old pattern. I couldn't trust myself not to choose another loser.

So, I'd remained withdrawn, wholly focused on working on my craft. That's what I should be doing now.

Instead, I let Killian drag me around without a fight. I couldn't muster up the same fears that had poisoned me since Derrek.

I even, maybe just a little, felt safe with his hand holding mine.

Felt healthier than I had in years.

It was a stupid feeling to have. Dumb. Idiotic.

And yet there it was. I wasn't afraid of Killian.

Not even a tiny bit.

The vendor saw us approach when we were still a few stalls away. She stepped from behind her crates of lush produce and smiled at Killian like he was the sun in her sky. She was an elderly woman with richly tanned skin, leathery and lined from days spent outside. She wore a faded denim shirt, rolled up to the elbows and a similar pair of worn jeans with gardening gloves sticking out of her back pocket. Her salt and peppered hair sat in a tight bun at her nape, a neatly folded scarf hung around her neck.

She was farm-life personified.

Killian let go of my hand, but not before her shrewd eyes noticed that he'd been linked to me. Momentarily forgetting about me, he stepped up to her and wrapped her in a tight hug, crushing her against his chest.

She wasn't a short woman, but she looked tiny against him. Her gray-streaked hair vanished beneath his beard as he momentarily rested his cheek against the top of her head. He gave her a quick kiss before pulling out of the hug, keeping one arm around her shoulders.

"Vera, I'd like you to meet Jo, my foster mom. Jo, this is Vera Delane."

Jo left Killian's side and extended a calloused hand to me. I took it, intimidated by her strength and direct gaze. "It's nice to meet you, Vera."

"Yes, you too," I told her genuinely. I wanted so badly to ask Killian about his childhood. I hadn't known he had a foster mom. I hadn't known he didn't have parents. Or maybe he'd been adopted at some point? Despite everything I'd learned or discovered via cyberstalking his rise to greatness, there was so much about Killian I didn't know.

Killian stepped in before the silence between us grew awkward. "Vera opened a food truck across the street from Lilou. She needs a good place to shop."

Jo's grin stretched across her face. "Well, you've come to the right place."

"I've been looking all over the city for a market like this. I didn't know it existed until Killian told me about it."

"He must like you then," she chuckled. "He doesn't usually share."

I nodded. "I've noticed."

"Alright," he interrupted. His hand fell to my lower back, and he nudged me forward, toward perfect looking produce. "Don't you have shopping to do, Delane?"

I could have grilled Jo for hours on Killian. What was he like as a kid? Has he always been a genius in the kitchen? Has he always been this cocky? Focused? Intense? Can I see pictures???

"Take a look around," Jo encouraged. "Killian's helped me plant over the years, so I should have whatever you need."

I raised an eyebrow at Killian. "That was nice of you."

"Yeah, well I didn't mean for it to be. I wanted Jo to be my personal gardener, but she's bound and determined to make money from other people. It's annoying."

She looked at the sky, slapping Killian with the back of her hand simultaneously. "Heaven forbid I pay the bills."

Killian's voice dropped low and frustrated. "I told you I'd help out with those."

She shook her head and moved back to her vegetables, lovingly reorganizing the ones that had been picked through. "How's Ezra by the way? I haven't heard from the greedy little bastard in a while."

Suddenly the cucumbers were super interesting. I picked one up and shamelessly eavesdropped on their entire conversation.

"The same," Killian replied evenly. "He wants to fire the chef at Bianca. He's dating again. He won't leave me alone."

Jo glared at a pretty pile of heirloom tomatoes. "He should fire that idiot at Bianca."

"He can't get anyone to replace him," Killian added as if reminding her.

I moved over to some plump, red strawberries. Jo softened, turning an affectionate smile on Killian. "What about the dating? I suppose that's going the same way."

Killian chuckled darkly. "Would you risk being turned into a restaurant?"

"He did that to himself. No respectable girl is going to go out with him only to be dumped for the sake of his empire."

The nosy busybody inside me perked up at this new information. Now if only they would turn the conversation to Killian.

"No respectable girl should date him anyway. He's not interested in settling down. He's married to the business."

Jo snorted. "I'm sure he loves hearing that from *you*. You're no better." I pretended not to notice when she turned her attention to me, staring directly without saying anything.

Killian didn't seem to notice her averted attention. "I stay out of his business. And he stays out of mine."

"Unless you're both in the kitchen."

Killian growled something I couldn't make out.

Jo's voice softened, gentled. "Don't leave him, Killian. You know he needs you."

"Jo…" Killian warned.

She raised her hands in surrender. "Alright, I'll stay out of your business. I'm just saying, you need each other. There's no reason to fight every day of your lives." I felt her gaze the second it snapped back to me. "And what about you, Vera? Are you having success setting up across the street from Lilou?"

I tried to pretend like I hadn't been listening to every single word of their conversation. I lifted my gaze from the strawberries and looked as innocent as possible. "Hmm?"

"Your food truck?" Jo pushed, unafraid of asking personal details. "How do you do over there across from Lilou? I can't imagine you have the same clientele?"

Jo seemed to know a lot about the food industry for looking like a simple farmer. I decided to grill Killian later.

"We don't," I agreed. "I cater more to the bar crowd. Our peak hours are different. When Lilou starts to close is when business takes off for me."

"Did you plan that?"

I met her stare with courage I didn't know I possessed. Her question was simple, but her meaning was deeper. She wanted to know if I had intentionally set up across from Lilou to use its success to my advantage.

"My brother owns the bike shop, Cycle Life. He lets me park in his lot rent free."

Her shoulders relaxed just a bit, and her claws retracted. Apparently, she believed me enough to move on. "Do you have a lot of family in the area?"

"Not really. Just my older brother and Dad."

"Oh, so you're from here?"

I subtly brushed my hand over my forehead, wiping the nervous beads of sweat out of sight. I felt like I should be under an interrogation lamp. Her questions were simple enough, but it was her direct gaze, her shrewd insight that made me jumpy. She saw way more than I wanted her to. "I am. I left for a few years to get my degree and check out life outside of Durham. But I moved back a few months ago when my dad was diagnosed with bladder cancer."

"Oh, my." She wrapped an arm around her waist and settled her other hand over her mouth. "I'm sorry, Vera. That is just awful. What stage?"

I cleared my throat and tried not to let the always bubbling tears surface. "Four. He's almost done with his first round of treatment."

172

Jo's hand slid to cradle her jaw. "Did they give him much hope?"

"I'm not sure," I answered honestly. "They didn't at first. His doctor and oncologist made it seem like he might as well plan his funeral. But since he started treatment, they've stopped treating him like a walking corpse. We're just kind of waiting to see. I don't know what's going to happen."

"My husband, Mac, died of colon cancer."

"Oh, no. I'm so sorry."

She waved me off. "That was years ago. Before Killian ever came to live with me. I'm just saying, cancer is a vindictive bitch. I hate that you have to watch someone you love go through it."

I was humbled by her succinct but authentic consolation. I found that most people didn't know what to say or how to reply when we dropped the C-bomb. Jo just got straight to it. Cancer sucked. There wasn't really any other way to respond besides acknowledging that.

"Thanks," I told her. "I hate it too."

She offered me a tight smile, then pointed at the strawberries. "Now let's get to it. I'm sure you're here to rip me off. I hate delaying the pleasure for you."

I laughed, thinking she was joking, but she remained stone-faced, so I didn't know what to think. She moved behind the counter and started to dig around for something. I looked at Killian for help and found his gaze already on me.

He was statue still, rigid and tight, coiled like a snake about to strike. I took a step back, not knowing what his problem was. Or why he was looking at me like that, like he couldn't decide what to do with me.

"You should have told me." His voice was nothing but steel and gravel, restrained aggression and cool control.

My voice, on the other hand, was a croaky whisper, two parts confused and one part embarrassingly flattered. "About my dad?" He nodded. "It's never come up. I don't know when I would have told you."

"I wouldn't have—"

I rolled my eyes. "Yes, you would have. Don't even pretend like you would have treated me any differently."

His lips quirked, ticking his beard on one side. "Maybe. But I might have been kinder about how I went about it."

"Well, now you know. I'll expect flowers and chocolate now instead of nasty notes scratched on the back of order tickets."

His smirk stretched into a full-blown smile. "I doubt the critiques will stop. But we can work in some chocolate. That sounds fair."

173

Before I could think of a clever reply, Jo interrupted with a calculator in her hand. "Were you wanting strawberries? Or was it something else that caught your eye?"

My gaze swept over her produce once again. "I get why you didn't want to buy from the other guy," I told Killian first. "I see the difference."

Killian tapped the wooden table with his pointer finger. "Jo knows her shit. She'll set you up with whatever you need."

I entered into conversation with Jo, haggling just like she'd accused. I realized that Killian hadn't stopped me from buying peppers because Jo didn't keep a stock that extensive. Although her lettuce was better than what I'd already bought. I ended up picking everything else I needed for the weekend from her except for protein and cheese.

By the time Killian said goodbye to Jo and helped carry all my packages to my car, I had dropped a significant amount of money. And I was okay with that. I felt better about spending it today than I had in a long time.

It wasn't as though I was completely destitute anymore. Foodie had been making enough money for me to continually put the profit back into the food and utilities and social media advertising.

If I had been living on my own and had those expenses to pay or had to rent a spot for my truck, I might have been in some unsustainable territory. With my family's help, I could invest a little more each weekend. It was a good feeling.

I hadn't crashed and burned.

Not yet.

"Do you want some help with your purchases?" I asked Killian when he'd put the last bag of organic goodies in my trunk and slammed it shut.

"Jo delivers straight to Lilou," he explained. "I have a standing order with her. She knows what I like."

I propped my hip against the passenger side door. "Must be nice to be the great Killian Quinn."

"Hey, we all have delivery services," he pointed out, referring to commercial kitchens. "I just have the best one."

"So, foster mom, huh?" It wasn't exactly a subtle question, but I was too curious to be polite.

He squinted, watching the market close for the day instead of me. "Yeah, the one that finally stuck."

"What do you mean?"

He dropped his gaze to mine, and I had to take a deep breath to steady my erratic nerves. How could I be attracted to someone as serious and intense as Killian? How could I even consider a man so similar to my ex? At least on the surface. It made no sense.

174

There had to be something wrong with me.

"That's a story for a different time," he answered. "It's kind of dramatic and I don't want to scare you off just yet."

I swallowed the disappointment and covered my reaction with sarcasm. "Too late."

His crooked smile made my insides melty. "We should make some time to talk about it, though. I'll share all the gory details of my childhood, and you can tell me about your dad. We don't even have to talk about food."

The bottom fell out from beneath me, and I was surprised I didn't have to flail as I regained my balance. "Are you asking me on a date?"

He lifted one shoulder. "Yeah, a date. It could be fun."

I licked dry lips and wished I could take a step back. "As fun as talking about my sick dad and your traumatic childhood sounds, I, uh, I can't."

His low voice softened, but not in a gentle way. Careful. Controlled. Curious. "You can't?"

His frown, his smooth voice, his intimidating tattoos that made him so much cooler than me, flustered me. I didn't know how to explain to him that it wasn't him. It was me. It was *all* me. But there were too many secrets that accompanied that truth. If I told him one, I'd have to tell them all. And I wasn't ready for that.

He wanted to keep his past a secret.

So did I.

"I just got out of a relationship," I braved. "It ended badly. I'm not ready to get into something new."

"I'm not asking you to marry me," he countered. "Just a drink. Share a meal with me. Have a conversation. Nothing crazy."

God, I wanted to say yes. Yes, to all of it. A drink, a meal, a conversation... him. I wanted him. "I know," I mumbled. I felt my chest start to crack, a thin fissure that snaked from breastbone to navel, starting the fracture that would split me open. But I'd stopped trusting myself to do the right thing a long time ago.

I couldn't give in now.

I couldn't undo everything I'd worked so hard to get back.

"I need more time," I told him, my voice thin with desperation. I needed him to understand. To back off before I crumbled under the light pressure of his interest. "I'm sorry, it was just a really bad relationship. How did you phrase it? Gory." Only I meant that quite literally.

A muscle in his neck jumped. "You broke up recently?"

"Before I left for Europe," I confessed. "Over a year ago."

His shoulders drooped, and I could have sworn his expression twisted with disappointment. "You're not over him?"

175

My heart tripped over its erratic beating, and I nearly fell over. He assumed I was still hung up on Derrek? And of course he would, because he didn't know any of the details, but he had no idea. The idea that I was still interested… that I could still want… My stomach twisted at the very thought.

Never again.

I would never give into Derrek again.

Even if that meant a lifetime of celibacy and no professional recognition.

"It's not what you think. I'm over what happened. I'm just… I just can't get a drink with you or a meal. I'm sorry, Killian."

"Don't apologize," he ordered, his voice unrelenting with the demand. "You said no. That's all I needed. I'm sorry to make you keep explaining."

He stepped back, and I immediately wanted to move into him. I also wanted to punch myself in the ovaries. God, could I just make up my mind?

I didn't want him.

I did want him.

I didn't want to lead him on.

I did want to go on a date with him and jump his bones.

My libido was at war with my head, and my heart wanted to abandon my body altogether. God, I needed to get my shit together.

And fast.

"I'm—" I stopped myself before I apologized again. "Thanks for understanding." That had to be the lamest letdown ever. As soon as he turned around, I was going to bang my head against my car door.

His shadowed bark of laughter surprised me. "I don't understand, Vera. I'm not even pretending to understand. But I'm not going to convince you to go out with me either. So, I guess I'll see you around."

I grabbed his wrist before he could walk away. He paused, half turned away from me. "Thanks for introducing me to Jo. And for showing me this place. I owe you."

His shoulders rose with a deep breath, calming some of his fierce energy. "You do. You owe me."

My hands dropped to my side, suddenly trembling from that dark promise. He turned around, changing his mind. He walked back to me, slowly, deliberately, trapping me between his hard, tall body and the solid wall of my car. His arms caged me in, pressing against either side of my head.

His chest barely brushed mine, hovering over me just enough to tease, to make me want closer contact, but denying me.

Just like I'd denied him.

I stared at him, waiting for him to do something. Say something. His green eyes held mine captive, flashing with thoughts I couldn't read and emotions I couldn't decipher.

Just when I'd decided to break the tension between us by speaking, he lifted his hand to my jaw and carefully cupped my face. His fingers were calloused and rough, cradling me with a softness that came from inside him, something you would never see on his outside.

"You like me, Vera. And if you haven't figured it out yet, you should know I like you too. I like you a lot. Get over this ex-boyfriend of yours so we can explore where this thing between us goes."

Before I could argue with him, his mouth dropped to mine, pressing a swift, intoxicating kiss to my lips. My eyes fluttered closed, and I drowned in sensation. Butterflies erupted in my belly, sending tingles soaring through my body, making my head swim and my toes curl. His beard brushed against my face, scratchy and soft at the same time. His lips lingered long enough for me to taste them, feel the shape of them, decide how perfectly they fit against mine.

He was gone just as soon as I'd decided to kiss him back. He stepped away from me, letting me slump against the car, disoriented and inwardly disheveled. He'd picked up all the pieces of me, all the puzzle pieces I'd been trying to sort through and put back together, and dropped them on the ground in a confused mess.

Nothing was where it was supposed to be now. Nothing fit like I thought it should.

"Bye, Vera."

I didn't even reply. I just watched him walk away while my knees wobbled and my heart tried to beat its way out of my chest.

Killian Quinn was nothing like I expected him to be. Charming when I wanted to be annoyed. Sensitive and thoughtful when I'd already decided he was only an asshole. Irresistible while I tried to do my best to resist him.

I was stubborn. Headstrong. Determined to see my isolation through.

But I was starting to realize he was more stubborn. More headstrong. More determined than I could ever be.

And that was very concerning.

Chapter Seventeen

The next Saturday night I'd perfected my shishito and skirt steak tacos. They were a huge hit.

I was super proud of them. And myself. Killian hadn't stepped in once to offer his advice. Well, except for the lemon suggestion, but since that had happened before I tried out the recipe, I let myself believe I might have come up with that one all by myself had I been given the chance.

The thing about lying to myself was that I had been doing it for so long that I hardly noticed anymore.

And I'd been lying to myself a lot this week, so it was almost impossible to divide the lies from the truth at this point.

I hadn't seen Killian since the Morning Market when I'd rejected his date request. I'd written him maybe three hundred texts, but deleted all of them before I accidentally pressed send. I'd also shown up to work way earlier than necessary in case I caught a glimpse of him, but he'd always been in his kitchen already. And unlike the weeks prior, he didn't leave it.

Last night, I heard his motorcycle pull away from Lilou, but I'd been plating to-go boxes in the safety of my food truck. He hadn't stopped by. And he hadn't sent anyone to spy on me as far as I could tell.

There were no notes or texts telling me what I needed to change.

Or add.

Or cussing me out for using salt.

And how pathetic was I? I'd done nothing but complain about the man all summer, and now he hadn't talked to me for three days, and I was seriously reconsidering my life decisions.

Even the ones I made post-Derrek.

"Are you sure you don't mind if I take off?" Vann's question pulled me out of my spiraling thoughts.

I looked down at the steak I'd been mutilating. Oops.

"No, it's fine. People will wait. And if they don't, their loss."

He lightly punched my shoulder. "That's the spirit."

Vann had waited for a lull in the crowd before broaching the subject. We'd been sporadically busy tonight. The bursts were big, but then the lulls were long and slow. It was a weird night.

"So, this is the second date?" I propped my hip against the counter and gave my brother my full attention.

"Second," he confirmed. "She's nice. You'd like her."

"Who cares if I like her? Do you like her?"

He nodded, his eyes remaining bored. "Yeah, she's nice."

"You already said that." My brother. Good grief.

He barely noticed. "Did I?"

"I don't know why you do this to yourself."

He jingled the keys in the pocket of his navy blue shorts. This was Vann dressed for a date—J. Crew shorts, crisp white, short-sleeved button up shirt, leather sandals. He looked like a preppy skater. If there was such a thing. "Do what to myself?"

"Date nice girls. You don't like them."

He gave me a look. "Of course I like nice girls."

"No, you don't."

He laughed like I was a lunatic. "You think I should date *mean* girls?"

"I think you should date a girl that makes you feel something other than *nice*."

He raised an eyebrow, not taking anything I said seriously. "Now you're a dating guru?"

"What? You couldn't tell from my super successful relationship and happily ever after kind of life?"

He stared at me for a minute, watching me, reading me. "I don't know, sis. I think all your wisdom comes from the bad experience variety."

I shrugged, my happy mask slipping momentarily.

"Are you ever going to talk about what happened?"

I breathed through my nose so he wouldn't notice the panic sizzling beneath my skin. He knew the story. At least I'd told him a version of what had happened when I first came home. But that had been the last time I talked about it. It wasn't worth bringing up again. "There's nothing to talk about. We didn't work out. Relationships end all the time."

"Not usually by one of them running away to Europe for the year. Did he even try to come after you? Or reach out and apologize for everything?"

I shuddered at Vann's word usage. Derrek had no idea where I'd gone. I'd made sure of that specifically because he would have come after me if he had. But he had bothered my dad for a long time. And if I wouldn't have deleted my email, social media accounts and canceled my phone, he probably would have found me and hunted me down.

Europe wasn't far enough away to stop him.

Hell, Jupiter wasn't far enough away.

Or maybe not. Maybe he finally understood that I was finished. Europe wasn't the first time I'd broken up with him. It was just the first time it had stuck.

And only because I didn't consult him on the decision. I just left. It was hard to convince someone to stay if they weren't there to manipulate.

My phone burned in my pocket. All of his unanswered Facebook messages felt extra heavy tonight.

"I flew straight to Amsterdam, Vann. What was he going to do? Hop on a plane and scour the city looking for me?"

For the first time in his life, Vann looked passionate about something. Not just serious. Not just involved, but zealous. "Yeah. That. Or the whole damn country. If you love a girl, if she's the one, you don't let an ocean stop you. You go after her. You don't let her get away."

My brother had been invaded by the body snatchers. It was the only explanation. Vann didn't do commitment. I'd never seen him date someone for longer than a couple of months. He didn't even take love seriously. He always said he was allergic to it. So, what was this?

"Where is this coming from?" I asked, shocked.

He looked out the window, avoiding my stare. "It's not coming from anywhere. That's just the way of it. You go hard after people you care about or you probably never cared about them to begin with."

"Then you should probably stop dating nice girls. You're not going to find Ms.-fly-across-the-world-to-get-her-back in your current pool of availables."

He shrugged and checked his pockets for his wallet. "You never know, Vera. She might turn out to be the one."

"You really think so?"

An amused smile lifted the corners of his mouth. "No, but she can be the one tonight."

"You're so gross."

"And late. I have to go. You sure you're okay on your own? Do you want me to send Dad over?"

"I'm fine. When Wyatt comes over for his break, I'll ask him to walk me to my car later."

"Alright sounds good. Lock the door behind me."

I saluted him because that's what little sisters did. He waved me off and headed out. I did as he asked and locked the door as soon as he stepped outside.

Oh, Vann. I didn't get his relationship issues. I had tons of reasons to swear off men and dating.

But his history with girls was so boring.

Busy. But overall, uneventful.

A few people walked up to the truck, and I threw myself back into my work. I hadn't been lying when I told Vann I'd ask Wyatt to walk me to my car later, even if I had to close up a little early. Killian might have been avoiding me, but I fully expected Wyatt at some point. He was like the stray puppy I'd accidentally adopted.

After I'd taken their money, I got to work, making tacos as quickly as possible and putting it in a box with sriracha esquites and a lemon wedge. I handed the boxes out the window, warning them that it might be a bit spicy.

Out of the corner of my eye, I saw someone step up to the order window, so I passed out some extra napkins and left them to enjoy their meals.

The side door of Lilou opened and captured my attention as I walked down the line of windows to the order side. My heart stilled in my chest, pausing just long enough for me to see it was someone taking out the trash—not Killian on break. Not that I was waiting to catch a glimpse of Killian or anything. Because I wasn't.

I let go of a frozen breath, and my heartbeat normalized again. But only for a second.

"What a relief to find out you're not dead."

His voice stopped me cold. Too late. I stood just inches away from him, separated by the thin siding of my food truck.

Derrek.

Derrek Hanover. Executive chef. Adjunct professor at CAI. Ex-boyfriend. Nightmare.

I wasn't a fan of horror movies. I could tolerate them, but they weren't my favorite genre. That said, I had always watched them with a sort of elevated sense of self. I would imagine myself in the exact shoes of the heroine in whatever movie and know exactly what I would do differently to save myself from whatever horrific situation she'd gotten herself into.

For instance, I would never run up the stairs if a serial killer chased me around the house. I would fight like hell to run out the door. Or car keys. I would get them in the lock in plenty of time not to be murdered. I wouldn't fumble around waiting to have my throat sliced. No simple task would stop me from survival.

And yet here I was, a psychopath just inches from me, and I'd taken the elevator to the top floor and thrown my keys down a well—probably the same well the girl from *The Ring* lived in.

Good lord, did I have a death wish?

"What are you doing here?" Again—I should have been dialing the police or running away or hiding. Instead, I was asking inane questions and allowing him space in my new life that had been constructed around the entire idea that he didn't belong in it.

He ignored my question. The answer was obvious. "I thought something happened to you. I called the cops. I filed a missing person's report. I didn't know where the fuck you went, Vera. You just up and left. Who does that? Who just fucking leaves like that?"

"I—"

"Shut up," he snarled. "You made me look like an asshole. Everyone wanted to know where you went and I had nothing to fucking say because *I didn't fucking know.*"

His eyes burned, pinning me in place with the intensity behind them. But it was nothing like Killian's, it wasn't the slow, delicious burn that licked its way up my legs and swarmed in my belly. No, Derrek's was nothing but searing fire that wanted to scorch me to ash, blaze through me until I was nothing but dust.

I tried to swallow but I couldn't. I couldn't even breathe. Panic welled up inside me like an overflowing dam, spilling over my brittle walls of protection in a rush of total destruction.

His voice dropped, gentled. His gaze softened too. He stopped being the terrifying avenger and transformed into the master manipulator. "You could have told me you were unhappy, Vera. You could have talked to me. I would have listened. I would have changed. For you. If you would have just talked to me first, we could have figured everything out. I could have made everything better. *For you.*"

"How did you figure out I wasn't missing?" I hadn't intentionally misled him to believe that something had happened to me. But I also hadn't done a whole lot to reassure him I was fine. When I said I just left, I meant it.

He went to work one day, and I packed up all that I could, took him off the one bank account I had and disappeared. I ran like the hounds of hell were chasing me.

And I didn't stop running until Dad had called with the cancer news.

"Your dad returned my hundreds of calls. Apparently, you had enough time to let him know where you were going. He said you needed to 'find yourself.'" He stepped closer to the window, wrapping his fingers around the ledge. I flinched at the sight of them, at the restrained strength that lay temporarily dormant inside them.

"I'm sorry I made you worry," I told him honestly. "I didn't mean for you to get the cops involved. I should have left a note."

His lip curled. "You think I care about that now? I was worried about you! Of course I called the cops. I loved you, Vera. I would have done whatever it took to keep you. I would have changed. I would have bent over backward to make you happy. But you didn't give me a chance. You didn't even involve me in the conversation." He paused, seeming to gather his thoughts. Then he added, "How could you just leave like that? How could you walk away from everything we had without saying goodbye?"

The night was hot as hell, but my fingers were ice cold. I took another step back. I needed to close for the night. I needed to lock the windows and turn off the lights and curl up on the floor until he went away.

A sob caught in my throat and I started blinking rapidly to hold back the tears. What if he didn't go away?

What if he didn't leave?

He sounded so nice. He was the penitent boyfriend, heartbroken by the girl he thought he was going to spend the rest of his life with. But oh, how his selective memory could play tricks on us both.

He didn't remember all the yelling, all the name-calling. He couldn't recall the time he slapped me. Or yanked me to the ground by my hair. He didn't remember the bruises on my arms I had to hide. Or the time he'd thrown a plate at me because he didn't like something I'd made. He didn't remember the days I spent walking on eggshells just to keep the peace or the nights spent curled in the fetal position trying not to shake the bed with my frightened sobs.

He only remembered what he wanted to. And he was going to use that idyllic history to paint a picture of our relationship that never existed. He'd done it a hundred times before.

The problem previously was that I always bought into the illusion. Everyone was flawed. He would try to change for me. He loved me. He didn't hit me that hard, I just bruised really easily. I should know better than to talk back to him by now. I shouldn't have made him so angry.

I should have kept my mouth shut.

I should have worn the dress he liked. Or made the food he wanted. Or remembered to record the show he'd asked me to.

It was always my fault. He always hurt me because of something I did. He didn't want to. He never wanted to hurt me. But sometimes I pushed him too far.

God, what a sick game.

I knew better now. At least my head did. I'd spent the last year analyzing everything I did wrong. And then every single thing he did wrong. I forced myself to relive traumatizing memories so I could guard myself against it happening again.

But my heart hadn't seemed to learn the lesson. Not that I still loved Derrek. I hadn't loved him in a very long time. But I couldn't stop from reacting when he laid on the guilt like this.

My instinctual reaction was to apologize. To him. For leaving him. See? This was why I couldn't trust myself in a new relationship. I didn't know how to stand up for myself. I didn't know how to be anything but a doormat.

And if it hadn't been for the past couple of months, I probably would have. But Killian had been good for something. He'd taught me how to fight. He'd taught me how to stand up for myself.

He hadn't meant to teach me this particular lesson, but he'd done it without demeaning me, without stripping me of dignity and self-worth.

If anything, Killian had helped me restore some of my confidence; he'd helped me find myself again.

And it was for that reason alone, I held Derrek's apologetic gaze and whispered as bravely as I could, "Do you really not know why I left you?"

A line of customers formed while he stood in front of me, wielding his sick magic. A few people had wandered out of Greenlight, the nearest bar. They laughed and chatted and didn't notice that I was crumbling to pieces right in front of them.

I was immediately embarrassed, ashamed, afraid they could look at the two of us and know exactly how I gave him permission to abuse me. It was crazy and they kept their distance, but I just wanted Derrek gone. I never wanted to see him again, let alone have this conversation publically.

His eyes flashed with hurt like I'd wounded him. "I really don't know, Vera. You were it for me. You were everything. And then you just disappeared. How can I move on when I don't even know what happened?"

"I can't do this right now," I told him. "I'm working." To the crowd, I said, "I'm sorry. I'll be with you in a moment."

Two people at the back of the line wandered off, not interested in waiting around while I sorted out my relationship drama. Another guy threw his hands in the air, frustrated with the wait.

"Derrek, you have to go. I have a restaurant to run."

"That's another thing. This isn't a restaurant. This is a trailer. You belong in a kitchen. You belong in one of the best kitchens. You're too damn talented for food like this."

I ignored his words, letting them bounce off me with little impact. At least for now. Later, when I was safely tucked in my bed with all the doors locked, I could fully absorb them. "Derrek, you need to leave. I mean it."

"You don't need this place, Vera. You probably haven't heard. Telltale Heart launched. It's getting great reviews. There has been some national buzz about it. About me. It's everything we wanted. You belong in Charlotte with me. By my side."

Fire seared through me, sparked by the original argument. I was good enough for a girlfriend, but not an employee. Not that I even wanted to work for him. But it was the principle. "By your side, but not in your kitchen?"

"What do you mean by that? Vera, God, I need you. Don't you hear what I'm saying? I need you with me. In my life, however I can have you. If that's in the kitchen, then fine. But just come home."

His words were like daggers in my gut. Or worse, letter openers- sharp enough to penetrate, but dull enough to hurt like hell. I threw all the steel I'd acquired over the last year into my tone and remained firm. "Derrek, I have to work. I need you to leave."

"When can I see you again?"

"You can't."

"I still have all your stuff. I need to give it back to you. We can meet tomorrow to discuss the details."

"Leave. Now."

"Not until you agree to meet me, to talk this out. It's a misunderstanding, Vera. You have to know I will do whatever it takes to get you back."

"Vera, are you okay?"

Oh, thank God. I nearly sank to my knees at the sound of Wyatt's voice. "Yes." Now that someone familiar was here, the grit oozed out of me, leaving me trembling and teary-eyed. "I need help, Wyatt. Can you step inside for a second? Vann had a date."

Wyatt glanced back at Lilou. For a second I was afraid he was going to tell me no. "Can you call Killian? Or text him. Tell him what's going on and that I'm going to help you for the rest of the night. I left my cell in the kitchen."

I nodded, afraid that if I spoke, I would crack.

Derrek's eyes narrowed on Wyatt and then me while I unlocked the door with shaky fingers and let Wyatt in. "Thank you," I whispered when he stepped inside. As soon as he closed it, I reached past him to lock it.

"That guy is bothering you?" he asked in a low voice.

"Yes. He won't leave."

"You text Killian. I'll deal with him."

Sending a quick message to Killian that explained I needed Wyatt's help for a few minutes, I whispered a silent prayer of thanks that he'd intervened when he had. Derrek wouldn't have listened to me. He would have stuck around until I gave in. Or called the cops.

I hovered in the corner of the brightly lit truck, wishing I could hide. Wyatt stepped up to the window, blocking Derrek from my sight. He was every inch of intimidating, huge male. Derrek might not have been intimidated, but he was forced to step back when Wyatt shoved the upper half of his body through the order window.

"Sir, you're going to have to leave. This window is for paying customers only."

"I have been trying to order something," Derrek insisted. "I just needed to talk to Vera first. So, if you'd move out of the way—"

"Nope. Not an option. She has the right to refuse service to anyone, and unfortunately, she doesn't like your face. You're going to have to leave, or I'm going to call the cops and have you escorted from the premises."

"You can't do that."

"I can and I will."

Derrek's voice turned to stone. "Do you know who I am? Do you have any idea who you're talking to?" He must have noticed Wyatt's chef's coat because he changed his tone from arrogant accolades to vicious threats. "You're finished in this industry. Done. From now on you'll be lucky to get a job bussing tables."

"Is there a problem?" I couldn't see him, but I heard him. Killian.

"This guy won't leave," Wyatt explained.

Now I wanted to throw myself on the ground and curl into a ball. I didn't need Killian involved. Or witnessing my humiliation. Wasn't he needed in his own damn kitchen?

187

"This guy is Derrek Hanover," Killian growled. "What are you doing here, Derrek? Why are you harassing a food truck three hours from your kitchen?"

"You'd be wise to stay out of my business, Quinn," Derrek warned.

Oh, God, they knew each other. Could this night get any worse?

"Not going to happen," Killian countered. "So, unless you want the cops called and this headline splashed all over every blog on the internet, I suggest you leave now."

"You wouldn't—"

"Have you forgotten who I work for? One tweet from Ezra and your shit is viral. Do you really want to push me?"

A heavy silence followed Killian's threat. Eventually, Derrek gave into the threat of public humiliation. At least for tonight. "I'll talk to you later, Vera," Derrek shouted at me. "This isn't over."

I couldn't see him, but he must have left, because Wyatt eventually stepped back. He stood in the middle of my galley, arms crossed over his chest like the bouncers that stood outside of Greenlight and Verve.

"Thank you," I told him. My voice had yet to recover, but a tiny bit of the panic had receded.

Killian's face appeared in the window. "How quickly can you close up?"

It took me several moments before I could answer him. I wanted to leave everything and lock the doors tonight. TBD if I would ever return. But I couldn't do that. Food was everywhere. I had fryers to turn off and messes to clean up.

"An hour. I can come back for most of it in the morning."

Killian's glare swung to his sous chef. "Wyatt, help her shut it down." To me he said, "I'll be back in thirty minutes to take you home."

My abrupt hysteria propelled me forward a step. "You don't have to do that—"

"Vera, whatever that shit was with Hanover, was not cool. I'm taking you home. End of discussion."

"What about your kitchen?"

"Fuck the kitchen." He rubbed a hand over his face, trying to calm down. "Besides, why do I hire the best sous chefs in the city if I can't count on them to handle one goddamn night for me? Clean up. I'll be back."

He didn't wait for my reply. Which was fine since I didn't have one to give him.

I looked to Wyatt with wide eyes, desperate for him to save me.

Instead of sympathy, he grinned like the cat that ate the canary. "Out of the frying pan and into the fire."

188

I glared at him. "Well, you're not helping." But I was afraid he was right.

Chapter Eighteen

Killian came back a half hour later just like he promised. He stalked across the street like an angry lion about to pounce on some poor, unsuspecting gazelle.

And I was the gazelle.

"What's Killian like to work with?" I asked Wyatt while Killian waited on cars to move out of his way.

Wyatt stood at my stove, scrubbing it until it looked better than when it had been brand new. He didn't cut corners or tackle the easy jobs. He went straight for the cooktop. That said something about the standard of work he was used to.

He kept scrubbing when he answered my question. "He's an absolute dictator. He requires nothing less than utter perfection all the time. He's not afraid to get in your face and yell. And he refuses to send anything out that isn't up to his insane standards."

I glared at his back. "You love working for him."

He shot me a playful smile over his shoulder. "He's the best, Vera. Yeah, he knows it, which makes him an asshole. But he can also back it up. I might plot his death in my head sometimes, but what I've learned in his kitchen is invaluable. I couldn't get that experience working for anyone else."

"There are other great chefs."

He tilted his head back and forth, deliberating. "Fine, I don't want this experience from anybody else. He's the kind of chef I want to grow into.

His style, his food, his command of the kitchen. I think it would be hard to find anyone that can rival him."

"God, just marry him already and get it over with."

He laughed at my lame joke and turned back to the stove. "Not that you wouldn't be fun to work with too, V. But I doubt you'd whip everyone into shape quite like Quinn. I swear there are handprints on my ass when I leave there every night."

"First of all, you're ridiculous. Second of all, I don't have room in my itty bitty kitchen to do any whipping." He grunted a laugh. I'd lost all will to take care of my own stuff. It was so much easier to have Wyatt do it for me. "I didn't mean to sound jealous by the way. I was so not comparing myself to Killian. I mean, there's not even a comparison there. He's, you know, him. And I'm just me."

He didn't look up. "Whatever you say, Vera."

Killian approached the truck, so I stopped talking. I needed to open the door for him, but I couldn't make myself move.

Nerves skittered through me. My belly flipped, and my feet refused to move.

He scared me. Granted, it wasn't in the same way that Derrek did, not even close. But I still couldn't let myself trust him. To trust him meant I had to be vulnerable, meant allowing him space in my life, giving him the ability to hurt me.

I knew, *I just knew*, that if I gave Killian that power, he wouldn't take a little bit. He would take as much as he could. He would pull and pull and pull and demand everything I had.

And then when he hurt me? It wouldn't be a small thing. It would be complete and total destruction.

His knuckles rapped against the door, punctuating the frantic beat of my heart with a harsh *tap tap tap*. When I didn't move, Wyatt did. He flicked open the deadbolt and stepped back to make room for Killian.

The tiny kitchen felt even smaller with the two of them taking up so much space. Killian looked around like he'd never been here before, absorbing every detail with his sharp gaze.

"What do you have left to do?" he asked.

I spun around and grabbed the last of the food that needed to be taken to the commissary. It was a pain to haul the food back and forth every single day, but at least I could park the truck here without worrying about it. Vann was awesome for that.

"I just have these," I pointed at the crates of food that needed to be carried to my car.

"This seems unnecessary," Killian sighed. "Why don't you just store everything at Lilou?"

I squinted at him, waiting for him to get all the conflicts of interest involved in that one question. When he didn't figure it out on his own, I gave him my reasons. "Because that's dumb."

He shook his head and grabbed a crate. "Where are you renting space from then?"

"The commissary."

He turned to Wyatt, not giving my answer a response. "Thanks for helping, man. I owe you."

There was a weird beat of silence where Wyatt and I simultaneously wondered why Killian owed him. Wasn't it me Wyatt did the favor for?

"It's no problem, Chef," Wyatt shrugged. "I'll just head back. Who's in charge now?"

"Kaya, but take over when you get there."

"She's going to be pissed."

"Who cares," Killian shrugged. "I told her you'd be back. Don't let her give you any shit and make sure she stays on track. I'm not dealing with her temper tantrums, yeah?"

"Got it." Wyatt swallowed thickly which made me think he was more nervous about standing up to Kaya than he wanted Killian to believe.

"And, Wyatt?"

"Yes, chef?"

"Don't fuck anything up."

Wyatt gulped for the second time. "Yes, chef."

Killian jerked his head toward the door, and Wyatt dropped the rag on the counter and backed away. "See you around, Vera."

"Thanks again," I told him quickly. "I really appreciate you showing up when you did."

His eyes flashed with concern and his mouth pressed into a frown. He hadn't asked any questions about Derrek, and I was grateful for that. But looking at him now I could tell he was worried about me. I just didn't have anything to tell him.

I was worried about me too.

He lifted a hand in a lazy wave and disappeared out the door.

I turned away from Killian and focused on the closing tasks. "I just need to shut everything down, then I'm ready to go."

He didn't say anything, so I went about double checking everything was off, closing the windows and locking everything up. It was a twenty-minute routine that got tedious, but Killian didn't complain.

193

When I was finished, he picked up two crates of food, one on top of the other, and headed down the steps. I grabbed the remaining crate and followed him.

He hovered over me while I set mine down again to lock the outside door. "Thanks for staying with me," I told him in a voice just barely above a whisper.

"Derrek Hanover is your ex-boyfriend? The one that drove you to Europe?"

Well, he didn't waste any time.

I knew he would have questions. What was worse, I knew he would want answers. My days of dodging the whole truth and nothing but the truth were over.

But, damn, I wasn't ready for this.

I also wasn't ready to see Derrek again, but apparently I didn't get to pick and choose my problems.

"Derrek Hanover is my ex-boyfriend," I confirmed. I swooped down and picked up my crate. It was easier to talk about this if I didn't have to look at Killian or acknowledge his existence altogether. I led him into the alley and toward my car.

"Europe?" Killian pressed, not giving me any wiggle room.

"He didn't drive me there. I went. Willingly." Which made it seem like I was the flighty one. I had no idea why I was still covering for Derrek. Four months ago, when I'd gotten back, I'd convinced myself I could talk about my relationship with him. I'd promised that I wouldn't bury everything. But the words were so difficult to spit out.

My shame was too great to admit. Especially to someone like Killian who would never let anyone intimidate or abuse him. And sure, he was a man, so the chances of that happening were minuscule. But it was more than that. It was his personality. He didn't put up with shit from anybody.

We reached my Taurus after a minute of tense silence. After enough nights of loading and unloading, I had the keys and trunk situation down to a science. Still balancing my crate packed with food, I unlocked the trunk and unloaded mine and then one of Killian's.

"The other one is going to have to go in the back seat."

He followed me to the side and slid it in. He stayed quiet the entire time.

His silence became a tangible thing in the air, heavy, dangerous and confusing. It was like he was mad at me for being involved with Derrek. And okay, I was mad at me too, but I didn't get it coming from him.

I closed the door and stepped back from him, not sure if I was ready to get into the enclosed space of my car just yet. "Do you know Derrek?"

"Do I know Derrek Hanover?" he repeated, only where my tone had been openly curious, his had an edge. "Yeah, I know Derrek Hanover."

I crossed my arms over my chest and shuffled my feet, kicking at a small rock. The night air had cooled down, and a refreshing breeze danced in the air. The clear sky allowed the half-moon to glow as brightly as it could, but it was still completely dark. A streetlight on the corner provided only a little light, casting Killian in shadow and hiding his features from me.

There wasn't an easy response to his biting remarks. I knew Derrek better than anyone. Killian was right not to like him. But this wasn't one of those situations where I cared about the whys of it. I wasn't interested in gossiping about my ex.

I just wanted to forget about him completely.

"Well, thanks for helping me close down." My voice sounded small, hidden behind old fears and fresh shock. "I appreciate everything you did tonight."

He stared at me for a minute, once again refusing to acknowledge my gratitude. His hand shot out, bouncing with impatience. "Here, I'll drive."

"What?"

"Give me your keys. I'll drive you home."

My thoughts bumped into each other in their rush to make sense of his offer. "That's not necessary," I assured him. "Derrek threw me off, but I can drive myself."

"You're shaking," Killian pointed out. "And you look terrified. Let me drive, Vera, for my own peace of mind."

"Your bike is here. How will you get home?"

"I'll take an Uber. Stop worrying about me."

My hackles raised, the hair lifting off the back of my neck in response to his pushy attitude. "You're the only one that gets to worry? How are you the boss?"

"I'm the only one stable enough to drive. So, yeah, I get to be boss."

"I'm fine, Killian." And because that didn't sound even the least bit convincing, I repeated myself. "I'll be fine."

"Did he hurt you?"

The darkness made the finer edges of his feature blurry, but the fury in his eyes was unmistakable. As was the harsh slash of his mouth and the rigid tension in his shoulders.

Still protecting my past, I tried an easy answer. "I left him, Killian. What do you think?"

He made a frustrated sound in the back of his throat. "Not in the generic sense, Vera. Not in the way that all bad relationships end. I mean, did he *hurt* you? Put his hands on you? Fucking beat you?"

How does he know? That was my first thought. I didn't have scars. At least not any on the outside. I had been lucky in that.

And I meant that. As screwed up as it was to associate my relationship with Derrek with luck, I knew I had been. There were women far worse off than I had been. There were women who couldn't just leave. Who didn't have a savings account to fall back on. Who couldn't get out. Who were knocked unconscious regularly—or worse.

When I looked at the grand scope of abused women, my case was mild in comparison to some of the true psychopaths out there.

That in no way made what happened to me okay. But I had perspective. And that was important to me.

"He got physical," I confessed, my words frail and broken and dragged from the deep recesses of my soul, the place I put things I never wanted to speak about out loud. The things I wasn't brave enough to face. "He didn't like, I don't know, hospitalize me or anything, but he was rough."

"That fucking piece of shit," Killian snarled. His hands clenched and unclenched at his sides. His chest lifted with his effort to breathe evenly. "What a slimy, lowlife *piece of shit.*"

I swallowed against the lump of regret lodged in my throat. "How did you know? I mean, how did you guess that he... that he..."

"My friend Natasha dated him for a few months a while back. She didn't let it get serious, but she told me some things that bothered her." He turned his head, showing me the full severity of his profile. "And I've worked with him before. We kind of, I don't know, rose in the industry at the same time. I've wondered about him. He's not right in the head, Vera. There's something seriously wrong with him."

I laughed, but it was a desperate sound, adrenaline fueled and easily broken. "Oh, I'm well aware."

"So Europe?"

Hugging myself tighter, the truth spilled out. "I tried to leave him more than once. I *did* leave him more than once. But I was stupid. I was..." I wiped my nose with the back of my hand, only just then noticing the tears leaking from my eyes. "I had convinced myself that I loved him. And he always convinced me that he would change. Every goddamn time."

"Tell me all of it. I want to hear everything."

So I did. While we stood behind my brother's bicycle shop on a balmy summer night, covered in darkness and tragedy and mutual hate for the man that had hurt me so deeply, I told him every hard detail of the two years I spent with Derrek.

I opened up about how he'd pursued me while I was still in school. I had been enamored with the adjunct professor that was ten years older than me and so incredibly hot. He'd taken the time to invest in my career and skill. He'd helped me become a better chef, a better person. He'd been so attentive and sweet and charming. I didn't stand a chance.

We started dating my last year. The day I graduated I moved into his apartment. He'd promised all these great things, everything I wanted to hear. He would keep helping me, introduce me to all the important people, get me into the best kitchens. I just needed a little more practice. I needed to establish a reputation first. So why not start somewhere small? Why not just work up slowly, so people didn't think Derrek was the only reason for my success?

He tore apart my world little bits at a time. He didn't like when I went home to Durham by myself, and since he didn't have the time to take off to go with me, I stopped seeing my family. My friends were all so much younger than him. He didn't have anything in common with them. So why didn't we just hang out with his friends? Besides, they were connections I could use.

He needed to focus on his career, so I should probably just work part time. That way I could help him reach the next level. After that, he promised to help me. He promised to throw all his resources at helping me move up. Just after he got to where he needed to be first.

After he'd picked apart my life and isolated me from everyone I cared about or knew… that's when the physical abuse started. Looking back, I realized the emotional and verbal abuse had started way earlier. He'd subtly slipped in his backhanded compliments and carefully woven doubts until my self-esteem had withered and died. I lost my confidence, self-respect and will to fight.

By the time he hit me for the first time, I'd been mostly convinced that I deserved it. It wasn't until two years later when he told me to quit my job and informed me that I would be staying home full time, that I realized he was going to take away the only thing I had left—my career.

That was the final straw. I should have stood up for my friends. I should have fought like hell when it had been my family. I should never, ever have let him hit me. But it wasn't until he threatened to take cooking away from me that I couldn't stand it for a second longer.

Killian had been winding tighter and tighter during my history lesson. His entire body looked ready to explode, a ticking time bomb of vengeance and justice. Beneath the milky moonlight, he was an avenging angel, nothing but hard lines and solid, unflinching resolve. "So you fled the country?"

"It sounds more dramatic than it is. I wasn't afraid he would hunt me down or anything." I thought of him outside my food truck refusing to leave. "Although maybe I should have been. But Europe was more about finally doing something for me. Finally, just, I don't know, crawling out of the hole I'd dug for myself. And cooking. It was a lot about cooking—the one thing I loved enough to protect from him."

"What do you mean?"

I shook my head, so humiliated... so wholly ashamed. "I couldn't leave him, Killian. I physically couldn't. I don't know what was wrong with me, but I just couldn't do it. I was afraid, yes, but it was more than that. It was like he had this hold on me that I just couldn't break. No matter how hard I tried."

He stepped closer to me, facing me again, watching me so closely I could feel his gaze on my skin, soothing the demons that still haunted me, calming my tattered heart—healing my battered spirit. He understood. "It wasn't your fault, Vera."

My eyes slammed shut as more tears poured out of me from a well that was so tainted with hurt and betrayal. Derrek was supposed to be my happily ever after. He was supposed to give me everything I'd always wanted—the blissful relationship, the financial stability, the hand up in my dream job. He had promised me love and given me pain instead. He'd promised me the world and locked me in prison.

I thought he was the answer to every one of my prayers. But he'd turned out to be the devil in disguise, the demon that ate at my soul and destroyed my hope.

But the worst part was that I let him. In my desperation to grasp the things I'd put on such a high pedestal, I'd let him bulldoze me. I hadn't even put up a fight.

And for that, I blamed myself. More than I blamed him.

Killian's hand smoothed over my jaw as he cupped my face gently in his overwhelming hands. His calluses scratched along my skin, but his touch was so gentle it made my heart hurt with a longing I couldn't define. He leaned closer until I could feel his breath on my lips. His beard scratched at my chin, and his scent filled the air around us.

"It's not your fault, Vera," he repeated. "You didn't make Derrek hurt you. He did that. He chose that. He decided to be the evil piece of shit that hits women and uses his size and stature to trap them. He has to answer to that. Not you. Not fucking you. *It is not your fault.*"

A slow tremble worked its way through my body. It was one part surprise and two parts relief. I hadn't realized the hold guilt had on me. Or the crippling shackles of blame.

I hadn't realized I needed to escape that prison as well.

Killian's grasp tightened on my face, his thumbs sweeping over my cheeks to collect the tears that wouldn't stop falling. "Tell me you understand. I need you to say the words."

"I can't," I hiccupped. "I want to but I can't."

He pulled me against his chest, wrapping his arms around me and holding me against the hard safety of his body. "You can," he promised. "However you see yourself or remember yourself is a lie. He hurt you Vera, and that is unforgivable. But what you did? Staying? Staying when you couldn't see a way out, when you lived in fear, when he lied to you over and over and over, that wasn't wrong. You didn't do anything wrong. That's his voice in your head, not yours. He's still feeding you the lies that kept you trapped for so long. You're brave. And you're strong. And you're so damn resilient. It might have taken you longer than you wanted, Vera, but you did it. That makes you the hero of this story, not the victim. You're the survivor. You're moving on."

I pulled back, opening my eyes to meet his gaze and it was one of the bravest things I had ever done. He held me there, captivated by his faith in me, by the grace and gentleness that was in such contrast to everything else I knew to be true about him. He wasn't judging me. He didn't think I was pathetic or weak or used. And he was asking me to see myself how he saw me.

It wasn't a switch that could be flipped. I didn't immediately feel like the brave, strong woman he promised I was.

But I took a step in that direction.

"Thank you." I licked dry lips and pushed through the emotion, trying again. "Thank you for being so kind. For saving me not just from Derrek tonight, but from me."

His head dipped toward mine, his arms tightened around me. "You still don't see it. You don't know how incredibly talented you are. You never needed Derrek to introduce you to anyone. Your food would have done that for you. You didn't need him to validate you. You didn't need his approval. You're brilliant, Vera. So naturally talented, you put me to shame. He saw how utterly precious you were and tried to capture your magic for himself. But he underestimated you. You're meant for more than him. More than the food truck you've sentenced yourself to. You're meant to shine, Vera. I saw it the first time I met you. You shine so fucking bright."

199

He closed the distance between us, pressing a kiss to my cheek. As soon as his lips touched my skin, a shockwave rocked through me. My fingers curled around clumps of his black t-shirt and I tipped into him, our bodies settling against each other as if letting out a satisfied sigh.

I didn't pull away. I couldn't. He had given me back a piece of myself that I'd been unable to find. He'd given me a gift that I would cherish for the rest of my life.

His lips lingered on my cheek, brushing once, twice, slowly peppering my cheekbone with the sweetest kisses. I shivered at the gentle seduction of it, the brush of his beard against my face, the fullness of his lips tasting my skin, the salty tears that had only just now stopped falling.

He'd told me I was bright, but not compared to him. He was the sun, and I was a flower turning my face to his heat. He was the stars in the clear summer night sky, and I was the stargazer mesmerized by the mysterious beauty I would never fully understand.

I turned my face toward his, seeking those lips that were driving me crazy. He let out a shaky breath, catching the corner of my mouth as soon as he could reach it.

Someone whimpered, but it couldn't have been me. I had never made that sound before in my life.

The next time he kissed me it was a real kiss, mouth to mouth, lips caressing lips, tongues seeking tongues. I melted into him, fully alive again for the first time in years.

He tasted as perfect as possible, all masculine need and hungry desperation. His mouth moved over mine, fully in charge, fully committed to kissing me as thoroughly as possible.

My hands wound around his neck, desperate to hold onto something stable as my knees trembled and my belly flipped and my core coiled, heating with delicious warmth.

He just kept kissing me, deepening until his tongue did wicked things to mine. His teeth nipped at my bottom lip, and then he licked a slow path that pulled another needy sound out of me.

His hands pressed me closer to him, while he walked me and leaned my back against the car. He held me there, trapped against the cold, dew-covered door and his hard, muscled body. His thigh slid between mine, not aggressively, just enough to tease me into wanting more.

I wanted him closer, harder. I wanted to strip his clothes off him and throw myself on top of him. This tension had been building and building between us. I didn't know if it was my emotional breakdown that had finally pushed us together or if we would have always ended up here, unable to resist the pull between us.

I'd tried to ignore it. Ignore him. But he'd never let me ignore the fire between us. He'd never let me get away with pretending we didn't want this.

And God, did I want this.

His mouth left mine to drag slow, sensual kisses over my jaw, to the tender spot just below my ear, down the column of my throat, where he spent a delicious amount of time at the hollow between my collarbones.

When he finally brought his mouth back to mine, we were nothing but lips and tongue and desire. His teeth bumped into mine as we learned the contours of each other, as we familiarized ourselves with each other's body and mouth and need.

It was everything a first kiss should be—irresistible, voracious and too short. Way, way too short.

He finally pulled back, and I slumped against him, breathing heavily and tingling with desire. My lips were swollen in a way they hadn't been in a very long time, and my stomach jumped with nerves and need and a thousand lust-filled butterflies.

He panted just as heavily as me, his arms still wrapped around my waist, supporting me so I didn't tumble over. His voice rumbled against the top of my head when he finally spoke. "You've wanted to do that for so long. I'm surprised you held off for as long as you did."

I smiled, surprisingly comfortable with his familiar arrogance. I didn't even bother standing up. I just smiled into his chest, inhaling him again and again. "I thought you'd be a better kisser, though. I'm trying not to be disappointed."

His chuckle vibrated his chest, and I closed my eyes at the sensation. God, I loved to make him laugh. "Since you won't be able to keep your hands off me now, I guess we're just going to have to keep practicing."

I finally stood up, hoping he meant right now. "I guess so."

He looked down at me, his dark eyes heating. "Not tonight, Vera. I need to get you home." I must have looked disappointed because he laughed again. "There will be more. I promise you that. But not after you've had to face your darkest demon. Not when Derrek is still infecting the air. Not after I've just decided on first-degree murder."

My blood turned to ice. It was that simple. Derrek still had the power to ruin every one of my moods, no matter how blissful or flawless. "Don't go to jail for him," I pleaded. "That wouldn't be fair at all."

Killian didn't seem convinced. "Let's get you home. I don't want to talk about him anymore tonight."

I tried to do the decent thing one more time. "You really don't have to drive me. I know it's inconvenient for you."

"Get in the car, Vera," he ordered, turning me toward the passenger side. "There's a goodnight kiss in it for you if you play nice."

I was ashamed to admit that got me moving. "You should know I live with my dad."

"He won't mind," he countered confidently. "He likes me."

"You're so cocky."

He flashed me a grin across the top of the car. "And you love it."

I rolled my eyes but didn't verbally respond. He was right. I did love it.

"Fine, you can take me home," I allowed. "But you better not be stingy with this goodnight kiss."

He smiled. Drove me home. And fulfilled his promise.

Very generously.

Chapter Nineteen

I smiled before I even opened my eyes the next morning. Yesterday had been traumatic on so many levels. I still had to deal with Derrek in a very real way. I had to make sure he knew he could never come back to my truck or my city or bother me ever again.

Until then, I chose to let Killian be the dominating headline of the morning. I lay there in the twin bed from my childhood and curled my toes into rumpled sheets.

It didn't seem possible. This man that had gone from idol to enemy, to reluctant friend, to fantastic kisser.

And not only had he kissed me beyond all reason and rational thought, but he'd given me back whole chunks of myself that had been missing. He'd said words I'd been too afraid to think and truths that had felt so wholly out of reach, I never believed they could be true for me. I'd purged some of my hurt and loathing.

Maybe not all of it, but some. It was like the first few shaky breaths after nearly drowning. They burned and clawed at my throat, they were painful and raw, but they were made of life-saving oxygen none the less.

I didn't know what to think about that or how to move on. Derrek was a darker cloud than ever, and yet Killian had inspired hope in a way that also healed where I had been only broken, that also breathed life where death had rotted and destroyed. He'd held out the person I used to be and offered it like a gift he had the right to give.

But the strangest part was that I didn't mind. I didn't even want to fight him for it. He had done something I hadn't been able to do myself, and I would always be grateful for that.

He even made me want to consider something more… something that wasn't just about me or my healing or my needs. He made me consider him.

He made me consider us.

The smell of coffee dragged me out of bed. I slid my feet into slouchy slipper boots and grabbed my robe for my dad's sake. I stopped by the bathroom to wash my face and throw my hair in a fresh messy bun, but other than that I looked like I did every morning- terrifying.

Shuffling to the kitchen, I found my dad at the table. He had a fresh cup of coffee in his one hand and a piece of toast and jelly in the other. It was earlier than I usually made an appearance, but then again, last night had been an earlier night for me.

Comparatively. It was after midnight before Killian had stopped kissing me.

"You're up early," Dad noted as he took a long drink of his super-hot coffee. I could have sworn he didn't have taste buds. For as long as I could remember, food temperature didn't bother him. It was unnerving how he just dove right into the hottest foods and drinks. Even now I resisted the urge to shout a warning to him. It wouldn't have done any good anyway.

"I closed up a little early last night," I answered honestly.

Dad set his newspaper down and gave me his full attention. "Did you run out of food?"

The story came out in a torrent of information. "Derrek showed up unexpectedly after Vann left for his date. I felt uncomfortable staying there by myself." For all my newfound courage, my explanation still trembled.

Dad's expression hardened. "Why would he do that? Why didn't he call first?"

"He doesn't have my number. And I wouldn't have answered anyway."

"Because you're a smart girl," he sympathized. I saw the questions bounce around in his head through the window of his concerned expression, but for some reason, he didn't ask them.

I wondered if he didn't need to. Maybe he already knew. Maybe he'd figured it out for himself. Either way, he patted the seat next to him and told me to grab some coffee before I sat down.

While I poured the perfect ratio of cream and coffee in my chipped Mickey Mouse mug, my dad asked a very practical question. "Are you going to have to worry about him showing up again?"

I'd already considered that possibility, and it made me nauseous. I didn't want to go to work every night worrying about Derrek lurking in the shadows. "I'm not sure," I answered. "He opened his own restaurant in Charlotte. So it's not like he has a ton of free time. But I'd love it if he never, ever showed his face again. Like if he could just bury himself upside down in the sand, that would be ideal."

Dad sputtered his coffee all over his newspaper. "Sorry," he coughed, wiping up the mess with the napkin he'd been clutching. "Warn me before you start plotting murder."

I hid my smile in a long drink of coffee. "Will do."

"What are you going to do about him?"

"I'm going to reach out to him today and tell him that I don't want him anywhere near the food truck or me."

He eyed me shrewdly. "And if that doesn't work?"

"I'm going to file a restraining order." There. I said it. The words were out in the world now, and I couldn't take them back. I couldn't even pretend they didn't exist. It was something I should have done a very long time ago.

Some of the color leached from his face, and I could tell he had his suspicions, but he hadn't put together the whole story yet.

He looked at me, blinking slowly. "Do you want to talk about it?"

I shook my head. Despite my brand-new mettle, I couldn't bring myself to tell Dad what happened with Derrek. The sunlight was too bright, too revealing. And my past was much too dark. My dad loved me more than anything, but the crippling embarrassment and fear of judgment kept the words locked inside me.

I justified my omission, by reminding myself I didn't want to stress Dad out any more than he already was. I wanted him as strong as possible for chemo and this gross cancer. He knew enough.

A restraining order was not something to joke about, and I hoped he knew me well enough to know I wouldn't just throw that threat around unless I absolutely needed it.

When I answered, "Not really," I pushed the guilt aside. I loved my dad more than anything, but I wasn't a little girl anymore. I needed to start fighting my own battles. Fight them. Not just run from them.

Knowing he would be there for me anytime I needed him gave me a whole new sense of daring.

"You can tell me anything, baby girl," he soothed. "I know you're all grown up and got your own business and all that. But I'm still your dad. I'll still go after any boy that breaks your heart. Or worse."

I took another sip of coffee to hide my emotional reaction. "I know, daddy."

His smile was sad, but genuine. "I love you, Vera May. There isn't a thing in this world I wouldn't do for you."

I sniffled and nodded. "Thank you."

He looked back at his paper, quickly hiding the tears that had filled his own eyes. Geez, all these heart to hearts were turning us into a bunch of softies.

My phone buzzed with a text message. I looked down to see Killian James Quinn's name appear in the bubble. I'd changed it from James Q because I couldn't erase the image of a middle-aged man in a bathrobe trolling me from his mom's basement. *Call me when you wake up.*

I blushed, surprised by the romantic message, even after everything that happened last night.

Just kidding. I didn't blush. And the message wasn't romantic. Leave it up to Killian to send me commands through text without even a please or thank you.

God, that man…

"Big plans for the day?" Dad asked while I decided what to do about Killian's message.

"Not really. I need to pay some bills and head to the commissary to do inventory. Oh, and manage my Facebook ads. And decide on next week's menu. I should make a trip back to the truck and do some deep cleaning before it gets out of control. At some point, I need a new pair of work pants. I still haven't found a bakery to work with either. I should swing by a few more today and drop off my card."

He stared at me with his cup halfway to his mouth. "I thought today was your day off?"

"It is. That's why I finally have time to do all the things I've needed to do for weeks."

He snickered, turning his attention back to the paper. "When you were a little girl you just couldn't wait to grow up. Remember that?"

I rinsed my empty cup and put it in the dishwasher. "Why didn't you warn me?"

"I could have, of course. But that would have spoiled all the fun."

"Who's having fun?"

He smiled at me, his grin stretching wide across his stubbled face. "Me."

I just rolled my eyes and put the creamer away. Since I really did have a ton to do today, I kissed him on the top of his shiny head and hurried to get ready.

206

My hair was a mess after sleeping on it wet, so I sprayed a half bottle of product on it and hoped for the best. I threw on a navy blue romper, with spaghetti straps and a bright orange belt to give it a pop of color. Rompers were a nightmare when it came to peeing, but I only had a couple more weeks of real summer and Sundays were one of the few days I didn't have to dress for work- even if I would be working the entire day.

After I'd brushed my teeth, applied minimal makeup and pulled my hair into a loose braid over my shoulder, I grabbed my phone and headed for my car.

Killian had called an Uber last night just like he'd promised and then he'd kissed me thoroughly until it arrived. My belly flipped just thinking about the way he pressed me against my front door and used his very talented tongue to drive me crazy.

I sat in my driver's seat tapping the back of my phone, deciding what to do. Had I changed my mind about dating? After last night, everything felt different.

I felt different.

Opening up to Killian had been freedom I didn't realize I needed, but did that change my decision to be single? I still had goals.

Foodie took up almost all of my time. And Lilou was even worse for Killian. We didn't really have time to pursue anything real.

Besides, as amazing as he'd been last night, I'd promised myself I would never date another chef again. It wasn't that I expected all of them to be violent psychopaths. But it wasn't a secret that Killian was arrogant, dominating and driven. The last thing I wanted to do was jump feet first into another unhealthy relationship.

I didn't want to put myself in another position to be trampled or forgotten about. I didn't want to ever compromise my dreams for someone else's again.

So, why did I pick up my phone and call Killian like he asked? Er, demanded.

Because obviously, my heart was a traitor that refused to listen to reason.

He picked up on the third ring and didn't bother with hello. "Did you just get up?"

"I'm actually on my way to the commissary. I need to check inventory for the next week before I go back to Morning Market."

"You're working today?" I could hear clanking in the background, voices calling to each other in an open space. He was already at Lilou.

"I'm catching up on everything," I told him. "Are you working today?"

207

I heard the smile in his voice when he answered, "I work every day. How long is that going to take you?"

I calculated everything I had to do, deciding to swing by Target first since it was on my way. "Two hours. Maybe three."

"Do you want to swing by Lilou afterward for some lunch?"

I bit my bottom lip, trying to restrain my smile. "Are you asking me instead of telling me?"

His voice dropped to a low rumble that did wicked things to my resolve. "Don't tempt me, woman. I have no problem telling you to get your ass over here. I'm not good at being nice, Vera."

Oh, my God.

I licked my lips and reminded myself I wanted a nice guy. I was done with assholes.

Only, Killian didn't feel like an asshole. Not anymore.

Not at all.

I cleared my throat and tested him. "Just say please."

His deep chuckle chased me through the phone. "Vera, please come eat lunch with me."

Holy cow. If I thought Killian was sexy when he told me what to do, the word please just rocketed him into an entirely different dimension of irresistible.

"Okay," I agreed breathlessly while my heart pounded erratically in my chest and my blood rushed with anticipation.

I heard the smile in his voice and knew he heard the same in mine. "See you soon."

"Bye, Killian."

I hesitated another three seconds before I made myself hang up. I was in very dangerous no-you-hang-up-first territory. Gross.

And at the same time—*swoon!*

I remembered belatedly that I was driving and refocused on the road, straightening out my car that had been gliding a little too freely to the left. Oops.

I determined not to think about Killian until lunch. I would focus on being a responsible driver, on finding the right black pants that I could destroy in the kitchen without regret, and on inventory at the commissary. I wouldn't think about him again.

Not once.

Starting now.

Chapter Twenty

*T*hree hours later, I parked in Vann's lot and realized I had done nothing but think about Killian since I hung up the phone with him. Which was obnoxious.

And secretly, *very secretly*, adorable.

I locked up my car and walked across the street, the August afternoon sun beating down on the top of my head. There was no breeze today, the air was thick with sticky humidity and sweat.

Hurrying across the street, I debated on whether I should go in the side door like Killian always did or through the front even though they weren't open yet. Nerves pinballed back and forth through my appendages, making me equal parts nervous and excited for a behind the scenes look at Lilou.

The enamored girl in me couldn't wait to spend more time with Killian. The curious professional couldn't wait to see the kitchen in all its famed glory or the dining room with the house lights fully up. It was hard to say which side of me was more anxious for lunch.

Wyatt pushed through the side door, carrying boxes to the dumpster and I decided to let him lead me inside. I felt like an imposter walking into the restaurant by myself.

When he turned around, he shot me a friendly smile and a cocked eyebrow. "What are you doing here? I thought today was your day off."

About thirty replies rolled around in my mouth, but I decided on the truth. So I just said it, with confidence as if it were the most normal thing in the world. "Killian asked me to meet him for lunch."

Wyatt's bark of surprised laughter was the reason I had contemplated going with something other than the truth. "Did he now?"

"Don't be weird," I scolded. "He's probably trying to steal more recipes."

"Well, that explains why he pushed our meeting."

"You can join us," I suggested casually, trying to downplay the idea that this was a date. "I don't mind."

"Not that kind of meeting. There's a critic from *Gourmand* stopping by tonight. He wants to make sure we don't fuck everything up." Before I could fully grasp how very cool that was, Wyatt swung the heavy steel door open and waved me inside. "But now we can just blame everything on you, so we're good."

I glared at him but only for a second because my attention was immediately diverted to the huge industrial kitchen that smelled like heaven and looked even cleaner. White subway tiles on all the walls made the gleaming stainless steel stand out in perfect lines and shiny surfaces.

A few employees in black coats and hats bustled around the kitchen, their hands busy with prep work and their gazes focused on their tasks. My heart kicked against my breastbone, jealous and happy and dreamy all at once.

The huge glass-doored refrigerators were stocked with fresh vegetables and cheeses, meats and more. A huge pot of broth simmered on one of the cooktops and the dishwasher was already buzzing from the morning's work.

My tiny truck kitchen could fit inside the walk-in cooler.

It hit me harder than it ever had what I'd given up when I came home. At least when I'd been in Europe living hand to mouth, I'd gotten to work in a kitchen. Even if I'd only been a peon in the hierarchy of restaurant staff, I'd still gotten to be a part of the organized chaos.

Nothing could compare to that. Not even the privilege of owning my own business. There was nothing like running around during dinner service, chefs shouting orders and tickets flying through the window. There was nothing like the different smells that tangled together or tired hands after prepping for hours. There was nothing like sending plate after plate of perfect food to a room full of diners that couldn't comprehend the amount of time, care and effort that went into each dish so they could have an experience instead of a meal.

Just when I thought I would burst from missing the rush so badly, my gaze fell on Killian. He hadn't noticed me yet. His focus was wholly on the dish at his fingertips, plating it just right so that the visual precision could change your life if you let it.

I stood next to the door, enjoying him in all his glory. He commanded the attention of everyone in the room just by his presence, by the sheer strength of his dominating will. His fingers moved steadily over the dish, never shaking, never questioning what he was doing. He orchestrated the plate. Not the other way around.

My mouth went dry watching him. My blood hummed beneath my skin. And every dormant part of me woke up and started paying attention. I decided I had never seen anything so sexy before, so fully my fantasy in every way.

His forehead wrinkled in concentration. His body bent over the plate as he moved it gracefully in circles deciding the perfect angle and position to add the sauce. He dipped a spoon into a tomato-based cream and slashed lines of it over lush stalks of asparagus sitting on top of creamy golden polenta. Plump mushrooms adorned a perfectly seared piece of filet mignon on the other side of the plate.

Seeing Killian in his element stole my breath and replaced my rational thought with unapologetic lust.

I must have made a sound because he finally lifted that intent gaze to find me hovering like a creeper against the door. His eyes softened and his mouth quirked up on one side. I tried not to melt.

"Hey," he said casually, like it wasn't an invasion of his professional privacy for me to be watching every single thing he did. Probably because he couldn't hear the very, very inappropriate thoughts running through my head.

"Hey."

"Hungry?"

I suddenly felt very shy. I hadn't done this with a guy in years. Flirt, I mean. I hadn't even been interested in someone since Derrek first started to pursue me.

And Killian wasn't just any guy. He was everything cool, strong and masculine. So very different than me—weird, weak and feminine.

We couldn't have been bigger opposites.

He couldn't have been more of what I was convinced I didn't want.

And yet here I was, quivering and interested and tired of telling my heart what it should want instead of letting it chase after what it knew it wanted.

"Yes," I answered succinctly.

Killian held my gaze, one hand shaping the side of his beard. "I have something for us out in the dining room. Is that okay?"

I pointed at the dish he'd been so focused on. "What's that?"

He frowned down at the plate. "Practice."

"For the guy from *Gourmand*?"

Killian's frown deepened. "Heath Noble."

"Yikes," I hissed, feeling his anxiety ratchet through the room. "That's not just any critic."

"No kidding," he sighed. "Plus, he already hates me. I wouldn't be surprised if he's showing up just to write a bad review."

I moved closer so I could inspect his dish. Obviously, I hadn't tasted it yet, but it looked perfect. It looked beyond perfect. It was everything good food should be. The steak was fat and juicy, sear lines making a plaid outline on the surface. The mushrooms had been sliced exactly evenly and the brown sauce coating them smelled robust and savory. The polenta was the right side dish, creamy, golden with tipped peaks and the right amount of substance without looking gluey. Despite everything on the plate, the asparagus refused to be ignored—a verdant green, pliable without being floppy, and crisp ends that would crunch in contrast to the soft polenta. It was flawless.

Immaculate.

My mouth watered just looking at it.

"It looks and smells amazing, Killian. You have nothing to worry about."

"It's not modern," he countered. "It's not interesting or pushy or anything but ordinary. I'm bored just looking at it."

"So make something else," I encouraged. I hadn't seen anything but the technical precision he'd used on the dish. But now that he suggested some problems, I could see what he meant. This wasn't a dish that was pushing the boundaries of the food industry. But not every dish had to be.

He glared at me. "This is what Ezra wants. This is what Ezra gets."

I leaned in until our shoulders touched, linking my pinky with his. "It's perfect. You know that it's perfect. Stop stressing out."

He let out a deep sigh and wrapped his arms around me, tugging me into a hug. I sucked in a breath, surprised by the intimacy in the middle of his kitchen. For a warm, delicious minute, he just held me against him, seeming to take as much pleasure in our innocent connection as I did. Finally, he dropped a kiss on the top of my head and stepped back. "Let's go eat. I'll worry about this later."

"I didn't take you for the nervous sort," I teased him as we weaved through the kitchen and out to the dining room.

He shot me a glance over his shoulder and then stopped at a corner table set for two. "It's not me I'm worried about. I know I serve the best. But I can't control him. You can't make someone enjoy good food. You can't convince them to appreciate the skill and taste and quality you put into every element. I learned very early on that food service is an art just as much as painting or storytelling. People either like it, or they don't. You can't argue with personal taste."

I sat down in the chair he pulled out for me. "Every other review of you or Lilou has been glowing. I know because I've read them all. You seriously have nothing to worry about."

He sat down across from me and pulled silver domes off the two platters waiting for us. One plate was the chocolate mousse I loved here. And the other was a conglomeration of meats and cheese, mustard, jelly, bread and nuts.

Killian grinned at me. "A charcuterie board."

"You're so full of it."

He nodded, waggling his eyebrows. "And you're impressed. It's okay if you want to tell me how much."

I just shook my head. Unbelievable.

"How was inventory? Do you know what you're going to serve this week?" He rearranged the plates so the charcuterie was between us and tore off a hunk of bread and meat, dipping it in the mustard before taking a bite.

I followed suit, kind of loving that he hadn't bothered to plate individually. "I was really inspired by those strawberries at Jo's stand. I was thinking about doing a deconstructed chicken salad sandwich with a strawberry-rhubarb compote over greens and like a Caprese salad on a skewer. I don't know. I'm just playing with the idea right now. I don't want the chicken salad to be too sweet."

His expression turned thoughtful. "Would you serve bread with it?"

"Maybe toast for texture? Or lavosh? Then layer it with butter lettuce, blackened chicken, the compote and a spicy-ish aioli to give it some heat."

"And the salad?"

"Fresh mozzarella balls and cherry tomatoes marinated in balsamic vinegar and roasted briefly with a basil pesto to dip it in."

He leaned forward, bringing us closer together. "Is that your style then? Fancy comfort food?"

I nearly choked on a curried pistachio. "What?"

"Your signature. You're doing upscale comfort food out of a food truck. It's clever, Vera. You should run with it."

I popped another pistachio in my mouth and let his words settle inside me. That was exactly my style. It wasn't a secret, but I hadn't had to explain it to him. He'd simply gotten to know my food and figured it out himself. There was satisfying validation in that.

My pride soared, and I settled into the style all over again. I loved to take ordinary meals that we were all used to and make them interesting, different. I wanted to take the thing that your mom made you on your sick days or the meals that reminded you most of home and spin them until they felt completely different. And then I wanted to make you love them just as much.

I smiled instead, appreciating Killian all over again. "Yes. That is my style."

"Are you ever going to expand beyond the truck?"

Was this his version of twenty questions? Geez. "Right now I'm about fifty thousand dollars in debt. First I'm going to pay off my student and business loans."

His eyebrows lifted at my candidness. Swiping a piece of cheese through the red pepper jelly, he said, "Yeah, but if the food truck continues to grow you'll need to capitalize on your success. I know you want a kitchen, Vera. And I know Foodie is taking off. A restaurant of your own seems like the next, most natural step."

"Derrek will never let me have a kitchen. I gave up on that dream the second I left him." I had doubts that I would be in the food truck business for another week now that Derrek knew where to find me.

His expression transformed from casual to furious in less than a second. He went from relaxed and fluid to angry, rigid lines, his fists clenched at his side, his jaw so hard it pushed his cheek muscles out. "Who cares what Derrek thinks? You're not still considering going back to him, Vera. That would be a huge fucking mistake."

"Geez." I felt my stomach drop to my toes. "Obviously not. I would never go back to him. I'm talking sabotage. He's been pretty clear on what would happen to me should I choose to work somewhere else besides his kitchen."

And just like that Killian slumped back in his chair, relaxed once again. Well mostly relaxed. The topic of Derrek still put him on edge, but at least he wasn't three seconds from turning into the Hulk. "Derrek doesn't get to decide where you work. Or what you do. Only you decide that, Vera. He doesn't get to control you anymore. And if he tries we'll take legal action."

I ignored his use of "we'll." I appreciated everything Killian had done for me, but I in no way expected him to help me fight Derrek all the way to court. I could never ask that of anyone, least of all Killian. But instead of explaining that, I changed the direction of the conversation. "I doubt he would do anything illegal. All he has to do is talk to the people he knows, get them to shun me and I'll be completely alienated. Un-hirable." Killian shook his head, refusing to agree. So, I repeated myself in simpler terms. "All he has to do is tell his friends in the industry whatever bad rumor he wants, and I won't be able to find a job at any good restaurant in the entire state."

"That's not true," Killian countered. "His circle of friends is smaller than you think. Most people can't stand the useless prick."

That made me smile. "Still, I'm a nobody. I haven't even worked anywhere notable, and I graduated over four years ago."

"Who cares," Killian insisted. "You're a hell of a chef. You can have my letter of recommendation any time you want it."

I was speechless. Completely. Utterly. Speechless. It wasn't like he'd offered another suggestion to my dishes, which I'd learned was both helpful and obnoxious. This was much bigger.

Killian freaking Quinn had just offered to give me a letter of recommendation. He'd called me a *hell of a chef*.

Obviously, I'd died last night. This couldn't be real. This wasn't my life.

I messed up. I always chose the wrong thing, the wrong path, the wrong boyfriend. I was the perpetual screw-up who had just learned to be okay with that.

What was happening?

"I wish you'd say something," he coaxed. "I can't tell if you're pissed or happy."

"Thank you," I whispered. "You're so generous. I'm just, I'm trying to process all your support. If we're honest, I'm still trying to process our friendship. So, this is like, I don't know, incomprehensible."

He snorted as he switched the charcuterie for the mousse and passed me a spoon. "We're not *friends,* Vera. If you haven't figured it out by now, I like you. And not in a way that's appropriate for *friends* to like each other. Whether we explore our non-friendship or not, you have my support in your career no matter what. Your talent isn't dependent upon me. You just kick ass in the kitchen. End of story."

"Oh."

"But if you want my honest advice, you'd be smothered in a kitchen that wasn't your own. You might think you'd enjoy working under someone, but we're all assholes. And you'd be stifled, pushed into a box that you don't belong in. Sure, you could work your way up, but you have your truck, so I don't know why you would."

215

"I don't know what to say."

He leaned forward, taking my hand in his and playing with the tips of my fingers. "Say yes when I ask you to go out on another date with me."

"Another?"

He waved his hand at the table. "I cooked for you. Don't I get credit for that?"

I pressed my lips together to keep from grinning like an idiot. "Yes."

"Yes, I get credit? Or yes to the date."

"Yes, to both."

And then he smiled at me again, soft, sweet, simmering with heat and affection and I thought my heart was going to blow up and kill me. He'd literally turned me into a Billy Ray Cyrus song—but like the happy version of *Achy Breaky Heart*.

I'd never felt like this with Derrek. Or any of the other guys I'd dated before him. I'd never been simultaneously this happy and this hopeful and this nervous. It was like my past was black and white, and Killian Quinn had finally given me color. He'd brought me back from a dead, lonely place and given me a reason to hope and smile and laugh again.

We finished the mousse, and he walked me outside, but only so he could press me against the cool side of the building and kiss me senseless. His lips moved against mine greedy with a different kind of hunger than I was used to feeding. He gripped my hips and held me against him, letting me feel all his hard, toned lines. My hands dove into his hair, kissing him just as relentlessly as he kissed me.

When he pulled away, my lips were swollen from his kisses, and my chin itched from the beard burn he'd left me with. We said goodbye, and I walked across the street to my truck, pressing my fingers against my mouth and trying to hold in the taste of him.

Was this really me swearing off men?

Maybe Killian Quinn was worth breaking a few of my own rules.

Chapter Twenty-One

...So for all these reasons, you need to stay away from me. I'm serious, Derrek. I will get a restraining order if I have to.

-Vera.

I read it over three more times before I hit send. I had tried to muster up the courage to call him several times over the last couple days, but I'd never been able to push the button. I had all these things to say to him, to yell at him. I wanted to eviscerate him with words and scar him with truth. For more than a year, I'd been mentally preparing the speech I'd give should I ever see him face-to-face again. And then when he'd inevitably shown up, I froze, paralyzed by fear and habit.

I had hoped disemboweling him over the phone would be easier. I'd sharpened my claws and practiced phrases like, "You made me fear, truly fear for the first time in my life. You were supposed to be the place I felt the safest, but you were my nightmare instead." In the end, it was all for nothing. I couldn't do it. Killian suggested I text him instead.

It had taken me another two days to work up the courage just to do that.

Since I didn't want him to have my number, I used Vann's phone. I hoped Derrek wouldn't go after Vann like he would me. But I knew Vann wouldn't put up with any kind of harassment.

I couldn't say the same thing about me. We'd already established that I was a doormat.

Setting the phone down on the counter between us, I stared at it like it was alive and dangerous, like any second it would sprout arms with talon-tipped fingers and lunge for me.

"Did he reply?" Vann asked from his stool by the order window.

I shook my head. "Not yet."

"Maybe he won't," Vann suggested. "Maybe he finally clued in that you don't want anything to do with him."

"Maybe," I agreed. "But not likely."

"Why didn't you tell me when it was happening? I would have moved your ass home the second you called."

My stomach turned with familiar regret. I'd opened up to Vann earlier when I filled him in on Derrek's surprise visit Saturday night. Vann had been as mad as I'd expected. He tried to convince me that he understood my silence. But I knew he didn't. He didn't understand why I'd never told anybody. And he didn't understand why I'd stayed with Derrek for as long as I did.

That made two of us.

He turned his face back to the window, stewing with useless fury and frustration. There wasn't anything he could do now, and that drove him crazy.

The weather had cooled significantly tonight, threatening a storm with heavy clouds blotting out the starry sky and the smell of rain perfuming the air. An occasional rumble of thunder and flash of lightning punctuated the building anticipation of a summer storm.

The promise of rain had emptied the plaza, making it a slow night even for a Thursday. I should have sent Vann home two hours ago, but I was too afraid to be alone again.

I couldn't help scanning the plaza every time I turned around. I half-expected Derrek to show up again now that he knew where to find me. I had big doubts that a stern text message would be enough to keep him away. He wasn't easily dissuaded.

"How was your date the other night?" I asked Vann, attempting to change the subject.

He shrugged, not changing his facial expression. "I don't think I'll see her again."

"Did she call you on your bullshit?"

Looking down at his crossed ankles, he suppressed a smile. "You might have been right about nice girls." At my huge grin, he amended, "Not in the traditional sense of being right. That's not what I meant. I just mean, maybe you were on to something."

I cupped my ear. "What's that? What did you say? Did you want to tell me how I'm right all the time? And emotionally intuitive? And awesome?"

He laughed at my theatrics. "Yeah, sure. You're all those things. And yet you have terrible taste in men. What's that about?"

I let out a heavy sigh and checked my phone for the umpteenth time tonight. Speaking of men... Killian hadn't texted all day. After enjoying a non-stop texting conversation since Sunday, I hadn't heard from him at all today. He'd been radio-silent, and rationally I knew he was probably busy working. But irrationally, I compared today with the previous few days and how he'd found time to text me then but not now.

I'd only analyzed what I could have said to piss him off two hundred times today, but I'd concluded that it wasn't me. He'd stopped by the truck yesterday afternoon, like he did every time I worked, and walked me to my car. There had even been some fantastic kisses against the driver's side door and a promise for a date just as soon as we could figure out our dumb work schedules.

Then this morning? Nothing.

I'd texted him a question about spices just to get a reaction from him, but he'd been radio silent.

The floodlights outside Lilou flicked off, and staff started to pour out the side door. Closing time for them. Usually, I stayed open for another two hours, but there wasn't any point tonight.

I watched the staff from Lilou walk to the parking lot, stripping out of their coats and bandanas as they went.

Nerves abruptly pricked at the back of my neck and forearms. I realized I'd been staying open, hoping to catch a glimpse of Killian. I'd been addicted to my phone today, hoping he'd text. I was becoming the girl that I hated. The girl I never wanted to be again.

"Let's go," I told Vann. "This isn't worth staying open for."

"You sure?"

I appreciated what a good sport he was, but now I was suddenly very anxious to get going. "Yeah, I'm sure. I just have to clean up a bit."

He nodded and started going through the money.

It wouldn't take long since we'd only had a minimum of customers tonight. A strong wind blew through the windows, rustling the papers and money, sending Vann scrambling after bills and order tickets. The menu sign hanging on the outside of the truck smacked against the siding and then lifted with the wind and slapped it again.

"Oh, geez." I left Vann to deal with the money while I rushed outside to grab the sign before it damaged the siding.

A fat raindrop landed on my forehead just as soon as I stepped outside. Sliding the menu off its hook, I turned around and nearly ran into Wyatt.

He squinted against the wind whipping him in the face. "Hey."

My hand landed on my frantically pounding heart, and I breathed in sharply through my nose. Apparently, I was terrified of Derrek showing up again if my reaction to Wyatt's surprise visit was anything to go by. I tried to appear unruffled, though. "Hey, sorry. We're closing. We want to get out of here before the rain gets bad."

"Oh, no, that's not why I'm here." He glanced over his shoulder nervously, and I immediately knew something was up.

"What's wrong?"

His lips pressed into a frown, and he played with his eyebrow ring nervously. "Have you talked to Killian today?"

"I haven't heard from him since yesterday."

He rubbed a hand over his face, pulling his bottom lip into a U. "You should talk to him," Wyatt coaxed.

It annoyed me that he was in my business. Especially after I'd just decided I didn't need to talk to Killian tonight. "Maybe."

"He got an early look at the review this afternoon, Vera. The *Gourmand* article. It's not good."

The menu dropped on the tips of my toes. "What do you mean it's not good?"

"Noble hated everything. Every single thing. And he didn't hold any punches."

I could not process his words. Like, they didn't make sense. They weren't in English or something. "That's not possible."

He gave me a look before ducking when another plump raindrop landed on his nose. "Ezra tried to get the magazine to retract the article, but they won't. It's going out next month."

"It's just one article," I argued pointlessly. "In one magazine. Killian can survive that."

Wyatt shrugged, stuffing his hands into his pockets. "He's not taking it well. He needs a friend."

"So, go talk to him."

He rolled his eyes so hard I thought one of them might get stuck. "Pretty sure I'm not the person he wants consoling him at midnight. Don't be mean."

I stared at Foodie for a long time, my shoulders catching sporadic raindrops. The temperature dropped another few degrees, pulling goosebumps from my legs and arms.

220

"I'll think about it," I finally admitted. "Thanks, Wyatt."

He took a step back, shoulders up by his chin. "At least make sure he actually leaves. I'm afraid he's going to burn Lilou to the ground in a fit of bad review driven lunacy."

I couldn't help but chuckle. Then I remembered Killian the night of my chicken and waffles nightmare. *I really hate bad reviews.*

He'd been nice enough to pull me out of my depression spiral, and that had only been a few dissatisfied customer complaints. Only two negative reviews had made it online from that night and neither of them were from a big magazine with household-name appeal.

I said goodbye to Wyatt and hurried back inside the truck. I spent the next thirty minutes keeping an eye on Lilou to make sure Killian didn't leave, cleaning my equipment and surfaces and packing up the remaining food. I had predicted tonight would be a slow night so I hadn't brought much with me. It all fit into two crates.

"Do you love me?" I asked Vann with the puppy dog look he couldn't resist.

"I'm not sure. What do you want?"

"Take the food to the commissary tonight? I need to check on Killian."

My brother's eyebrows shot up to his hairline. "Check on him how?"

"He thinks he has crabs," I deadpanned. "I'm going to go inspect the situation."

His nose wrinkled and his face paled. "I can't tell if you're joking."

I shrugged. "I could go into more detail if that would help you decide."

He chuckled, then took the crates of food and the key to the commissary. "Just don't catch them yourself," he warned. "I would have to call the health inspector on you. They'd probably tent you. I'd hate to see my sister bug bombed."

Now I was confused if *he* was joking or not. For the first, and hopefully only, time in my life I worried about my brother's sexual education. "I feel like you should go to a doctor to learn more about sexual health. The clinics will give you free pamphlets. It might be beneficial if you had some more information. I'm starting to worry about these nice girls you date."

He showed me his middle finger—because he was a mature, responsible, small business owner. "Oh, don't you worry about me. Or them for that matter."

I shuddered. "Go away, pervert."

Shooting me one last mischievous grin, he said, "Text me if you need anything. I mean that."

I waved him off, thankful that he did mean that. That I could rely on him. Trust him. It turned out I didn't hate all men. There were a few that still had my respect and affection.

Locking up Foodie, I headed across the street to the one man that had my respect and affection and wasn't related to me. The rain had started, and it wasn't being shy. I crossed the street in a veritable torrential downpour. By the time I made it to the alley next to Lilou, my hair and chef coat were soaked.

I expected the side door to be locked, but when I tugged on the handle it swung open easily. I stepped inside to a dark kitchen. The dining room lights were still on, filling the in and out doors with golden light.

Shedding my wet coat, I threw it on the nearest counter and listened for the sound of anyone still here. A glass clinked not too far away.

I tugged my hair out of the wet ponytail holder and scrunched it while I followed the sound. Suddenly nervous that it wasn't Killian out there, but Ezra or someone else instead, I moved with caution. Nerves made the pulse in my throat jump with anticipation.

But my feet kept moving, and my urgency kept increasing. I had been irritated with Killian for making me care about him. But now all I could do was care for him.

This wasn't the end of his career. At most it was a blip, one of those jarring, thin speed bumps that made everyone bounce around wildly even if you were driving super slowly, but over quickly enough. He would move on. His reputation would be barely tarnished.

His ego on the other hand...

I found him not far from the kitchen. He sat sprawled in a chair with a bottle of Glenmorangie in one hand and a crumpled piece of printer paper in the other. His entire body was reclined, his legs spread apart and casual, even while he radiated tension. He'd unbuttoned his chef's coat and revealed his sinewy, chiseled chest beneath a thin black t-shirt.

A jolt of something hot and fizzy slid through my belly. He was a fallen angel; a Greek god brought low by the reality of life. He was Killian Quinn, and he wasn't perfect.

And I wanted to lick him from head to toe.

He'd made some serious progress on the bottle of whiskey in his hand. His glossy eyes took me in without surprise. I doubted that he'd been expecting me, so it had to be the alcohol.

The realization that he was drunk did nothing to slow my thumping heart or buzzing nerves.

At the same time, my gut clenched with sympathy. The review had clearly gotten to him. He looked miserable, completely upended by the harsh words of someone who had judged him based on one visit.

He had been right at lunch, about critics. The reality of our business was that you couldn't argue with someone's taste.

We were artists, creating beauty with something ingested. No matter how well-crafted our dishes were, if a person hated an ingredient inside the dish, they judged us on what they thought of that one aspect of the dish. Or sometimes they just didn't like it. It wasn't anything that could be logically explained. It was an opinion, as unique and personal as the person holding it.

And if people didn't like the taste of something, it didn't matter how visually appealing the dish was or technically perfect or difficult to make. In the end, our reputation depended on enough people liking the taste of what we created.

We were as subjective as ballet or opera.

It was easy to tell ourselves that truth when the logical part of our brain was in charge. It was harder to believe it after a hurtful review.

Especially an important one.

We stared at each other for several long minutes. He didn't say anything, and I didn't either. And the longer we stayed silent, the thicker the silence became, the heavier.

Seeing him like this, realizing he had taken this review about as hard as anyone could, I just wanted to soothe the pain away. I wanted to make this better for him. I wanted to take this from him and remind him how amazing he was—how incredibly talented and innovative he was.

I had decided thirty minutes ago that I didn't want to see him tonight. That I'd gotten too wrapped up in us, too wrapped up in him.

But looking at Killian like this, so completely at the end of himself, I realized I didn't care about any of that. Because I cared about this man. I cared for him deeply. Somehow over the summer, he'd wormed his way into my heart and made a permanent home there.

He wasn't Derrek. He was nothing like Derrek.

Yes, he was arrogant and bullish and demanding. But he wasn't mean. He wasn't cruel. He wasn't selfish.

And yes, he was a chef. But he was also a friend. And a confidant. And a mentor. And everything I believed a good man was.

He wasn't Derrek. And I wasn't in danger of getting myself back into a bad relationship. Whatever this was with Killian was healthy in a way that I'd never experienced before. Healthy and hopeful and heady.

Sucking in a steadying breath, I walked over to him. His eyes tracked my every movement. The rain had soaked my coat and left my white t-shirt damp, clinging to me everywhere. I'd worn black leggings tonight instead of practical pants, and he noticed them with a searing gaze that moved over my hips and thighs with hungry interest. He took a slow sip of expensive whiskey straight from the bottle, and I watched his tanned throat work as he swallowed without flinching.

I took the bottle from him when he finished, setting it carefully on the table next to him. He relinquished it without a fight.

He sat up straighter and moved his legs together when I stepped over them, straddling him. The emailed review fluttered to the ground forgotten.

I gently placed my hands on his broad shoulders, loving the feel of muscle and bone beneath the starchy fabric of his coat. I rubbed back and forth once, twice. His lips met mine halfway when I leaned in for a kiss.

It was like we'd been doused in gasoline, and someone had thrown a lit match on us. We exploded in hunger and passion and the familiar push and pull we'd always had.

He tugged me down, settling me firmly against him, while his lips moved over mine. He nipped roughly at my bottom lip, pulling it into his mouth, sucking, biting, licking before he moved to my tongue, repeating every aggressively delicious action.

His hands gripped my waist, yanking me closer against him, fitting our bodies as tightly together as possible. The feel of him under me, my legs wrapped around his waist, my hands holding on to his shoulders for balance sent shockwaves of sensation rocking through me.

I felt him beneath me, the button to his pants through the thin material of my leggings. The hardness of the thighs I straddled. The hip bones that framed his tapered waist. And the part of him that made him oh, so very male.

My fingers curled into his shoulders at the feel of him growing hard beneath me. I rocked forward, unable to stop myself. He caught the whimper that fell out of my mouth and deepened the kiss, making the moment even more intense, more erotic.

I clung to him as he held me against him, letting me fidget and grind and work my body against his the way a man and woman should move together. His beard left an intimate burn over my chin and lips, reminding me who was kissing me—never letting me forget it. He tasted like whiskey and oranges and every hot fantasy I'd ever had.

Before I could talk myself out of it, I started pushing at his coat, needing it off him, needing to have it out of my way. He tugged his arms free, revealing those toned, tattooed arms. Once unrestricted, one of those big hands I'd been obsessed with for months slipped beneath my shirt.

We both gasped at the contact. His hand so hot against my ribcage, his palm so hard against the softness of my skin. Our mouths crashed back together, greedier than ever. He palmed my breast under my shirt, kneading until I couldn't catch a full breath. Until I was nothing but want and need and trembling desire.

He shoved the cup of my bra to the side, and his fingers did wicked things to my nipple, pulling sounds from me I had never, ever made before. And the whole time my legs squeezed his waist while he moved against us, our clothes the worst kind of obstacle in the history of obstacles.

"Killian," I moaned when he yanked my shirt up, exposing my soft stomach, my breasts, my peaked nipples.

He groaned deep in his throat and then captured my nipple in his mouth, licking, sucking, biting again in a way that mimicked how he kissed me but better. So. Much. Better.

"More," I pleaded. "Please more."

He made a very agreeable sound in the back of his throat and moved to the other breast. His talented fingers tugged my bra cup down, giving me the pleasure I was so, so desperate for.

I leaned into him, giving him as much of me as he wanted. Taking as much of him as I could get. One hand supported my back, the other played with the waistband of my leggings. His fingers dipped inside, and I shivered at the tickling sensation.

He sucked harder on my nipple, and I nearly exploded. Adjusting his grip, he leaned me back further, exposing me like his own personal feast. He kissed his way from one breast to the other, taking his time on my breastbone, then over my heart as it raced in my chest. His fingers dipped further inside my leggings, playing with the seam of my panties.

His fingers brushed over my core, separated from my most intimate part by just a thin scrap of fabric. He moved his fingers again in a way that was so perfectly timed I bucked against him.

I dug my fingers into his hair as we kissed and kissed and kissed. He moved my underwear to the side and his fingers dragged over my center deliberately slowly. My breath caught in my throat as I waited for more, barely holding onto the tether of reality.

One finger slid inside me, and I stopped kissing him. I couldn't multitask anymore. I couldn't even think coherent thoughts anymore. I rested my forehead against his and accepted the pleasure he was intent on giving.

He moved that one finger achingly unhurried. Deep. Deeper. *Oh, God.*

A second finger joined his first, and that was all it took. I held onto him as fireworks burst behind my closed eyelids. My body clenched around his fingers while my head swam in the best way, dizzy and disoriented. The orgasm burst through me, tightening every single muscle as I gasped and clung to him, unable to let go until I'd landed back on earth, fully sated.

Oh, my God.

There was more I wanted to do. More I *needed* to do. But first, I had to catch my breath. Our temples were pressed together, his breathing as erratic as mine. The only difference between us was I had my pleasure, and he was still hard and tense beneath me.

Which was perfectly fine with me. I could help him out with that.

And I planned to.

Unfortunately, he had other plans.

When my breathing had finally evened out, he pressed a sweet kiss to the corner of my eye and stood up without warning. I let out a squeak of surprise as his hands went under my bum, taking me with him.

Apparently, the fun part of the evening was over. Killian was officially on a new mission.

Chapter Twenty-Two

"*W*here are we going?" I laughed as he moved through the restaurant.

He didn't say anything. He just continued to stalk through his kitchen, his domain, flipping light switches as he went.

The kitchen was just as beautiful as the first time I'd been here, only bigger without all the activity that brought it to life. Nevertheless, my breath caught, and my stomach flipped, feeling the deep, familiar pull that whispered I belonged here.

Maybe not here-here. But somewhere like it.

I loved Foodie, but this was what I wanted. I wanted it to be mine. I wanted the staff and the space and the rush of dinner service. I wanted the acclaim and the challenge and every single thing.

No matter how satisfying running my food truck was, it would never compare to this. And I wasn't made to settle for it. I couldn't shut off the need to be something better, something more... something great.

If I could, I would. Truly. It was like a burden that I didn't know how to carry. I just wanted to put it down and walk away from it, leave it for someone else to find.

But I couldn't.

Killian set me down on the center counter, the stainless steel cold against the backs of my thighs. He stayed between my legs, playing with the ends of my hair.

His eyes had lost the listlessness from disappointment and too much whiskey. They were now clear, green and endlessly deep.

227

He dropped my hair and brushed the backs of his fingers over my jaw. "You're incredible, Vera."

I reached up and grabbed a handful of his beard, bristly to the touch, and tugged. "I've wanted to do that since I met you," I explained. "Sorry."

He smiled patiently at me, but untangled my hand from his facial hair so he could link our fingers together. "Hungry?"

A blush stained my cheeks, and butterflies buzzed in my belly. "Mmm-hmm."

He dropped a lingering kiss to the corner of my jaw and spoke against my skin. "Me too. But how about some food instead?"

I shivered at his implication. "Are you going to cook for me?" Apparently, I'd been body-snatched by a horny alien with a much sexier voice. *Was that really me?*

He pulled back, and I watched his mouth spread in a slow smile. "Don't move."

I laughed when he held up his hands, wiggling those unfairly attractive fingers. He walked deliberately over to the sink and washed his hands, sending me a quick wink.

We shared another searing look, a promise for more, but then he got down to business. He moved around the kitchen, turning things on and gathering ingredients. I decided watching him cook was my new favorite activity.

Who knew prepping vegetables could be sensual? Or spicing meat? Or filling up a pot with water?

This was crazy.

Those things weren't erotic.

They were just normal, everyday things that had no sexual connotation whatsoever.

I gripped the edge of the counter, digging my fingers into the hard edges of the lip. Yeah, no. It wasn't working. Killian Quinn was sexy as sin in this kitchen. He could have been deboning a fish right now, and I'd want him deboning me.

See what I did there?

"He's a prick."

My thoughts were way too far in the gutter to have any context for his comment. "Who?"

"The critic. Noble. He hates Ezra, which means he hates me. The review was a setup to talk shit about Lilou. I should have known better." He shook his head, giving the food at his fingertips all his attention. "But I'd been cocky. I thought I could outcook his opinion of me." He lifted his head and met my gaze. "I was wrong."

228

"Why does he hate Ezra?"

He chuckled darkly. "A lot of people hate Ezra. That doesn't mean the review was less true."

My chest squeezed with sympathy. "The review is tainted by a bully with an agenda. You can't let it get to you."

A bitter smirk lifted one side of his mouth, unamused and surprisingly self-deprecating. "Trite. Unimaginative. Formulaic. Those were the words he used. They're the truth I've needed to hear for a while, but nobody has been brave enough to say them to me."

He wasn't any of those things. Not even a little bit. But his menu was, and there was nothing he could do about it. "What's the deal with you and Ezra? Why are you so loyal?"

"He's my brother."

"Wait. What?"

Killian moved around in the kitchen, pulling ingredients from the fridge and pantry. "Well, foster brother. But we might as well be blood. He's the closest thing I have to family other than Jo."

My eyes widened in shock, but he didn't notice. "She raised you both?"

"I wouldn't say that." When he laughed this time, the sound was lighter, full of warmth. "She whipped us both into shape. Ezra and I were both products of the system. Me, because my parents were absolute degenerates. Drug dealers. Drug addicts. The state pulled me from their care when I was five. Ezra's mom was a decent human; she died when he was ten and didn't have family to take care of him." He paused for a minute as he moved to the stove and started a sauce over hot flame. "Not surprisingly we turned into troubled teens. Ezra was smarter than me and got caught less, but both of us bounced around in the system never fitting in with the foster families that couldn't handle us. He got to Jo first. By the time I showed up, Jo had her hands full with one rebellious teen; I had figured the last thing she wanted was another."

"So, you pulled it together?" I guessed.

His smile was full of memories and nostalgia. "No. I got myself arrested for stealing her car. She called the cops on me, then made me sit there overnight and think about what I'd done wrong. The truth was Jo didn't put up with shit. She'd already whipped Ezra into some shape, and he'd only been there for weeks. I knew she'd try to do the same thing to me. But I had never had an adult in my life that cared about me before. I mean, maybe my case worker. He seemed to care if I lived or died. But other than that, there was no one. I knew Ezra's story because we'd housed together more than once, but never for long. I saw the way he

229

looked at her like he trusted her. I watched him do what she asked and use manners. It was the most terrifying thing I'd ever seen. I didn't want to turn into him."

"But you did."

"Well, I'd like to think I'm the better version. But yeah, there's just something about Jo that crawls under your skin and makes you want to love her. She finally got me out of jail, but informed me immediately that I needed a job to pay all my court and legal fees off.

"I thought she was joking at first, but Jo doesn't joke. She put me to work on her farm. I was only fourteen, and the only food I had ever eaten was what was put before me. Depending on the foster family, sometimes it was nutritious and tolerable. Sometimes it was a soggy TV dinner and a beer. Jo put real food in my hand and told me to grow it. She said I couldn't count on anything, not even a steady meal. If I was tired of not knowing where my next meal was coming from, then I should learn to cook it myself. So, I did.

"She taught me how to grow food and judge it, pick out the best and recognize the not-good-enough. When I turned out to be decent at growing, she moved me into the kitchen and showed me how to turn my harvest into a meal. It was the first time I had ever loved something."

"Jo?" I guessed where this was going. But I was wrong again.

He shook his head. "Cooking."

The ache in my chest needed to hear he had a happy ending, though. I needed to hear him tell me she became a mother to him and gave him the life he'd always wanted. "But you did love Jo, didn't you?"

He chuckled. "Later. Much later. For the most part, Jo was more of a drill sergeant than a mom. She didn't tolerate disobedience or laziness. Ezra and I worked hard for her. We earned our room and board from the sweat off our backs. We hated her at first. Ezra still hates her sometimes, but then again, Ezra is prone to hating a lot of things. Anyway, she got the job done. She turned Ezra and me into functioning adults and encouraged us to go to college. In return, we helped her turn her garden into a farm and grow her business. To this day, it's still a give and take relationship. She provides us with the best produce; we give her our exclusive business."

He'd seared steak, made a sauce and poached eggs during his story. Now he plated them with grace and poise and precision. He was everything a great chef should be.

Everything a good man ought to be.

"Does she still take foster kids?" I asked out of sheer curiosity.

His affectionate smile lit up his face. "Who else would work her farm?" He lifted his gaze, revealing deep loyalty and sincerity. "I hope you know I mean that in the best way. She's not a slave driver. She gives kids that have never loved or cherished anything the chance to have something of their own. It's more about developing a strong work ethic and sense of accomplishment than her crops."

I smiled reassuringly. "She's like the Mr. Miyagi of farming."

He nodded, turning back to the plate. "Exactly."

"So you left her farm and went to culinary school? And Ezra?"

"Ezra's real dad found him his senior year of high school. It's a pretty messed up story, but basically, his dad was very wealthy and really sick. He'd always known Ezra existed but had trouble finding him because of something his birth mom did. Anyway, long story short, Ezra's dad died two years later, leaving Ezra and his half-sister Dillon a pretty substantial inheritance. Ezra turned that money into more money. It turns out Jo taught me how to cook and Ezra how to work twenty hours of every day."

We fell silent for a few minutes while he finished plating and I digested his story. My heart hurt for the child he'd been, for the troubled teen that had needed so much guidance, for the man that he was today that only loved two things—cooking and Jo. And at the same time, I marveled at how well he'd done for himself, at the man he'd become despite his circumstances.

He walked over, handing me a fork, a plate of food and a glass of wine he'd borrowed from the restaurant cellar. He'd sliced steak over crispy hash and nestled the poached egg in the middle. A creamy yellow sauce crisscrossed over the top. Hollandaise?

"I can do fancy Americana, too," he said by way of explanation.

"Steak and eggs. Very creative."

He nudged me with his elbow. "Smart ass."

We dove into our food, and I tried not to have another orgasm. First, from the excellent Cabernet he'd picked out. Then from the meal he'd cooked for me. *Oh, my God.* The steak was probably one of the best I'd ever had. I didn't need fussy food, I just wanted it well-flavored and perfectly cooked. Killian accomplished both so effortlessly that it was hard not to be jealous of him.

"Ezra paid for culinary school."

I looked over at him, surprised by his statement. "Is that why you stay at Lilou?"

He took another bite of steak without responding. "We have our differences, but he's been there for me when I had nobody else."

231

Reaching over to steal one of his strips of steak, I very casually said, "But there are other chefs out there. Chefs who would kill for this job. Maybe even murder you for it. Here's the thing, when Ezra paid for you to go to school did he know he wanted to open restaurants?"

Killian shook his head. "No. That came much later."

"He didn't send you to school so he could have a personal chef, right?"

"Right."

"And you're paying him back?"

"I did. Years ago."

"What do you have to feel guilty for? If you think it will destroy your relationship with Ezra, I mean maybe I understand your hesitation. But Killian, you can't live your life for someone else. You hate it here."

Setting his plate down next to him, he leaned back on one hand and stared at me. "I don't hate it here. I'm just frustrated. And I feel... stagnant."

"Then you have your answer. You're too good at your job to feel stuck."

"And what about you?" Those green eyes burned straight through me, obliterating whatever line of defense I'd still try to use against him. "We both know the food truck isn't your end game. You want a kitchen, Vera. How are you going to get it?"

"Listen, I made my bed. I'm happy to lie in it. There are worse things than owning your own business and setting your own hours."

One side of his mouth lifted in a sardonic smile, calling me on my bullshit. "We both know the truck isn't big enough for you. And if you ever figure out how to set reasonable hours, let me know your trick."

I didn't want to get into this right now. My life was complicated enough without having the great Killian Quinn reminding me of everything I didn't have. He was held back by loyalty to someone he considered a brother. I was trapped because of a series of bad, unfortunate decisions. They weren't the same thing.

Just to get him off my back, I decided to suggest the most preposterous thing imaginable. "Fine. You want something bigger, I want something bigger, let's just open a restaurant together. It can be all modern American and convenient hours. For us. Not our customers."

He slid off the counter and took my glass of wine from me. Carefully setting it off to the side, he stepped between my legs again and rested his hands on my waist, beneath my t-shirt. Skin to hot, rough, glorious skin.

He tugged me forward so that my thighs wrapped firmly around his hips. He stood tall enough so that we were perfectly lined up, his chest pressed against my chest, his heart beating in rhythm with mine.

"I've been thinking the same thing," he murmured, dropping slow kisses along the line of my jaw.

My mind was already swimming with lust, but not far enough gone to recognize how preposterous that was. "You have not." I laughed, trying to play off his serious tone and the ridiculous idea.

His lips found mine, and he kissed me deeply, tangling our tongues, bringing our bodies as close together as possible with our clothes still on. "Since your lamb meatballs."

I pulled back, stunned by the honesty in his tone and the timeline of events. That was so long ago.

He had to be lying.

This was a trick to get in my pants. *But newsflash, Killian, I wasn't exactly playing hard to get!*

He didn't let me dwell on it, though. He closed the distance between us, devouring my mouth like it was the best thing he'd ever tasted.

My fingers slid through his silky hair, holding him to me while we spent time getting to know each other in intimate ways. He removed my shirt completely, exposing me to the cool air and his sizzling gaze.

He laid me back on the stainless steel prep table, taking in every inch of my body in such an appreciative way that it was impossible to feel self-conscious. I wasn't skinny. And while I had never been overly embarrassed of what I looked like, it was impossible not to be nervous. But the voracious hunger flashing through those deep green eyes took away whatever anxiety I had.

Killian liked what he saw. Every piece of me.

And then he showed me. Using his mouth, his tongue, his teeth, to taste every inch of my body. He started at my throat and worked his way down. My collarbone. My breasts. Especially my breasts. My stomach. My hips.

He spread my legs apart and spent a maddening amount of time at the apex of my thighs. By the time my panties disappeared, I was a panting mess of desire and need. He coaxed me to relax and whispered about wanting dessert.

My thoughts alternated between, *Oh, my God!* And *Oh, my God, we're at Lilou!*

Then his head disappeared between my legs, and I stopped thinking altogether. He turned me into nothing but feeling and sensation and pleasure.

He was as relentless with my body as he was with everything else in his life. He demanded. He pushed. He took what he wanted. But he gave, too.

He gave so much.

By the time he walked me to my car, I was fully sated—and completely, utterly wrung dry. And so far gone for this man that I didn't know if I would ever recover.

Derrek had convinced me to love him with tempting possibilities and groundless promises. They hadn't lasted. They hadn't been enough. Even without the abuse, Derrek and I wouldn't have made it. He wasn't what he said he was. He didn't live up to everything he offered.

He was less than.

He was empty.

Killian was the opposite. He didn't convince me to love him; he'd given me so much of himself that the only thing left to do was care about this man. He'd proven himself time and time again to be the man he said he was, the man he wanted to be.

The man I needed.

He hadn't asked me to trust him; he'd just always been trustworthy. He hadn't needed me to need him. He was just the man I needed every single day. He hadn't manipulated me through sugar sweet lies and baseless compliments I wanted to hear. He told me what I needed to hear and left everything else up to me.

He kissed me goodbye one last time, and I drove home with a smile on my face and hope in my heart. For the first time in a long time, I knew who I was, and I knew who the man I loved was.

Love.

Maybe it was only the beginning of love. Maybe the roots were still shallow, and the feeling was still new and green, but it was love.

And it was love for a man I thought I would only ever hate. A man that was my complete opposite in every way and the opposite of everything I thought I wanted.

Thank God for that.

Chapter Twenty-Three

*T*he next three weeks passed in stolen make-out sessions behind Lilou and morning phone calls that lasted hours. For as much as I'd fought for a place in the food industry, I was starting to hate being a chef.

Or at least, having the hours of one. And Killian's were worse.

We loved what we did, but officially hated working. I wanted a date. A real one that didn't involve either of us cooking. I wanted to laugh over dinner and cuddle during a movie, and then I wanted hours and hours to explore his body and finally—*finally*—take our relationship to the next level.

I was ready. So. Ready.

Which honestly surprised me. Sex with Derrek had been an obligation I fulfilled because I was scared of the consequences if I didn't. The intimate part of our relationship had been another aspect of my life to control, to assert dominance. It had been enough to scare me away from sex for eternity.

And yet with Killian, I couldn't seem to hold onto those same skeletons. The ghosts of that traumatic time slipped through my fingers, bone turning to ash, tangible fear disappearing in the wake of trust. *Actual trust.*

I didn't fear Killian. I didn't fear what he would turn sex into or how I would just become another object to use.

It was hard to believe. Especially after so many years, convinced I didn't need or want sex ever again. I had been happy to ignore that part of me, the part that wanted, desired and hoped. That was easier than imagining opening myself up to a man again. So much easier than letting myself be vulnerable not just physically, but emotionally as well.

Before Killian, the thought of intimacy with any man made me physically ill.

With Killian? With Killian, I couldn't wait to discover what it would be like, what *he* would be like. When we kissed, I only wanted to keep kissing. When he touched me, I only wanted him to keep touching me—to never stop.

Because of trust. Because he had opened himself up to me first. Because he was honest and sincere and intentional with me and my heart. Because he had cultivated my confidence, gently at first, then deeper and deeper and deeper until I knew I trusted him. I *could* trust him in everything. Including a relationship.

He wasn't Derrek.

He would never be Derrek.

And I would never be the girl that dated Derrek. Never again.

"Hey, V," Molly greeted as she stepped inside Foodie. She brought a cool breeze with her, and I stood frozen still, trying to get the most of it.

The end of September had brought a change in the weather. The leaves on the trees had started changing color and began to crisp. The evening breeze now smelled like campfires and football. And I wasn't drenched in sweat by the end of every night. Still sweaty of course, just not completely soaked with it.

"Hey, Molls." I spun to face my best friend as she put her stuff down and pulled her hair into a high ponytail, fiddling with her bangs so they didn't get swept up with the rest. "Guess what?"

"What?" she asked around the hair tie in her mouth.

I held up the money pouch for her. "I'm going to pay you tonight!"

She blinked at me. "Why?"

"What do you mean, why? Because you're here practically every night and you deserve at least minimum wage."

She snorted a laugh. "Well, as flattering as that sounds, no thank you. I don't need money. I'm here because I want to be."

"No way," I argued. "I'm paying you. I've totally taken over your life since I've been back in town. I keep you from your other friends and fun Friday nights. You don't even date anymore, and it's because of me."

"Please, I don't have other friends. At least not ones that mean as much as you. And I don't want to date. That has nothing to do with you. I'm sick of dating boys playing dress up as men." She dropped her hands to her hips and held my gaze. "Plus, I don't want to be anywhere else but

236

here. That's enough payment for me—that you're here and you're happy. And that you're far, far away from Chef Douchebag."

My heart hiccupped with the mention of Derrek and the relationships I'd damaged when I was with him. It was hard for me to forgive myself for not coming to Molly sooner or being honest with her. I hadn't been the only one going through something at that time. Derrek had shut me away from my friends and family, but Molly had lost her best friend too.

It would have been easy to blame everything on Derrek. And don't get me wrong, he was responsible for a lot. But I also had to own up to my part. I had to be honest with myself about what I'd let him do and say and turn me into.

If for no other reason than to make sure it never happened again.

"Well, I'm still paying you," I told her smartly. "So just accept it."

Molly pushed the stool over and sat down next to the open window. "I won't. It's like stealing from a charity. I feel too guilty."

"Are you calling me a charity?" I couldn't believe her.

She avoided my eyes. "You only just got back on your feet, Vera. I'm not taking any of that away from you. You deserve every penny."

My eyes misted with tears I refused to let fall. "I couldn't have done it without you, Molly. I probably couldn't have come home if you weren't here."

"You would have come home for your dad," she chided. "That's not even a question. How is he doing by the way?"

It was so like Molly to steer the focus of the conversation away from her. She hated being the center of attention. And she hated whenever anyone made a big deal about anything she did. Which was why she was a graphic designer instead of an artist.

I took a deep breath and let it out slowly. "He's okay. He finally gave into surgery. So that's scheduled for the end of the month."

"I thought he wasn't going to do it?"

Swallowing through a lump of emotion, I said, "Vann and I have finally convinced him to stick around a little while longer. He's doing it for us."

She nodded, absorbing the information with thought. "And then more chemo?"

I mimicked her head bobbing. "Only if the surgery doesn't work."

Reaching out she squeezed my hand. "He's going to pull through, Vere. He's too strong to let this defeat him." I hoped she was right. "Oh." Molly sounded so disappointed that for a second I panicked thinking her sudden emotional shift had something to do with my dad.

"What?"

She slid off her stool and walked to the back of the truck. "You have a customer."

Sure enough, I did. Ezra Baptiste approached the window looking like an editorial for GQ. He fiddled with the cuffs of his crisp white oxford, tugging one in place above a matte black watch. He appeared bored and casually aloof, and so handsome it hurt to look directly at him.

Molly had scurried to the back of the truck like a scared church mouse, and that left me in charge of the window. But my feet refused to move. Ezra was the most intimidating man I would probably ever meet.

Almost as much as Killian had been at first.

He didn't wait for me to walk to the window. His shrewd gaze focused with laser-like accuracy over me in a quick, assessing glance. "Vera, right?"

I finally mustered the courage to walk over to him, wondering if this had something to do with Killian. "Yes."

His expression remained serious. "What's on your menu tonight, Vera?"

Narrowing my gaze, I tried to figure out if he was for real. He wanted to order from me? "Cubano and duck fat fries."

His eyes flickered over the truck, the front, the signage, the inside through the windows. He took his time deciding whether the dish sounded appealing or not. Finally, with a sharp nod and another tug on his sleeve causing his cufflinks to wink in the light coming from the truck, he said, "I'll take it. One, please."

This had to be a joke. "Are you Killian's spy tonight?" I asked, mostly kidding. Killian stopped sending his version of secret shoppers a while ago. There was no need when he stopped by every night to tell me his opinion in person. He'd also helped me craft the weekly menu option, so his opinions were a lot more positive recently.

He made a sound in the back of his throat. "Killian's spy? I'm not sure what that means, but I can assure you, no. Killian didn't send me. In fact, he probably wouldn't be the happiest if he knew I was here." He held out his money, and since I had no idea how to respond to that ambiguous explanation, I took it.

Attempting a confident smile, I pointed to the other window. "Give me a few minutes, and I'll have it ready for you down there."

He nodded, taking a step back. His gaze once again inspected the inside of the truck, absorbing every inch he could see through the windows. The second he found Molly hiding out in the back, his frown turned into… more of a frown. He glared openly, not seeming to like seeing her at all.

I threw her a questioning look, but her attention was firmly on her feet.

Ignoring all the weird vibes coming from *everyone*, I started his order.

"What does he want?" Molly asked in a low voice so he couldn't hear her outside the open window.

I chuckled dryly, not believing it was true. "The Cubano."

She huffed a disgruntled sound. "He's so pretentious. I don't know how Killian works with him."

"They grew up together," I explained. "I think he's the closest thing Killian has to a BFF, although he would never admit that."

Molly let out a wobbly breath that could have been a laugh under different circumstances. "Can you imagine what those two are like together? No offense, Vera, and by the way I'm super happy for you, but I feel like they would just sit around discussing politics and retirement plans. Never smiling."

My laugh was less subtle. "You might be onto something." I focused on the food for a few minutes, thankful that no other customers had shown up yet because I didn't think Molly planned to move from her spot in the corner until Ezra Baptiste had officially disappeared. "What's your deal with him?" I finally whispered. "Why are you hiding from him?"

She threw me a look that screamed *duh!* "He has terrible taste in design."

"Oh. Right. Then do you also hate me?"

Stepping closer to me, she dropped her voice even lower. "You don't have terrible taste in design. You have *specific* taste in design. There's a difference."

"Seriously, Molls, what is it with him that's got you all flustered?"

She rolled her eyes and crossed her arms at the same time—the universal body language for *back the hell off*. Of course I didn't. I paused what I was doing to poke her in the arm.

"I just don't like him, okay? He asked for my opinion on his website when we were at Lilou, so I gave it to him. He didn't like it apparently, so he picked it apart completely. He didn't really want my opinion. He just wanted me to tell him what he wanted to hear. When I called him on it, he got even more defensive. We just don't see eye to eye. And on top of that, he's super intimidating. He makes me uncomfortable."

Well, she had me there. He *was* super intimidating. I finished plating his food and walked it to the window. He stood away from the truck, typing furiously on the small keyboard of his phone.

I hesitated for a second not knowing how to address him. On one hand, he was Killian's good friend, which made us kind of familiar, right?

239

On the other hand, he was a super important titan in the industry I was trying to survive in, and that had made me spend five extra minutes on his food to make sure it was perfect in every way.

Ezra? Or Mr. Baptiste? Or Mr. Ezra Baptiste?

Just kidding. The last one was overkill. *Definitely, overkill.*

I cleared my throat and went with my instincts. "Um, your order is ready."

He looked up from his phone, clicking it off and shoving it in his pocket when he saw me half-hanging out of the pickup window. Closing the space between us in five smooth paces, he grabbed the box from me with robotic efficiency.

As I explained where the napkins and plastic utensils were, he studiously ignored me in favor of checking out his order. He flicked the top of the French bread with his pointer finger, but it stretched in protest, anchored by a heavy amount of Swiss cheese. He made that sound in the back of his throat again and pushed the decadently greasy fries around with the same finger.

When he finished jabbing at his order, he reached for a napkin and wiped his hands clean. Then he lifted his gaze and inclined his head toward the sidewalk. "Do you have a few minutes to talk?"

"Uh, sure." The words were out before my panicked brain could stop them.

Ezra stepped to the side of the truck to wait for me. Molly's eyebrows were scrunched together over her nose as I gave her a helpless shrug, wiped my hands on my apron and left the safety of my truck.

The cool night settled on my heated skin like a sigh of relief. I inhaled deeply, enjoying all the different smells of the city and the kitchen I could never quite wash off.

I found Ezra several yards away from Foodie, closer to the alley than the street. He'd polished off half the sandwich and fries before I caught up to him by taking gigantic bites that didn't fit his polished style. He appeared all tailored professional, but he'd just inhaled his order like an animal.

Uhh… I took his voracious appetite as a compliment. Sort of.

Spotting me, he wiped his hands on his napkin again and extended it. "We haven't had a proper chance to meet yet."

I shook his hand for the second time in my life and resisted the urge to text Killian and demand he get over here and explain his friend's bizarre behavior. "Thanks for stopping by the truck," I told him sincerely. "Killian has spoken so highly of you."

He gave me a look that said he didn't believe me. "Killian doesn't speak highly of anyone."

Well, he had me there. I didn't know what to say to that, so I stayed silent, hoping he would get to the point.

"Except you."

Ezra's words caught me so off guard I took a physical step back. "W-what?"

"Except you," Ezra repeated, slower. "He can't stop talking about you, in fact."

I attempted a coherent sentence. "Uh, yeah, we, uh… yeah." And failed.

He stood up taller, squaring his shoulders, his expression shifting from serious to very, very grave. Oh, God, this man was going to make me cry.

Not in an emotional way. But in the visceral, slice me apart professionally way. I could feel it coming, like electricity in the air before a big storm.

"Be careful with Killian."

What??? "What?"

"He doesn't care for things easily. It's even harder for him to care about people."

My mouth dried out and my chest burned with the need to defend myself from what I was realizing was a warning. Not wanting to jump to conclusions, I said, "I don't understand what you're trying to say."

In a moment of what I could tell was rare weakness, he ran his hand through his hair, messing it up. On a bitter chuckle, he explained. "I trust too easily. My restaurants can attest to that. But Killian is the opposite. He doesn't trust people. He doesn't let them in. Work is his life and, until you, that's always been enough for him. I just… I worry for him. I'm asking that you're careful with him. Don't break him."

Fire burned through me, engulfing my esophagus with angry flames that spilled out of my mouth. "I won't. I would never." What I didn't say was that I had been broken by someone else. I would never hurt another person in the same way.

Especially not Killian. The person that had healed big parts of my shattered heart. The man that had pushed his way into my life uninvited and demanded that I ask for more, do more… be more.

He stared at me, taking in my furious eyes and firm frown. Seeing something he approved of, he nodded. "Thank you."

"I'm not doing it for you." I struggled to explain. "I… what you don't know is… Just know that I won't hurt him. I care about him too much."

He jerked his chin in concession one more time, his shoulders relaxing just barely. "There's one more thing."

I resisted the urge to turn my back and end the conversation. Ezra barely knew my name, let alone anything about my relationship with Killian. His warning didn't endear me to him at all. But all of Killian's comments about Ezra finally made sense.

Reminding myself that this was Killian's friend and the owner of three highly successful restaurants, I bit my tongue and waited.

He held my gaze, unflinching. "I'd like you to apply for a job."

I blinked at him, trying to decide if this was real or if I had started hallucinating. "What?" When I'd first handed Ezra his order of food, I'd hoped to impress him. In reality, I'd basically just said "What?" for fifteen minutes straight.

Because that always made a lasting impression. *Good job, Vera.*

"Are you familiar with Bianca?"

Oh, my God.

Oh, my God.

Oh, my God.

This isn't happening. This couldn't be happening. HOW WAS THIS HAPPENING???

"I am," I croaked.

"I recently let the head chef go, and I'm having trouble replacing him. I'm wondering if you would like to audition for the position? Killian only has good things to say about you. His opinion is important to me. And he knows food. That said, I'd still need to see what you're capable of myself. I'd like to see how you are with meal progression, so a five-course would be appropriate. Although, we do have a pastry chef at Bianca, so you wouldn't need to worry about dessert long term. I'd just like to see your range, what you're capable of. I'd also like to see a few variants of appetizers, soups, salads, entrees, sides, etc. You could use Bianca's kitchen and pantry. I'm sure you'll find that it has whatever you need. If not, just let me know what you're missing, and I'll make sure it's available. I can email you the details, and we can go from there."

He stopped talking, and I just stared at him. I didn't know how to respond. He was offering me... everything. Honestly, everything I had ever wanted.

Bianca? *Was he kidding?*

Bianca was a dream kitchen. No, not a dream kitchen, *the* dream kitchen. With a reputation as good as Lilou's, my reputation would be catapulted to the next level. Or the next five levels. People would know my name, associate it with one of the best kitchens in the region. I would

242

be somebody. My budget would be nearly unlimited. I would have an entire staff working for me. I would have a reservation list that was impossible to get on.

Executive chef.

I would be the executive chef.

His hand reached out between us. "Vera?"

Clearly, he thought I was having a stroke. To be fair, I might have been. I couldn't even mentally wrap my head around his offer. "I'm sorry, I'm just trying to process everything."

His mouth twitched in an almost smile. "I understand. This is really out of the blue."

Out of the fucking blue! But I didn't say that part out loud. "Can I have some time to think about it?" My voice shook as words I hardly expected ever to say escaped. "I, I... I just opened my food truck. I'm still getting my legs under me."

His almost smile disappeared, a frown turning down his mouth instead. "Of course," he clipped out politely. "I wish I could give you all the time you need, but this is a position I need to fill soon. Can you let me know what you decide by Monday?"

It was Friday. "Yes. I can do that. I can let you know by Monday."

He nodded and began to walk away.

Realizing I had just made the biggest mistake of my career to date—which was saying something—I panicked. "Wait, I'm sorry. I hope you don't think I'm comparing my food truck to Bianca. I'm not. I just opened it, and I have quite a bit of financial responsibility tied up in it. I need to figure a few things out is what I'm saying. I apologize if it came out differently."

This time he allowed a full smile, and I nearly had heart palpitations. Good grief. No wonder he had so many ex-girlfriends. "It's fine, Vera. Really. Just because I'm used to getting my way all the time, doesn't mean I should. You deserve time to mull this over. Executive chef in any one of my kitchens is not for the faint of heart." I gulped audibly. His expression softened, taking pity on me. "But if Killian thinks so highly of you, I can't help but believe you're cut out for it."

My insides became all melty chocolate for this man that had so completely captured my heart.

Killian. Not Ezra. I barely knew Ezra.

And like I said, I was fully gone for Killian.

"Thank you, Ezra. I really appreciate this opportunity." I smiled, settling into confidence I had never felt before. Partly because I'd just been offered a dream position. Partly because Killian thought so highly of me, he'd convinced his friend I was worthy of the position, but mostly because I did feel worthy of it.

I could run Bianca. It wouldn't be easy. It would take an insane amount of work and practice and hours. But I could do it.

I'd made Foodie a success in only a few months. I could tackle Bianca, too.

The question was, did I want to?

"I'll look forward to your answer." Ezra tapped the top of the cardboard box he held. "This was delicious, Vera. Killian has impeccable taste."

My smile stretched and my chest squeezed. He'd complimented my food, but I could see in his warm expression that he meant it twofold.

I walked back to my kitchen on cloud nine, grinning from ear to ear.

"I take it you don't hate him quite as much as I do," Molly grumped. A line of people had formed, and she had a handful of order tickets.

"He offered me a job," I told her gleefully. "But even better, he approves."

"Approves of what?" Her eyes were as big as possible.

"Of Killian and me."

At that, her eyes softened, and her expression turned adoring. "Of course he does. You're perfect for each other. Now cook these before you run yourself out of business."

I took the order tickets from her unable to break my smile. The differences between Derrek and Killian went on forever. But this was one of my favorites—the best friend support. Molly's seal of approval felt amazing.

There was nothing to hide from Molly or Vann or my dad. There was nothing to keep secret or manipulate into sounding better than reality.

More of the pieces of my lost self clicked into place. I found more of me. I became more of me.

And it felt good.

For the first time in so long, I felt like me. Completely, wholly me.

Chapter Twenty-Four

"*W*e need to talk about something." Killian showed up later that night, all black t-shirt, tattooed skin and sexy beard.

I cut my eyes to Molly, wondering if I needed a rescue. Talk about what? I suddenly felt like I was in trouble for something. "Why?"

He crossed his arms, resting them on the window and leaning in the truck. "When are you out of here?"

Uh, oh.

"Things have died down. I can be done soon." I cleared my throat and focused on the bread crumbs clinging to my chef's coat. "Unless it picks up again. Then, it could be hours before I close." I looked up. "Days even."

His lips twitched. He rubbed a hand over his mouth, hiding his reaction. "That busy, huh?"

I held my poker face. "Yep."

He patted the inside of the truck, the muscles in his tanned forearms flexing and shifting. "I'll be back in an hour."

He said goodbye to Molly and started walking backward. I panicked and called after him. "Then what?"

He quirked an eyebrow at me. "Then we talk."

I stepped to the window. "About what?"

He smiled, flashing white teeth surrounded by dark, alluring beard. "Don't be so nervous, Delane. If I bite, I promise you'll like it."

Turning around, he darted across the street, leaving me nervous for an entirely different reason now.

"Vera," Molly asked in a quiet voice, "Do you just spontaneously orgasm all the time when he's around?"

I leaned against the window and bugged my eyes out. "Yes," I agreed. "All the time."

"Seriously, though, are you okay? What does he want to talk to you about?"

I shook my head, tension curling inside me once again. "I have no idea. He makes me so nervous."

She released a bubbly laugh, reminding me my fears were probably unfounded. "Why?"

Shrugging, I moved back to the galley so I could start cleaning up. "Habit, I think? I don't know. He's so intense. I never know whether to call him on his bullshit or just strip naked so he can have his way with me." I looked up at her. "Maybe I'll try shrinking into a ball and seeing what that gets me."

Molly lifted a finger, wiggling it at me. "No shrinking. You're done shrinking, Vere. You were meant to shine, friend. End of story."

I wrinkled my nose and tried to believe her. "That's not as easy as it sounds."

"The best things in life never are," she reminded me. "Doesn't mean they're not worth pursuing."

My breath of relief came from some deep recess of my soul, filled with truth and understanding and hope. For the first time in a long time... hope.

"Thanks, Molly. For tonight, and for everything else too. For being there for me even when I shut you out and became someone I'm not proud of."

She closed the distance between us, wrapping me up in a hug. I hugged her back, finding closure in our relationship I hadn't let us breach before. "It doesn't matter," she promised. "All that matters is that you're someone I'm beyond proud of now. You're someone that didn't break beneath the weight of something so ugly. You got out. You left. And you fought and fought and fought until you made something amazing. You're my hero, Vera."

I squeezed her tightly. "You're my hero too, Molls." And she was. For being the friend that didn't judge and only supported. For being the woman who didn't get herself into bad relationships. Not just because she was quiet, and so sweet and nice, but for always sticking up for herself.

246

For never being the doormat. For being beautiful and kind and giving. She was exactly who I wanted to be when I grew up.

"Now do what you need to do before Killian comes back and bites you."

I stepped back from her laughing, smiling, happier than I could remember in a long time.

Killian returned an hour later, just like he'd promised. He stepped inside the truck without an invitation and picked up a crate of leftover food. "I'm taking these to Lilou tonight, so you don't have to drive all the way over to the commissary."

"Do I get a say?"

He raised an eyebrow at me. "It's one-thirty in the morning. Do you want a say?"

I repressed a smile. "Is it okay? I mean, I don't want to get you in trouble."

He moved toward the door. "It's my kitchen. I decide what goes in it."

Okay, then.

After he'd dropped off my crates of food in *his* kitchen and locked up Lilou, he stood by while I locked up Foodie. There was something about the moment that sent warm tingles spiraling through me. The late fall night, the sounds and smells of a city I had come to adore, Killian at my side after a long, fulfilling night of doing something I loved so much... it felt *right*.

He wrapped his arms around my waist and tugged me back against his chest, resting his chin on my shoulder. "Where's your car, Molly?"

She pointed at her Jetta parked on the street. "Just there."

"We'll watch to make sure you're okay?" Killian told her.

There was an awkward silence where Molly and I had a nonverbal conversation using only our eyebrows. Eventually, she waved at both of us, a grin plastered across her smug face. "Call me tomorrow, Vere."

"Drive carefully," I answered noncommittally.

True to his word, Killian and I stood there until she'd gotten in her car and safely driven away. His arms tightened around my waist. "Ready?"

I struggled to swallow through a suddenly very dry throat. "For what?"

He kissed the spot just below my ear. "Our talk."

"Do I have a choice?"

I felt his smile against my neck. "You always have a choice, but I'd like it if you stopped being such a little chicken, got on the back of my motorcycle and let me take you home with me."

Nerves pelted my insides so abruptly I jerked in his arms. "I thought you wanted to talk?"

247

"We'll start with talking," he amended. "We can see where it leads."

This was a trick. I knew it was a trick. He hinted at fun things to get me to say yes to the un-fun things.

But it worked.

I linked my hand with his and let him pull me across the street to where his bike was parked. We decided to leave my car at Vann's shop so I could ride with him.

He threw on his leather jacket and pulled out the helmet for me. I had to redo my hair in a low ponytail to get it to fit, but I made it work. He gently cradled my helmet-covered head with two hands and grinned at me. "Fucking sexy as sin," he murmured. Then he climbed on his bike and tilted his head for me to join him.

I had jealous flashbacks of watching him take a different girl home on the back of this bike. But I quickly shooed them away. We'd both been tested since our naughty night at Lilou. We were both clean and committed to this thing between us. I didn't have to worry about nameless blondes riding home with Killian or riding him.

I just had to worry about me doing those things.

Gulp.

Leaving my chef's coat on to protect my arms during the drive, I climbed on the back of Killian's motorcycle feeling beyond bad ass. My thighs hugged the backs of his, and I linked my arms around his solid core. A shiver rippled through me, heating my body with bright awareness.

"Hold on," he called over his shoulder. I did as he said.

He started the bike and took off out of the plaza, zipping through the cool night with smooth efficiency. I clung to him, enjoying the ride and the flight of butterflies tumbling around my belly.

To calm my racing pulse, I focused on the city zooming by. The night air was crisp and just damp with the heavy dew that settled on the ground in these middle of the night hours. The streets were mostly dead, leaving plenty of room for Killian to navigate smoothly.

I stared into darkened shop windows and down dark, quiet streets. The stoplights gleamed red and green, glittering on the pavement under a night sky filled with sparkling stars.

There was something about this time of night that made me feel so achingly at home, comfortable. These were the hours I lived for and the life I was getting used to living.

I would never have a traditional nine to five job. I would never wake up with the dawn and get home in time to make a normal dinner. I would, hopefully, always head to work at odd hours and stay until everyone else was safely tucked away in bed. I would always fall asleep closer to the time that everyone else woke up and drag myself out of bed not long after so I could get to the market in time for the freshest ingredients. I would never look forward to the weekends because I got them off. No, I would anticipate them for their busy chaos, for the crowd-filled dining rooms and even later nights.

This was the life I chose. The life I fought to have.

The life I fought to keep.

Killian turned down a tree-lined street with a gorgeous limestone church on the corner. Tall, narrow spirals reached toward heaven, a golden bell nestled between the two. My heart thumped at the quaint beauty of his street and then twice more when we pulled up to a cool looking bungalow, complete with a covered porch and blue front door.

He parked his bike in the garage behind the house and grabbed my hand as soon as I'd slid off the seat. We didn't talk as he led me through his back door and into his kitchen.

Love at first sight. Maybe not with Killian, but definitely with his kitchen. Granite countertops, glass-door refrigerator, huge, stainless steel range. The center island stretched long and wide, scattered with fresh fruit and a massive wooden cutting board, one side was sprinkled with flour and a discarded dish towel. His house smelled like baked bread and roasted garlic and everything wonderful.

Killian went about flicking on lights and setting his things down. I unbuttoned my chef coat feeling silly in work clothes.

I imagined the first time at his house to be better planned. I'd pictured a sexy outfit and hair that hadn't been smashed beneath a helmet and wild from a night working in my kitchen. I'd also hoped to be perfectly groomed in all the right places and not covered in kitchen grease and pickle juice.

But to be fair, Killian never did what I expected him to do. And we never happened like I expected us to happen. So, this was all fair play.

He swung open his beautiful refrigerator. "Water? Beer? Wine?"

"Water and wine, please?"

He pulled out two cold bottles of water and tossed me one before stepping into his pantry for the wine. As he opened the bottle and set it aside to rest for a few minutes, I took a seat at one of his iron barstools. "Your house is gorgeous."

One of his shoulders lifted in a casual shrug. "It's a little much for just me. But it's like my one hang-up from growing up in the system. I wanted a nice place to come home to. And I wanted space. I wanted privacy."

I stared at him, wondering if maybe that wasn't all. Maybe that was all he wanted to admit to me tonight, but there was more from his life in foster care that left scars.

Not that he hadn't come out perfectly adjusted, but I knew better than anyone that our pasts marked us in ways we couldn't escape. They shaped us into the adults we were destined to be whether we wanted them to or not.

It was up to us how we used those experiences. We could let them own us, or we could let them be the journey they were meant to be, the stepping stones to a better life, a better self. Each moment, good or bad, a tool to give us the strength we needed to be the person we were supposed to be.

Finally, he poured my glass of wine after I'd downed most of the water. He brought it over to me, taking the stool next to mine. "How was your night?"

Twisting the stem between my fingers, I swirled the crimson Cabernet until it made a tornado in the glass. "Ezra stopped by," I said without looking at his face.

When I looked up, Killian's shoulders were tense, and the humor had drained out of him. Tension thickened the air. "He told me."

I found myself ensnared by his heated glare. "Is that what you want to talk about?"

His chin dipped once. "He mentioned that he offered you Bianca."

I swallowed against the absurdity once more, still unable to believe that happened. I'd replayed the conversation so many times by now I had started to wonder if it had actually happened or if I'd somehow imagined it. "Crazy, right?"

"No, completely understandable. Ezra's not an idiot—I knew he'd come for you eventually."

My chest hollowed out, my heart dropping to my toes in disappointment. "You don't sound pleased." I wanted to make an excuse for Killian's boorish behavior. I wanted to explain away his disappointment with me being offered a full kitchen. What was it with men and trying to keep me locked away? Fury boiled in my belly, spreading with acid-fueled frustration through my blood.

Killian shook his head, adamant. "I knew this was going to happen for you. I just didn't realize it was going to happen so soon."

"Well, not everyone thinks I have an issue with salt," I bit back. I was so done with defending my career to egotistical maniacs. Done. Over it.

But before my head could explode with irrational anger, I breathed out slowly, realizing for the millionth time that Killian wasn't Derrek. That maybe my defensiveness could be dialed back until I heard him out.

Killian's open gaze bored into mine. "Is that what you want then? Bianca?"

I nibbled on my bottom lip, before answering honestly. "It's what I thought I wanted, before Foodie. But now I don't know what to think. Honestly, at this point, I'm just happy to have been considered."

"You're kidding, right?"

His tone caught me off guard, and I leaned away from him, afraid I'd pissed him off and not able to squash the instant reaction to run and hide. "What do you mean?" I whispered.

Not catching my panic attack, Killian sat up straight and leaned forward. "You're not a consolation prize, Vera. You're a phenomenal chef. Ezra figured it out in the shortest amount of time, but soon the entire city is going to be buzzing with your name. There will be more offers for kitchens, more head chef positions to choose from. I'm glad you're happy to be considered, but think bigger... better. Don't just take the first thing thrown at you because that's all you think you'll ever get. Decide what you want in life. What do you want out of a kitchen? If Bianca is what you're looking for, then take it, but don't do it because you're afraid there won't be anything else. There will be, Vera. There will be everything else."

I stared at him, not knowing what to say or think or feel.

"I'm just saying, decide what you want. You have options."

I blinked. "Like what?"

He'd been full of energy when he'd told me I deserved Bianca. His body had been vibrating with enthusiasm and sincerity. His hands moved animatedly, and his eyes practically glowed with intensity.

Now he was still and stoic. It was like stepping out of a hurricane and into an air-conditioned room. His body stopped moving, his expression shuttered, his eyes darkened, a wall falling in place and hiding his thoughts from me.

I preferred the hurricane.

Until he spoke. And then I realized he was protecting himself. He'd pulled back to ready himself against my reaction.

But what he should have done was warn me to do the same thing. If I thought his words of affirmation were shocking, I had no way to prepare myself for what came next.

"Like me," he pitched gently and at the same time with so much weight and possibility that my knees nearly buckled beneath it. "Like us. We could do something together. Open something together."

I tried to take a deep breath and failed. "Us? You want to open something with me? You're serious?"

He must have seen something in my expression because his wariness turned soft and tender. His distance became a careful touch as if he were handling something so incredibly fragile and precious. "I'm serious. Modern American with flare. It's not original, but our dishes would be. It wouldn't be your own kitchen, per say. But you would have someone to share the burden with... the commitment."

I tried to breathe deeply again. And failed again. "Killian..."

He wrapped his hand around mine, closing it into a fist. I hadn't even realized I was reaching for him, that I'd perched on the edge of the stool readying to throw my arms around him. "Don't answer now," he said quickly. "Think about it. Take your time. I'm asking a lot."

He had no idea what he was asking. It was so much more than a restaurant or business venture. He'd looked all the way down the road and decided he wanted me to take a chance with him. He'd promised commitment in either a relationship or partnership that extended into a potentially very messy future. "You want to open a restaurant with me?" My voice was small, delicate. Breakable.

His gaze held mine with bewitching clarity, a faint smile lifting the corners of his mouth. "Yes, Vera, I want to open a restaurant with you. I want to do a whole lot more than just open a restaurant with you, but we could start there. This thing between us is real. I'm not going to stand in the way."

"How do you know?"

"What?"

"How do you know that it's real? That we're real? That you want to tie yourself to me in such a permanent way? What if we break up or end up hating each other? What if we end up hating each other because of the restaurant? This is a huge commitment, Killian. How do you know I'm the right person?"

His face relaxed, and so did his shoulders. He tightened his grip on my hand and slid to the edge of his stool too, so that our legs were slotted together and his body heat warmed my exposed skin, pulling goosebumps from my arms. "It's here." He put my hand flat against his chest. "You're here."

His heart thumped against my open palm. Fear strangled me. Panic clawed at my stomach and settled in my bones. "But what if I don't stay there?"

He shook his head, a look of utter determination transforming his expression. "It's not like that. You can't just come and go as you please."

252

He tugged on his beard with his free hand and thought about it for a second before explaining. "It's more like… like this. When I got to Jo's and got to know Ezra, for the first time in my life I realized I didn't have to be alone. I'd found my family. It was a poignant moment in my life that I can still picture to this day. I probably wouldn't have picked them myself." A playful smile danced across his mouth. "But once it happened, it was done. I can no more stop loving them than they can stop loving me. And when I found cooking. It was like this thing that just clicked. Or fastened. Or came together. I knew it was my calling. I'd found my purpose in life." His green eyes glittered with truth. "And with you. I found you, and there was this tug to get to know you, to find out everything I could about you. I couldn't ignore it. Hell, I didn't want to ignore it. As soon as I opened the door, you became more. You were significant and important and *right*. You settled inside me like you were always meant to be there. I found you, Vera, because I was supposed to find you." It was impossible to breathe at this point. This man, this brilliant, talented, gorgeous man had just poured out his heart to me, and I was going to die before I could respond because I'd stopped breathing. He continued. "At some point, we'll fight. In the future, things might get difficult. I'm never going to be an easy person to get along with. But, Vera, on the other hand, we can fight for each other. Life will likely get difficult whether we're together or not, so why not tackle it together? And I might be an asshole, but I'm an asshole that cares a very great deal for you. In fact, I might even love you."

Basically it was impossible to breathe now. I had probably turned purple. "You what?"

His hands moved up my forearms, gripping for support. Whether it was for him or me, I didn't know. "I love you, Vera. I do. I love you."

My heart fluttered, jumped, and then threatened to climb into my head, taking control of my body. It was staging a military coup against my brain and my ability to think logical, rational, clear-thinking thoughts. And I was just so close to letting it. "I love you too." The words were out of my mouth before I'd fully decided to say them. And there went my heart again, clapping… applauding… deciding right along with me that I did. I loved him. These feelings, so soul deep and life changing, were more than temporary or fleeting. They had been fought hard for. First by us as we struggled to make sense of each other. Then as we pushed beyond our pasts, beyond everything that had damaged and scarred us. Deciding I wanted to say it again, this time with clarity, I whispered, "I love you, Killian."

Awe and joy and that same emotion, that confident *love*, shown from his eyes. "I love you. And I believe in you. I believe in us."

Remembering his initial restaurant pitch, I asked, "You believe in us like as business partners?"

He slid closer to me, pressing his legs against mine, settling his hands on my hips. "Yeah, sure, business partners. I believe in us as business partners." He dropped a kiss on my nose. "And other partners too." Another kiss to the corner of my lips. Just beneath my ear, in that spot that drove me crazy. "Actually, any kind of partners. I think we make a good team."

I laughed, because honestly, this man. "You think we make a good *team*?"

His mouth found mine, kissing away the laughter. "Yes, we make a good *team*." He kissed me again, his lips moving and tasting and worshiping, making my toes tingle and my belly heat with anticipation. "Just think about the restaurant idea. If you decide it's crazy, tell me. But if you decide maybe it's not so crazy… you know, tell me that too."

Yes, sat on the tip of my tongue. But I had thrown myself into a relationship with another chef that made oh, so sweet promises before. It hadn't ended well. And while I knew that Killian was nothing like Derrek, I still hesitated. "You're out of control, Killian Quinn. I hope you know that."

He nudged my knee to the side so he could fully step between mine. I wrapped my legs around his waist and held onto his t-shirt with two fists. He didn't bother with a verbal answer. He just started kissing me again. And that was all it took.

All it took for me to relax into this very new relationship of ours. All it took for me to stop questioning and doubting and fearing every little thing.

All it took for me to give up whatever control I had left and give into his kiss and his touch and his crazy ideas that could never, possibly work.

Open a restaurant together? That was insane.

Insane.

And also brilliant.

My mind spun and spun and spun with pros and cons and the different scenarios and possibilities. But there were just too many unknowns. I couldn't possibly predict what would happen if I gave up on the two tangible futures I had- Foodie or Bianca- and went *wild card* with my future.

I pulled back from Killian when my thoughts would no longer stay silent. "You would really give up Lilou to risk everything with me?"

254

He cupped my face with his strong, calloused hands and held my gaze. "Didn't I just tell you I loved you? I would give up a hell of a lot more to risk everything for you, Vera." He shrugged one shoulder in an easy up and down bounce. "Lilou is replaceable. I know I can work in any kitchen in any restaurant and cook anybody else's food. What I want to do is work with you in our kitchen in our restaurant making our food. I want to be challenged and pushed and held accountable for this talent of mine. I can think of no other person that does all three of those things as effortlessly as you. Challenge me. Push me. Make me a better chef and a better person. And I promise to do the same for you. I promise not to stop challenging or pushing you until we find out just how crazy genius you are."

I blinked at him, terrified and overjoyed and panicked all at the same time. "I can't believe I'm thinking about this."

He kissed the corner of my mouth, teasing me with his mouth and hot, roaming hands. "I can't believe you haven't said yes yet," he countered on a rumbled murmur. "I'm not going to rush you, Vera. I want you to take your time and think it over. And then, go with your gut."

I laughed gently, brushing my lips along the scruff of his jawline, his beard softly scratching against my skin. "You think my gut will lead me to you."

He nodded, not even trying to hide his smugness. "I know it will lead you to me. Just like mine would lead me to you." Without giving me time to respond, he kissed me.

And kept kissing me.

He kissed me so thoroughly I eventually wrapped my entire body around him and let him carry me to his bedroom.

Leaving the lights off, he tossed me on cool sheets and a rumpled comforter, then followed me down. Our bodies fit together in tangled seduction as he kissed me and kissed me and kissed me. Our hands moved over each other—greedy, seeking, discovering. And then our mouths joined in the chase, tasting each other's skin and bodies and secret places as we gasped for breath, numb and tingly with satisfaction.

Our clothes disappeared, one piece at a time until we were nothing but naked, hot skin and blinding desire. Need pooled in my core, want pulsing through every inch of my body.

Killian hovered over me, sitting back on his knees to take a moment to admire my body. Even in the darkness, it wasn't easy to stay still. Insecurities twisted the beauty of our moment, whispering poisonous lies about my body, about what he would think of me. I wanted to be confident and clear-minded, but his gaze was too hot, too searing.

When I covered my breasts with a self-conscious arm, he tsked and reached for my hand. He laid it against my side so he could look at me once again. "Lovely," he whispered with a husky, lust-filled voice. "So fucking lovely."

My heart kicked in my chest. I wanted to say the words back to him, but I doubted he wanted to hear that I thought he was lovely too— gorgeous. He was *perfect*. All toned muscles and tanned skin. His tattoos blurred in the dark room, but I had them memorized by now. He made my mouth dry, and my insecurities melt away.

This man was mine.

Lifting my hands, I circled them around his neck and pulled him back to me. Our mouths found each other instinctively, and our hands moved over each other's bodies, learning the way, discovering all the wonderful, intimate things that drove the other crazy.

When at last, his knees spread my thighs open, I was gasping desperate pleas for more against his mouth. He reached for a condom from the nightstand and fumbled for longer than I would have liked.

"Killian!" I growled.

He figured it out and swooped down. His chest brushed against mine, his length pressing at my core. "So impatient," he murmured.

And then there was no more reason to complain. He moved inside me, filling, satisfying, driving me to a breathless precipice. We found our rhythm, pushing, pulling, the way we always were together.

My legs wrapped around his waist, needing him deeper. His kisses trailed over my throat, down to my collarbones. He took a nipple in his mouth, and I arched against him, desperate for more... for everything. And then he gave it to me. We came together in a panting, sighing, gasping harmony. Fireworks exploded behind my eyes and every part of me tensed in delicious climax.

He was all tight muscle and hungry need until it was over, then he settled next to me in a languid pile of satisfaction. "I love you, Vera Delane."

It was less of a shock now, now that I was half dazed from sensation and bliss. "I love you too, Killian Quinn."

We fell asleep bare naked and totally intertwined, legs, arms and torsos wrapped together in sated intimacy. He held me through the night, and my heart responded to the sweetness of his touch with clear acceptance.

I woke up thinking crazy thoughts about our future together... about our kitchen. I woke up smiling and laughing and delirious with happiness. Which was probably why I stayed with him all morning. He kept me close, never taking his hands off me, not even when he made the best pancakes I had ever had. I mean, ever. I mean the best pancakes in the history of pancakes.

It was also probably why I didn't shut down his restaurant idea. Not the night before. Not in the morning. And not when he dropped me back at my car.

I didn't even shut it down when he sent me a reminder text later that afternoon to just "Think about it."

So instead of going away, this impulsive, short-sighted, irrational idea grew like a weed instead.

Or a flower.

It grew like a tree that had started as a fragile seed but now stretched toward heaven with heavy, fruit-filled limbs, a thick, sturdy center and roots that plunged deep in the dirt. Maybe his idea wasn't totally crazy.

Maybe, just maybe, I'd started to realize how very brilliant he was instead.

Chapter Twenty-Five

I flung the door of Foodie open and practically threw the crates of food inside. Thank God, Killian had insisted I store them at Lilou because I was running way too late to have made it to the commissary today.

Granted, I decided my hours and if my customers had to wait, then so be it. Except I couldn't get myself to relax! I'd stayed way too late at Killian's this afternoon. Then I'd wasted even more time sitting on the edge of my bed thinking about his offer.

Killian Quinn wanted to open a restaurant with me.

With me.

He wanted to open a restaurant with me.

It was so crazy I almost didn't believe it happened. Throw on top of it the offer to audition for Bianca? What was happening to the world!

This was the end. It had to be.

I leaned out the window and looked for the giant meteor on its way to obliterate Earth. Nothing. The North Koreans then.

It had to be.

Realizing I'd frozen, and instead of *mise en place*, I'd gone back to staring blankly while I tried to make sense of Killian's offer, I shook myself out of the stupor and got to work.

Prepping everything for a night of orders took some time, and I lost myself in chopping, dicing, julienning and all the other knife-involved tasks. When Vann showed up three hours later, I was only just starting to believe I could open on time.

He stepped inside Foodie and whistled low. "Whoa, Vera. Last minute menu change?"

I wiped sweat from my brow with the towel tucked in my apron, pausing for a second to say hi to him. "I got a late start today."

"I can see that."

I rolled my eyes at my brother's self-righteous attitude. As if he'd never been late to open Cycle Life. Please.

"If you want to help, I'm not going to stop you," I told him.

He made a noncommittal sound in the back of his throat but grabbed an apron anyway and tied it around his waist. "Give me a job."

I grinned at him. "Don't you just love learning all these new life skills? Just think, without me, you wouldn't even be able to make your boring steel cut oats."

He washed his hands which I interpreted as his expression of eternal gratitude. "Why are you so happy?"

"Happy?" I tried to suppress a smile. "Me?"

"Yeah, you. You're like you used to be, all bubbly and shit. Why?"

"Bubbly and shit?"

He gave me a look. "Stop answering all of my questions by repeating my questions."

I covered my stupid grin with my hand and turned away from him. "I don't know what you're talking about."

"Vera," he chided. "Is this some weird after sex mood or something? Because that's gross. I shouldn't have to be subjected to this."

He started to take off his apron, even though he'd just put it on. "Stop!" I held up a hand, the smile finally breaking free even though he was acting a fool. "Seriously, this has nothing to do with sex." Mostly nothing to do with sex. "I'm just happy. Can't I be happy?"

His expression softened. "You know I want you to be happy. It's all I want for you."

My smile stretched wider. "Thank you."

He pointed at me. "But something else is going on. This isn't just normal happy. This is psychotic happy. Are you on drugs?"

Groaning, I finally gave into the truth. "Ezra Baptiste asked me to audition for the head chef position at Bianca yesterday."

Vann blinked at me. "You're kidding?"

"I'm not."

"That's incredible, Vera! Congratulations!"

"I'm still freaking out. I can't believe it."

"Believe it, Vere. You deserve it."

I stared at my brother, wondering what he would think of my next announcement. "There's more."

He laughed at the absurdity of there being more. "What?"

"Killian counter-offered. He wants me to open a restaurant with him."

"Holy shit!" Vann exclaimed.

"I know."

"He was serious?"

My eyebrows drew together at my brother's doubt. "Yes, he was serious."

"Right." Vann nodded unconvincingly. "Of course he was."

"Vann, he was." I went on to explain our conversation last night and some of the sweeter things Killian had said and promised. I left out the more intimate details of course.

Vann listened attentively, absorbing my words with thoughtful consideration. I had been worried about sharing everything with Vann, but now I realized how silly that was. My brother was incredibly wise. I should have gone to him first when everything happened with Derrek. But I was so glad I came to him with this. I was a lucky little sister to have a big brother so willing to listen, so invested in her life. He was my hero. Hands down.

"What are you going to do? I mean, a restaurant with Killian? Kind of risky, huh?"

"Super risky. But Bianca would be too, I guess."

Vann thought about it for a minute, rubbing his fingers along his jawline. "But the food truck is risky too, I suppose. You're kind of gambling any way you decide."

He was right. The food truck had no certain future. And the Bianca job wasn't even a sure thing. It was just an offer based solely on Killian's very biased opinion of me.

"That's true." My exuberant mood chilled into pensively serious. "It's crazy right? Tell me it's crazy."

"Which thing? They're all crazy to me."

I smiled at my brother's dry humor. I hoped it was humor anyway. "The Killian thing. I mean opening a restaurant with a man I'm only just getting to know? That's insane."

"You keep saying words like crazy and insane and risky, but Vera, the best things in life are all of those things. You can't reap big rewards if you don't take big risks."

My stomach clenched with fear and anticipation. Also with hope. "What should I do?"

Vann stuck his hand into his pocket and pulled out a quarter. Rubbing it between his thumb and forefinger, he said, "Let's take the food truck out of the equation for just a minute. We can add it back in later. But first, let's tackle your two offers." He held up the coin. "Heads it's Bianca. Tails it's Killian. Yeah?"

I sucked in a steadying breath. This was a technique he'd taught me a long time ago. "Yeah."

Vann flipped the coin up in the air, the silver of the coin glinted against the steel ceiling of the food truck. Vann reached out to grab it, but I moved for it at the same time, suddenly afraid of what it would reveal. Our hands bumped into each other, causing both of us to miss.

The clinking of the quarter against the floor resounded through the galley like a fire engine. Or at least that was how it felt. We both looked down.

"Heads, Vera. Bianca."

Vann raised his eyes to meet mine that had nearly bugged out of my head. "Heads," I confirmed.

"So how do you really feel?"

That was the trick of the coin toss. The answer always revealed your true feelings. If Bianca made me feel relieved, I would have known Bianca was the right answer. If Bianca had caused disappointment, then I would have known Killian was the right answer.

"Vera?" Vann pushed. "What's it going to be?"

"Vera."

My answer died on my tongue when that familiar, grating voice called my name through the window. Vann and I both turned to look at the same time.

Derrek stood in the window looking like he did the first time he'd visited. Only this time it wasn't dark yet. Dusky evening swirled in the sky turning clouds to rosy pink and grayish purple. His features were clearer in the natural light, not exaggerated like before under the glare of Foodie's spotlights, not twisted from my personal fear or agony.

I was in no danger of going back to Derrek anymore. There was nothing that could tempt me from my new life. Even if things with Killian went badly, they wouldn't go violently.

They wouldn't leave me a shell of myself, broken, bruised, beaten.

And I would still be better off than when I was with Derrek. I'd tasted freedom and finally found healthy. I wasn't willing to go back.

I'd settled back in my body. My bones were mine again. My thoughts belonged only to me. My future was mine alone to decide.

It was the best feeling in the entire world. Better than head chef offers and boyfriends that made me smile like a lunatic. Better than this career I loved so very much or the dreams I was just beginning to chase again.

Knowing myself... *being myself* was better than anything else.

It was the very best thing.

But before I could say any of that out loud, Vann stepped to the window and clenched his fists, hammering them on the ledge. "Are you fucking kidding me, man? It was the wrong move to show up here."

"I just want to talk to her, Vann. Relax."

Vann's spine turned to granite. He jabbed a finger in Derrek's direction. "Don't tell me to relax, asshole. I will annihilate you."

I hoped Derrek believed Vann because I did.

Derrek held up his hands. "I'm not trying to start trouble. I would just like to talk to my girlfriend."

"Ex."

Both men turned to me. "What?" Derrek asked.

"Ex-girlfriend. I'm your *ex*-girlfriend."

He shrugged. "That's what I meant."

That wasn't what he meant. He'd already started his manipulation game. I didn't even think he noticed. It was such a part of who he was that he couldn't stop it.

When I didn't make a move or open the conversation further, he pushed forward with his agenda. "Will you talk to me, Vera? I drove all the way here. I closed my kitchen for tonight. For you. I just want the chance to talk. That's all."

I stared at him, taking in his worth with a glance. This man that I had once been so enamored with, that had wowed me with his talent, smooth compliments and good looks was so lacking now. So... unimpressive.

A flush of embarrassment washed over me. I couldn't believe I'd fallen for him... gotten sucked into something so toxic *with him*.

I surprised myself by saying, "Yes."

Vann swung to face me, his eyes bugging out of his head. "Vera, you can't be serious."

"We can talk," I told Derrek. "But that's it."

Derrek glanced at Vann. "Can we go somewhere?"

I pointed to the side of the truck. "We can go right there. I'm not closing my kitchen for you. Ever."

A sour look of disappointment crossed his face, but he quickly hid it behind penitent remorse. "Fine."

He stepped back, moving to the place where my customers usually stood around eating their orders. Orders I made for them. Out of my truck. From the safety and success of my new life.

"Are you sure?" Vann asked in a low voice as I moved to walk past him.

I held his gaze. "If he touches me at all, you have my permission to beat him to a bloody pulp."

Vann grinned at me. "You're not going out there to make up with him?"

"I'm going out there to tell him to leave me alone and never, ever come back."

My brother pressed his hands to the sides of my head, squeezing like only big brothers did and kissed my forehead. "Proud of you, Vere."

I ducked under his arm. "Even if it's just like a finger, Vann, beat his ass."

Vann's chuckle followed me out the door to where Derrek waited for me. I approached with wariness, but determination too. This needed to happen. He wasn't going to leave me alone until he realized I was no longer scared of him. Till he understood that we were never, ever going to happen again.

Derrek's sneer reminded me of so many bad nights with him. And yet this time it couldn't touch me. Even if it still turned my stomach. "Vann's playing bodyguard now?"

"Well, I need one when you're around. So, yeah. I guess he is."

"Vera," he groaned. "You're not serious."

"Derrek, I realize that you are living in some delusional alternate reality where you've convinced yourself that you didn't do anything wrong and that I'm at fault for all that happened between us. But the truth is, you're a horrible person. The way you treated me is completely unacceptable. I am lucky to have gotten away from you, and that's where I'm going to stay."

A muscle in his jaw ticked, and he shoved his hands in his pockets, probably restraining them from what he wanted to do. "What happened to you?" He leaned forward, getting in my face. "Did you join some kind of cult I don't know about? You're a completely different person."

I looked at the sky, hoping to find patience, but then my glare returned to Derrek's face because even if I'd found myself, I still knew exactly who he was and I didn't trust the slimy bastard. "The problem is not that I'm a different person, but that you're the same person. I can't be with you, Derrek. Frankly, I don't want to be with you. Burn my things or give them to charity or whatever, but we are so over."

"Therapy," he threw out. "Is that what you want? Couple's therapy? Because, Vera, I can do that. You're making me out to be some kind of monster, but you're not perfect either. It's not fair to pin this all on me."

I swallowed back the need to defend myself. It wasn't easy. I wanted to scream at this man, this *idiot* that couldn't see his own faults and wanted to make this about our relationship problems instead of the real issues.

But I couldn't get sucked into his manipulation game. If I engaged his rhetoric, then he got to dictate the direction of the conversation.

And he was right. I wasn't perfect. I might be justified. I might be right. I might have had every reason to flee. But I wasn't perfect.

"Derrek, I don't want to go to couple's therapy. I want you to acknowledge that it's over between us."

"So that's it?" His sneer came back, twisting his features into a terrifying snarl. "You're just going to give up on us? Walk away after all the time and energy I put into making you happy? You're going to turn your back on me after *everything*?"

I nodded, surprised to find tears lurking in the corners of my eyes. "I am."

"Vera," he growled, low and menacing. "This is a big mistake."

The next words took the most amount of courage I had ever used. It was one thing to run away without facing him. It was one thing to have the men in my life chase him away when I couldn't protect myself. But it was an entirely other thing to stand up for myself, to speak the threat that needed to be said. "And I'm filing a restraining order. Today. I told you in my text that I would if you bothered me again. You chose not to listen to my warning. So now I have no choice but to follow through."

He lunged forward, bringing us nose to nose. "Bullshit!" he yelled, snapping whatever restraint had been holding him back. "Bullshit, Vera! A restraining order? Are you fucking kidding me? *What is wrong with you?*"

"Hey!" Vann rushed out of Foodie at the same time Killian darted across the street, shouting the same thing.

Both men surrounded me, pulling me back from Derrek and stepping in between us. "Back off," Killian yelled.

"Get out of my way, Quinn," Derrek barked. "This isn't your business."

"Wrong." Killian rolled his shoulders, and even under his chef coat, they were intimidating. "She's absolutely my business. What she isn't is yours. She wants nothing to do with you, man, so back the fuck off."

Vann stood at my side, his arm wrapped around my shoulders protectively. "Leave, Derrek, before we call the cops."

Derrek laughed, but it sounded slightly hysterical. "That's ridiculous! I haven't done anything wrong. We were just talking."

Killian had zero patience for his lies. "Leave," he ordered. "Or I'm going to make this very public. And that would be very bad business."

Derrek ground his teeth together, the muscles in his jaw popping and flexing. He looked at me, ignoring the men at my sides. "This is really what you want? After all we've been through? This is how you want to end it?"

I felt sick, irrationally guilty and overwhelmed at the same time. "Yes." My voice was stronger than I felt. Despite my earlier bravado, this was *hard as hell*. "This is what I want, Derrek. It's over between us. I'm filing the restraining order today. I don't want to see you again."

"It's done then," he spat. "You don't have to file a fucking restraining order. I get the message."

"Okay." I wasn't going to argue this with him. He could leave and maybe I really would never see him again. But I wasn't going to take the chance.

He glared at me for another long moment, conveying hate and anger and maybe even something like surprise. But eventually, he turned around and walked back to his car. He didn't look at me again. His tires ground against the pavement as he peeled away from the sidewalk, plunging into traffic like a bat out of hell.

His silver Lexus disappeared in the crush of Saturday evening traffic, and then he was gone. Hopefully forever.

My entire body slumped with relief. Vann caught me against him, squeezing my arm tight with encouragement.

Killian turned around and practically snatched me from Vann's arms. He crushed me against his chest, holding me tightly to him as if I'd just been through some traumatic life or death accident.

The truth was, Derrek hadn't even gotten physical. This last exchange of ours was mild compared to others. And yet it felt like a kick in the gut.

Adrenaline slipped from my blood, leaving me weakened and shaky. I couldn't get over the feeling that I'd just fought some major battle and won. From the outside, it might have seemed anticlimactic, but to me, to my heart, to my fragile spirit that had fought so hard to get away from Derrek, that confrontation had been years in the making.

I'd gone through hell to get here. My soul had been razed and rebuilt. My dreams had been lost and then found again. I'd given myself up to someone who didn't deserve me, and then I'd fought tooth and nail to have a life I did deserve—the happiness and relationship and man I deserved.

Killian's strong arms were like a brace around me, holding me up and reminding me that he was here for me, that he wasn't going anywhere.

When my mind finally stopped spinning and my body evened out, I pulled back and looked at him, traced the lines of his face and the depths of his eyes. I saw the answer to the coin toss there. I felt the disappointment fresh and fierce as I remembered the coin showing Bianca on the floor.

I didn't want Bianca.

And I didn't want Foodie unless Killian was involved.

I wanted this man. I wanted him more than I had even wanted culinary school or my own kitchen or the food truck that saved my life. I wanted him and a future with him and to work side by side with him for as long as I was able.

He cradled my face in his hands, calloused palms scratching against my jawline. "I love you," he whispered. He didn't ask if I was okay. He didn't ask me how I felt. He told me the words I needed to heal, to move on, to remember the life I wanted and the future I was willing to work so hard for.

"Yes."

One side of his mouth lifted in that arrogant smile and his green eyes twinkled knowingly. "Yes to what?"

"Yes to everything."

His smirk became a smile. "And what else?"

I laughed, because seriously. This man. "And I love you."

His eyes warmed, and he looked down at me with so much adoration and awe that I felt it all the way to my bones. "Yes, to everything." His thumb slid over my cheekbone. "And I love you." When he kissed me, it wasn't gentle or sweet, it was demanding and desperate. He kissed me with the promise of a future in front of us. He kissed me with the truth of who he was, the man he would always be, but also the man he would become because of me. And I kissed him back, promising those same things.

When he pulled back, I missed him immediately. A secret smile still danced in the corners of his mouth, hidden by his beard unless you knew where to look. He held me close and said, "Now can we please go file that damn restraining order."

Laughing because I couldn't contain my happiness, I looked across the street. "What about Lilou?"

"They're going to have to learn how to survive without me. They might as well start tonight."

"But there's no chef!" Even through my happiness, I knew that Ezra Baptiste was not someone you made an enemy.

"Eh," Killian shrugged, knowing, confident, cocky as hell, "I was planning on recommending Wyatt for the position anyway. Ezra won't notice."

"Ezra's going to notice," I protested.

Killian gave me a mischievous side eye, "But what can he do about it?" While I sputtered for an answer, Killian grabbed my hand and pulled me toward Foodie. "Now let's lock up and get to the police station. I have other plans tonight, so we're going to need to wrap this up as quickly as possible."

"What other plans?"

Vann stepped away, reminding us both he was still there. Covering his ears, he said, "I don't want to know. For the love of God, wait until I'm gone."

Turning to my brother, I said, "Thanks for everything, Vann."

He grinned at me. "Looks like you finally hired some help, yeah?"

Killian squeezed my hand. "It's about time."

"I think I'll make him work the window," I told Vann, ignoring Killian's smug satisfaction. "He might just be pretty enough to bring in some extra cash."

"As long as I get to control the salt, I don't care where you put me," Killian countered.

I slapped his chest with the back of my hand, which he then caught and pressed against his heart. The message was there in that sweet, subtle gesture. I was in him, and he was in me. We were complete opposites, but we'd been made for each other.

We said goodbye to Vann and locked up Foodie. Then together we went to the closest police station. Filing a restraining order wasn't as easy as I thought it would be. It took work and a lot of standing up for myself, which was hard since it was practically a new concept for me.

But I had Killian there with me, supporting me when I needed it and stepping in for me when I needed that too.

At the end of this journey, I so wanted to be the tough girl. I wanted to kick ass and take names every damn day. But some things, I was learning, were personality based. Conflict wasn't my thing. Making people do exactly what I wanted them to do was hard for me. And if I never got myself into a Derrek situation again, I could be okay with that.

By the time we left the station, the sun had been down for a while. It was Saturday night, and we were both supposed to be working. This was the busiest night of the week. We had kitchens to run, food to cook, money to make.

Instead, we climbed onto Killian's motorcycle and ignored everything but each other.

"Let's go grab some dinner," he said over his shoulder.

"Like a real date?"

He gave me his profile so I could see the smile and his beard and his gorgeous face. "Like a real date."

Chapter Twenty-Six

I stepped inside Foodie and quickly shut the door behind me. I wouldn't need to open the windows to let cool air in today. It was frigid outside.

Well, maybe not frigid, but the November breeze was biting as it chased the sunlight outside. I rubbed cold fingers together and wished for warmer days. I'd rather be sweaty and overheated than frozen.

Or so I told myself now. Just wait until the middle of summer. I might feel differently then.

I looked around the familiar space and brushed my fingers over the cool surfaces and smooth steel. It was going to be one of the last times I got to stand inside her and not just because winter was almost here.

I'd sold her.

I couldn't believe it either.

But after much thought and consideration and many, many business meetings, we'd decided that it was for the best.

We were moving on from the food truck business and dipping our toes in the restaurant business. Or rather, plunging headfirst into the restaurant business.

Killian and me.

I smiled at my blurry reflection, unable to believe it even after all this time.

Killian and I were opening a restaurant together. Killian and I were moving in together. Killian and I were... together.

And I had never been happier.

Or more myself.

It turns out I wasn't such a doormat after all. I just needed the right relationship to push me. I needed the right man to challenge me.

It was easy to stand up to Killian. Not because I didn't care about his feelings or what he thought, but because I had confidence that he cared about me, that he wouldn't leave me because of a dumb fight or my unflinching opinion on how the dishwasher should be filled.

I fought back because he mattered to me. I wasn't just surviving with him. I was living, really, truly living.

And because it weirdly turned him on.

The door opened and Vann stepped inside, closely followed by my dad. "Hey there, baby girl," my dad greeted gently. "How are you?"

I eyed the bottle of wine in Vann's hand. "Better now that you're here."

Dad ran his fingers over the hammered wall. "It's hard to believe you're already sending her on her way. It's like she just became part of the family. Now I have to say goodbye."

Vann sighed. "Yeah, we'll all miss those nights you worked us to the bone and didn't pay us."

I stared at my brother. "It's really hard for you to sit at the window and make change? That was really difficult?"

He glared at me, but my dad stepped in and said, "Now, Vera, you know he's more sensitive than you."

I smothered a smile while my brother contemplated falling on the wine bottle like a sword. My dad went on without noticing.

"I should have bought her," he said. "I could have tried my hand at this whole cooking thing. Taken her around the country. You know, lived out my retirement on the road."

Vann and I shared a look. A relieved look. It was nice to hear dad talk about the future again. He'd been through hell with this cancer and paid the price with his health. He was practically gaunt from how much weight he'd lost. He'd stopped looking like our dad and turned frail... old.

It broke my heart to see him now, a shadow of his former self. But I also knew he was finally at the point where he could start to recover, put his weight back on. Thanks to surgery, he was cancer free! There had never been better news than that.

The door opened again, and Vann and Dad moved out of the way so Molly could step inside. She had a bottle of champagne in her hand.

"What's that?" I asked her.

"To celebrate." She held it up. "Aren't you supposed to smash it on the front before you sell it?"

I stared at her for a second, trying to decide if she was for real. "I think that's for ships. Before you sail them. Not sell them."

She hugged the bottle. "Oops!"

The door opened again, and Wyatt stepped inside. Now it was so crowded that we all had to squish around the galley. I slid onto the counter with my feet dangling, hoping to make more room. "I didn't realize this was going to be a party."

Wyatt smiled and stepped over by Molly. "We all wanted to say goodbye. I'm going to miss this truck. Now where am I going to get my fourth meal from?"

"You're head chef now, bucko. You're not going to have time for fourth meal."

He nodded solemnly. "Or third meal. Maybe not even second meal."

My dad patted him on the shoulder. "Well, there's always breakfast, son." Wyatt looked up at him curiously, and Dad added, "Most important meal of the day, you know."

While we laughed at my dad's joke, the door opened, and Ezra Baptiste stepped inside. He blinked at the five of us huddled in the galley and glanced at the door as if he wanted to run away. "Hello."

Wyatt was the quickest to recover. "Hey, boss."

Ezra stared at Wyatt. "Who's in the kitchen?"

"Killian's saying goodbye," Wyatt explained. "It was too emotional for me. All the crying and shit." He looked at me. "From Killian."

Nobody believed him.

The door opened for the fifth time and when Jo squeezed in, I knew something was up. "Okay, what's going on?" Then feeling rude, I smiled at Jo. "Hi, Jo. Welcome."

She smiled back at me and then told Ezra to shove over. "Hello, Vera Dear."

I couldn't help but ask her, "What are you doing here?"

She held out her hands. "I wanted to see what all the fuss was about. You've talked so much about the truck, I just wanted to see it for myself."

"Okay, something is going on." Glaring at each of my visitors in turn, I waited for someone to confess.

They just smiled at me like dorks.

The door opened and Killian finally stepped in. Obviously, this was his doing, but I didn't know why. Was it just a thoughtful gesture because he knew how much Foodie meant to me? I'd been bugging him all week with dramatic tears and second guesses.

273

Foodie had been everything to me when I needed her to be everything, but now it was time to chase after what I really wanted.

This truck had healed me. And introduced me to this man I loved so much. And for those two things I would always and forever be grateful.

But I also couldn't wait to see what else I could do.

Killian had given his notice to Ezra the day after I'd agreed to open a restaurant with him. He'd also recommended Wyatt to replace him. Ezra had been furious of course. And he had a right to feel that way since he still had to replace the head chef at Bianca too. Eventually Killian had convinced him it was for the better or at least that they should still be friends despite Killian's abandonment.

We'd all been a little surprised when Ezra had agreed to let Wyatt take over though. It showed just how much Ezra trusted Killian after all. Even if Wyatt wasn't totally convinced yet. Killian had spent the last two months training Wyatt in all things Executive Chef. Yesterday was Killian's last official day at Lilou, although he had to tie up all the loose ends today.

Tomorrow we would officially be self-employed.

It was awesome.

And scary as hell!

Killian squeezed through the sea of surprise guests so he could stand by me in the middle of everyone. The second he walked in the door our gazes locked. I watched him as he moved, reading the excitement and worry on his face, reaching for him as soon as he was close to me.

God, I loved this man.

"Hey."

He bent down to drop a quick kiss on my lips. "Hey."

"You invited a lot of people to a very small space," I told him.

"How do you know I invited them?"

I looked at our friends. "Because it would be weird if they just showed up."

He smiled at me, his green eyes sparking with fire and love. He held up one of my cardboard to go boxes. I wondered when he'd grabbed that since I'd cleared the excess equipment two weeks ago. "I made you something."

I stared at the closed box in his hand. The light glinted off the shiny cardboard. "You made me something?"

He shrugged, that one shoulder lifting and lowering with careless ease. "Kind of a last hoorah in the Lilou kitchen."

A tingle of anticipation zinged up my spine. "Thank you?"

He held the box out for me to take it. "I need your advice, though."

My eyes slid to Molly, but she gave nothing away but a huge, dopey smile. "About what?"

He leaned forward, our foreheads almost touching. "The flavor."

I took the box from him with trembling hands. My mind couldn't seem to make coherent thoughts. There was a part of my brain that suspected what was happening, but mostly I was numb with excitement and hope.

Opening the lid, I gasped, sucking in a sharp, needed breath of air. A glittering diamond ring winked at me from the inside, not food. He didn't need my opinion on salt! That liar!

I looked up at Killian, the box violently shaking in my hands now as I tried not to pop.

Killian's expression was filled with the kind of hope that cut straight through me, that settled in the air like a tangible, permanent thing. "I have another idea of something we can do together," he said.

"Yes," I whispered, my voice choked with emotion. "Yes, to everything."

He cradled my face in those familiar, strong hands. "And I love you?"

"And I love you," I whispered, my voice thick with emotion.

Our friends cheered and clapped, and a champagne cork popped while he swooped down to seal my answer with a kiss. Happy tears tracked down my cheeks as I struggled to kiss him through my smile.

It wasn't easy! I wanted to do both things, but the smiling was winning.

He pulled back just enough to take the ring from inside the box and my trembling left hand. He slid it on my ring finger, unable to hide the quiver in his own hands. Once it was in place, I stared at it in awe for a long, heart-fluttering minute, then he kissed me again.

"You all knew!" I accused once we'd remembered there were witnesses and we could save the fun stuff for later. I pointed at Wyatt who was recording us with his phone. "Unbelievable!" I turned to Molly. "And you! No head's up? You could have at least warned me to dress cute!" I patted my face. "Or wear makeup!"

"You're beautiful," Killian murmured, his face dipped close to mine as if he couldn't pull away. "Always."

I blinked away a fresh wave of tears, repeating, "I love you."

He smiled, that full smile that was cocky and confident and adoring and everything I loved. "I love you too, chef."

We celebrated with our loved ones long into the late hours Killian and I were so comfortable with. We made the truck home for one last memorable night, laughing and talking and planning futures that would be spent together.

And when our friends and family went home, Killian and I stayed, talking about our future together both as a married couple and as business partners. We shared hopes and fears. We laughed and held each other and then we came together on the floor of the truck unable to stay apart for a second longer.

Killian took me home on the back of his bike. I wrapped my arms around him, knowing he was everything I didn't know I wanted. He was the opposite of my plans. He was the opposite of the kind of guy I thought I wanted.

But he was everything I needed.

Thank you for reading The Opposite of You! I hope you enjoyed Killian and Vera as much as I enjoyed writing them! The second book in the Opposites Attract Series, The Difference Between Us, is coming this July. Each book is a standalone romance following a different couple! Keep reading to find out more about Molly Maverick and Ezra Baptiste.

The Difference Between Us coming July, 2017!

I'm cursed.

At least when it comes to finding Mr. Right.

I'm tired of men that only want one night stands or blind dates that are nothing but awkward and uncomfortable. I'm tired of avoiding inappropriate text messages and the constant disappointment of always meeting Mr. Wrong.

After all these years of dates that lead nowhere, I can admit that it's me. I'm the problem. I'm shy and picky and cursed. Definitely cursed.

So I've decided two things.

The first? I'm giving up dating and relationships and men in general. Maybe, possibly, forever.

The second? I'm going to have to try harder to avoid Ezra Baptiste.

If I couldn't hack it in the kiddy pool of dating, I certainly can't swim in his deep end. He's too successful. Too intense. He's all man when I'm used to nothing but boys pretending to be grownups. He's everything I'm afraid to want and so far out of my league we might as well be different species entirely.

So he'll need to find a different artist to paint his mural. And a different graphic designer to help him with his website. He'll need to find someone else to glare at and flirt with and kiss.

It can't be me.

We're too different.

Acknowledgments

To my God who is sovereign and merciful and self-sufficient. You don't need my gratitude but you have it. Thank you for this gift and for this crazy, beautiful life and for loving me so much more than I deserve.

To Zach, thank you for every single thing. This book couldn't have happened without you. You are my favorite human. I love you and your beard.

To my kids, thank you for keeping our lives so interesting. Thank you for making me pick up my head and pay attention. I love you more than the sun and the moon and the stars in the sky.

To my mom, thank you for being the strongest woman I know. You love deeper than anyone. You believe deeper than anyone. You forgive deeper. You live deeper. Basically, you're my hero.

To Lindsay, you're welcome for all the F words! I'll just never be able to read this book out loud. Ha!

To Lenore, my dearest beta. I love you, sweet friend. Thank you for always offering your smart edits, your awesome encouragement, for getting my sense of humor and for being so freaking awesome.

To Katie, Tiffany and Sarah Jo, thank you for earrings and cheesecake and laughing until it hurts. #dingledangle

To Samantha Young, Georgia Cates, Amy Bartol and Shelly Crane, thank you for friendship and advice and so much understanding. I love you girls to pieces. And without you there wouldn't be words or sanity or ads.

To Caedus Design Co. thank you for the amazing cover. You're a genius. That's a fact.

To Amy Donnelly of Alchemy and Words, thank you for your patience and expertise. Thank you for putting up with my rambling emails and unfinished projects and forgetfulness. I have so much fun working with you. I don't just love you as an editor, I love you as a friend.

To the Rebel Panel, thank you for unending support. Even when I disappear and quit social media and have a baby. You are incredible, beautiful women and I am so blessed to have you in my life.

To all of the bloggers that helped so very much with this release. Thank you for spending your time with Vera and Killian. Thank you for supporting The Opposite of You and for being just incredibly amazing! You are so very appreciated.

And to the reader, thank you for taking a chance on The Opposite of You! And these characters that mean so much to me! I wouldn't be an author without you! I am so grateful for every book you pick up and every review you leave.

About the Author

Rachel Higginson was born and raised in Nebraska, but spent her college years traveling the world. She fell in love with Eastern Europe, Paris, Indian Food and the beautiful beaches of Sri Lanka, but came back home to marry her high school sweetheart. Now she spends her days raising their growing family. She is obsessed with reruns of *The Office* and Cherry Coke.

Look for The Difference Between Us coming July, 2017!

Other Books Out Now by Rachel Higginson:

Love and Decay, Season One
Volume One
Volume Two
Love and Decay, Season Two
Volume Three
Volume Four
Volume Five
Love and Decay, Season Three
Volume Six
Volume Seven
Volume Eight
Love and Decay: Revolution, Season One
Volume One
Volume Two

The Star-Crossed Series
Reckless Magic (The Star-Crossed Series, Book 1)
Hopeless Magic (The Star-Crossed Series, Book 2)
Fearless Magic (The Star-Crossed Series, Book 3)
Endless Magic (The Star-Crossed Series, Book 4)
The Reluctant King (The Star-Crossed Series, Book 5)
The Relentless Warrior (The Star-Crossed Series, Book 6)
Breathless Magic (The Star-Crossed Series, Book 6.5)
Fateful Magic (The Star-Crossed Series, Book 6.75)
The Redeemable Prince (The Star-Crossed Series, Book 7)

The Starbright Series
Heir of Skies (The Starbright Series, Book 1)

Heir of Darkness (The Starbright Series, Book 2)
Heir of Secrets (The Starbright Series, Book 3)

The Siren Series
The Rush (The Siren Series, Book 1)
The Fall (The Siren Series, Book 2)
The Heart (The Siren Series, Book 3)

Bet on Love Series
Bet on Us (An NA Contemporary Romance)
Bet on Me (An NA Contemporary Romance)

Every Wrong Reason

The Five Stages of Falling in Love

Connect with Rachel on her blog at:
http://www.rachelhigginson.com/

Or on Twitter:
@mywritesdntbite

Or on her Facebook page:
Rachel Higginson

Keep reading for an excerpt from Rachel's second chance romance, Every Wrong Reason.

Please enjoy an excerpt from Every Wrong Reason, a second chance adult romance.

Prologue

1. He is the most selfish person I know.
2. I would be happier without him.
3. He can't take a shower without leaving water everywhere.
4. If I have to clean up his toothpaste smears one more time I'm going to go insane.
5. How hard is it to put the milk away?
6. I don't love him anymore.
7. We were never right for each other.

How did we get here?

Again?

I just wanted to go to bed. I had the most obnoxious day of my freaking life and all I wanted to do was come home, take the longest, hottest shower in the history of showers and face plant into my pillows.

Instead, it's three o'clock in the morning and I have a migraine the size of the moon. Goddamn it.

"This isn't about the water all over the bathroom floor, Nick. God, honestly! It's about the principal of the water all over the bathroom floor!"

"Are you kidding me? What the hell does that even mean?" His handsome face contorted with frustration. He wouldn't even look at me.

I thought back and tried to remember the last time he looked at me, *really looked at me*, and couldn't remember. When was the last time he saw me? When was the last time we hadn't been fighting long enough for his clear blue eyes to look into mine and make a real connection?

It had been years.

Maybe he had never seen me.

"It means there's water all over the floor! Again! How many times have I asked you to clean up after your shower? I'm not asking for much! I just want the water cleaned up off the floor so that when I go in there I don't soak my socks *every single time!*"

"You're going to take your socks off anyway! Why does it matter?" His long arms flew to his side as he paced the length of our bedroom.

I flopped back on the bed and the pillows depressed with the weight of my head. I felt like crying, but I wouldn't let something this stupid bring me to tears. I *wouldn't*.

Not again.

This whole argument wasn't really about the water. He was right; I had been planning to take my socks off. But I was so sick of asking him to do something so simple. Why couldn't he just listen to me? For once?

"Fine," I relented. "I don't care. Let's just go to bed."

"Typical," I heard him mutter.

I peeled my fingers away from my face and propped myself up on my elbows. His back was to me as he stared unseeingly at our closed blinds. I could see the tension taut through his broad shoulders. His thin t-shirt pulled on the sculpted muscle he was so proud of.

It was so late and both of us had to work in the morning, which only proved to fuel my frustration. His run had lasted forever tonight. He left shortly after dinner and hadn't come home until close to ten. I had started to think something had happened to him.

When I asked him where he was, he told me his running group had gone out for beers afterward. He'd gone out for beers and hadn't bothered to text or call or let me know he was alive and not dead in the ditch somewhere.

I'd had a terrible day and my husband got to go out for beers at the end of an excessively long run while I did the dishes, cleaned up the kitchen, started his laundry and graded papers.

And then at the end of all of it, I'd walked into an inch of standing water on our bathroom floor because he couldn't be bothered to clean up after himself.

And he wants to throw around the word "typical."

"What was that?" My voice pitched low and measured, in complete opposition to the pounding of my heart and rushing of blood in my ears.

This was not the first time we'd had such a lengthy blow up. In fact, we fought more than we got along. If I were truly honest with myself, I couldn't remember the last time I'd enjoyed being around him.

"It's typical, Kate. Just when I finally get to the bottom of why you're so pissed off, you decide to shut down and turn yourself off. You're ready for bed and I just finally figured out what crawled up your ass. So what am I supposed to do with that now? Just forget it? Move on and pretend you didn't keep me up all hours of the night yelling about it? God knows, *you* will."

"I'm tired, Nick. It's three o'clock in the morning. We both have to work tomorrow! What do you *want* me to do? I guess we could sit here and talk in circles until the sun comes up, but like you said, you finally get it!"

"God, you can be a bitch."

His words hit me like a slap across the face. "And you can be a selfish asshole."

I watched his face fall. It was that perfect kind of hit that took all of the wind right out of his sails. His entire body deflated and I knew I hurt him as badly as he hurt me. Except instead of making me feel better about myself, I realized I had never felt worse.

He slumped down at the edge of our bed and buried his face in his hands. His tousled, light brown hair fell over the tips of his fingers and reminded me of the times I used to brush it back, out of his eyes.

Even now, after seven years of marriage, he was still one of the most gorgeous men I had ever seen. His tall frame was packed with lean muscle and long limbs. His face was blessed with sharp angles and deep, soulful blue eyes, a square jaw hidden behind a closely cropped beard, like he'd forgotten to shave for a few days. His wild hair was a little longer on top than on the sides, but despite his unruly hair he had always been casually clean cut. No piercings. No tattoos. And his lips had always been dry, for as long as I could remember. But he had this way of dragging his tongue across them that used to make my mouth water.

I fell in love with him on our second date. We shared mutual friends that introduced us. My roommate Fiona was dating his track teammate, Austin, and one Saturday in October during our junior year of college, she finally hauled me along to one of their local meets.

We hit it off after he took first place in the thirty-two hundred and he was in a celebratory enough mood to not stop smiling. *I* couldn't stop staring at his lonely dimple or his bright blue eyes. He had the keen insight to know he'd charmed me.

Or maybe he just read the very obvious signs. I was not good at hiding my feelings.

Our first date was an absolute disaster though. I was awkward and he was nervous. We didn't find much to talk about and when he dropped me back at my dorm, I swore to Fiona that he would never call me again.

I never understood why he asked me out for our second date, but it was that next time, when he took me to my favorite Italian restaurant and then out for a drive that ended with trespassing and a moonlit walk through random fields in the middle of the country, that made me realize I would never find another man like him.

He had something I decided I couldn't live without. His intentional questions and quick sense of humor held my attention and his big smile made my insides melty. I had never met anyone that made me feel that way... that made it seem as if I were the only person alive that had anything interesting to say.

If every night could be like that second date I would never doubt what was between us, not even for a second. But after struggling to put up with each other for all of these years and knowing that whatever chemistry we had with each other fizzled a long time ago, I was exhausted.

I was starting to realize, I was also broken. Or if not broken, then breaking.

I couldn't keep doing this.

And while I was deciding these things I had started to collect reasons for why we weren't right for each other... why he wasn't right for me. I was organized by nature. I was a list-maker. I couldn't help but compile all of the reasons we were wrong for each other.

Even if they broke me.

Even if they destroyed us.

"What are we doing?" he mumbled into his hands.

Hot tears slipped from the corners of my eyes, but I wiped them away before he could see them. "I don't know," I whispered. My hands fell to rest against my flat stomach. "We hate each other."

He whipped his head around and glared at me over his shoulder. "Is that what you think? You think I hate you?"

"I think we've grown so far apart, we don't even know each other anymore."

It was his turn to look like I slapped him. "What do you want, Kate? Tell me what you want to do. Tell me how to fix this?"

I recognized the pleading in his voice. This was how it always happened. We would start fighting about something mundane that neither of us would give in to, inevitably it would reveal our bigger issues, the ones we usually tried to ignore, then finally we would round out the night by Nick promising to do whatever it took to make this work between us. Only, the next morning we would wake up and nothing would be changed or fixed or forgotten and we would start the delusional cycle all over again.

I was sick of it. I was sick of feeling like this and walking on eggshells every time we weren't fighting. I was sick of feeling bad for how I felt and the things that I said. And I was really sick of that look on his face right now, knowing I was the one that put it there.

I wanted to get off this crazy train. I wanted to wake up in the morning feeling good about myself and I wanted to go to bed at night knowing I wasn't a huge disappointment.

My hands clenched into tight fists on my belly and I squeezed my eyes shut before they tried to leak out more painful memories. I glanced to my left, taking in my appearance in the mirror on the door that led to our bathroom. My long hair looked black in the dim lighting and my skin was so pale it could have been see through. I stared at my eyes, as equally dark and empty as a black hole, and wondered if they were reflecting my broken spirit.

"I don't think we can." My words were a shattered whisper, but they felt like clarity... like truth. They were hurtful, but they were freedom. "I think we're too broken, Nick. I think it's too late for us."

"What are you saying, Katie?"

I ignored the agonized rasp to his voice. If I started to feel bad for him now, I would never get this out. "This is over, Nick... *We're* over. I think it's time we were both honest with ourselves and admitted that."

His response was immediate, "You're for real? You really don't want to try at this anymore?"

My temper shot up again and my face reddened from the hot anger pumping through me. "I have been *trying*! What do you think I've been doing for the past seven years? I've been trying every single day! And it's not enough! It's never enough! I cannot keep doing this day in and day out. I can't keep pretending that things are okay and then falling apart every time we start arguing. Nick, I'm exhausted in my *bones*. You're a good person, but it's like... it's like I bring out the absolute worst in you. And the same is true about me! I'm fun. I'm a really fun person. People *like* me! All of the people except *you*. And I don't blame you! When we're together I'm a nag and I'm ungrateful and I'm just... ugly. And I hate that person. I hate the person that I am with you. And I hate the person that you are..."

His head snapped up. I hadn't meant to go that far or finish that thought, but Nick was too perceptive to miss it. "You hate the person that I am with you. Is that what you were going to say?"

I shrugged one shoulder, ashamed that I'd let those words slip out. I shouldn't have said it, even if it was true. If nothing else, it drove my point home. I was a terrible person with Nick. *To Nick*. We'd made each other into horrible people.

Our relationship was toxic. He was slowly poisoning me.

I was slowly poisoning him.

289

"So what are you saying?" he demanded on a rasp. "You want a divorce? Is that what you want? You think we should get a divorce?"

I nodded, unable to get those precise words beyond my lips. "We aren't good together. We hate each other."

"Yeah, you've made that abundantly clear tonight."

"Can you think of any reason that we should stay together? Give me one good reason that we should keep doing this to ourselves and I will try. I swear to you, if you can come up with one reason to stay together, I'll keep doing this. But, Nick, *god*, this is ruining me. I don't know how much more I can take before I just fall apart."

This time when the tears started falling, I didn't wipe them away or try to stop them. My chin trembled from the force of my emotion and a devastating sob racked my chest. It was true. All of it. I hated myself and I hated him because he was the one that had turned me into this awful person.

I could not do this anymore.

If he came up with a valid reason, I didn't know what I would do. I knew I told him I would stick it out, but at this point, I couldn't do it. I would never really try again at this broken relationship. I had nothing left inside of me to give.

He watched me for a long time. I could see him processing everything behind his veiled eyes. I knew he thought he was hiding his emotions from me, but after seven years of marriage and ten years of being together, I could read him like an open book.

This was his analytical phase. He had to weigh each piece of information, emotion against truth, accusation against reality, before he could come to a logical conclusion.

My husband, the cold-hearted thinker. Logic and reason outweighed everything else. If it wasn't a fact, then it didn't exist to him.

Or at least it didn't matter.

"If this is what you want, then fine. A divorce, legal separation... whatever will make you happy."

Whatever will make me happy. Is this it? Is this what I want? But I had already told him it was. Immediately I regretted everything about tonight, everything I had said and everything I'd accused him of. But I couldn't keep feeling this way. I couldn't go through this again, only to have it happen tomorrow and the next day and the day after that. It was time to stand up for myself and fight for my happiness. Nobody else was going to do it for me.

Not even Nick.

"Thank you," I whispered.

There was a long weighted silence, as if he were waiting for me to take everything back, to make my final words disappear. Eventually, in a hoarse, tortured voice, he said, "I'll, uh, sleep on the couch tonight. I can move my things out tomorrow morning."

I sucked in a sharp breath. Was he serious? Were we really doing this? "Where will you go?"

"I'll stay with my brother until I can get a place of my own."

"Jared won't care? I mean… what will he think?"

"You can't have it both ways, Kate. You can't ask for a divorce and then hope to keep it a secret. Besides, it's better than staying at a hotel."

"No, you're right," I whispered. I rubbed my stomach and tried to ignore the sinking feeling in my gut. I asked for this. I practically demanded the divorce. So why did I feel such a horrific feeling of disappointment.

My body felt like it was being pulled apart in every direction. My heart felt trampled beneath a stampede of bulls. This was supposed to make me feel better. This was supposed to feel like freedom. I was finally digging myself out of the wreckage of our marriage and yet, I felt more wrecked in this moment than any moment leading up to this one.

"We're really doing this?" My words couldn't seem to come out stronger than a weak whisper.

"You tell me. You're the one that started throwing around divorce. It's not the first time you've asked for one, Kate. I'm frankly sick of trying to talk you out of it."

"I just… I don't know where else there is for us to go. Nick, we've tried. We gave it our best and now I think it's better if we move on… away from each other."

"Yeah," he breathed. "Tried and failed, I guess."

I wanted to argue with him. I wanted to tell him that he was wrong and that we hadn't failed, that there were as many good times between us as there were bad, but I couldn't bring myself to put up the effort. He was right. We failed.

We were failures at our marriage.

When I didn't say anything else, he grabbed his pillow and stomped downstairs to the living room. I rolled over in bed, pulled the duvet over my shoulders and cried until I passed out.

When I woke up in the morning, he was already gone.

Chapter One

8. My life will be better without him.

The bell rang and my stomach growled. I looked at my classroom, at the kids shoving papers and notebooks into their backpacks and the energetic chatter that warred with the high-pitched ringing of the fourth period bell, and wondered if I had some Pavlovian response to that sound.

I had been conditioned to know hunger, but I hadn't felt it in months.

I smiled at my students as they filtered from the room and reminded some of them about homework they owed me, but I barely heard the words that fell from my lips or acknowledged the concise instructions I was notorious for.

Behind my smiling mouth and teacher responsibilities, I was made of brittle glass and emptiness. I was nothing but paper thin defenses and sifting sand.

I had never known this kind of depression before. I could hardly tolerate my soon to be ex-husband and yet his absence left me unexpectedly battered.

Once my English class filled with a mixture of juniors and seniors had left me behind, I let out a long sigh and turned back to my desk. I dropped into my rolling chair and dug out my lunch from the locked bottom drawer.

I set it on the cold metal and stared at the sad ham sandwich and bruised apple I'd thrown together last minute this morning. I couldn't find the energy to take a bite, let alone finish the whole thing. I'd lost seven pounds over the last three months, one for each year of my disastrous marriage. And while I appreciated the smaller size I could fit into, I knew this was the wrong way to go about it.

My friend, Kara, called this the Divorce Diet. But I knew the truth. This wasn't a diet. I'd lost myself somewhere in the ruins of my marriage and now that my relationship was over, my body had started to systematically shut down. First my heart broke. Then my spirit fragmented. Now my appetite was in jeopardy and I didn't know what to do about it. I didn't know if I would ever feel hungry again.

I didn't know if I would ever *feel* again.

I used to eat lunch in the teacher's lounge, but lately I couldn't bring myself in there to face other people, especially my nosey colleagues.

Everyone had heard about my failed marriage. They stopped me in the halls to offer their condolences or hitman services with empathetic expressions or playful smiles. They watched me with pitying eyes and sympathetic frowns. They whispered behind my back or asked invasive questions.

But none of them cared. Not really.

They liked having someone to talk about that wasn't them and a topic that didn't dive into their personal lives. I was the gossip martyr. As long as they could tear apart my bad decisions and argue whether it was my frigidness or Nick's playboy tendencies that hammered the last nail in our coffin they shared a macabre sense of community.

They didn't care that each callous comment shredded me apart just a little more or that I could hear them cackling from down the hall.

They didn't take into account their own divorces or unhappy marriages or faults or hypocrisy or shortcomings. They only saw mine.

And now so did I.

The creaky door swung open and my best friend and fellow teacher, Kara Chase popped her pretty red head in the room. Her pert nose wrinkled at the sight of my untouched lunch and she smoothed down some of her wild frizz with a perfectly manicured hand. She had endless, luscious curls, but as the day went on and she dealt with more and more apathetic high school kids, her beautiful hair would expand with her impatience.

"That looks… yummy." Her stormy gray eyes lifted to meet mine and I couldn't help but smile.

I wrinkled my nose at her. "Don't judge! It's all I had."

She walked all the way in the room and leaned against the white-washed cement wall with her hands tucked against her back. "You used to be better at going to the grocery store."

The small dig cut deeper than it should have. "I've been busy."

Her lips turned down into a concerned frown that I mildly resented. "You can't wallow forever, Kate. Your marriage ended, not the world."

But he was my world. I kept that thought to myself. Now was not the time or the place to sift through my complicated feelings regarding Nick. I wanted this. *I wanted this divorce.* I had no right to be this upset or depressed.

Deep breath. "You're right," I told her. "I just haven't gotten the hang of cooking for one. Last time I went to the store, I ended up way over-shopping and then I had to throw half of it out when it went bad."

As gently as she could, she said, "You'll get the hang of it."

I pushed off in my chair until the back of it slammed against the white board behind me. "I hope that's true."

Because if it wasn't...

Had I just made the most colossal mistake of my life?

No. This was right.

But then why did it feel so... unbearable?

"Until then, let's sneak out and grab something better than... than whatever is on your desk now." Her expression brightened until I felt myself smiling at her. We had been friends since we started at Hamilton High School eight years ago. We had that kind of natural connection you only find once or twice your entire life. We were instantly inseparable. Even though Nick and I were already together we were only engaged at the time. Kara had been my maid of honor at our wedding and my closest confidant over the years. She knew the lowest lows of my marriage and the hard adjustment I'd faced since I ended it.

I didn't want to think about where I would be without her.

I looked at my wrist and checked the time. "I have twenty minutes. Can we be back in time?"

"We'll hurry." Her kitten heels clicked against the polished floor as she moved to hold the door open for me.

She was the only teacher at this school that had any sense of style. Her expensive taste didn't mesh well with her public high school teacher's salary, but thankfully for her, her wealthy parents supplemented her meager income.

My parents questioned my choices and thought I was a failure at life.

And yet we both knew what it was like to struggle to please impossible expectations and feel insignificant in the wake of our parents' cold assessments.

I might not have had a designer wardrobe, but at least my parents didn't try to buy my love.

I grabbed my purse out of the same locked drawer I'd tucked my lunch into and straightened my pencil skirt as I stood. I felt my spirits lift immediately.

Kara usually had that effect on me. And it helped that we were sneaking out of our jobs, to do something forbidden.

I loved breaking rules.

Just don't tell my students.

We were halfway down the hall and laughing with each other when we were caught.

"And where are you ladies off to today? I'm certain Ms. Carter has class in a few minutes." The deep voice made my skin feel too tight and my insides warm slowly.

I turned around and met Eli Cohen's rich brown eyes and tried not to smile too big. "Checking up on me?" I raised a challenging eyebrow.

Eli moved closer. "I was just in the lunchroom and heard a pair of junior boys discussing their hot English teacher."

That wiped the cocky expression off my face. "Gross. Don't tell me which ones. I don't want to know."

Eli's face split into a grin and a rich baritone rumble of a laugh fell from his full lips. "On one condition."

"This is blackmail!"

He laughed at me again, but when he raised his dark eyebrows and gave me an expectant look, I couldn't help but soften toward him. He was adorable. "Bring me back something from Garman's."

I couldn't believe him. "How do you know we're going to the deli? We could just be… just be… going to the bathroom together."

He shook his head slowly at me and grinned. "I see the determined look in Kara's eyes. I know that look. She's hungry. And she's enlisted you to help her sneak out."

"He's good," Kara mused. "I think our science teacher is a little too good."

"I'm starving," he admitted. "I've been watching the hall for five minutes hoping to catch a teacher on their way out." He held out his empty hands. "I forgot my lunch at home today and I have a meeting in three minutes."

I looked at Kara and tried to figure out what she was thinking. Eli had transferred to our school two years ago and over that time I had gotten to know him slowly. I could now say I counted him as my friend, but for a long time I had kept him at a distance. He was too good looking, too perfect. His skin was nicely bronzed, his hair perfectly quaffed and for a science teacher, his body was surprisingly filled out. I had found him intimidating at first and then, because I was married to a handsome man and supposedly in love with that man, I found it utterly ridiculous to be so affected.

I was a mess. Even back then.

But I had kept my distance until a few months ago. Until after Nick moved out.

"I suppose we can take pity on him," Kara sighed. "He does look famished."

I ran my eyes over his broad chest and flat stomach. "He's practically starving."

"Should I get you the cobb salad?" Kara asked innocently.

Eli pointed a playful finger at her. "Don't you dare. I wouldn't know what to do with something green. I'd probably make my students dissect it."

It was my turn to shake my head. "You're hilarious."

He smiled at me, wide and carefree. "I'll owe you one."

"Sure you will." Kara and I started walking again. "I'll be sure to collect."

"I'm counting on it." His low voice followed us down the hallway and I had to turn around before he saw an inflamed blush spread across my cheeks.

I pressed my cold hands against my face and tried to ignore the burn in my abdomen. It had been a long time since I flirted with someone, even longer since that someone wasn't Nick.

Kara's elbow found my side playfully. "What was that?"

"A favor?" I turned my wide eyes to her and silently begged her to tell me it wasn't as forward as I thought it was.

She pressed her lips together to hide her smile. "Sure it was."

"We're just friends."

"And now you're single."

A shuddering breath shook my lungs. "Not really. Not yet."

"Soon," she argued. "When the divorce is finalized, you'll officially be back on the market. Obviously, Eli knows that."

The flirty tingle turned sour in my stomach and suddenly I'd lost my appetite all over again. The blush drained from my cheeks and I felt myself turn pale and see-through.

Kara noticed immediately. "I'm sorry, Kate. I didn't mean to... to upset you. I just thought... It's been four months, babe. Nick hasn't even reached out to you. Not really, anyway. I thought you might be ready to move on."

Ready to move on after four months? Was that all it took to get over the last ten years of my life? To delete seven years of marriage? I had been with Nick in some form or capacity for a decade, but I was supposed to erase him completely from the important parts of my heart in four months?

How?

I wasn't against the idea. In fact, I would have loved to forget about him and the poisonous relationship we'd created. I would love for this pain in my chest to dissipate and the sickness that seemed constant and unrelenting to ebb.

But it wasn't that easy. I couldn't shake our relationship or the hold he had over my heart.

Not everything about him was bad. In fact, most of him was good and beautiful and right. But with me, he wasn't those things and I wasn't either.

But how was I supposed to let go of him? I loved him. I loved him for ten years and knew nothing else but loving him.

How could I walk away from him and even entertain the idea of another man after everything I had been through? I wasn't sure if I ever wanted to date again, let alone so quickly after my last relationship failed.

No. *Epically failed.*

Nick was supposed to be my forever. Nick was supposed to be my "until death do us part." And now that the rest of my life had taken a sharp, life-altering turn, I didn't know where I was headed anymore.

I was lost.

I was rudderless.

I was floating in a sea of confusion and hurt. I needed something to tether me, to pull me back to shore. But I knew, more than anybody else in my life that I wasn't going to find that with a new man.

"It's okay," I told Kara with a throaty whisper. "I just wasn't… I wasn't expecting that from him."

She squeezed my forearm and gathered her thoughts. "I know that what you're going through with Nick and everything is intense, but you're still young. You're still gorgeous. You still have a lot of life left to live. I don't want you to give up, just because the first try wasn't successful. You're a catch, friend. You have to know that Eli isn't the only man lining up to take advantage of Nick's colossal mistake."

"The divorce was my idea," I reminded her. "I'm the reason we ended it." The words felt like stones on my tongue. I felt their gritty, dirty wrongness and I wanted to spit them out and wash my mouth out with something cleansing.

Something like bleach.

Or battery acid.

"Yeah, maybe," she sighed. "But he should never have let you get away with it."

Something sharp sliced against my chest. I felt the same way too. If he had really loved me, he wouldn't have let me go through with it. Right? If he really wanted things to work out between us, he wouldn't have moved out.

He wouldn't have stopped talking to me.

He wouldn't have left.

Desperate to change the topic, I pushed through a back door and blinked against the bright fall sunlight. "So, lunch?"

"Yes!" She smiled at me. I could see the concern floating all over her face, but she held her tongue in an effort to keep me together. "Garman's has the freaking best pastrami on the planet."

I would never understand how Kara could eat so much and stay so thin. She did what the rest of us did, which was an insane amount of cardio and limited sugar. But she could eat whatever she wanted.

I looked at a piece of chocolate and my thighs expanded.

Well, until recently.

We hurried across the lengthy parking lot and busy Chicago street until we reached the tiny corner deli that boasted whole pickles with every purchase and sandwiches the size of my head. It was a favorite spot for everyone that worked on this block, but especially for the teachers at Hamilton. When given the choice of bad cafeteria food, a quickly packed lunch from home or a thickly-meated, moist-breaded, delicious deli sandwich from Garman's, the choice was obvious.

But after an incident last spring, in which a group of students had left school to corner and threaten a teacher off school grounds, our administrator had banned teachers from leaving campus during the school day and so technically we were sneaking out and breaking rules.

Hamilton was located in one of the under-privileged sections of Chicago. We were firmly in the city proper, not skirting the affluent suburbs or near a wealthier area of downtown. No, Hamilton was directly in the middle of gang violence, low-income housing and race wars.

I'd been offered jobs at some of the more stable schools in the city and even one at a prestigious private school in a well-off suburb. But when I chose Hamilton, it was with my heart. I had examined all of my options, and I knew that taking this job was a risk professionally, but I couldn't deny that I felt something meaningful for these kids.

I wanted to make a difference. Not the kind that you see on TV or that moves you in a heart-warming movie, but a real difference. I wanted to empower these kids with knowledge that would never leave them and tools for a future that was beyond this neighborhood. I wanted to inspire something inside of these neglected teenagers that had all of the odds stacked against them and had to fight to just show up on a daily basis.

I fought a losing battle every day and I was exhausted. But it was worth it.

I could feel it in my bones.

Kara's heels clicked against broken sidewalk as we hurried to Garman's, mingling with the sounds of angry traffic and city melee. The warm sun heated my exposed arms and face and I lifted my closed eyes to soak it in.

There was healing in this industrial chaos. There was a beautiful surrender to the noisy madness that felt cleansing and therapeutic. It wouldn't last. I would pay for my sandwich, go back to my desk and the reality of my broken life would come crashing down on me.

But for a few seconds, I had the flirtatious smile of an attractive man in my memory and a minute of reprieve from the demands of my life. I sucked in a full breath, taking in the exhaust and grit from the city. And yet, my lungs felt full for the first time in as long as I could remember.

"It's going to get better," Kara said so softly I barely heard her.

I opened my eyes to keep from tripping and they immediately fell to the cracked sidewalk and patchy grass on either side. "I'm not sure it is," I told her honestly.

She dropped her hand on my shoulder and squeezed, pulling me into a side hug. "There's more to life than Nick, babe. I promise you. And it won't take you long to figure it out. You just need to get the divorce finalized so you can move on." Her laugh vibrated through her. "And Eli would be a very good place to start."

"Maybe," fell from my lips, but I didn't feel any sentiment behind it. More sickness roiled through me and a cold sweat broke out on my neck. I swallowed against rising nausea and convinced myself not to throw up.

I was getting a divorce, but even the thought of another man still felt like adultery. Whatever our faults, Nick and I had always been faithful to each other. Moving on seemed impossible when I had dedicated my entire life to one man.

To the one man that had let me down and stomped on whatever remained of my happiness.

Nick and I were over, I promised myself.

I would move on eventually.

And Nick would too.

We grabbed our sandwiches, but I let Kara drop Eli's off. I had lost any desire to communicate with other people. I practically crawled back to my classroom and sunk into my chair. My deli sandwich went uneaten, just

300

like my one from home, because I couldn't bring myself to feel good enough to eat.

Kara had meant to encourage me, but she'd done the opposite.

I realized that she was right. That one day I would move on.

But that I was right too. Nick would move on as well.

I knew I could find someone better for me. I knew my life would be better off without him.

I just couldn't swallow the hard pill that his life would be better off without me too.

That he would find someone better than me.

Pick up Every Wrong Reason now!